# Vale of Shadows

*A Novel*

*By*

Rob Dakin

Charleston, SC

Charleston, SC 29418
©2010 by Rob Dakin
All rights reserved. Published 2010
First edition published 2010
Printed in the United States of America

ISBN (Trade Paperback): 1-4392-5462-1

EAN13: 9781439254622

Vale of Shadows — First Edition

Cover Design by Aubrey Dakin
Interior design by Aubrey Dakin
Cover Photo by Rob Dakin

www.robdakin.com

*This novel is lovingly dedicated to my wife Karen.*
*My sons Josh, Jeff, Jon, and Joe.*
*My daughter Aubrey.*
*My daughters-in-law Shelby and Letitia.*
*my granddaughter Emma, and my*
*new grandson Zander.*

# I

You betrayer will be betrayed.
You slayer will be slayed.
What do you believe to be true about fear?
All that you know will be of no use to you when
you fall under the
blackness of shadow.
Your terror will know no bounds when the evil of
the jinn finds you.
How do I know?
I am imprisoned in the residence of the Terror.
I languish in the Vale of Shadows

Baba Moush
1452 A.D.

# TheBeckoning

Tropojë Province, northern Albania
25 February 1475

His was not a life well lived.

Brutality and treachery were the epitome of his character.

Was it really so long ago that he stood in triumph in front of his lord, Gjergi Kastrioti? Will none of his victories against the Turks count for anything?

Kastrioti is dead. All of his comrades in arms are now dead. Only he remains, a pathetic specter of his former stature. These last days have seen him a writhing wretch, and all the glory that was his has melted into hopeless despair. The acclamations of his conquests now long silent.

He now lies dying.

This drafty sheep shack is no shelter from the fierce winter blast that pummels the high mountain meadow. He squirms under the weight of his guilt. The wolf fur pulled tight under his chin cannot protect against the bitter cold.

He groans. Not in pain. He groans in fear. Fear of the torment-filled death that awaits him. Përparim Lleshi knows there will be no peace for him on the other side. He knows there will be no redemption.

The comforts he extracted at the expense of others now lie in ruins. Misery and paranoia have been his steady companions in a life trudged out as a fugitive. A torment haunts his soul for his ill-deeds. No consolation can ease his agony.

A haze envelops him as terror sinks its insidious talons into his heart. He fights against a memory. A terrible day he wishes had never happened. A terrible possession he wishes he had never possessed. Oh, if only he had died in battle, he laments. He cries for help in his mind, knowing it is futile. The knifepoint of recognition of his own mortality causes him to cry out to the God he neither acknowledged nor reverenced in life. The struggle against Creator by the created will pass unremarkably into judgment.

His eyes meet that of the witch, Valbona, as she stands over him. Only she understands his plight, and she has no words of comfort. She knows what haunts him. She knows what he has been running from, what he has been hiding from, and she knows that this is his forsaken doom. She returns his pleading gaze with pitiless, cold, dark eyes.

A shriek is carried by the wind over the top of the mountains. Lleshi, wild-eyed and gasping in terror, pulls the wolf fur higher over his beard. He struggles to remain silent as another shriek echoes through the valley. The evil comes his way. Hunting.

Lleshi's stare suddenly focuses on a point above the witch. A strange glimmer of hope surges through him as he sees an apparition through the stick and straw roof of the shack. He struggles to form a word, but only a barely audible whisper escapes his lips. "Come."

Valbona turns to see the object of his attention. A meager smile stretches across her ancient face. She beckons with her gnarled hand, and utters a single command. "Come."

# 1. Malevolent Shadow

European Istanbul
22 July 1956, 9 p.m.

Hamdi stumbled over the curb and crashed into the moss covered stone wall that ran along Dolmabahçe Boulevard. Blood from the cut above his left eye coursed along the wrinkles and creases in his face, blinding him until he wiped it away with his open palm. He stared at the blood smear in disbelief until a droplet fell from the tip of his nose and plopped into his upturned hand. He tried to blink the blood out of his eyes but was forced to wipe again. Terror had dulled him to the pain. Weak and uncoordinated, he fell back against the wall separating the Dolmabahçe Palace from the road. He frantically grabbed at the stones to keep from falling to his knees. Turning, he stared back down the boulevard toward the Beşiktaş pier. Streams of people walked inland after disembarking one of the larger ferries.

Wild-eyed and exhausted, he continued running up the slope of the road. His only thought was escape. He careened from tree shadow to tree shadow, avoiding the glare of the full moon as much as possible. He stopped breathlessly beneath the canopy of an ancient sycamore and peered into the shadows before and behind him. His pursuer was not in sight.

The voices of the people coming off the ferry began to fade as they dispersed into the night. No one walked in his direction, but he knew he was being stalked. As he turned to continue his trek toward Taksim, the heaviness of doom returned. He fought off a wave of panic, and steeled himself to push forward.

A whimper escaped his lips as he prayed under his breath that Dr. Yay's laboratory was close. He forced himself to take one step and then another under the growing weight that was crushing down on him. "Please help me make it," he gasped as he staggered drunkenly.

Hamdi came to a fork in the road. He was from the other side of the Bosphorus, the Asian side, and was not familiar with this part of İstanbul. He decided to go to the right and continue the upward journey. A series of hairpin turns in the road disappeared into the darkness ahead. A shrill cry in the dark distance behind him sped his decision to cut across the landscaping that defined the switchbacks.

He took in big chugs of air as he flailed through the shrubbery. The weight of his legs seemed to increase with every stride. The cry drew nearer. He dared not look over his shoulder, but he sensed that the demon that had been hounding him over half of Turkey was about to take him. Crashing through the hedge, he fell off the curb into the street in front of a yellow *dolmuş* rounding the curve. Hamdi threw himself into a roll making it back to the gutter before being run over by the cab packed with people heading down to Beşiktaş from Taksim square. "Allah, be merciful!" he exclaimed, startled by the sound of his own voice.

He chanced a quick glance down the way he had come to see the *dolmuş* weave its way down the serpentine road. In the peripheral beam of the headlight, Hamdi saw movement in the shrubs tracking the way he had come. He gazed in horror at the black void floating toward him. His vocal cords were paralyzed with terror. He tried to scream for help, but only a low gurgling sound escaped.

The thought of his imminent death spurred him into a pell-mell run up the middle of the road. Turning one more corner, he could hear the sound of traffic and people in the square. A group of smartly dressed teenagers waited patiently at the corner for another *dolmuş* to take them down to the *iskelesi*, or pier. They were deep in conversation and did not see him approaching. He tried to call out, but no sound escaped his lips.

The shapes of the teenagers became blurred. The loss of blood and exertion made him feel light-headed. He rubbed desperately at his eyes. The images before him came in and out of focus. Light and sound distorted. Hamdi was falling under the shadow. He made one last desperate lunge toward the teenagers; no more than a squeak escaped his mouth.

One of the youth casually looked in his direction. "Hey, look there's a drunk coming." The teens laughed and pointed at Hamdi as he collapsed to the pavement. Soon their shapes vaporized before his eyes. Hamdi made one last gasp, and then darkness overtook him.

The shadow lingered over the lifeless body, and one of the teenagers began to walk slowly toward the collapsed man. "Hey! I don't think this guy's drunk. I think he's dead," said Altin as he crept closer. The group moved timidly toward the fallen man. After a few steps, Altin noticed the shadow. He looked up at the moon through the trees to try to determine its source but could find no natural explanation.

"Do you see it?" he asked in a strained whisper.

"See what?" responded Melda, cautiously coming up behind him.

"That shadowy thing hanging over him," said Altin, not daring to point.

"Yes, I see it," said Ümët coming up from the back of the group.

The shadow hovered for a few seconds, and then moved with lightening speed to the top of the trees, vanishing out of sight. The astonished teens stared into the sky, and then looked down collectively in horror at the body of Hamdi. They gasped at the blood smear covering his face in finger-furrowed streaks. The body lay in a contorted heap as if every muscle had flexed violently just before death. Its teeth were clenched with the lips pulled back into a sardonic grin. Wild, wide eyes stared up at them, nightmarishly fixating their own stares.

Finally Altin was able to pull his gaze away from the corpse. Blinking in disbelief at the sight, he said, "We've got to call the police." The others individually came to their senses as if they had been in a trance. Slowly the girls backed away holding hands for support.

"He looks so horrible," mumbled Zenap. "What could have done that to him?"

Only Ümët stood his ground as he stared at the fallen man. He mumbled something unintelligible as Altin tried to tug him away. Ümët jerked his arm violently from Altin's grasp and took a step closer to the man. He disregarded the shadow as it hovered in the tops of the trees. He bent down and leaned over Hamdi, studying his face in the dim light.

"This man is my cousin," he finally said with certainty. "He is from a village east of here." Ümët straightened Hamdi's body, and patted down his pockets. The crackle of paper could be heard through the vest fabric. He reached gingerly into the pocket and pulled out a yellowed, soiled paper folded in fourths. As he began to open the paper, the shadow moved closer. Ümët scrambled to get back to the others.

Altin screamed at the shadow out of sheer desperation, and not knowing what else to do hurled the only thing he had in his hand, a half-eaten apple core. The apple passed through the shadow and splattered on the pavement on the other side of Hamdi, falling short as if it had met some resistance in the shadow. The shadow retreated to the tops of the trees as the six friends stood in awe and terror unable to move. A low voice resonated just loud enough for only Ümët to hear.

"My time is done for now," it hissed menacingly. "We will meet again." It moved off quickly to the east as if drawn by an unseen power.

Ümët dared not move; too afraid to take his eyes off the last place he had seen the shadow. "Did you hear that?" he asked Altin, who crept up slowly to his side.

"I didn't hear anything but the sound of the rushing wind,"

Ümët pulled the crumpled piece of paper from his trouser pocket where he had inadvertently stuffed it. Altin and the others crowded closer to see over his shoulder. The paper was yellowed with age, and charred along the edges as if someone had tried to burn it. It was filled with tightly written Arabic script.

"Are you able to read it?" asked Zenap.

"It's old Ottoman script," said Ümët. "My dad has been teaching me, but the calligraphy is so ornate I can't read it in this light. It looks like a genealogy or something. I'll take it to my dad and see if we can figure it out."

The group ran back into the square to find a policeman. No one wanted to be left alone. They turned and moved quickly back up the road, glancing over their shoulders as they went to make sure they were not being followed by the sinister shadow. When they reached the corner to walk into Taksim square, Altin turned to take one last look. The body of Hamdi was gone.

# 2. Uncle Ümët

Jeff sat in his stranded car with the engine idling. He had been sitting in the same spot in traffic for the last two hours. Snow was still falling, bringing the bustling city to a standstill. Literally. He watched with detached amusement at the *Istanbullus* trying to outmaneuver each other so as to gain two to three more inches in the traffic jam.

Horns honked incessantly. Men stuck their heads out of their car windows to yell at each other, waving their hands in such a way as to say, "Hey, come on! What are you trying to do?" As if this would actually make any difference. What made matters worse was that occasionally someone would get out of his car either to yell at someone else or run into a nearby shop to grab something to eat. Of course, it would be at that time the traffic inched forward, causing even more of a bottleneck while other motorists tried to pull around on the medians or sidewalks. This got the pedestrians involved in the yelling match causing more of a tie-up since, of course, they would have to come out into the street to argue their point.

Jeff began to realize that Turks, cars, and snow should never be used in the same sentence. He smiled to himself as he tried to concentrate on the language tape he was listening to. "Türküm...I am Turkish," parroted the voice with a distinct British accent. Jeff pushed the eject button impatiently. "I am neither Turkish nor British," he said as he came to realization that mastering a language like Turkish was not going to happen for him any time soon. He wiped his face with his gloved hand

9

and gazed out the window. Time loped slowly onward leaving that hopeless impatience that made him feel he had lost precious moments of life that would never be recovered.

He realized that he had moved far enough forward in the line of traffic that he was now stuck at a perpendicular intersection. The road that ran straight off to his left rose with a distinct incline. He peered through the snow at the little melodramas going on around him, tapping his fingers on the steering wheel, when suddenly out of the corner of his eye he caught a glimpse of a large model Mercedes sliding on the ice down the perpendicular road toward him. The Mercedes was still about halfway up the hill, but Jeff began to have a terrible feeling that it was not going to be able to stop before it skidded into him.

He looked nervously for a way to escape through the congestion. The other motorists around him seemed oblivious to the impending catastrophe. Jeff started honking his horn but realized that he was just adding to the mayhem. He looked back up toward the oncoming Mercedes just as it bumped into the curb and stopped about three-quarters of the way down. Jeff shook his head in relief. "Crazy Turks," he muttered.

The driver of the Mercedes got out of the car along with his three male passengers. They walked around the car while thoughtfully massaging their bearded chins. After some contemplation three of the men stepped around to the back of the vehicle and grabbed the bumper, while the driver leaned into the car and put it in neutral. With a "*Bir...iki...üç...*" the four men began to heave and pull with the intent of getting the car back up the hill.

Jeff watched in utter shocked amazement. "No way!" he exclaimed out loud. "You've got to be kidding me."

After a few failed attempts at even budging the Mercedes in an upward direction, the driver stopped pushing against the doorframe and walked off to the middle of the street.

This only allowed the car to begin rolling forward since the three men in the back had no chance of holding the weight. The driver frantically jumped back into the car and took it out of neutral. He climbed out of the car laughing while the other men cursed him.

Two pedestrians making their way down the icy sidewalk were pressed into the ill-advised endeavor by the driver. Soon, all six men were tugging and pulling to get the Mercedes up the hill backwards. After fifteen minutes they hadn't moved an inch. Finally, they gave up. The four occupants of the vehicle began walking back up the sidewalk leaving the car bumped up against the curb. The other two made their way down as was their original intention. It wasn't long before they all disappeared from sight into the snowy night. Meanwhile, Jeff was still stuck.

He decided that the only way he was going to keep from going crazy was to take a nap. He rested his head back against the seat, scrunching down as best he could around the steering wheel, and closed his eyes. Just as he got situated, his cell phone rang in his pocket, startling him. He fumbled for the phone that he had just purchased that afternoon. Its tone pinged out "Dance of the Sugar Plum Fairy." Jeff made a note to change the ring ASAP. He pushed on the call button. "Hello?"

"Hey, Jeff, where are you, man?" asked Orhan.

"I'm still stuck in traffic," sighed Jeff shaking his head. "I'm somewhere near Ortaköy. This snow has sucked the brains out of all the drivers around here. It's crazy!"

"It's the worst snow we've had in thirteen years," said Orhan. "No one is used to driving in it."

"Well, it makes me want to get my cattle prod out and do a little selective zapping. You won't believe what I just saw some guys try to do," Jeff replied. "Does your uncle really need me to come tonight?"

11

"Well...yes. If you can. Uncle Ümët has been looking forward to meeting you for a long time. He remembers your father with great fondness," said Orhan.

Jeff's father, Altin, left Istanbul when he was a teenager to study in America. Since he had left before he had fulfilled his military obligation, he never returned. He met Jeff's mother after he graduated from the university, and fell in love. Altin had kept in contact with his old friend Ümët over the years. The two men exchanged letters and photos of their children, and called each other when special events happened in their families or careers.

"Well...I'm not exactly sure were I am," said Jeff peering through the snowfall for a landmark he recognized.

"Is the Bosphorus at least still on your right?" gibed Orhan.

"Yes. I'm still heading in the right direction. Oh...wait! There's that mosque you were telling me about. The one that was in that movie...uh, *Armageddon*," said Jeff. "It's just up ahead to the right. Traffic is starting to move a little better now."

"Good! You're in Ortaköy. Just keep on that road. You'll go under the Bosphorus Bridge, and then just keep going until you get to Bebek. You are still about an hour to an hour and a half away in this weather, but we'll wait up for you," said Orhan.

"OK," said Jeff. "Traffic is starting to move pretty good now. I'm just about ready to go under the bridge. See you in a few." He clicked off his phone and stuck it on the dash of his car. The road congestion was opening up due to more and more people giving up and finding alternate side roads to get back home, and soon Jeff was traveling along the Bosphorus through old neighborhoods. The snow began to let up a little, so his visibility was much better. He pulled the car over for a moment to study a crude map that Orhan had sent him.

As he studied the map by the light of the overhead lamp, he was startled by a loud thwack against the driver's side window. Then another and another. He was amused to see a group of children heaving wet, sloppy snowballs at him. He was a sitting duck. He jumped out of the car and scooped up two handfuls of snow off the roof of his car. He formed a missile with precision for the best aerodynamics, and flung accurately at the tallest of his assailants, hitting him right in the back of his neck as the boy turned to avoid the cold projectile. Snow cascaded under the boy's collar and down his back prompting a frantic dance to wiggle the snow quickly away from his skin.

"Ha! That'll teach ya," laughed Jeff.

Suddenly a barrage of snowballs came from all sides splatting against the car and his uncoated body. Jeff realized much to his chagrin that he had stopped in the middle of a snowball war between children on both sides of the street. Outnumbered, he dove back into the car in the nick of time as another, fiercer barrage pounded him. "OK...you win," he said as he drove off.

He finally came up to the ferry landing in Bebek and pulled over near the taxi stand. Orhan had arranged to meet him there and continue on with him to Uncle Ümët's house.

"That didn't take too long," said Orhan as he slid into the front seat. He noticed Jeff's appearance in the overhead light. "Why is your shirt all wet?"

"I had a little trouble with a marauding band of snowball warriors," exclaimed Jeff. "I didn't have a chance."

Orhan smiled to himself. Jeff's playfulness always amused him. After a short drive, he instructed Jeff to pull over and stop in front of an old *yalı*, or villa. "This is it," he said easing open the door and pausing to look over at Jeff. "Just to warn you, my uncle is very big into Ottoman history. He is a little eccentric; I'm afraid, but harmless."

Jeff got out of the car and looked up at the grand Ottoman mansion before him. "Wow! This is cool," he exclaimed.

"*Cool* is not exactly the word I would use," said Orhan. "More like *cold*. You'll see what I mean later."

# Rob Dakin

The *yalı* had been built around the 1850s by a pasha of the Ottoman Empire. Its elaborate Baroque style overwhelmed Jeff as he passed through the front entrance into a courtyard with a fountain. Jeff and Orhan entered a grand sitting room through ten-foot-tall French doors. The sitting room was lavishly furnished with antique Ottoman fixtures. On the far side of the room was a *cumba*, or bay window that jutted out over the water of the Bosphorus. The entire wall was glass pane, and offered a spectacular view of the Bebek Bay.

Jeff stood in awe with his mouth open. The floor was covered with plush Hereke carpets, once reserved only for the palaces of the sultan. He was dazzled by a huge crystal chandelier that hung in the center of the room casting prisms of light across the walls. Jeff followed Orhan's lead and removed his shoes at the front door. As he struggled with the last shoelace, Uncle Ümët strode gracefully into the room. He wore a sumptuous floor-length silk *kaftan* that barely exposed his slippers embroidered in silver filigree. Around his robe was a sash of crimson silk. Jeff half expected to see a *cembiyes*, an Ottoman curved dagger, sticking out of his sash, but as this was a social visit, Ümët wasn't wearing one—much to Jeff's relief. He did, however, wear a silk turban fastened in the front by an ornate broach with an Arabic calligraphy design. Ümët noticed Jeff staring at his forehead.

"It is a sultan's *tuğra*, a personal monogram used in place of his signature. It is very beautiful, is it not?" said Ümët. "This one happens to be of Sultan Abdül Mecit the First. He was the sultan that moved from the Topkapı Palace to the Domabahçe Palace about the same time this *yalı* was built. The calligraphy is exquisite, is it not?"

"Yes, it is very beautiful," said Jeff. "I've seen drawings of them, but I never knew what they were."

"They represent an era long gone, but not forgotten," said Ümët. "Some think I am eccentric for all the time and money

# Vale of Shadows

I spend reviving Ottoman nostalgia, my nephew included." He gave Orhan a sidewise smile. "For me, however, remembering the glory and splendor of the past helps me cope with the misery of the present. Forgive me, though, I do ramble on. I am Ümët Aziz. *Hoş geldiniz.* Welcome to my home, humble as it is." He cordially shook Jeff's hand.

Jeff took an instant liking to Orhan's uncle. He wanted to greet Ümët in Turkish, but his mind froze, and he went completely blank. So he just stood there in mid stammer.

Orhan bit his lower lip and smiled. He had heard all this before. His uncle had bought a rundown *yalı* and renovated it during a time when most of the old villas were being torn down to put up apartment buildings, or were subdivided into apartments. The problem that Orhan had with his uncle's passion was how much had been spent on this old mansion to fix it up. Even with all of the renovation, it still provided little protection from the north wind and the bitter cold of winter, perched as it was right on the water's edge. The heating bills were astronomical, and even then everyone in the household had to either wear robes like his uncle, or heavy wool sweaters. Orhan felt the money could have been better spent on a new, modern house. At least they would all be warm.

Despite the problems, living in the grandeur provided by his ancestors wasn't without its perks. All he had to do to impress a girl he was interested in was to tell her that he lived in a *yalı* in Bebek, and he pretty much had her wrapped around his finger. His uncle's villa was well kept and stood out easily with its brightly colored paint. Other *yalıs* along the waterfront were more dilapidated, their wood blackened by cold and humidity. It was almost impossible to keep paint on them. So Uncle Ümët spent part of his fortune repainting every two to three years.

A young boy about eight years of age came from a side hall with two pairs of slippers for Jeff and Orhan. He knelt down and gently lifted Jeff's foot off the floor so he could place the slipper on it. Jeff tried to pull away but was restrained by the soft touch of Orhan's hand on his elbow. "It's OK, "said Orhan."It is our way."

"*Teşekkürler*," said Jeff as he accepted the second slipper onto his foot. "Did I say that right?" He looked at Orhan for confirmation.

"Yes. Your Turkish is getting very good. You will be fluent before you know it," said Orhan patting Jeff on the back.

"Yeah, right! The more I learn, the more I realize I don't know."

Another servant, a teenage girl, came from the same hall and helped him on with an ornate *kaftan*, not as fancy as the one Ümët was wearing but still a whole lot nicer than the raggedy terry cloth robe he had been wearing at home since he was thirteen years old.

"Please accept our hospitality. This old house has many drafts. It is the price we pay for living in the past," said Ümët apologetically.

"Thank you for inviting me," said Jeff. "I love everything about the history of this part of the world. This house makes me feel like I'm taking part in a magnificent past."

"I am pleased you feel that way. Come, have a seat here on this couch. The cushions are very comfortable." Ümët led Jeff and Orhan to the couch closest to the bay window. Jeff took a seat and gazed out across the Bosphorus. He could barely make out the lights on the Asian side partly obscured by the fog that had settled over the water. The snow had stopped but had blanketed everything in a thick, fluffy carpet.

A male servant in his forties bowed into the middle of the seated companions caring a *nargiles*, or water pipe, with three pipes and placed it on the round copper tray baring the *tuğra* of Sultan Ahmet that sat in front of the couch.

"Would you like to smoke?" asked Ümët as he took up one end of the hose, placed the mouthpiece between his lips, and inhaled.

Jeff had seen these "bubble pipes" in the bazaar. He had always wanted to try one so he grabbed up an end and inhaled, going immediately into a violent coughing jag, smoke and mucous snorting out of his nose. Orhan patted him on the back.

"You have to suck slowly with these water pipes," he said. "The smoke is far denser than a normal cigarette."

Jeff tried to regain his composure. "It *is* just tobacco, though, isn't it?" he asked still in the midst of uncontrolled coughing.

"Oh, yes. It *is* just tobacco," laughed Orhan. "Anything else would be illegal."

"Yeah, right," said Jeff as he took another puff, but this time more slowly.

All in all, once Jeff got used to the bubble pipe he rather enjoyed the leisure of it. The three men sat comfortably, lounging on the cushions, and drew quiet puffs of tobacco smoke while absentmindedly staring out over the Bosphorus. No one spoke for a time. Jeff felt as if he had been drawn into an 1819 Melling's engraving of the sultan's court two hundred years ago.

As he became more relaxed he began to look more closely at his surroundings. "Tastefully extravagant" was how he decided to summarize all that he saw. His eyes were soon drawn to a crack that ran across the ceiling and down the wall opposite from where he was sitting.

"I notice you have a crack in your wall," he said breaking the silence. "Is it from the earthquake?"

"Yes," sighed Ümët. "I'm afraid that August seventeenth, nineteen ninety-nine will be remembered with great sadness for generations to come. We felt the quake even though the epicenter was a hundred miles away to the east. I understand this is the reason you are here in Turkey."

Jeff nodded. "Yes. After Orhan contacted me and told me of the devastation and what you all were going through, I felt I needed to come and help in whatever way I could. I came in October and have spent most of my time in Golcük, but I have also spent quite a bit of time in Adapazarı."

"I am grateful that you and Orhan have become such good friends," said Ümët. "Who would have believed how fate would bring the son of one of my closest friends into the life of my dear nephew?"

Jeff and Orhan met for the first time when Ümët arranged for Orhan to go to the United States to explore attending a university in Jeff's hometown of Wichita, Kansas. The two became fast friends and decided to room together after Orhan was accepted to Wichita State University and granted a student visa. The years passed quickly for the two men. Jeff finished his degree in biology, and Orhan got a masters degree in business to help him when it was time to take over the family business in Istanbul.

After graduation, Orhan moved back to Turkey and began working in the shipping company started by his great, great grandfather under Sultan Abdül Hamit II. His father had died suddenly of a heart attack when he was just a boy. Since that time he had lived with his father's brother, Ümët, who had no children of his own.

Jeff was always a good student and applied to medical school but was put on an alternate list. He worked as a teacher's assistant in the biology and chemistry labs while he reapplied to med school, but then the earthquake hit Turkey so he came to help.

Now, he noticed how respectful Orhan and his uncle were of the servants. They seemed to treat them almost like family. The male servant stood off to the side of the room with his hands folded waiting on any bidding from his master. The young girl and boy were nowhere to be seen, but Jeff could hear them shuffling around in the adjoining rooms as they prepared his bedroom for the night.

"Your servants...have they been with you long?" asked Jeff.

"Yes. Ermal here has been with our family for many years. Ermal's wife, Moza, is our chef, and their children Esma and Aydın you met earlier when you arrived. They are as much a part of my family as Orhan. They are all very dear to me," said Ümët reflectively as he drew from his pipe again. "You see, Jeff, our family descends from the Ottomans. We are in fact Ottomans. Our heritage is rich and glorious, which makes our present condition even more miserable. We were not in favor of the revolution that resulted in the new republic. We adapted to the new order under Atatürk because we had to, not because we wanted to. I, and not just a few others, would like nothing better than to see the greatness of the past restored under the sultans, but alas that will never be."

"I didn't realize that there were Turks who still wanted the old empire around," said Jeff.

"Yes, well...the revolution that replaced our last sultan, Mehmet the Fourth, came, as do all revolutions, at a time when the government was weak, and carelessly extravagant, and completely uninvolved in taking care of the needs of its people," said Ümët. "We made the mistake of forgetting who it was that made us great. We were so consumed by our own pleasure that we foolishly thought our inferiors would gladly live and die in their squalor just to provide us with luxury. It is a different world now. Human blood no longer drips with divinity." Ümët put his pipe down and fixed his eyes on the crack in his wall and ceiling. "We are, in fact, in ruins."

Jeff couldn't help but notice that Uncle Ümët included himself in the indictment against the Ottoman Empire. He caught Orhan's eye, and the two men smiled at each other, drawing more smoke from their pipes. Orhan began blowing smoke rings. Jeff tried to imitate him, but being a nonsmoker his comical attempts fell flat.

Ümët continued. "There is a melancholy that is woven into the very fabric of every *İstanbullus*. We call it *hüzün*. It is a melancholy that you will see in the eyes of everyone native to İstanbul. The city is ancient, so we have ancient grievances. Ancient pain and sadness. From the Byzantines that are still represented by the Greek population here to Ottomans like our family to the Republicans that replaced us. We all have a right to maintain this melancholy throughout every aspect of our lives. We almost cherish it, and pass it down to our children as a legacy. We have earned the right to keep it closely guarded against outsiders who come here with their Western ideals and see only the exotic."

Jeff stopped smoking and put his pipe down. He was fascinated by Ümët's social study, but he was beginning to be a little upset in his stomach from the smoke. He gazed around the room. Ümët, Orhan, and Ermal all stared absentmindedly at the floor in front of them for several moments without speaking, the words spoken being all too true. Jeff sighed and suddenly realized how extraordinarily hungry he was, as his stomach thundered like a calving glacier. He hoped quietly that Moza was preparing a big meal and strained his olfactory senses to pick up a scent of food above the reek of the tobacco smoke.

After a moment of reflection, Ümët spoke again. "Alas, these earthquakes have made matters even worse, and have affirmed our melancholy. Those who are religious blame those who are not for bringing the wrath of God down on us. There was actually a surge in mosque attendance for the first months after the quakes, but that has slowed a bit now. Those who are not religious blame fate, which plunges them deeper into irreligious philosophies. You will find thousands of people tonight sleeping outside their perfectly good homes for fear that another quake will strike and trap them in their apartments. A gloom has settled over the city; you can see it in the eyes of everyone you meet in the markets, buses, trams, ferries, and underground. You may ask us why we don't seem friendly. It is because we have earned the right not to be." He paused for effect. "There you have it in a nutshell, as they say."

Jeff had experienced this *hüzün* firsthand. He didn't blame the people for their feelings. Although he had spent the last few months here, he was still an outsider. He hadn't lost anyone or anything in the quakes, so he couldn't really know what they were going through. All he could say was what he had been told to say by the mission organization he was with: "*Geçmiş olsun*, or may it pass."

There was an unspoken shift in the atmosphere of the conversation. Ümët swung his legs off the couch and settled them on the floor. He leaned forward with his elbows on his knees, hands clasped together in front of him, and tapped his thumbs together as he furrowed his brow mentally forming his next words carefully before he spoke them.

"So...tell me, Jeff," queried Ümët as if emerging from a dream. "What did your father tell you about the night of July twenty-second, nineteen fifty-six?"

# 3. Old Journals and Water Pipes

Jeff looked across the *nargile* at Ümët, and then glanced over at his friend Orhan. He knew that the reason he had been asked to come tonight was to discuss this very topic—a topic that had haunted his father until the day he died. Jeff had never discussed the specifics of that night with his father. He had, however, always sensed that there were things that terrified his father stemming from that night so many years ago.

"I know that the chief reason my dad left Turkey was because of that night," said Jeff. "He tried to tell me details a number of times over the years, but he was never able to come to grips with telling it out loud. He was very superstitious, and I think he thought that if he spoke of it openly somehow the evil would track him down even in America. So at this point I'm pretty much in the dark about the whole thing."

Ümët nodded thoughtfully. "I know how he felt. I have often looked over my shoulder in these past years. The urgency to meet you has been thrust upon me in recent months as I am now the soul survivor who witnessed the horror of that night." Ümët ground his teeth as he stared out the window toward Asia. "There were six of us that night, including your father. We were on our way tc Sultanahmet to drink tea at our favorite tea garden. It was between the Hagia Sophia and the Blue Mosque. We had just come from the cinema and were going to take a ferry from Beşiktaş to Eminönü. We could have taken a taxi, but the ferry at night on the Bosphorus was more romantic. We were, after all, teenagers in love."

Jeff repositioned himself on the couch. He could finally smell the aroma of food coming from the kitchen. The prospect of a meal lightened his spirits, and he smiled over at Orhan and turned toward Ümët to encourage the resumption of his tale. The old man studied him for a moment, and then continued.

"We had just missed a taxi going down to the waterfront, and we were waiting for another when we saw a man staggering toward us. We thought at first he was drunk, but it quickly became apparent that something was seriously wrong. When he collapsed, your father and I started to walk over to him. I was terrified when I recognized the man as the son of my father's brother. I could not believe it was random chance that he had died right in front of me. It was several days later, after translating a document I found in his vest pocket, that I began to form theories. I was too afraid to share them with anyone, and it was many years before I wrote to your father about what I concluded."

He cleared his throat and pondered his next words as if wondering whether Jeff and Orhan would believe him. "We all saw the shadow," he said. "We tried to dismiss it at first, and attributed it to hysteria, maybe, or just the fright of seeing a man die right in front of us. The girls were terrified and wanted to leave immediately, but Altin felt we should call the police." Ümët paused again. "Did your father ever mention the disappearance of the body of the man on the street?"

Jeff shook his head no. He knew he needed to show that he was seriously listening to the elder sitting across from him, but he was afraid of making a wrong comment or having a wrong body posture that would offend Ümët. He decided it would be best if he just kept quiet and let Ümët continue with his story.

"Well, of course, none of us could believe what we saw. For a while we even tried to convince ourselves that we hadn't seen it. When the police came, they were very skeptical. We didn't blame them. No body. No blood. No sign of a struggle. Nothing. The more they made us tell our story, though, the more we became convinced that we really had seen what we had seen.

The police took us off one at a time and compared our stories, then came to the conclusion that we had at least seen *something*. That in itself kept us out of jail for wasting their time.

"We were all afraid to talk about it later. That night we split up and went home. The police said if they had any questions they would contact us. As it turned out they never did. Your father became obsessed with solving the mystery of what had happened to the body. He asked questions of everyone he met on the road and at school. Unfortunately he became known as the 'crazy guy,' and most of his friends began to shun him. The six of us decided that whatever really happened may never be fully explained, but we made a pact that we would stick together.

"It was about three weeks later that Altin was contacted by a professor from the university named Dr. Özhan Yay. He asked to meet with all of us in his laboratory in Taksim. We were apprehensive at first, and we blamed Altin for asking too many indiscreet questions.

"We arrived at Dr. Yay's laboratory together. He was very matter-of-fact and serious in such a way that it frightened us. No small talk. No cordial greeting. He jumped right in and asked about what we had seen that night. He told us that he had heard about Altin asking questions in the neighborhood, and so he had contacted a friend of his at the police precinct and was given a copy of the report.

"He told us that the man we had seen die was a mayor from a village where a number of villagers had mysteriously disappeared. He told us that this man and another man, a policeman from Adapazarı, were supposed to have come to his lab that night. He waited for them until the next evening, but when they did not come he decided to contact the police in Adapazarı. They told him that their man had not reported in when he was supposed to, so they sent out two other officers to the village. They also failed to report back.

# Vale of Shadows

"The police at this point were taking no chances and called in the military. The soldiers and police arrived at the village to find it completely deserted. No sign of life anywhere. Neither man nor animal. There were no bodies, carcasses, or signs of carnage...nothing. Dr. Yay concluded that the death and disappearance of the mayor we had witnessed was more than likely the same fate of the villagers, police officers, even the animals. A full-scale investigation followed, but after a couple of years with no leads, the interest in the case and the initial panic subsided. Most people just slowly forgot about it. The village was small, and apparently there was no follow-up with any of the villagers who had previously left for bigger towns.

"The investigation in İstanbul fell by the wayside even sooner. When İstanbul police found out that the investigation was being conducted in earnest elsewhere, they were more than happy to cross it off their list of things to do.

"After Dr. Yay recounted his story to us, he made us swear that if we got any additional information we would contact him. I finally got the courage to tell him about the paper I had found in the dead man's vest. I told him that when I had arrived home much later than I should have, my father was very angry. He made me tell him the whole story right down to the paper. When I showed it to him, his face turned ashen, as he immediately recognized our family genealogy written in the old Ottoman script—a genealogy that included my name and his, and that of the dead man, Hamdi.

"I then recounted to Dr. Yay my father's belief that our family had an ancient curse placed on it several centuries ago, and that this paper had been thought lost. He didn't know how it had come into Hamdi's possession, or how it had been updated in the Ottoman script, as he was sure that his brother, a true Republican, had neglected to pass on the knowledge of that language to his family.

25

"Dr. Yay pondered these words for a moment, and then asked to see the paper. I had it folded in my pocket, and handed it to him. He studied it for a time and then looked at me gravely, but he also included Altin in his stare. He told us that he had heard rumors of an ancient curse that had been placed on two families: one Albanian and one Turk. He had been doing research for a book he was writing and had heard of the disappearances in Hamdi's village. He had gone to Adapazarı to meet with Hamdi, who had reported to the magistrate the disappearances in his village over a period of three to four weeks. He said that Hamdi was to bring him a document that he had found in a cave in the mountains when he sought shelter with his sheep from a storm. He said that Hamdi claimed that he could not read it, but that the disappearances of the villagers began shortly after he found it. Dr. Yay said he was waiting for Hamdi to come to his lab in Taksim that night.

"That dark moment had changed each of our lives from that time forward. We soon found ourselves spending less and less time together. Our other friends accepted us better when we were not with 'the group.' When we were together, we could sense the unspoken insults from the others. The jokes at our expense. The outright ridicule. As time passed our friendships faded.

"Your father was so convinced that the shadow had marked him somehow that he fervently petitioned his parents to allow him to leave Turkey and to study in America."

Ümët paused for a moment and popped a piece of Turkish Delight in his mouth from the bowl Ermal had just placed on the table in front of him. Although he didn't care for Turkish Delight, it was too sweet for his taste, Jeff was compelled by hunger to take a piece as Ümët continued.

"At the request of your father after he had lived in America for a few years, I tried to look up Dr. Yay. I found that he had moved to Izmir about five years after our incident. When

# Vale of Shadows

I finally tracked him down through the university, I was told that he had died suddenly. I asked if the university had any of his papers or notes that I could read, and they told me they would contact me after they had made a search. Two days later I was invited to go to Izmir and meet with one of his colleagues.

"When I arrived I found the colleague to be extremely nervous about talking to me. I asked him why, and his only answer was to thrust a worn-out old notebook into my hands. I looked at him, puzzled, and he told me that all my questions would be answered in these yellowed pages. He apologized for not being able to do more, but he told me that it was all he was prepared to do. He then advised me to leave and go back to İstanbul that very afternoon. He did not so much as offer me a drink or anything to eat.

"By his fearful demeanor, I took his inhospitality to be a warning, so I followed his advice and took the first bus back to İstanbul that same day. The eight-hour bus trip gave me a chance to read Dr. Yay's notebook. It was full of newspaper clippings and handwritten accounts of bizarre and malicious events that dated back hundreds of years. There was a large bibliography of books that documented murders and disappearances of humans and animals alike. Dr. Yay had written his own comments, beliefs, observations, and conclusions in the margins. In some cases it looked like he had torn entire pages of text and pictures out of these books."

"I'd hate to see his library fine," Jeff interjected.

"Excuse me?" said Ümët.

"I'm sorry. I was just making a joke," Jeff apologized. He had forgotten that humor seldom translated well between languages. He sat back and folded his hands, hoping he didn't look as foolish as he felt.

Ümët gave Orhan a puzzled look. Orhan smiled and just shrugged, saying something in Turkish to his uncle, who just smiled and shrugged back. Jeff sat like a chastised schoolboy.

Orhan smiled at his friend then looked back over at Ümët in a conciliatory fashion indicating that his uncle could continue with his story without further interruption.

"Well...what I could gather from the professor's notes was that for centuries occurrences like this had taken place. Most of the accounts were sketchy because people were so terrified that they refused to say much about the incident, let alone write it all down. The professor, who was a scientist, even went so far as to blame superstition and religion for the lack of accurate accounts being kept. He called it 'religious malpractice.' But the professor still had a pretty good collection of stories and accounts that dated back to the early years of the Ottoman Empire.

"Based on these accounts, he concluded that an evil entity was unleashed one time in a generation. These periods of time seem to correlate to a relationship between solar flares, planetary alignment, catastrophic events, and a pedigree moon."

"Excuse me, Uncle, but I am not familiar with the term pedigree moon," said Orhan.

"A pedigree moon is the time in which the moon is closest to the earth, and therefore, feels the most pressure from the moon. It only happens one or two times a year. This, along with the occurance of at least one of the other events I mentioned had the effect of beginning what has become an unpredictable cycle which starts at the beginning of a pedigee full moon and ends at the next full moon wrecking havoc during that month on the objects of the curse. As I told you, back in the summer of nineteen fifty-six, an entire village was annihilated. What happened to all those people of that village, plus the three policemen from Adapazarı, no one really knows. The only eyewitnesses that remained to tell their tale were your father and I, and the four others. But as I said, no one took us seriously except for Dr. Yay."

# Vale of Shadows

"What did Dr. Yay think about it?" asked Jeff. "I mean, did he write any theories or hypotheses down. Did he make any guesses?"

"Yes, he did," said Ümët. "He felt that based on what he could gather from our account and historical accounts, the evil was described most commonly as a solitary shadow. It was described as 'darker than dark,' 'blacker than black,' and capable of movement at great speeds. It was said that it could inhabit any creature it wished and thus had the ability to move about physically. It seemed to thrive on fear. Dr. Yay theorized that the entity would appear as a shadow in mercurial form, and then feed off of the fear of its victims.

"He wrote of the meeting he had in Adapazarı in nineteen fifty-six. The first disappearances were a shepherd and his family in a small village about forty kilometers southeast of Adapazarı. The mayor of that village reported the disappearances to the magistrate of the area, who at first dismissed them out of hand. But when the mayor came back and reported that more disappearances had occurred, the magistrate decided that he needed to act.

"He contacted the university in İstanbul, who put him in contact with Dr. Yay. Dr. Yay was an anthropologist and historian who had written a book concerning ancient, unsolved murders and abnormal deaths. The book was considered at the time to be merely a collection of myths and folklore, but the magistrate felt he needed all the help he could get. A meeting was arranged with Dr Yay, who went to discuss his theories with officials in Adapazarı.

"He wrote in his notes, which at this point seems to be in the form of a journal, that he found himself without answers. After his visit, he had arranged for a policeman and the mayor of the village to come to his lab in Taksim. He had a theory that the murders had something to do with specific family trees. He wrote that the mayor had mentioned that the village was made

29

up of members of the same clan. He was hoping to get more details from the mayor to see if there were indeed any familial links between his village and the victims of the past. But he never heard from the mayor or the policeman again. It wasn't until he heard rumors of Altin questioning people around the neighborhood that he had any leads at all."

Ümët slipped back into the cushions of his couch more comfortably, eyeing Jeff and Orhan. Jeff could tell that the recounting of this story was very taxing for Ümët. The older man took his gaze off of them and began staring blankly out the window into the night.

"It has been now nearly forty-four years since the last known incident," continued Orhan's uncle. "I began adding to the notebook, doing research of my own. It seems that at the same time another mass murder took place in northern Albania, in the Balkan Alps. The inhabitants of the village of Prifti simply disappeared without a trace. This village was situated in a high mountain valley with two other small villages near it.

"In this case, however, there were two other villages all three within an easy half-day's walk of each other. The mayor of Bitaj, the village farthest north and deeper into the valley, reported that his brother from the village of Prifti told him of the disappearance first of all the shepherds who had spent the night in the pasture. His brother was, of course, very distraught, stating that none of the other villagers would venture from their homes. They believed a murderer had fled the city and was hiding in the mountains.

"The brothers discussed the matter and decided that the best course of action was to consult a witch who lived higher up in the mountains. The conversation they had with her was never recorded, but with resolve and haste they went back to Prifti only to find every living soul missing…as if they had just vanished off the face of the earth.

# Vale of Shadows

"With deepened fear they made their way toward the third village, which was farther south, and nearest to the mouth of the valley. They reported that when they had walked about halfway to the village of Rrapëz, they saw a deep black shadow that seemed to move parallel to their trail but kept to the edge of the trees. They ran with all their might to the third village, howling and crying the whole way. By the time they reached Rrapëz they were so distraught and exhausted that they were accused of being drunk on *raki*. The brothers never saw the strange shadow again.

"The story of the two brothers was largely ignored by the authorities. This was in the summer of nineteen fifty-six. The Communist dictator had an iron grip, and the people of the northern mountains were a nuisance at best to him and his regime. Many of the people in the north wanted democracy and gave the government no little trouble. Because of this the Communists sought to punish them by not building roads or power plants to them. They were left in the Dark Ages. So in essence the government turned a deaf ear to the brothers' story.

"I found this account of their story in a journal of a Catholic priest who had been smuggling Bibles into that region. He heard about the brothers and tried to find them, but according to his journal he never did. He gathered what information he could from people who knew the brothers and had heard their story before he was eventually forced to flee due to threats by the local Communists. He escaped in a fishing boat heading for Italy one night, and never was able to follow up on the story. After his death his journal passed to his Order and somehow ended up in the papers of an estate in Tuscany. I just happened to find it in a book market in Milan when I was on holiday there.

"Between Dr. Yay's notebook, the priest's journal, what my father has told me, and the document found in Hamdi's pocket, I have been able to slowly piece together some answers

31

at least in part, to the questions that have haunted us since that night in nineteen fifty-six." He turned to his nephew. "To summarize, our family, Orhan, is under a curse. A curse placed on us by a sorcerer betrayed by an ancient ancestor. I am sorry to say that I have not found out all of the details of this curse, except to know that it also includes Jeff's family because of that shared betrayal.

"I believe that we do not have much time. The next full moon phase will be a pedigree moon. With the recent earthquakes in August and November I fear that makes the year two thousand significant to us. I believe the urgency has been placed on us by the arrival of a package. The content of this package is both terrifying and magnificent all at once."

As he said this, Uncle Ümët rose from his couch and went to an ornate chest in the corner of the room. He pulled out rolled linen and placed it on the table. Unrolling it, he carefully removed an animal skin parchment and brought it over to Jeff and Orhan.

"This is lambskin," he said as he placed it on the copper table. "The writing is ancient Persian. I have had no time to study it. I do not know who sent it or why it has been sent now. My feeling is that the resumption of the curse is eminent. Just as the genealogy came into Hamdi's possession just before the cycle in nineteen fifty-six, so now I believe this parchment heralds the beginning of the next cycle." He paused. "I fear we are soon to be in grave danger."

"When did this arrive?" asked Orhan.

"Today," replied Ümët. "It has been preceded by several days of my feeling more and more apprehensive...like something has been watching me, or at times even following me. I have had a sense of doom that goes well beyond *hüzün*. You two are the first to see this."

"Do you really believe that all this is related, Uncle?" asked Orhan.

32

"Yes, I am afraid I do," said Ümët. "This curse may be passed down along family lines. The deaths of the past were linked along bloodlines." Ümët sighed a deep sigh. "Our bloodlines. It seems that maybe this *evil*, whatever it is, may seek you, Jeff, because of your father. It may seek you, Orhan, because of me. I just don't know for sure."

"Well, if we are at risk," said Orhan, "then we better be prepared. What should be our first step?"

"I don't know," said Ümët. "Ermal here has advised that we wait."

The two men turned to see Ermal standing patiently at his post by the hall. He stepped closer and stood next to Ümët, suddenly looking less servile to Jeff.

"My family will know what to do," he said in an accent that Jeff determined was not Turkish. "We will wait for their counsel."

Jeff saw that Ümët and Orhan seemed satisfied with Ermal's input, so he decided to accept it without comment. He sat back in his couch and stared out the window trying to make sense of Ümet's story.

At that moment Moza came in and took the *nargile* away. When she returned a short time later, Jeff was relieved to see her carrying a large platter of mixed grill. Just the thought of eating made him feel better. His mouth watered at the sight of chicken shish, *donar* kebab (spiced meat), *iskender donar*, onions, peppers, tomatoes, pita bread, yogurt, *acı biber* (red pepper), and mint. Moza sat the platter down on the brass table between the three men, and then stood off to the side.

"Ah, good," said Ümët. "I hope you like our humble fare."

For the sake of politeness Jeff tried to control his excitement and not just dive into the platter with both hands. He deftly held a piece of pita in his hand and placed a portion of *donar*, along with yogurt, onions, and tomatoes sprinkled with the red *acı biber* pepper, and folded it in half taking a big bite. "Ummm, this is my favorite," he said to no one in particular.

The three men finished the platter to its last morsel with little conversation. Afterward Ermal brought in a tray with two teapots stacked one on top of the other, along with tea glasses and cubes of sugar. Jeff told him that he wanted his *çai*, or tea, light with a little sweet. Ermal took the top pot and poured about a quarter of the glass with dark brown steaming tea. He then took the bottom pot and filled the rest with boiling hot water, dropping in one sugar cube. Jeff took up the glass by the rim but found it too hot to hold. He put it back down and grabbed his earlobe with the forefinger and thumb that he had used to pick up the glass; the heat from his fingers transferred to his earlobe, taking the sting away so he could pick up the glass again.

Orhan smiled at his antics. "You know that doesn't *really* work," he said.

"Yes, it does," defended Jeff. "I learned it from a villager. The heat from the glass is transferred from the fingers into the fat of the earlobe so that you can drink the tea more quickly."

"It doesn't work. It's just an old wives tale."

"Have you ever tried it?"

"Well...no."

"Don't knock it until you've tried it," smiled Jeff taking another sip after pinching his lobe. "See, I've been able to take two sips already."

Orhan followed his friend's lead. He looked up, surprised. "Hey! It really does work!"

"I told ya. You city people think you know everything," said Jeff. He gave a big stretch, and a yawn. The meal was settling well with him. He looked out the window and noticed the running lights of a large tanker heading north toward the Black Sea. Giving a deep sigh, he felt as if he could curl up and go to sleep right there on the couch. He slowly turned his attention toward Orhan and Ümët. "I suppose I could hang with you guys for a couple of days until you get this thing cleared up."

Ümët smiled at Jeff, and then looked over at Orhan, who felt the penetrating gaze of his uncle. He had known that gaze since he first came to live with his father's brother many years ago. There was no use fighting it. "OK. I don't know if I believe all of this yet, Uncle, but I will wait as Ermal says. If this is a wild goose chase, as they say, I will have to return to work. We still have much to do in rebuilding the docks since the earthquake. *Tamam*?"

"*Tamam*," said Ümët.

"Well, if I'm going to be expected to fight ancient evils, I better get some sleep," said Jeff.

No sooner had he said this than Ermal came in and announced that the bedroom was ready for him. Jeff didn't have to be told twice. He jumped up off the couch and followed Ermal after bidding goodnight to Ümët and Orhan. He passed by the kitchen, where he saw Ermal's wife and two children cleaning up after the supper. Moza stopped drying a pan and caught Jeff's eye as he passed. She glared at him for a moment, and then went back to her drying. Jeff shrugged and continued to where Ermal was waiting for him at the door to his room.

The man bowed slightly as Jeff passed in front of him. Jeff returned the bow and entered the room, walking toward the large window that overlooked the bay. He heard the door close softly behind him.

He removed his robe and slippers, and began draping his clothes over the chair next to the window. He picked up the silk pajamas that had been left for him at the foot of the bed, and smiled to himself. "This beats my sweaty old T-shirt."

As he pulled back the comforter, a small gold cross fell onto the floor at his feet. He picked it up and examined it in the light cast by the sconce on the wall above his headboard.

"Hmm...now there's something you wouldn't expect to find in an Ottoman household." He placed the cross carefully on the nightstand and turned off the light. As he snuggled under the blanket, he clasped his hands behind his head and stared up at the ceiling in the dimly moonlit bedchamber.

"Books about monsters and Albanian witches," he sighed under his breath. "What have I gotten myself into?"

# 4. Turkish Coffee

Orhan entered the grand room the next morning to find Jeff sitting in front of the window in a large overstuffed chair with his feet propped up on an ottoman. He held a small saucer and demitasse containing thick, black Turkish coffee. He took a careful sip of the steaming hot drink and replaced the demitasse on its saucer. Then he turned, craning his neck to look at Orhan as he entered the room.

"I can't believe how hard it is to get Turkish coffee here in Istanbul," said Jeff. "I haven't been able to find any in the restaurants, so I asked Moza for some this morning, and she asked me if I really wanted Turkish or if I wanted instant Nescafe. I thought Turkey was famous for its coffee. What's the deal?"

"Well, Nescafe is about the only coffee available in restaurants. Some places you can get Turkish coffee, but not very many," said Orhan.

"Why is that?" Jeff asked as he drained the last drop of liquid off the thick grounds in the bottom of the cup.

"That is a common mistake made by foreigners. You see, coffee was the official drink of the Ottomans, but tea is the official drink of the Republic," said Orhan. "You can get about a hundred different kinds of tea, but at most restaurants you are out of luck unless you want Nescafe." He walked over and sat down on the couch near Jeff. "How long have you been up?"

"Oh, about a half hour or so," said Jeff. "I've just been sitting here counting the boats on the Bosphorus."

Orhan smiled. "That has always been a favorite pastime for me also. I used to spend hours daydreaming about where each boat was coming from or where it was going."

Jeff and Orhan stared silently out at the clear, sunny morning. The snow clouds of yesterday had been replaced by a brilliant blue sky. Snow blanketed the hills, with Judas, plane, and cypress trees on the Asian side. Everything below the sky was a surreal black and white. The ships and boats in the strait glided slowly in their perspective lanes. Tankers from Russia and Greece. Merchant ships from Bulgaria and Italy. Jeff became excited when he saw a large cargo ship flying a United States flag off of its stern. Bosphorus ferries of the "City Line" darted in and out between the steel behemoths. A French warship made its way from the Black Sea to the Marmara Sea. Jeff smiled as he remembered seeing that same ship heading in the other direction two days before as he was crossing by ferry from Asia to Europe.

Orhan sat forward in his chair and waved a hand in front of Jeff, who was staring trance-like off into the distance. Jeff blinked himself back into consciousness with a chuckle. "You're right. I could spend all day just sitting here counting ships. It's mesmerizing."

"I used to go out in my father's *caïques* and row out to just outside the shipping lanes," said Orhan. "I would wait for a Turkish ship to come along and then make a tugging motion with my arm in the air to see if I could get the captain to blow his foghorn. It used to scare my mother to death, but my father confided in me that he used to do the same thing when he was a kid."

"That's funny you should say that," said Jeff. "I used to do the same thing with truckers on the highways in Kansas. This is so cool, though, watching all these ships. About the best we can do back home is watch the sailboats on Cheney Lake. It's not exactly the same thing."

The two friends continued their tranquil assessment of the Bosphorus ecosystem in silence for several more moments. They both wished that they didn't have anything else to do for the rest of the day. Finally Jeff broke the silence.

# Vale of Shadows

"So what do you think of your uncle's story?"

"I don't know," responded Orhan. "When he gets his mind set on something, it is really no use in trying to change it. I told you before that my uncle was a little *eccentric*." Orhan accepted a cup of Turkish coffee offered by Moza, who had entered the room without either Orhan or Jeff noticing her.

"That was scary," said Jeff, secretely hoping she didn't understand English. "She always moves around so quietly."

"I think you'll have plenty of opportunity jumping at shadows later," laughed Orhan. "You don't need to start with the hired help."

Jeff smiled at Moza as she passed in front of him to take his demitasse away. She simply glared at him, and mumbled something under her breath. Jeff frowned, and looked over at Orhan, who seemed to have ignored the whole exchange.

"That didn't sound like Turkish," said Jeff.

"It wasn't," said Orhan. "Moza is a Gypsy, as well as Ermal. She was speaking Romani. They are from an eastern European clan of Roma as they call themselves."

"Well, what did she say?" asked Jeff.

"I have no idea," said Orhan. "They won't teach me any."

"I thought your uncle said that this family had worked for your family for a long time."

"They have, but the Gypsies are still very secretive. There's something about the past that has created a special bond between my uncle and Ermal. The details are a little fuzzy to me, but if you are really interested I'm sure that Uncle Ümët or Ermal would be happy to enlighten you."

"No, that's OK," said Jeff watching Moza's back as she left the room. "But I get a distinct feeling that she doesn't like me."

"She just needs to get to know you better, and then you will know for sure that she doesn't like you," teased Orhan.

39

"Hey, that was almost like a joke. Very funny," said Jeff. He stretched the last bit of sleep from his bones and settled back in his chair, pushing the ottoman out of the way so he could cross his legs. "

"I don't like the idea of just waiting around," said Orhan. "But Ermal says we will know more soon."

"How does Ermal fit into this whole story?" asked Jeff.

"Uncle Ümët told me last night after you went to bed about Ermal's dedication to our family. His clan swore fealty to our family some eighty years ago. It was just after the First World War when the battle cry was 'Turkey for the Turks.' There was a lot of bloodshed...Armenians, Greeks, Gypsies, and others. Somehow my grandfather had something to do with saving Ermal's clan from death. So they have been watching out for us ever since. It hasn't always been the same immediate family, but it has been the same clan. They are apparently scattered all over Eastern Europe. Ermal and Moza have been with my uncle for fifteen years or more. Before that it was someone else, but they were gone before I came to live with him."

Uncle Ümët came into the room with the lambskin parchment in one hand and a piece of stationary in the other. On the stationary was a partial translation of the parchment written in Turkish Latin script. Jeff noticed the ornate seal on the letterhead as Ümët sat the parchment and paper down on the table next to him. It reminded him of a sultan's *tuğra*.

"I was just noticing this letterhead. It's pretty impressive," said Jeff picking the stationary up from the table and studying the imprint more closely. "The calligraphy is one of the most beautiful I have ever seen. This is for *your* family?"

"Yes, it is the Aziz family crest, so to speak," said Ümët as he settled into a chair. "Our family descends from Sultan Abdül Aziz. He ruled from eighteen sixty-one to eighteen seventy-six. He did much in the way of modernizing administration and government. He built the Turkish navy to be the third largest in the world behind England and France. For a while he supported a constitutional government, but later when he changed his mind he was dethroned during a student-led revolt. Some accounts say he committed suicide by cutting his wrists four days after he lost power, but there is pretty strong evidence that suggests he was actually murdered. Alas for our poor family. We have had so much ruin."

"Wow. So you are actually royalty!" Jeff smiled over at his friend. "Should I bow or something? Kiss your feet…anything like that?"

"You can if you want," chuckled Orhan. "Actually, our lineage is a little dubious. You see, the sultan had a pretty fair-sized harem. The women all vied for their own children to inherit the power of the sultan, so there was a lot of pushing and shoving going on. Most Westerners don't know all the little conspiracies and intrigues that went on behind the harem walls. Lots of wives and concubines meant lots and lots of kids. There was no end to the bickering between all these women and children."

"Of course, the sultan would have his favorites," continued Ümët. "And that, of course, would just lead to more jealousy and conniving to get ahead. There were actually quite a few murders that were never brought to the attention of the outside world. Over the centuries many a 'prince' or 'princess' from the sultan's household were tossed into the Golden Horn like so much rubbish.

"Our lineage comes from a lesser wife, but a wife nonetheless, who had the cunning to leave the palace and build a *yali* of her own. When things began turning bad for Sultan Abdül Aziz, she and her young son were far enough away from the intrigue to escape the violent repercussions that followed the dethronement of Aziz. Other wives, concubines, princes, and princesses were not so fortunate."

41

Jeff studied the seal for a moment longer."Hmmm…who would have thought?" He replaced the stationary on the table.

Ümët explained, "I have been working on translating this parchment. As I said last night, it is written in ancient Persian. I have only translated a very small portion. Today I have made an appointment with a friend of mine who is a linguistics professor at the university. Hopefully he will be able to shed some light on it. I have very limited knowledge of this language. It appears to be poetry, but I am not sure."

"Why would poetry be sent to you?" asked Orhan.

"Like I said, I am not really sure it is poetry. It just has the meter like poetry," replied Ümët.

Jeff suddenly had an uneasy feeling as his hand brushed against the lambskin. "Who knows of this parchment?" he asked.

"At the moment, Ermal, myself, you two," replied Uncle Ümët, "and whoever sent it to me."

"So we will just wait then," said Jeff with a sigh.

Orhan and Jeff raised eyebrows at each other and decided that this would be a good time to get ready for the day. They had a breakfast of bread, cheese, sliced meat, fish, and tomatoes. Jeff ate all he could since he was not sure where his next meal would be coming from.

After they had eaten, he said, "I have to take the car back to Taksim this morning. I borrowed it from a friend I met in Golcük. I also have some running around I wanted to do today."

"I will be at our office all day," said Orhan. "If you need me you can call my *cep*. You are welcome to spend the night here again if you'd like."

"Thanks, but I have a hotel in Taksim. I wanted to go to Sultanahmet and check out the Covered Bazaar. I haven't even had a chance to see the Hagia Sophia or the cisterns yet," said Jeff getting up from the table. "This could be my last chance."

"Sounds like you'll be having a tourist day today. Will you be alone?" asked Orhan.

"No. The friend I met in Golcük is from the States who has lived here for about a year and a half. She's going to be my guide. It's her car that I borrowed."

Jeff went to the front entry and bent over to put on his own shoes. As he began tying his laces, he caught Moza staring at him out of the corner of his eye. He turned to make eye contact with her, but she quickly darted down the hall. Jeff shook his head slowly. "There's something wrong with that woman."

"I will find out from Uncle Ümët what he has learned from his linguistics friend, and give you a call," said Orhan as he followed Jeff out of the door to his car. The two men shook hands.

As he got into the car, Jeff said, "*Görüşmek üzere*. See you later."

"*Güle güle*," said Orhan waving as Jeff started the car.

"What does that mean again?" asked Jeff sticking his head out of the rolled down window.

"It literally means, 'go with laughter,'" said Orhan.

Jeff smiled as he drove down the road. He was the type of person that enjoyed learning new things, and he felt very good about the time he had spent in Orhan's uncle's home. He had a new appreciation for this marvelous, ancient city. For a time, as he drove along the Bosphorus, he was able to block out all the tragedy of the last several months. The earthquakes that had shaken the region last August and then again in November had killed thousands and left many more homeless. For the moment, however, he had an inexplicable sense of peace wash over him. He realized that at least for now there was no other place on earth he was supposed to be.

Snow covered the street but was not difficult to drive in. The craziness of the night before on the roads had not yet reconvened. The whole landscape seemed to be one scene after the other in black and white. It suddenly dawned on Jeff that

43

there was a strong smell of woodsmoke in the air. He rolled down his window. The briskness of the air was tainted by the smoke of a thousand fireplaces and wood-burning stoves. In all its glory, thought Jeff, Istanbul was still much as it had always been: unchanged by the rapid advancement of the rest of the world. He wondered, respectfully, if this also contributed to the melancholy that hung over the city and its inhabitants.

# 5. A Day with Aubrey

"Dance of the Sugar Plum Fairy" played from within Jeff's coat pocket. With a towel wrapped around his waist, he crossed his small hotel room to retrieve his phone. "I've got to get that changed," he said reminding himself again as he answered his phone. "Hello? Yeah, I just got out of the shower.... You're here already? ... OK, I'll be down in about ten minutes."

He tossed his phone on the bed and finished getting dressed. He had decided to wait to take a shower until getting back to his hotel room. The *yali* on the Bosphorus in Bebek was just a little too cold for him to relish getting wet there. Clean and dressed, he grabbed his key and headed down to the lobby where his friend Aubrey was waiting.

He exited the elevator to find Aubrey sitting with her back to him looking out the window at the hustle and bustle of Taksim Square. She heard him coming up from behind and stood to face him. In Jeff's eyes she had a tough beauty that he was infatuated with.

"Hi. Sorry I wasn't there this morning when you dropped my car off. I had to go to the bakery."

"That's OK," said Jeff. "Your roommate told me where you were. Thanks for coming today."

"No problem. I'm glad to help. What did you want to do while you're in Istanbul?" she asked, picking up her small backpack and slinging it over her shoulder.

"Well, my plans have changed. I may be on kind of a tight schedule after talking to my friend and his uncle last night." Jeff gazed at Aubrey from the corner of his eye trying to capture every detail of her appearance. Her shoulder-length red hair was

45

pulled back under a blue bandana. She wore a black leather coat with a fur-lined hood that lay tight around the back of her neck to keep the chill out. She picked her way through the snow piles along the sidewalk, keeping her attention on the slick pavement.

"What do you want to do first?" she asked.

"Well, I haven't seen the sights yet in Sultanahmet. I thought maybe we could go there," said Jeff.

"OK. Do you want to go the fast way or the scenic way?"

"How 'bout the scenic way."

She made a quick about face and headed back toward the corner where Jeff's hotel was. When they rounded the corner, she quickened her pace toward a yellow *dolmuş*. A small group of people was already getting into the cab. "We're in luck," she said.

They crammed in next to two others already seated in the back. The driver slid shut the door with a bang, and then climbed in behind the steering wheel. Aubrey handed a four hundred thousand Turkish lira note over the middle seat for the passengers ahead of them to pass to the driver. Jeff was amazed at the exchange rate between U.S. dollars and Turkish lira. It currently sat at about 1.3 million Turkish lira to one dollar, making their short cab ride down to the Beşiktaş pier only about thirty-five cents apiece.

"Do you know the word for 'stuffed'?" asked Aubrey.

"No."

"It's *dolma*. This is where the name dolmuşeş comes from. These minivans won't go anywhere until they are filled or *stuffed* with people. We got lucky to get this one without a wait. Sometimes when I've been by myself, I've had to wait fifteen to twenty minutes until more passengers come to fill the cab. It's a real drag if you're in a hurry."

The cab dropped them off at the pier where a City Line ferry was docked. Aubrey led the way through the turnstile and pressed in her *akbil*, an electronic token, twice to pay the fare for both of them. Jeff stopped to get two *simit* from a street vendor pushing a cart through the crowded dock. He handed one to Aubrey. "I just love these things," he said as he took a bite out of the bagel-shaped sesame seed bread. "Where are we going first?"

"First of all we'll take this ferry to Eminönü. Then we can grab a tram to Sultanahmet. We can walk over to the Hagia Sophia and the Blue Mosque." Aubrey saw a figure running through the crowd of people on the dock. She turned her attention toward the shore to see a young girl jump past the turnstile and leap onto the ferry, bypassing the passengers boarding on the gangplank. She headed straight toward Jeff. He had been looking out toward the Bosphorus and was startled by her sudden appearance at his side. She thrust a small black burlap poach into his hand, then turned and jumped off the boat just as one of the crew was about to snatch her.

Jeff stared after her in bewilderment as she skittered between taxis and buses, and disappeared from sight.

"What was that all about?" asked Aubrey staring after the girl. She turned her attention to the black pouch in Jeff's hand. He rolled it over in his palm studying it. It was about two inches square and was sewn roughly with a blackish brown twine made from sheep wool.

"I have no idea," said Jeff. "That kind of creeps me out a little bit."

The two looked out through the congestion of people and vehicles trying to pick up a sign of the girl. Aubrey squinted between the two buses the girl had run between. "There!" She pointed. "There past that red bus on the curb. See her?"

"Yeah, I see her now," said Jeff. The girl watched them pull away from the pier. She was wearing a mid-calf length skirt with several mismatched patches sewn to it. Her legs were covered by a worn black leotard that had holes in the knees. She wore heavy rubber overshoes that were obviously three sizes too big for her and layers of handmade wool yarn sweaters of

47

various bright colors. Her face was weatherworn and chapped from the cold, and her stringy black hair was pulled back under a scarf tied under her chin. She couldn't have been more than nine or ten years old.

As the ferry surged out toward its lane in the Bosphorus, Jeff and Aubrey saw an older woman similarly dressed come along side the little girl, and take her hand. They stood watching Jeff's ferry move on around the bend in the shore. He didn't take his eyes off of them until they were completely out of sight. Then he looked back down at his hand and squeezed the pouch between his thumb and forefinger. The contents seemed to be seeds of some kind. He frowned down at the oddity he was holding.

"What do you suppose it is?" he asked.

"I've actually seen something like this before," said Aubrey. "Before I came to Turkey, I did some mission work in villages of central and northern Albania. I met a man who was a Bektashi Muslim who wore one around his neck on a leather thong. He called it a *hajmali* and said it brought him luck and protected him from evil spirits. I told him it was stupid to believe in such things, and he said he had had it since he was a child. He said it was a 'gift from God,' and that it had fallen to earth from heaven. He said that because of it he had had a good and honorable and safe life. When I tried to take it from him to look at it, you would have thought I was trying to kill him. The scene he caused not only frightened me but everyone standing around. I decided to leave well enough alone, and he walked away from me looking terrified.

"I stood there with my mouth hanging open, feeling completely stupid, when another man came up to me from the crowd and identified himself as the local *dervish*. He asked me if I had ever read *Hamlet*. I had to admit that I had skipped it when I was supposed to have read it in school. He said to me, 'There are more things in heaven and on earth than are dreamt of in your philosophies.' I didn't really know what he was talking about at the time, but I figured it had something to do with me minding my own business.

"The village welcomed me in spite of myself, even the *dervish*, but I never saw that little old man again. I learned a valuable lesson that day and that is even though I might not believe in something doesn't mean that someone else doesn't believe in it, and the consequences of their beliefs will dictate everything they do."

Jeff looked from Aubrey back to the *hajmali* in his hand. "So do you think this is like a curse or an amulet for good luck?"

"Well, I think it's for good luck," said Aubrey. "After all it *is* a 'gift from God.'" She smiled at Jeff but noticed the concerned look on his face. "This wouldn't have anything to do with your change of plans, would it?"

"Gosh, I hope not," said Jeff. "After what Orhan's uncle was saying last night, though, I'm not so sure. There has been some pretty creepy stuff going on around here, and my dad apparently witnessed some of it years ago. Who do you think that little girl was? Did you understand what she said to me before she ran off?"

"Well, no, but I don't think she was Turkish. I think based on her appearance she is more than likely a Gypsy. They're everywhere around here."

"A Gypsy! What is it with me and Gypsies?" Jeff said exasperated. He caught the inquisitive look on Aubrey's face. "Orhan's uncle has Gypsy servants and I have a strong feeling they don't like me."

Aubrey smiled, but said nothing. She made a subtle move to sit closer to Jeff pretending to straighten her coat tail until her thigh touched his. When Jeff made no move to pull away their eyes met briefly and neither could hide the smiles that flickered nervously across their lips.

# Rob Dakin

"This snow reminds me of home," said Aubrey as she gazed out over the Bosphorus at the snow laidened landscape on the Asian side.

"Really? Where's home?" asked Jeff, surprised that they had not had this conversation before.

"Colorado," said Aubrey. "Crested Butte, Colorado."

"Really? I've skied at Crested Butte. You were born there?" he said as he turned his body on the bench to face Aubrey."

"Yes. My parents were hippies and moved there in the early 70's. I learned to ski before I was two. I was a ski instructor and eventually on the ski patrol.

"You know I actually took lessons there. It was the first place I ever skied!" Exclaimed Jeff.

"I thought you looked familiar. You were the guy that kept falling down on the bunny slope," giggled Aubrey as she nudged his arm.

"Very funny," said Jeff. "I actually got pretty good for a flatlander. That always looked like a fun job."

"Yeah, it was fun, but I wanted something more. I went to Northern Arizona University in Flagstaff— another ski town. My dad said it was a good university for hippies. I got a degree in music and became a music therapist. After graduating I worked with kids with disabilities, and found the organization I am with now. So far I've worked with kids in Albania and Turkey."

"I can't believe your parents were hippies."

"Well if that shocks you, it gets worse. I was actully a *love child* conceived in the back of a psychedelic painted VW van after a *Bread* concert. That's pretty wild, huh?"

"There was actually a band called *Bread*?"

"Sure. My folks loved them, but it gets even more weird— I was named after one of their songs. Don't tell me you never heard the song *Aubrey*."

"Uh...no."

"And Aubrey was her name, a not so very ordinary girl or name, but whose to blame, I loved her name." Sang Aubrey. "You've never heard that before?"

"I guess not," apologized Jeff. "It does sound nice though," he said rolling his eyes.

"You're a jerk," she teased. "Some of my fondest memories are of my mom singing *Bread* songs while she worked in her garden tending her marijuana plants."

"Your mom had marijuana plants?" blurted out Jeff.

"Sure. Didn't you grow up with pot plants in your house?"

"No way! I can't believe..."

Aubrey cut him off. "I'm just kidding." She gave him a broad smile as he stared at her in shocked silence. "I'm just joking with you." She gave him a gentle nudge.

"Whew, you had me going there for a minute," said Jeff.

"Yeah, she didn't really sing *Bread* songs in the garden."

"You're terrible," he said trying not to smile.

The two sat in silence for the rest of the trip. Jeff looked out over the Bosphorus. He had begun to recognize some of the landmarks that dotted the shores on the European and Asian sides. After a short time, the ferry engines flared then cut out as it was maneuvered expertly into its berth on the pier in Eminönü.

As Jeff disembarked via the gangplank, he looked out into the sea of people coming and going. He really hoped he didn't see any more Gypsies staring at him. Aubrey caught up with him and hooked her arm in his as they walked. Her touch took his mind off of all things sinister.

"Now where?" he asked.

"Just up here is the end of the line for the tram. We can take it up to Gülhane Park and Topkapı Palace then walk over to the Haghia Sophia and the Blue Mosque if you want. From there we can grab the tram again to Beyazit and 'shop till we drop' at the Grand Bazaar. How does that sound?"

"Sounds great to me," said Jeff.

They walked with caution on the snowy street toward the tram stop. Jeff was amazed at how many people were already out and about.

"Those stairs lead down to a little bazaar under the street." Aubrey pointed toward wide stairs that led down underneath the intersection that they were crossing. "Normally I would go down there to get across the street because the traffic is so bad, but today because of the snow it seems like we may make it just fine."

They walked up the concrete steps to the tram platform and stood with a group of others who were also waiting. After a few minutes, Jeff looked down the tracks to see the bright headlamp of the tram coming around the bend. The transients jostled for position to board as the tram drew nearer. Aubrey pressed her *akbil* into the meter twice to pay for their ride. They quickly boarded, and each grabbed a strap that dangled from a bar to steady themselves as the tram jolted to gain momentum.

The passengers swayed back and forth with the motion of the tram. A recorded woman's voice announced the upcoming stops. Jeff tried to pick out any words that he knew but found she spoke way too fast for him. It didn't take long for the tram to come to a stop at another platform. Aubrey pushed her way to the door. "Stay close," she said over her shoulder. Jeff found himself being pushed from behind right into Aubrey's back.
With the press of bodies they nearly exploded from the tram door onto the platform.

They crossed the street and made their way to the gate of the gardens and Topkapı Palace. Aubrey stood facing the street and looked up and down the causeway. She turned back to Jeff. "So what would you really like to do? If we tour everything here, we're going to run out of time."

Jeff peered through the gate at the gardens and the palace. "This looks pretty cool. Is there a charge to get in?" he asked craning his neck around the wall so he could get a better look.

"We can walk through the gardens, but there is a small ticket price for the palace," said Aubrey. If you would like to do some shopping later, I suggest we maybe walk on over to the Haghia Sophia. Tour that. Then we can walk around the pillars of the hippodrome."

They decided to take a short walk through Gülhane Park. The snow-covered trees gave a ghostly beauty to the palace in the background. Jeff secretly wished Aubrey would slip so he could come to her rescue, and then not let go of her hand. She was too sure of her steps, though, and the more he thought about it, the more he realized his thoughts were that of a desperate, pitiful man. He decided to be content with walking by her side.

"What is that little button you keep using to pay our fares with?" he asked as they rounded the corner to the ancient church/mosque/museum that is the Haghia Sophia.

"It's called an *akbil*," she answered. "It's electronic, and I can recharge it with lira. It's really handy and is used for the buses, ferries, and trams." She took it out of her pocket and handed it to him. Jeff noticed for the first time that it was attached to her key ring.

"It looks like the electronic buttons they use to activate those laser tag guns," he said after he examined it. "Umm…it has the word *Dallas* on the back. Do you think that means it is made in Dallas, Texas? That would be wild."

"I used to think that also, but I think it actually is the name of the company," she said. She was becoming more and more amused by the playful way in which he viewed and interpretated his surroundings.

They bought tickets to the museum for the equivalent of about three dollars apiece. Aubrey led the way, and began talking in hushed tones.

"I have been here before so if you would like I can tell you quite a bit of the history, but I can't look like I'm a tour guide or we will get in trouble with the *real* tour guides," said Aubrey. Jeff noticed a group being formed by an official tour guide. He sauntered toward them to see if he could hear what the guide was saying. When he got closer he was disappointed to hear German being spoken.

The pair walked down the marble floored hall and entered the main structure through a huge door. The acoustics were spellbinding to Jeff. He had seen other magnificent cathedrals throughout Europe but nothing compared to this as far as historical prowess. Designed as an "earthly mirror of the heavens," its interior dwarfed everyone and everything inside. Scaffolding was erected to the very dome itself for repairs. The massive pillars that supported the dome were adorned with eight gigantic calligraphic roundels that reminded Jeff of huge, round shields. "What is that calligraphy?" he asked, pointing.

Aubrey gently grabbed his arm and lowered it. "Don't point," she whispered. "These roundels are inscribed with the names of Allah, the Prophet Mohammed, the first four caliphs, and a couple of martyrs. They are Islamic." She continued her lecture, "Did you know that in the Koran there are ninety-nine names for God? There are actually a hundred names, but the hundredth name is known only to the camel. That is why it has an arrogant smile and looks down on men." She smiled at Jeff when she saw his reaction. "Or so I have been told."

"It's hard to believe that we're standing where Byzantine Kings were coroneted, and knights were knighted," said Jeff in awe. "These mosaics appear to be in Greek," he noted as they walked back into one of the side galleries.

"Yes. The Byzantines were Greek speaking, but when they were defeated by the Ottoman Turks this great church that dates back in part to Emperor Constantine was modified to be a mosque," said Aubrey as she and Jeff studied a mosaic of Jesus as a child and a man. "The Ottomans being Muslim still regarded Jesus as a great prophet, so even though other Christian symbols were destroyed these mosaics were simply covered over with plaster. Right now they are being restored, but some plaster is being left to remind people that this was also a mosque. Right now it is a museum. Since the Christians and Muslims claimed it as an important part of their history, the new republic made it a museum. So *now*, they have to share it."

"So the Turkish Republic is not necessarily religious?" asked Jeff.

"No, not necessarily. It tolerates religion, but its goal is to be 'Western' and 'secular,'" said Aubrey. "Most everyone is Muslim around here, though."

They began to ascend a cobblestone ramp that switch-backed to the second floor balcony. Jeff noticed a crack reinforced with metal stays and bolts, which had calibrations. Aubrey saw his interest. "Those are to try to stabilize the walls. There was some damage during the earthquake. Those markings are so they can gage the shift. You see them in many buildings in Istanbul now."

When they reached the balcony, they looked out over the nave and eavesdropped on the German tour below. The balustrade they leaned against had been defaced, its Christian cross bas-relief chiseled off. Jeff chuckled to himself and shook his head. Although the bas-relief had been chiseled flush with the rest of the marble, it still left a scar in the shape of the cross. *Craziness*, Jeff thought to himself.

They continued walking around the upper gallery, Jeff taking pictures. A museum guard eyed them warily. They tried to look nonchalant as they made their way back to the cobblestone ramp. Jeff placed a hand on Aubrey's arm to stop her. "I want to take a picture of you up here." He took her by the shoulders with both hands and gently positioned her for the right pose. He pretended to focus his lens on her but actually focused over her shoulder at the museum guard who was still staring at them. Aubrey could tell that he wasn't looking at her, and began to turn.

"What are you doing?" she asked.

"No. Stop. Don't look around," said Jeff. "I want to get a picture of that guard gawking at us. He has the most remarkable sour-puss look on his face." Jeff refocused over her shoulder. "Say cheese." He took the picture of the guard with only a small portion of Aubrey's shoulder in the corner of the frame. "There. That will make for interesting conversation later."

"You're crazy," chuckled Aubrey as they descended the ramp. "Wouldn't this be fun to go down on roller skates?"

As they were the only ones on the ramp, they thought it would be fun to race down, but after running into the wall on the first landing they realized that this idea was a broken ankle waiting to happen, so they slowed down. They met the group of Germans about halfway down as the tour was coming up. The tour guide was busy making sure everyone was careful with his or her footing. As he passed Jeff and Aubrey, he said in English, "Be careful you don't fall."

Jeff experienced the dread that all international travelers have when they suddenly find out that someone speaks their language that they didn't think could. He hoped he had not said anything that would get him into trouble.

Exiting the Haghia Sophia, Jeff and Aubrey began to walk toward the pool and fountain that lay picturesquely between the Haghia Sophia and the Blue Mosque. To the right was the hippodrome. A vendor with a cart full of hot chestnuts had positioned himself along the sidewalk of the park.

"Do you want some chestnuts?" asked Jeff. "They're 'roasting over an open fire...'"

"No thanks. They turn your hands black," said Aubrey.

They crossed the street and walked toward the mosque. Children came running up and crowded around them trying to sell postcards of the Blue Mosque and Haghia Sophia. Jeff tried to push through them, but Aubrey stopped to look at what the children were selling.

"You American? Five dollars," said one of the boys. Aubrey began to walk off. "OK. Nice lady, four dollars." The other children pushed maps, postcards, and books about Istanbul in their faces.

"I'll give you one dollar for two postcard albums," said Aubrey.

"Aw...you're killing me," said the boy. "Two dollars for two. OK?"

"OK," said Aubrey smiling as she pulled two dollars out of her little Turkish carpet coin purse. "It really is a good deal," she said to Jeff. "These are full of photos of the inside of the mosque. They're better than you'll be able to take with your camera."

Jeff ended up buying several postcard albums and a book in English about Istanbul. He haggled the price down to ten dollars, and then put his new acquisitions into his book bag.

They walked up the steps to the entrance that led to the courtyard. Jeff was amazed at the architecture of arches and domes. Six minarets jutted skyward, four from the four corners, and two towered over the entrances to the courtyard front and back. Each had two or three balconies. In the center of the courtyard was an ablutions fountain, but Aubrey informed Jeff that it now was strictly ornamental. Standing at the fountain, Jeff turned to face the mosque. A cascade of domes and semi domes gracefully fell in architecture toward the courtyard.

"All these rooms under the arches and small domes around the courtyard once housed the seminary here," said Aubrey. "See these six minarets? They have an interesting story." She waited to see if Jeff was paying attention.

"Go ahead, teacher. I'm listening," he said with a grin.

"Well, the mosque was commissioned to be built by Sultan Ahmet the First back in a time when the Ottoman treasuries were pretty depleted. He wanted his new mosque to be taller than the Haghia Sophia. When the builders had finished with the dome, it was found that the mosque was about six inches shorter than the Haghia Sophia. So the sultan had his unfortunate imperial architect beheaded. He commissioned a new imperial architect to finish, who just happened to be an Albanian by the way, with the instructions that the minarets were to be covered in gold. The sultan then went on a long journey to Persia. Well, the poor architect knew that there was not enough gold in the treasury to finish such a task, so the ingenious Albanian decided to make six minarets instead of the usual two or three. When the sultan returned to find that his minarets were not covered in gold he was furious, and wanted his imperial architect's head. The architect explained that he thought the Sultan had requested six minarets not gold minarets because in the Turkish language the word for gold is *altin* and the word for six is *altı*. The sultan believed this to be an honest misunderstanding and let the imperial architect keep his head. After all, no mosque in the world had six minarets, so the sultan still got a glorious edifice to dedicate to Allah. Or so I have been told."

"Pretty clever," stated Jeff, nodding his head approvingly.

"Yeah, it just goes to show you that BS'n is an ancient and time-honored art," laughed Aubrey.

# Vale of Shadows

They walked out of the courtyard up what appeared to be a back stairway outside of the mosque. Aubrey began to take her shoes off to go in.

"It's OK for us to go in here?" asked Jeff.

"Oh, sure. This is a real mosque, but it's open for a tourist like you." She nudged him in the ribs playfully. "All you have to do is show respect, and don't do anything stupid like putting a New Testament in the Alms box. That will get us both thrown in jail for sure."

Jeff slipped off his shoes and was handed a plastic bag to carry them in by the attendant at the door. Aubrey put her shoes in her plastic bag and handed them to Jeff while she put a scarf over her head like the Muslim women wore. They walked onto plush carpets in their stocking feet. Around the huge, thick piers that supported the dome were shelves that encircled the pillars at their base for the "regulars" to store their shoes. Jeff felt a little uneasy as he walked quietly around one of the piers. There seemed to be some kind of class being held in the center of the mosque.

Aubrey and Jeff circumvented the worshippers and tried to discreetly take a few photos. Aubrey pointed out the Mihrab or prayer hall with her chin. "That is a prayer hall and marks the direction of Mecca." She said. "Next to it is called the *minbar*, or high pulpit. The Imam will give a sermon from there on Fridays." From the dome hung a massive chandelier that at one time held candles but now was illuminated by light bulbs.

As they neared the exit, an old man hobbled over to Jeff and took his hands. He gave Jeff's hands a little shake and said something that Jeff didn't understand. Jeff smiled politely at the old man, sensing that he was just trying to be friendly. He looked over at Aubrey to see if she could tell him what the old gentleman was saying.

"He said that you are welcome here, and asks if you are a 'believer,'" she interpreted.

59

Jeff nodded his head stupidly. "Tell him thank you. And yes I am a *believer*, but probably not in the same way that he is."

"OK, I'll tell him, but get ready to run."

"What?" exclaimed Jeff somewhat in a panic.

"Just kidding," said Aubrey. She talked to the old man at length, explaining to him that they were Christians in Turkey to help with earthquake relief efforts. The man continued to hold on to Jeff's hands. When Aubrey explained that they were there to help Turks in their time of need, the man raised Jeff's hands to his forehead then lowered them to his lips and kissed them. "He has just thanked God for you and asks a blessing on you," said Aubrey.

Jeff felt a little embarrassed but also honored by the sincerity of this little man. He looked around at the other people in the center of the mosque. No one seemed to mind that they were there. He was pleasantly surprised when the little old man agreed to let Aubrey take a picture of the two of them together. *This is one of the coolest things I've ever done,* he thought as the flash stung his eyes.

# 6. Dance of the Sugar Plum Fairy

Jeff and Aubrey left the mosque and replaced their shoes only to be swarmed by postcard-selling children again. This time the pair pushed on through them despite the cacophony of pleas. Clouds began to darken overhead; the sunshine of the morning was being replaced by the promise of more snow in the afternoon. The children finally gave up chasing Jeff and Aubrey for easier prey as the German group made its way from the Haghia Sophia towards the Blue Mosque.

"Just across the street are the Basilica Cisterns. Do you want to go look at them?" asked Aubrey as she sat down on a bench shadowed by trees along the Hippodrome. She finished lacing her shoes as Jeff sat next to her. The snow had been cleared from the bench by a couple of young lovers who had just left walking off hand in hand down the walk toward the ancient columns. Jeff's mind daydreamed of a time when he would go walking hand in hand with Aubrey. His dream was interrupted by the "Dance of the Sugar Plum Fairy" emanating from his coat pocket. He fumbled to get the phone out of his pocket quickly to shut off the ring.

"Nice," teased Aubrey. "Very manly."

"I know. Isn't it great?" Jeff said sarcastically. "I just got it, and I haven't had a chance to read the instructions on how to change the tune." He finally wiggled the phone free and answered it. "Hello...hello?" Jeff took the phone away from his ear and stared at it for a moment. "No one there," he said to Aubrey, who was looking on inquisitively. Just then the phone tune played again. Jeff answered it more quickly this time.

"Hello. Oh, hey, Orhan," he said cheerfully, but his face immediately turned serious as Orhan quickly went into a rant.

"When? … OK, I'll be there." He hung up and stared at the phone in his hand.

Aubrey shifted around on the bench to face him. She looked at him with great concern and asked, "What's wrong? Who is it?"

"That was Orhan. He said his uncle came home after meeting with his friend at the university. He is very agitated and wants to meet with Orhan and me later at my hotel," Jeff toyed with his phone as he hunched over and rested his elbows on his knees. "His uncle didn't take time to explain and left the house again without saying where he was going. All he said was we have to be in Ephesus in two days."

"Ephesus? Do you know why?" asked Aubrey.

"Not yet. Ümët had a pretty wild story last night. It had to do with ancient curses and Persian parchments, and a bunch of other crazy stuff. I don't know that I buy into it. It's just too weird."

"That might explain the Gypsy girl, and the *hajmali*," said Aubrey reflectively. "We probably shouldn't ignore it."

"*We?*"

"Well, yes. I can't let a greenhorn like you go traipsing all over Turkey by himself," said Aubrey with a smile. "Besides, I heard about your little fiasco with the wrong bus going in the wrong direction. You obviously need a babysitter." She gave Jeff a playful nudge.

Jeff cringed at the memory of what Aubrey was alluding to. Two months ago he had been working in Adapazarı, and had really worn himself out. He boarded a bus he thought was going west to Istanbul, and fell dead asleep. When he awakened he found he had boarded the wrong bus and had no idea where he was. He didn't recognize any landmarks. He didn't speak the language and had no cell phone. If it hadn't been for a helpful university student who spoke English, he would have been in real trouble. As it turned out he had boarded a bus to Ankara, and had gone in the opposite direction from Istanbul. His friends had since teased him that he was lucky he hadn't ended up in Iraq.

"What time do we need to meet Orhan?" asked Aubrey as she stood, and placed her book bag over her shoulder. "Do you still feel like sightseeing?"

"Not really. We need to be back to the hotel by around four thirty," said Jeff standing up next to her. It was already almost two. He looked down the hippodrome in the direction of the Egyptian Obelisk. The two young lovers were still holding hands, studying the column. Snow began to fall gently like the floating cottonseeds that drift from the cottonwood trees in the spring back in Kansas. Aubrey began to walk towards the Fountain of Kaiser Wilhelm. Jeff followed her with his eyes. She suddenly realized that he was not with her, and turned and met his gaze.

"What?" she said, smiling at him slightly embarrassed.

"Nothing," he said. "I was just thinking." He shuffled through the snow to catch up with her, and the two turned up the walk passed the fountain. Aubrey was leading them to the Sultanahmet tram stop just up ahead. Through the snowy stillness came the afternoon prayer from the Firuz Ağa Mosque. They crossed the street and ascended steps that were part of a garden under the shadow of the mosque. Jeff made a mental note that as the prayer was blasting through the loudspeakers on top of the mosque's minaret, no one seemed to be paying any attention to it.

"This prayer is called Zuhr. It is supposed to call people to search for God in the middle of their busy day," said Aubrey. "Most people, as you can see, are too busy to pay much attention."

They crossed the street and climbed the stairs to the tram platform. The snow was falling heavier now. The silhouette of the Haghia Sophia was blurred in the distance by snowflakes the size of one hundred thousand Turkish lira coins — or the size of a quarter mused Jeff.

"What's your poison?" asked Aubrey. "We can go down to the covered bazaar or head back to Taksim. Do you feel like shopping?"

"Not really, but I am getting pretty hungry. Do you know any good spots to eat around here?"

"Sure. We can go eat at a Turkish restaurant, or there's a McDonalds next to the Beyazit tram stop. That's just across the street from the bazaar."

"I vote for Turkish," said Jeff.

The tram heading up toward Beyazit came around the corner, and Jeff and Aubrey boarded an already crowded compartment. The basic color for *Istanbullus* is black. Black leather jackets, black trousers, black shoes, black hair, dark complexion, and dark moods. Jeff tried to smile at a man whom he was being pressed against only to have his smile returned with a surreptitious scowl. Aubrey bumped up into Jeff from behind with a little "Oooh!"

"Are you OK?" he asked.

"Yes, but I just got my Christmas goose a little early," she said as she repositioned herself under Jeff's arm hanging from the ceiling strap. "Someone just pinched my rear."

"You're kidding!" exclaimed Jeff.

"No. It happens all the time," she said. "You don't mind if I snuggle a little closer to you, do you?"

"Remind me to send that guy a Christmas card," Jeff said under his breath.

"What was that?"

"Oh, nothing."

\* \* \*

They got off at the second stop and found a Turkish restaurant that looked interesting. Aubrey ordered them each *lahmacun* and *gözleme*. "These are like pizzas with lamb and spices. The *lahmacun* is the flat one. The *gözleme* is the rolled up one," she explained as she took the plate from the man behind the counter, and handed it to Jeff.

After lunch Jeff decided that he was distracted by Orhan's call to go shopping, so they boarded another tram that was heading back to Eminönü where they were able to get a *dolmuş* back to Taksim Square. The snow fell heavier. Traffic began to crawl again, and Jeff had flashbacks to the sluggishness on the streets the night before. The *dolmuş* inched across the Galata Bridge. Automobiles, trucks, and buses packed the thoroughfare; pedestrians dressed in black overcoats with shoulders hunched against the cold packed the sidewalks on either side of the bridge. Jeff suddenly felt a sense of the melancholy that Uncle Ümët had been talking about as he gazed out of the window toward the confluence of the Golden Horn with the Bosphorus. He shivered as he stared through the now thickly falling snow and tried to block out of his mind what Orhan might have to say.

Aubrey felt him shiver and saw the darkness of his mood in his unblinking eyes. She pressed closer to him, placing her arm in his. He smiled slightly and patted her gloved hand. The *dolmuş* finally moved off the bridge. Once they were past the bottleneck in the traffic, they made better time through the streets of Beyoğlu going toward Taksim.

They came to the *dolmuş* stop across the square from Jeff's hotel. A tram circled the monument on its roundabout tracks as it began its ascent back up İstiklal Street. Jeff and Aubrey waited for it to pass then crossed the street, picking their way through the piles of snow. Jeff was tired of being cold, but he didn't dare say anything knowing that he would soon be back in Kansas with central heat while Aubrey would continue to suffer in her apartment with only a small space heater.

"I know a place up the street that has really great *profiterole*," she said trying to lighten his spirits.

# Rob Dakin

"What's *profiterole*?" asked Jeff.

"Oh my gosh!" she exclaimed. "You've been here how long, and you've never had *profiterole*?"

"I guess not," he said impatiently.

"It's actually a French pastry. Kind of like a chocolate-covered cream puff. They are great," she explained. "We'll go get one. It will make you feel better." She pulled the cuff of her glove down and looked at her watch. "We have a little over an hour before you are supposed to meet with Orhan and his uncle. Plenty of time."

She led the way down İstiklal Street crossing back over the tram tracks to a small pastry shop, where she ordered them each *profiterole*. There was a small, two-seater table in the corner, so they sat down to enjoy their treat. Jeff played with the thick chocolate syrup that covered the cream puff with his spoon, and then took a scoop of the succulent pastry.

"Whoa! This is good," he mumbled with his mouth full. His phone tone played inside his pocket startling him and causing him to jump. He fumbled to get it out of his pocket, eying Aubrey nervously across the table.

"Hello?"

"Jeff, where are you?" demanded Orhan.

"I'm in Taksim eating *profiterole* with Aubrey," he said trying to quickly chew and swallow the bite that was already in his mouth. "Why? What's wrong?" Jeff could tell by the urgency in Orhan's voice that he was upset about something.

"Have you had anything strange happen to you today?" asked Orhan.

"Yeah. In addition to your call earlier I had a creepy little Gypsy girl give me a strange good luck charm," said Jeff. "What's going on?"

The long pause caused Jeff to think they had been disconnected. Orhan's voice finally broke the silence. "We are in *big* trouble. Be extra careful."

66

# 7. Persian Utterances

"Uncle Ümët is dead," said Orhan flatly. "He came home after his meeting at the university. He was very agitated and said he was sure he had been followed going to the university and then coming back from it. He left the parchment with Ermal, and then said he had to make a quick errand. The next thing I knew the police were at our door and told me that Uncle Ümët had been found dead on the street. "

"That's horrible!" exclaimed Jeff, flabbergasted. "Are you OK?" He then turned to Aubrey, cupping his hand over the phone, and said to her, "Orhan's uncle is dead." She gave him a look of shocked disbelief, but said nothing.

"I'm physically all right. I will have to grieve later," responded Orhan, "I am already on my way to your hotel. I should be there in about another half an hour as long as it does not snow any harder. I will meet you in your lobby." With that he hung up.

Jeff studied the expression on Aubrey's face. It was one of concern, but he saw fear begin to shadow her features. They did not feel like finishing their dessert, and soon they got up and walked back to Jeff's hotel. The snowfall was lessening as the horizon turned a darker gray over the tops of the buildings as dusk began falling behind the clouds. Jeff looked up into the sky and blinked the falling snowflakes off his eyelashes. Aubrey stopped beside him and followed his gaze skyward.

"I don't think it's such a good idea that you stay here," he said to her, not taking his attention off the horizon. "Orhan will be here in a few minutes."

"Jeff if you're in danger, I don't want to leave you alone," she said squeezing his hand in hers.

# Rob Dakin

"All right...you can stay until Orhan comes, but after that...we'll see."

They went into the lobby of the hotel and sat down on a sofa facing the street. Through the plate glass window they saw Orhan approaching from around the corner. They watched him pause and turn, facing the way he had just come. The snow on his shoulders and stocking cap gave evidence that he had been walking for some time. He finally came into the lobby, stomping his shoes free of snow. He looked up at them without smiling and approached the sofa carrying a thick folder of papers.

"My uncle has been murdered," he said without greeting.

"Are you sure he was murdered?" asked Aubrey.

"Yes. The police are certain of it, but they have no clues as to how, or who, or why. He left a note, sealed, with both of our names on it. I haven't opened it yet, but along with the note he left a key to his safe. Inside was all of his research since nineteen fifty-six. I haven't had a chance to do anything but scan through it."

Jeff and Aubrey stood up on either side of Orhan, and peered over his shoulder as he began to open the seal. But Orhan suddenly looked up, and Jeff and Aubrey followed his gaze to several men sitting in the lounge of the lobby staring at them. Thinking better of it Orhan slipped the envelope back underneath his coat. "Let's go up to your room."

When they arrived in Jeff's third floor hotel room, Orhan immediately went to the window, which faced out toward the square and pulled the curtains closed.

"Do you think you were followed?" said Jeff.

"I don't know. I can't believe I'm here and not taking care of my uncle, but Ermal told me I need to come here. He was very insistent." Orhan took a seat in the desk chair as he turned on the lamp. He took a hotel letter opener from the stationary packet and gently pried it under the sealed flap opening the envelope. Jeff and Aubrey moved closer hovering over Orhan's shoulder. He pulled out a piece of stationary with the Aziz *tuğra* embossed as the letterhead. The note was written in a script neither Aubrey nor Jeff recognized.

"It looks like Arabic," said Aubrey with disappointment in her voice.

"It is similar to Arabic, but it is actually Ottoman Turk script. Atäturk had the written language Westernized with the Latin alphabet as one of his attempts to make the new Turkish Republic more like the West and less like the East."

"You can read it?" asked Jeff.

"Of course. I am, after all, Ottoman Turk," replied Orhan incredulously. He began to read out loud:

*Orhan and Jeff, I cannot stress enough what great peril you are in. I am sorry you have been dragged into this horror, but alas, it is your fate. It is your destiny. Today my worst fears have been confirmed with the translation of the ancient Persian text. There are men who have aligned themselves with the Evil that haunts us. They have been following me and are now ready to make their move against me. I know this to be true. There is no escape.*

*Ermal has been bound to this family by oaths taken, but today his service passes from me to you, Orhan, and to you, Jeff. It is a very long story that goes back centuries to the times of our ancestors, who sold their souls for power. The selling of their souls brought about a harsh and relentless curse that unfortunately by your blood you are now a part of.*

*I do not have time to explain to you everything now, but in my papers locked away in my safe you will find all that you require.*

*Ermal will meet with you two days hence at the Cave of the Seven Sleepers in Ephesus. It is a place mandated by ancient magic. You must listen to him. You must not delay. Time is precious. Farewell, my beloved nephew. May Allah be merciful.*

*Your loving uncle, Ümët Aziz*

Rob Dakin

The three companions sat in the gloom of the hotel room illuminated only by the single lamp on the desk. They pondered heavily the words that Orhan had read. Jeff felt the hair on the back of his neck stand up. He finally spoke after a long silence.

"Did your uncle say anything else about the translation of the parchment before he left on his errand?"

Orhan nodded. "He said that although it was written in ancient Persian, it was actually a translation into Persian from another language. In Persian, Ümët's friend said it made no sense and therefore would mean nothing if it were translated into Turkish or any other language. My uncle left immediately after telling me this." Orhan paused. "Ermal said that when the words are spoken they create powerful magic, and they are not to be uttered casually."

"Yes, but in what language would it be spoken?" asked Jeff.

"I have no idea," said Orhan in frustration. "Ermal took the parchment and went off to study it privately. Shortly after that the police came."

"Your uncle mentioned the Cave of the Seven Sleepers; what do you know about it?" asked Aubrey.

"Not much," said Orhan. "I know that it is a Christian site at the ruins of ancient Ephesus. Uncle Ümët had a history of it in his papers that I happened to notice as I was scanning through them." He thumbed through the papers until he found the information he was looking for. "OK. Here it is. Apparently there was a dispute between the Christians and the Roman Empire over an imperial cult that everyone was supposed to honor. The Christians refused to sacrifice animals at the imperial temple to Roman gods, and so they were considered enemies of the state, and were treated as such. Around two hundred fifty AD, during the reign of Emperor Decius, seven young Christian men fled the city and hid in a cave because they refused to sacrifice animals at the temple. After a while they fell asleep, and

70

when they woke up they went back to the city to buy food only to find that they had not slept for just one night but for two hundred years. By that time, Christianity had spread to every corner of the empire. The news of the seven young men reached the ears of Emperor Theodosius the Second, and he declared it as proof of the Resurrection. When these men died they were buried in the cave, and a church was later built at the site. For hundreds of years, people have wanted to be buried as close to the "seven sleepers" as possible because they were considered holy. According to local Christian legend, Mary Magdalene was buried there also."

"Wait a minute. How could Mary Magdalene be buried at that site when she would have died four hundred years before the so-called seven sleepers?" asked Jeff.

"I don't know. How does any legend or myth get started?" said Orhan. "The point is, this cave has been considered holy ground for centuries, and that makes it powerful according to my uncle's research."

"So when do we leave?" asked Aubrey.

Orhan studied her for a moment but decided not to press the issue. "*We* need to go first thing in the morning. I wanted to drive my car, but it does not do well on the icy and snowy roads. Besides, it is a very long way. It would be best if we took a bus, so we can sleep. We may not have much of a chance later."

"So what do we do now? Study your uncle's papers?" asked Jeff picking up the folder of research papers.

"Exactly. We need to know all he knew before we do anything else." Orhan took a stack of notes from Jeff and divided it, giving Aubrey a share. "If you are going, you need to be up on all this also."

The threesome studied in silence for over an hour, each taking up a comfortable position. Orhan stayed at the desk hunched over his stack of notes. Jeff situated himself in an overstuffed chair by the window and propped his feet up on the heating and air conditioning register. Aubrey stretched out on the bed with her back propped up with pillows.

When Jeff pulled the curtain back slightly and peered out into the square, night had fallen. The pristine snow had given way to the dirty, slushy tracks of streetcars, buses, and automobiles. The square was dimly lit by yellowish orange streetlights and a collage of neon signs and billboards situated around the periphery. As a tram made its pass around the monument in the center of the square, Jeff saw a woman and a child standing across the street from his hotel looking straight up at him. Their clothes were ragged and patched. His heart skipped a beat as goose pimples covered his arms. Startled, he quickly dropped the edge of the curtain hoping he had not been seen.

Orhan noticed his sudden movement out of the corner of his eye. "What is it?" he asked. "What is wrong?"

Aubrey looked up from her reading, "Did you see something?"

"Yeah. More Gypsies," Jeff exclaimed. "Across the street, staring up at us." Orhan and Aubrey set aside their pages and came to the window. The three of them crouched down below the sill and peered out from under the bottom of the curtain.

"You must be seeing things," sighed Orhan in relief.

There was no one there. Jeff didn't know whether to be disappointed or relieved. "Well, they were there just a second ago," he said defensively.

"I believe you," said Aubrey. "From what I've read already, I would believe just about anything right now."

"Have you finished your pages yet?" asked Orhan.

"I need a little more time," said Jeff.

"Me too," said Aubrey.

They continued their study for about another thirty minutes. Then Jeff looked up with a smile. "You know, I just realized this is all in English."

"Yes. My uncle translated it. We have the Turkish copies as well. Who wants to start?"

"Well, mine has to do mostly with the journal of an Italian priest who reported an incident in Albania," said Aubrey.

"Yes, we heard all about that last night," interjected Jeff. "Anything else?"

"It has a pretty detailed report of a...I guess a witch, in northern Albania. Uncle Ümët never met her, but he found people who knew of her. She lives up in the mountains and is accessible only by foot. It has a hand-drawn map to a cave and a description of her powers according to the locals. One thing that she claims to be able to do is conjure and control *djinn*. Whatever that is. This tidbit is underlined and circled, so your uncle must have put some stock into it. There's other stuff, but mostly it's about Albania, so I don't see how that's going to help us."

"Orhan's uncle said we had to eventually go to Albania," said Jeff scratching his head. "We can file it for future reference. My pages had to do with the *djinn* you were talking about," he continued. "Ümët became convinced that this evil was actually a djinn, or jinn. It is known as a *marid*, which is a powerful and usually evil djinn by nature. This marid is even more malicious than most of its kind and seems to thrive on fear and murder. It is bound by certain rules placed upon it by spells and incantations, which could explain the cyclic nature of its appearances. It can change shape or inhabit the bodies of other creatures."

"What is a jinn exactly?" asked Aubrey.

"Well, we would call it a genie in America," said Jeff, "but that would take away from the fearsomeness of it."

"I thought that that was all make-believe," said Aubrey.

"No, actually the jinni are a very big part of our Islamic lore," explained Orhan. "Their stories actually predate Islam by thousands of years. Jinni are even mentioned prominently in our Most Holy Koran."

"Well, what are they?" asked Aubrey.

"There is quite a bit of information about them in these notes," said Jeff. "First of all, they are created beings like humans. Muslims believe that they are made of smokeless fire by Allah. Humans, on the other hand, are made of clay. Jinni have free will. They have communities, eat, marry, etc. They can die, although they live considerably longer than humans. They can be good or bad. They can see humans, but humans cannot generally see them. The jinni that are malicious or bad toward humans usually behave this way because they resent their position being usurped by humans before God. Muslims believe that Satan is a jinn, and his rebellion against God was because humans were elevated above jinn in God's sight. Angels are of light, jinn are of fire, so apparently that's where they get that idea about Satan. They can change their shapes into animals or humans. They can be controlled by spells and incantations. They can be bound to objects and places through magic."

"So your uncle believes that what we are dealing with is a genie, basically," stated Aubrey.

"Yes," said Jeff, "but it would be a big mistake to confuse what we have here with a Disney character. I don't know if I go along with all this, but one thing is for sure: strange and terrible things have been going on whether we believe in them or not."

"I agree," interjected Orhan. "I never have personally believed in jinni, but until we figure out what it really is, we should keep our minds open."

"There's a phrase in my set of notes that has been underlined," said Jeff. "It's written in our alphabet, but it sounds like it might be Arabic. The note to the side says it must be spoken to protect someone against the jinni."

# Vale of Shadows

Orhan rose up and came over to Jeff's side. Jeff held the page up for him to see in the light. "It is Arabic," he said. "*Bismillahi! Allahumma inna 'audhu bika minal khubthi wal khabaa'ith.* I have no idea what that means."

"It probably wouldn't hurt to memorize it anyway," said Aubrey, taking the page from Jeff and writing the phrase on a small notepad. "So can this jinn be killed?"

"My guess is that it can be since it can die, but I don't have any info on how to do it," said Jeff. "Hopefully that's were Ermal comes in." Jeff and Aubrey looked over at Orhan expectantly.

"My pages contain some history of this particular jinn gathered by my uncle and Dr. Yay. It seems that all the incidences throughout recent history, or at least the last few hundred years, has been the work of probably two jinni; one here and one in Albania. They weren't sure; it's a little sketchy in the details. The jinni are bound by a spell placed on them by a sorcerer back five hundred and forty some years ago. It seems their apparent immortality is actually due to the dormancy, like hibernation, that they undergo between cycles. This jinn in Turkey was enslaved by a general serving Sultan Murad the Second to defeat his enemies. His chief rival was another of the sultan's generals named Scanderbeg, who betrayed the Sultan by going back to his homeland of Albania and using his knowledge of the Ottoman tactics to fight against them. I will tell you more about Scanderbeg later."

"I've heard about Scanderbeg in Albania," said Aubrey. "He is a national hero there."

"Yes, he is a hero, and not just to the Albanians," said Orhan, finding a page torn from a history book. "He was born in 1405, in Albania, and as a young man he was taken as a hostage by Sultan Murad the Second. His family was Christian and would not convert to Islam, so as was the custom, the Ottomans took as hostages the children of nobles who would not convert.

"Scanderbeg's real name was Gjergj Kastrioti. He was educated in Edirne, Turkey, were he was given the name Iskander, or Alexander, and given the rank of *bey*, hence Scanderbeg or Skënderbej. He became a great general for the Ottomans, but in 1443 he abandoned the Ottoman army, went back to Albania, embraced Christianity, and fought the Ottomans for the rest of his life. He is credited with keeping the Ottomans from extending any further west."

"So this explains, at least in part, the connection between the Albanians, and Turks," said Jeff, "but what does that have to do with Ermal, and us?"

"I don't know yet," said Orhan. "Hopefully we find out tomorrow."

\* \* \*

Jeff looked at his Timex Ironman watch. It was already past midnight. He was feeling the effects of a long day. He watched Aubrey bobbing her head drowsily. She blinked her eyes trying to keep them open, but before long she had nestled into the pillows and fallen sound asleep. Jeff smiled and looked over at Orhan, who had also noticed Aubrey nodding off.

"Well, I guess she gets the bed," Jeff said. "Looks like you and I get the floor."

Orhan rose from his chair and went to the closet, pulling out a couple of blankets and another pillow. Jeff gently took one of the pillows off the bed without disturbing Aubrey. He pulled the bedding up over her and tucked her in. He suddenly became self-conscious and embarrassed when he noticed Orhan smiling at him.

"We can go over the rest of these notes tomorrow on the bus," said Orhan.

Jeff settled into the makeshift bed he had made on the floor near the window while Orhan took up a spot at the foot of the bed. Even the floor felt good. It had been an eventful and tiresome day.

76

# Vale of Shadows

"What will happen with your uncle?" Jeff asked through a yawn.

"The Imams are reading the Koran over him right now. It will take most of the night; then he will be buried in the morning," said Orhan.

"You are not planning on going to the funeral?" asked Jeff. He could sense his friend was hurting but was trying hard not to show it.

"No. My uncle expects me to take care of business. 'No time to mourn,' he would say." Orhan heard a long yawn come from near the window. A faint light seeped from the edge of the curtain, casting an eerie pale over the room. Orhan heard Aubrey snoring softly on the bed above him. He placed his hands behind his head. Whatever horror awaited them tomorrow, at least tonight they would rest safely.

* * *

Outside in the shadows just out of reach of the street lamplight stood a lone figure dressed in layers of shabby clothing. He kept his ungloved hands warm by jamming them deep into his coat pockets—a coat he had found in the garbage behind the mansion of a well-to-do İstanbullus. The collar was pulled up high above his ears. His head was covered with a scarf, the loose ends wrapped around his neck. He stood with his left foot resting slightly on top of his right to keep the snow from soaking into the hole in his shoe. He kept his gaze fixed on the dark curtained window on the third floor of the hotel. He shifted his position to be certain that the room had become lightless through a small crease at the curtain edge. Under his breath he repeated an incantation: "*Bismillahi! Allahumma inna 'audhu bika minal khubthi wal khabaa'ith.*"

# 8. Silent Visitor

At 5:05 in the morning, Jeff catapulted up in a sitting position on the floor. He had squirmed in his blankets in the night and was now jammed against the side of the bed in which Aubrey was still sleeping. He stared into the darkness trying to ascertain where he was. For a moment he couldn't figure out who was snoring softly on the bed next to him. His eyes slowly grew accustomed to the dim saber of predawn light that pierced from between the curtains.

He rolled over on to his knees and fixed his eyes on the form in front of him. It finally dawned on him that he was in his hotel room. He remembered with a chuckle to himself that Orhan and Aubrey had stayed the night. *That is so weird*, he thought to himself. Waking up confused in the middle of the night was common when he traveled.

His mind began to clear as he recognized the call for morning prayers echoing through the alleys and streets. The city was already waking up to another cold winter day. He heard Orhan stir at the foot of the bed. He shuffled on his knees and leaned across the corner of the bed to peer at his friend. "You awake?" he asked.

"No" came Orhan's groggy reply.

Aubrey rolled over on her side and sat up on her elbows. "What time is it?"

"A little after five a.m.," said Jeff. "Something woke me up. I don't think it was the prayer call, though."

"What do you think it was?" asked Aubrey as she sat up with her feet dangling over the edge of the bed."

# Vale of Shadows

"I don't know. A premonition, maybe?" Jeff crawled over to the window and lifted the curtain slightly. The only occupants of the square were city workers clearing the road and sidewalks.

"We need to get ready to go. It will take about an hour to get to the Harem bus station, and our bus will leave around eight o'clock," said Orhan through a wide yawn and a stretch.

Orhan and Aubrey began gathering what they needed for the trip. They collected the pages of research notes that had been left scattered around the room since the night before. As he bent over the bed to pick up Aubrey's notes, Orhan found a small, dark brown burlap pouch lying on her pillow. He picked it up and examined it suspiciously. "What is this?" he called to Aubrey who was in the restroom combing her hair.

"What is what?" she asked stepping back into the room.

"This," he said holding up the pouch for her and Jeff to see.

She squint her eyes in the light to see what Orhan was holding up and furrowed her brow, puzzled. "It's the *hajmali* a Gypsy girl gave Jeff yesterday at the pier."

"Well, it's not mine," said Jeff pulling his *hajmali* from his pant pocket.

"Where did you find it?" asked Aubrey.

"On your pillow," said Orhan. He walked around the bed toward Aubrey so she could see it more clearly. As he stepped over his own makeshift bed on the floor, he caught sight of a similar pouch next to where his pillow had been resting. He leaned over and picked it up, comparing it to the one he had just picked up from Aubrey's pillow. It was similar in size and shape but was obviously handmade and not mass produced. He palpated the oddities between his thumbs and forefingers. "Someone has been in our room while we slept," he said with distinct concern in his voice.

79

"Who, and how?" asked Aubrey. She turned toward the hall door. It was locked with the security chain still in place. "How could someone get in here?"

"I don't have a clue, but I'm betting that they left these things to protect us. It could be part of Ermal's clan, but how they got in here and why they left them the way they did is a puzzle."

They quickly finished packing up their belongings. Orhan and Aubrey made sure to put the charms securely in their pockets.

"Man! I feel like I've been rode hard and put up wet," said Jeff through a cavernous yawn. "I don't think I slept well."

Orhan laughed. "You have some of the strangest sayings."

"Yeah, well..." Jeff unlatched the security chain and opened the door, turning to face his companions. "I'm starved," he said waiting for them to join him in the hall.

They went up to the top floor dining room, which was just opening up, and ate a good buffet breakfast. Jeff loaded his plate with sliced meats, cheeses, fruits, a hard-boiled egg, and pastries. He joined Orhan and Aubrey, who were already seated at the table due to the fact that they had not filled their plates nearly as full as his. "What I wouldn't give for a good strip of bacon right now," he said as he scooted his chair up to the table.

They ate in silence for a few moments. Jeff gobbled down his food like it was going to be his last, then got up and got another plate full. As he sat back down he noticed that the sun was beginning to come up, and he could now see out of the window instead of seeing their reflections in the darkness. The window faced the Bosphorus, which could be seen through the buildings. Jeff smiled at the promise of a sunny day, but then became somber at the thought of what lay before them.

Orhan, seeing Jeff gazing out of the window, cleared his throat to speak. Aubrey and Jeff focused their attention on him.

80

"I think it would be best to take a taxi all the way to Harem. The traffic won't be too bad this time of day, so we should get there in time to catch the early morning bus."

The other two nodded in agreement, and continued eating their breakfast. After a few moments Aubrey's curiosity could not be contained any longer. She reached into her backpack and pulled out the *hajmali* placing it on the table in front of them.

"How in the world did this get on my pillow?" she asked. "And why didn't we hear anything. I mean, didn't you say you didn't sleep very well?" She looked at Jeff out of the corner of her eye.

"No, I didn't, but I still didn't hear a thing," said Jeff. "I was actually going to throw mine away, but I never got a round to it."

"Why were you going to throw your talisman away?" asked Orhan.

"Well, for one thing I don't believe in all this hocus pocus. I think it's crazy to assume that some ancient curse has been passed down to us just because my dad and Orhan's uncle witnessed some bizarre death forty-some years ago." Jeff had his mouth full and began talking faster and faster through his food. "We don't have anything but a bunch of papers of—I'm sorry, Orhan—of dubious origin." Jeff was talking adamantly with his hands, a fork full of food in one of them. Aubrey moved a little farther away, fearing she was going to be pelted with breakfast projectiles. "I mean really," continued Jeff, "how did a curse from a genie end up in our laps? I think it's just plan stupid."

Orhan tried to calm his friend. "I know it sounds stupid, but my uncle was absolutely convinced, and he went to his death sure of what he believed. I think it would be imprudent to not take these notes seriously…to not beware of the danger that it seems others believe we are in."

"Like the Gypsies," said Jeff.

81

"Yes. Like the Gypsies," responded Orhan. "I agree we definitely don't have many answers, and to go off to Ephes may be a wild goose chase, but we need to go anyway. We need to find out all we can, and if Ephes is the place with the answers, then I say we get there as fast as we can." He sat back in his seat realizing that he, too, had become quite animated. He continued more calmly, "As far as these little burlap pouches are concerned, I say we keep them in our pockets. I don't seriously believe they have any special power either, but it won't hurt anything to keep them around just in case."

"When we get to Ephes we may find out that there is nothing to all this stuff," Aubrey said, patting the folder with the research pages, "but if there is a curse on you guys, the sooner you find out how to get rid of it, the better."

Orhan let a few moments pass in silence then spoke up again. "Two things that we cannot ignore. First, my uncle is dead by an unknown murderer, and second, let us not forget that my uncle knew the man murdered that night, who was in fact a relative. A segment of my uncle's clan that had moved or fled to the mountains generations ago." He looked at Aubrey and then to Jeff. "I am afraid that there really is something to all of this 'stuff.'"

The three finished breakfast and went downstairs to the lobby to check out. Orhan talked to the neatly uniformed bellman standing at the ready. The bellman went out into the street and flagged a taxi, which pulled up from just around the corner. As Jeff climbed into the back seat with Aubrey, he glanced over his shoulder to the corner from which the taxi had just come. He had an odd premonition that made him shudder.

"You know," he said, "I think that, according to those notes, this is the very corner where my dad and your uncle saw what they saw."

Orhan looked out the windshield toward the corner. "I think you're right."

# Vale of Shadows

"What do you think that means?" asked Aubrey leaning slightly over the front seat so she could see out of the front window of the cab. "Do you think this place is significant? Like maybe it has some secret history that somehow binds all this craziness together?"

"I don't know," said Orhan. "Who knows? Hopefully we will get some answers by tomorrow."

The taxi pulled away from the curb, and began its journey through the winding streets and boulevards toward the Bosphorus Bridge. The trio rode in silence, each deep in their own thoughts, staring out their respective windows at the snow-laden neighborhoods. Istanbullus went about their business as the sun began to climb the early morning sky.

The bridge was packed with commuters making their way into the city. On any given workday, the population of Istanbul swelled to nearly eighteen million people. The crowdedness and confinement of the city made Jeff homesick for the wide-open spaces of Kansas. The taxi driver proficiently made his way across traffic to exit the freeway onto the shore road on the Asian side. At the Üsküdar pier, Orhan had the driver pull the taxi to the curb.

"I have to drop off a packet for our business," he said turning halfway in his seat to face Jeff and Aubrey. "It's just up the street. I will not be long." With that he exited the cab and walked toward a side alley. He disappeared behind a bus that was passing by, and then was lost to sight in the crowd.

Jeff and Aubrey decided to stretch their legs and got out of the taxi but stood close by. Jeff wondered at the magnificent sight across the Bosphorus of the Dolmabaçe Palace. Its extravagant white facade, punctuated with high arching windows from corner to corner, shone brilliantly in the early morning sunlight. He was suddenly awakened from his daydream by a tugging on his pant leg. He looked down to see a young street urchin beginning to polish his shoes. He had already put a smear of brown polish on Jeff's shoes before Jeff could stop him. Jeff tried to pull his foot away, but the child held firmly.

"Please, I make good shine," the kid said.

"I don't need a shine," argued Jeff haplessly. "The streets are snowy, muddy, and slushy." The shoeshine boy continued his craft despite Jeff's objections.

"It's no use, he doesn't understand you," Aubrey laughed. "You might as well not fight it. He only knows enough English for the tourists. Besides, it's only going to cost you a few pennies."

"Yeah, but it's not even the right color," Jeff said staring down at his mismatched shoes. Aubrey laughed so hard her eyes began to water. Jeff decided that if his little misfortune could bring her so much pleasure then he would just go along with it.

After the boy was finished with both shoes he held out a shoe wax stained hand. "One hundred thousand," he said.

Jeff took out a one hundred thousand Turkish lire coin and handed it to the boy, who immediately gathered up his shine box and looked around for another victim. Jeff held his foot up and turned it side to side to admire the new color.

"It's not so bad," snickered Aubrey.

"You're really having fun with this, aren't you?" scolded Jeff teasingly.

"It's just that the shoe-shine boys are notorious on both sides of the Bosphorus. I think it's funny that you got to sample it firsthand. I had a friend last summer who was wearing sandals, and when he walked by a shine boy, the kid literally swiped a stroke of polish across his sandals so he would have to get a full shine."

"So did he?"

"No. He was so mad that he chased the kid down and made him wipe it off," said Aubrey with a big grin on her face as she looked back on the memory.

Jeff spied a *simit* vendor across the way. "Do you want a *simit*?"

"Are you always hungry?" she asked, astonished that he wanted to eat again.

"Only when I'm about to die," he said jokingly.

Aubrey sobered up. "That's not funny."

"Sorry," he said "but really do you want one?" She nodded that she did, so he walked over to the vendor. As he stood there waiting to get their sesame seed bagels, he felt a tug on his foot. To his dismay another shoe-shine boy was trying to give him a shine. "No," he said kicking his foot free. "Aubrey! Help." Aubrey just stood by the cab laughing and clapping. Jeff ran away from the boy and dove back into the back seat of the taxi followed quickly by a giggling Aubrey. The boy ran to the taxi carrying his shine box awkwardly by a strap around his neck. He pounded on the passenger window.

"Please, I need to buy food for my little brother and sister," he pleaded through the glass. Aubrey rolled down the window a few inches.

"I don't need another shoe shine," Jeff said, "but here's five hundred thousand lira if you just leave me alone." He leaned across Aubrey and handed the boy the coins through the window. He was pleasantly surprised when she didn't try to move away from him. The boy pocketed the money, and then quickly turned to go back to work.

"You know, I bet these kids are probably filthy stinking rich. I bet their parents drop them off every morning in a fancy Mercedes Benz on their way to some expensive spa somewhere," Jeff said.

"You may be right," said Aubrey, "but I doubt it. I've seen where some of these kids live. It's not pretty."

Just then Orhan reappeared crossing the street toward the taxi. He jumped in the front seat, and the driver started the car and took off without a word. Orhan turned slightly in his

85

seat and looked over his shoulder so he could speak to Aubrey and Jeff.

"I made a phone call," he said. "My uncle's funeral is this morning at ten. He apparently left instructions to the staff and rest of the family that I was not to be detained. I wish I could be there, but..." his voice trailed off as he stared blankly out at the passing traffic.

*   *   *

After a few minutes, the taxi pulled up to the busy Harem bus station and the driver let them out at the curb as close to the ticket office as he could. Orhan glanced at his watch. A little before eight a.m. They had just enough time to purchase a ticket and board. He paid the driver, and the three trotted into the building to buy tickets. A small, ragamuffin child followed close behind them as they made their way through the congestion of buses. Jeff was the first to notice the little girl. She grabbed his sleeve and tugged on it.

"Please. One dollar," she said holding up three packs of travel sized facial tissue. Jeff's first impulse was to refuse out of a matter of principal, but then he realized that he really did need some for his runny nose. He pulled out a dollar and handed it to her. Her smile beamed through a dirty smudged face. Her little red nose was running, and her lips and face were chapped from the bitter cold. Jeff smiled back at her. He couldn't help thinking about his little sister, who was about the same age as this girl. He wondered what life would be like for his sister if she lived in this part of the world.

Aubrey stepped closer to Jeff's side.

"I have a little sister about her age," he said to her. "My folks had her when I was fifteen." He squatted down to eye level with the girl. "How old are you?" he asked in English. Aubrey translated in Turkish.

"I am ten years old," the girl replied in English.

"Oh, you speak English. Great!" Jeff said with a smile.

"I only speak little," she said. "Why go bus you are?"

"I have to meet someone in another city," Jeff said as he straightened up.

"You go, you have bad thing happen," she warned.

Jeff frowned at her. Her statement shocked him into silence. Aubrey and Orhan were shocked by her candid comment also. Aubrey was the first to regain her composure. "Why do you say that?" she asked kneeling down to face the little girl.

"I know. We all know. Bad thing waits."

"Where does the bad thing wait?" asked Jeff.

The little girl just stared blankly at him, as if she did not understand his question. Orhan repeated the question in Turkish, but before he could get an answer she ran off into a crowd of travelers that had just arrived on another bus.

"You know, I'm getting tired of weird little girls coming up to me and saying or doing weird things to me," said Jeff as he boarded the bus. Aubrey followed him up the steps and turned to see the little girl watching them. She raised her hand to wave good-bye, but the girl vanished behind an arriving bus.

\* \* \*

They had just made it in time. They were the last passengers to take their seats. It always amused Jeff that the buses in Turkey had assigned seats. He found himself sitting toward the back next to an old woman, while Aubrey and Orhan were seated together near the front. Jeff smiled at the old woman, who glared back at him moving closer to the window to get as far away from Jeff as she could. He gazed forward and shook his head biting his lower lip slightly. Aubrey turned to find where he was sitting.

"OK?" she mouthed quietly.

"Yeah," he mouthed back with a subtle eyeroll towards the woman. They smiled at each other as Aubrey squared back around in her seat. Jeff looked back over at the woman, who was obviously trying to ignore him. He looked passed her out the window. In the shadow of the station's awning stood the little girl staring at him. A cold chill ran down his spine. Even from this distance, he could see her coal-black eyes fixed right on him. Could she really see him through the glare of the bus windows and the shadows within? He tried to pull his gaze away from her as the bus backed out of its parking space, but he couldn't.

He suddenly felt himself becoming disoriented. His body seemed to be feather-light, as if even the slightest puff of air would cause him to float away. He began to sway as dizziness clouded his vision. He envisioned himself in a billowy cloud gliding in slow motion. Suddenly he was jerked back to reality by a rough hand that grabbed the back of his collar, straightening him back up in his seat. He roused himself from his stupor and saw the old woman looking at him with concern. He realized she had saved him from falling out of his seat.

Orhan and Aubrey were unaware of anything wrong. Jeff wondered if he had just imagined the dizziness, but the old woman's grip had been tangible. He sat and pondered the events of the last two days, trying to make sense out of what was happening and what was being said. He was too tired to make sense out of any of it. He decided to rest his eyes as the bus made its way through the congested, snow-covered streets.

# 9. Not to Be Confused with Vampire Cows

An hour later he was awakened from his nap by a heavy nudge to his side. He sat up in his seat and noticed the old woman nodding in the direction of the aisle. A porter was standing next to him offering a small carton of orange and apricot juice and a packet of hazelnuts. Jeff took what was offered, thanking the women and the porter. Aubrey came back and leaned over the seat in front of him since the occupant of that seat had moved and was now sitting double across the aisle next to a small child.

"So, how are you holding up?" she asked brightly.

"I've been resting for about the last hour," said Jeff. "I started feeling kind of dizzy when I saw that little girl again just as we were pulling out of the station."

Aubrey gently touched his face. First his forehead, then his cheek, just like his mother used to do when he was running a fever.

"I'm really concerned about you, Jeff," she said softly. "I'm afraid of what you guys might be getting yourselves into."

"I know. I'm getting a little worried myself," he said, thinking what a gross understatement he had just made. What *was* he getting himself into? He took a sip from his juice box and smiled brightly at Aubrey.

"So, tell me what your father was like," said Aubrey trying to take their minds off of their present circumstances.

Jeff smiled at her obvious ploy at changing the subject; the new topic of his father brought them right back to where they were. "Well, for one thing I'm sure he would have tried to stop me from coming to Turkey had he been alive. I really didn't have any idea about all of this. Just snippets of stories, really. It seems that all of his memories of his youth in Turkey were clouded by what happened that night all those years ago, but he never wanted to talk about it in any detail."

He paused for a moment while Aubrey traded places with a man across the aisle from him who was willing to move in order for them to talk. "My dad left Turkey when he was nineteen. He got into college after working odd jobs for about three years. He had always been interested in engineering, so he ended up getting a degree in aeronautical engineering. He moved to Wichita to work at Boeing, and that's where he met my mom. They got married after a long engagement, almost six years. My dad was several years older than she was."

"Wow, six years is a long time to be engaged," interjected Aubrey.

"They were older than most when they started having kids. They waited almost ten years before they had me. They had my little sister fifteen years later." Jeff paused and looked out the window over Aubrey's shoulder. "My dad was a good father and husband, but he always seemed to be nervous about everything. My mom was the risk-taker of the two. That's where I get my adventurous streak."

Aubrey smiled at him kindly. Jeff had proven over and over to have a little more than an *adventurous* streak. It really bordered on reckless abandon with total disregard for his own safety. She thought back to the first time she had met him in Adapazarı. An apartment building had collapsed back in November during a strong aftershock, trapping a dozen children in a daycare. Jeff had charged into the building ignoring the yells of warning from the other rescue workers. Before it was all over, he had managed to drag five of the children to safety, spurring on the bravery of the other volunteers to follow him, and all the children were pulled out alive. Jeff was a hero, but he downplayed his own part and gave great accolades to the others who had followed.

Jeff continued, "My dad died a couple of years after my sister was born from what we thought was a heart attack, but now...from what Orhan's uncle told us it may not have been a heart attack at all. Who knows for sure," he said with a sigh.

After another half hour or so the bus pulled into the station in Adapazarı. Jeff's friend Jonathan Michaels was there to meet them with a minivan.

"Hey, Jeff. Hey, Aubrey," he greeted them with an outstretched hand. "Your phone call this morning caught us all by surprise. We thought you were going to be in Istanbul at least another week."

"I was," said Jeff shaking Jonathan's hand, "but something has come up."

Jonathan gave Aubrey a cheek-to-cheek kiss, and then turned back to Jeff. "What's up?" he asked.

"Well, it's a long story," Jeff replied. "I don't know really where to begin, but I came back here mainly to get a couple of things I left in the apartment that I might need."

Jonathan smiled at Aubrey as he addressed Jeff again, "So I see you finally got the courage to hook up with Aubrey. I'm glad I'm not going to have to listen to you moan about how much you miss her."

Jeff's face suddenly reddened with embarrassment as he made a mental note to strangle Jonathan later. He didn't dare look over at Aubrey, though if he had, he would have been encouraged by her pleased expression.

Just then, Orhan joined them after buying tickets for the night's trip to Kuşadası. He nodded respectfully at Jonathan, who nodded and shook his hand.

"Well," Jeff exhaled heavily and nodded toward Orhan. "This is my friend from Istanbul. We were roommates together back in college." The two men shook hands again, and then Jonathan led them to his minivan.

Jeff was impressed with the newness of the vehicle. "Hey, when did you get the new van?" He had grown accustomed to riding around in old beat-up vans or trucks that looked like they were on their last mile.

"The organization got it yesterday," explained Jonathan. "It was pretty crazy. We had to pay cash for it, so Ara and I went to the dealership with a suitcase containing three-point-nine billion Turkish liras. We could hardly carry it. It was wild." He shook his head in an amused fashion. "It's about thirty thousand dollars," he said anticipating Jeff's next question.

They piled into the dark blue Mercedes van, Jonathan and Orhan sitting in the front while Aubrey and Jeff taking the middle bench seat. They drove past the rubble of fallen buildings. Mangled rebar and concrete were heaped in piles. The once beautiful city now lay in muddy, bleak ruins. Brick sidewalks that had once been laid out in tightly packed patterns were now rippled like the breakwater of ocean surf. They passed the Tozlu Mosque, its minarets fractured in fragments. The main dome and semi-domes lay askew as if they had collapsed as a single unit. Some of the buildings looked normal at first, until they looked closer to see that the second floor was now at the level of the street and the first floor was subterranean. One building had fallen over at about a forty-five-degree angle and rested against the building next to it. Jeff was amazed that none of its windows were broken. It had tipped over during the quake completely intact. The plate-glass windows mirrored passersby as they had always done.

Every park, school, and stadium had become a makeshift tent city. Everywhere they looked shanties of cardboard, wood palates, and plastic tarp pocked the landscape. People whose apartment buildings had not collapsed were still too afraid to go back inside, so they lived in tents or whatever else they could find. All this was made worse by the fact that it had been the worst winter in thirteen years.

# Vale of Shadows

Jonathan deftly maneuvered his van through the crater-infested streets. Water mains had ruptured, and deep pools of standing water made driving treacherous. Finally, at about ten-thirty a.m., they arrived at Adapazarı Hotel where Jeff and Jonathan had shared a room. "Home sweet home," said Jonathan as he pulled the van around to a parking place situated between mounds of debris. They paused for a moment before going into the building.

"Not too much has changed since I was here last month," said Aubrey as she sniffed the brisk morning air.

"No, it's going to be a long haul to clean this mess up," said Jonathan propping the door open for the others to enter.

He started up the stairs even though Orhan had gone over to the elevator and pushed the Up button. Jonathan stopped on the second stair and turned to Orhan. "We haven't used the elevator since the quake. You just never know when another one will strike, and I'm not getting stuck in one of those death traps if it does."

\* \* \*

Orhan was already pulling the file of notes from his pack as they entered the hotel room. "I finished reading through all the papers on the way here. Between my uncle's research and the research of Dr. Yay, I think I have a pretty good understanding of what went on. At least back in nineteen fifty-six." The others crowded around him, including Jonathan who still didn't have a clue what was going on.

"What we are dealing with is a jinn. A specific malicious jinn that was bound by a spell five hundred and forty-four years ago. He absolutely hates everything that has to do with humans...uh, specifically our families. He was actually betrayed by our ancestors when he was bound by the spell. His sole source of energy is fear in others. He is driven by it. Murder and carnage are only a means to elicit this fear. He is released from his bondage at various times when a pedigree moon is

93

accompanied by a massive solar flare, or the alignment of the planets, or some geological catastrophy like an earthquake. In the last five hundred and forty-four years there have been twelve cycles. This year will be the thirteenth cycle."

"That's just plain weird," said Jeff. "So what are we supposed to do about it?"

"Well, just wait and listen. In the summer of nineteen fifty-six, this jinn was loosed. At that time there was a great deal of posturing about science, and ridiculing of superstition. People were 'more enlightened.' They didn't believe in 'ghosts.' At least here in Turkey, the general population was being taught to be more logical and to use reason instead of relying on myths and old wives tales. Religion was some what less influential than it had once been."

"Thus enters the village," said Jeff, comprehending Orhan's point.

"Exactly. Less education in the villages meant more potential for fear and panic. So the jinn went after villagers. He entered the bodies of cattle first and behaved in such a way as to make the superstitious villagers terrified to go out into their fields. The animals were then slaughtered, which caused more fear. Eventually the jinn murdered the villagers one by one using the suspense to heighten their fear. The speculation is that the policeman who went to the village with the mayor was murdered first because he, being combat experienced, wasn't as fearful as he was wary. This, of course, caused more fear in the mayor, who fled to İstanbul. There is a side note here stating that the policeman had been a Korani."

"What's a Korani?" asked Jonathan.

"They were the first Turkish soldiers of the Republic to fight in a foreign war. They were fierce fighters, and part of NATO in the Korean War," explained Orhan. "They are still shown a lot of respect. You can see the old men wearing their pins on their lapels. People will jump up from their seats to let them sit.

"To continue, the jinn could have taken the mayor anytime, but he seemed to be playing with the man like a cat plays with a mouse. The jinn stalked him to Taksim, and then killed him in front of my uncle and your father. Ümët and the mayor were cousins. It was no accident, therefore, that Altin and Ümët witnessed the murder. I don't have any idea why Altin and Ümët weren't killed that night if they really were part of a curse, and a relative of the mayor. But if fear is the driving force that could explain why not everyone who has had an encounter with the jinni have been killed; for example the Albanian brothers mentioned in the priest diary."

"Is there a way to kill the jinn or at least make him impotent?" asked Aubrey innocently. The men smiled to themselves and decided to let her question go without a risqué comment.

"There is a way," said Orhan, "but I have found nothing in the papers to explain how to do it. Ümët mentioned that the jinn needed to be killed, but he didn't say how. Hopefully Ermal will have something to say about it when we get to the Cave of the Seven Sleepers."

During this whole time Jonathan had been sitting on the edge of his bed listening to Orhan's oration without comment. Finally the suspense was too much for him.

"What in the heck are you guys talking about?" he asked.

"Haven't you been listening?" grilled Jeff with mock intensity. "We have been marked for death by *vampire cows* and *ware-cows*. They come out at night during a full mooooon and suck your blood." Aubrey laughed hysterically, which gave Jeff all the encouragement he needed to keep going. "Yeah, once you are bitten, you become a *ware-cow* yourself, and turn into a cow during a full mooooon and stalk other poor, unsuspecting farmers."

"Stop, Jeff," pleaded Aubrey still laughing. "You're making my sides hurt." She gasped for air with her arms across her stomach. "Man, I must be more tired than I thought. Sorry. It's really not that funny."

Orhan and Jonathan just glared at Jeff and Aubrey for a moment, and then broke into to smiles themselves. Jeff could always be depended on to lighten the mood.

"Seriously," continued Orhan, "if it were just a matter of *vampire cows...*" He chuckled — "where do you come up with this stuff? Anyway, if it were just a matter of vampire cows, we would at least recognize it when it came after us. As it is, this jinn can take the form of just about anything. We need a plan."

"I say we attack it before it attacks us," said Jonathan.

"What do you mean *us*?" asked Jeff. "You don't need to be a part of this."

"I'm already a part of this," argued Jonathan. "You're my friend and roommate, and if you have some boogeyman coming after you, then I want to be there to help.... To help you," he said in jest, "not the boogeyman."

"OK," said Orhan, "but we're not dealing with a make-believe monster, like a vampire cow or a boogeyman. It is a creature that is real, and hateful, and a proven killer. We can't just the four of us go off carefree without a plan."

"Well...so it looks like our starting point has to be in Ephes," said Aubrey. "Hopefully *there* we will get some answers to solve the problem."

\* \* \*

They decided to pass the day resting. The weather outside was cold, and light snow flurries fell from the sky. The room remained cold throughout the day. The central heat of the hotel was supplied from a boiler, which sent steam into individual radiators in each room. Unfortunately, the main pipe from the boiler had been fractured during the earthquake, and no amount of duct tape was able to patch it.

Jeff stretched out on the floor with his head propped up by a pillow from the bed. He continued reading the notes from where he had left off the night before. Much to his delight, Aubrey grabbed her notes and lay down beside him. He tried to cover his broad smile as she squirmed to get comfortable. Orhan and Jonathan began a game of chess at the small table near the window.

After a time Jeff asked, "When exactly is the full moon supposed to start?"

"Tomorrow night," answered Orhan.

"OK, so if this jinn is not to be released from his spell-induced bondage until tomorrow night, why am I having these weird things happening to me?" asked Jeff.

"Because you're psycho," teased Aubrey with a playful elbow to his ribs.

"Well, yeah, that goes without saying," said Jeff elbowing her gently. "But seriously though. Why?"

"I don't have any idea," said Orhan moving his queen's knight into position to take Jonathan's advanced pawn. "Maybe we're just like the pawns in this game. We have no control over our fate."

"Well, that's not much of an answer, but I guess it'll have to do." Jeff rested his head back on the pillow. "Maybe the men that are in league with the jinn have played their hand and the Gypsies have caught on to it. They have murdered Uncle Ümët which seems a little careless at this point. Why didn't they murder you also? I guess it could be that they are just trying to build the fear factor preparing for his arrival."

"That sound's really terrible," said Aubrey rising up into a sitting position. "If it's true, then there could be a bunch of the jinn's helpers or minions just following us around. We won't know where to turn."

Jeff sat up and put his arm around Aubrey's shoulders. She was visibly upset. Her usually laid-back demeanor flustered by the prospect of multiple enemies.

"We don't know that for sure," comforted Jeff. His tone was dramatically less cavalier than it was a moment ago. "I only said *maybe* that's what's going on."

"Yes, but what you said does make sense," said Orhan. "Why else would Uncle Ümët be dead, and you be having these encounters with the Gypsies? If the jinn has no power until tomorrow at the rise of the full moon, then how else could we explain everything unless it is these men that Ümët told us about in his letter?"

Jonathan sat with his head in his hands, elbows propped on the desk. He had come over with the same organization as Jeff but had only arrived last month. He came from a large family in Louisiana and had grown up in the bayou not far from Baton Rouge. He was used to hearing stories of swamp creatures and mysterious goings-on from his older brothers and sisters, who made it their sport to frighten him. As he listened to his companions, he had a hard time not dismissing their discussion as just another swamp tale.

Now he said, "Do you really believe there is a murderous creature out there that has made it his business to target you two out of all the people in the world he could go after? I mean...why you? Why are you the ones in danger, and not some other shmoe on the streets? It sounds a little too far-fetched for me." Jonathan stood up and stretched wide, then looked at his watch. It was only just noon. "I mean, I'm with you all the way," he continued, "but you should know that I think you're full of something that I won't say in front of Aubrey." He smiled at her in mock condescension.

"I think it *would* be great if we weren't the ones being targeted," said Jeff, "but unfortunately we've had too many weird things happen in the last twenty-four hours."

"Like what?" pressed Jonathan. "I haven't heard anything that would make me believe a hundred percent that anything really out of the ordinary has happened."

"You don't call Orhan's uncle being murdered and leaving an ominous note behind along with all of his life's research 'out of the ordinary'? You don't call little freaky Gypsy girls throwing beanbags at me 'out of the ordinary'? And what about Aubrey and Orhan waking up to find those little bean bags on their pillows in a double-locked hotel room?" Aubrey and Orhan decided to let Jeff continue with his tirade. "We have had nothing but 'out of the ordinary' things happen to us." Jeff was waving his hands in the air by this time.

"Don't forget your dizzy spell," offered Aubrey.

"Yeah, that's right. I've never had dizzy spells in my entire life. Not even when I ran triathlons in the heat. No, something is very *out of the ordinary*, and we better quit messing around or we'll end up ten toes to the sky."

Jonathan tried to wipe the smile off his face. He had seen Jeff get wound up before, and he knew now wasn't the time to argue. He changed the subject. "So is anyone else hungry?"

Jeff stared at him blankly. "Is all you can think about your stomach?" he accused.

"You have a lot of room to talk," said Aubrey as she took Jonathan's cue and got her coat on. Orhan threw his coat on and the two of them went to the door and waited expectantly for Jonathan and Jeff to join them. Jeff's face softened as he realized what his friends were trying to do.

"OK," he said, "I'll calm down. Let's go eat."

# 10. Without Adult Supervision

> Adapazarı Bus Station
> 10 p.m.

Jeff was the first to board the bus. He didn't want even the remote possibility of being approached by another Gypsy child. He quickly found his seat and sat down, nearly knocking over an elderly gentleman who was trying to squash his plastic sack, acting as his suitcase, into the overhead. Jeff peered cautiously out the window, keeping his face shielded by the seat back in front of him. No sign of creepy little girls. He sighed quietly in relief.

Aubrey waited her turn, making her way patiently down the narrow middle aisle of the bus. She finally arrived at her seat, which much to Jeff's relief was right next to his. Orhan and Jonathan had seats together closer to the front. The bus driver mounted his seat promptly, and the bus began to pull out of its stall before all the passengers were safely seated. This suited Jeff just fine. The less time in the station, the better, as far as he was concerned.

Aubrey placed her head back against the headrest and closed her eyes. Jeff saw how tired she looked, so he decided not to bother her and laid his head back for a nap also. But he was unable to get comfortable in the seat. The armrests were non-retractable, and the seatback only reclined about a half an inch. Jeff looked over at Aubrey with envy seeing how easily she melted into her seat. Her petite physique allowed her to fit comfortably in her seat with plenty of room between her and the seat back in front of her. Jeff, with his six-foot-one stature, felt like he had been poured into the space.

He heard Aubrey's soft, purring sigh as she nestled into her seat. He slouched down in his seat as much as he could and raised his knees up against the seat back in front of him. This immediately resulted in a firm, over-the-shoulder frown from the man in the seat ahead. Jeff quickly straightened up and resigned himself to the inevitable fact that he was going to be uncomfortable for the next eleven hours.

After a torturous hour, he perceived a shadow hovering over him through his partially closed eyelids. Startled, he opened his eyes only to find the porter standing in the aisle next to him. The young man was neatly dressed in a white shirt, dark pants, and a bow tie, and he carried a clipboard. When he saw Jeff was awake, he said something completely unintelligible. Jeff tried hard to pick up any word in the man's sentence that he recognized, but with the vowel harmonies that make up the Turkish language, it was just a garbled mess to him. He finally determined that the porter must have wanted to know if he wanted something to eat or drink. He looked around desperately for help from anyone, but Aubrey still slept soundly next to him. Even though he was a little hungry, he decided to take the easy way out and simply shook his head, saying, "No thank you." The porter's shoulders slumped in frustration as he realized that Jeff did not understand. Jeff could envision him thinking, *Stupid American*, as he futilely repeated his phrase.

Aubrey suddenly awoke and looked up at the porter, who was still standing with his pencil at the ready on the clipboard in hand. "What does he want?" she asked.

"I think he wants to know if we want something to eat," stated Jeff out of the side of his mouth.

Aubrey looked up at the young man, and said with a polite smile. "I don't believe I will have anything." She had no sooner said that when the word for ticket popped into Jeff's mind, *bilet*, and he recognized it as being within the phrase of the porter's sentence.

"Oh, he wants our tickets," Jeff said as he fumbled through his pocket to retrieve the bus tickets he was holding for himself and Aubrey. He handed the porter the two tickets with a sheepish smile. The porter took them and abruptly made two check marks on his clipboard. He shook his head irritably, and moved on back to the next row.

After he had passed, Jeff and Aubrey turned their heads to look at each other and simultaneously said, "I don't believe I'll have anything." They both giggled at the comedy of the situation, fully aware that the young porter did not share in their amusement.

They settled down in their seats again, and Jeff craned his neck to look out the window peering into the night sky for any sign of the moon. The reflection of the interior running lights against the glass hindered his search. From what he could see, the sky appeared featureless. He surmised that it was overcast.

After two hours, the bus pulled into a roadside restaurant for a scheduled stop. Jeff was unaware at first that the bus had stopped, but he was awakened from a shallow nap by the commotion of the other passengers exiting the bus. He looked up ahead to see that Orhan and Jonathan had already disembarked and were walking stiffly toward the entrance of the restaurant. Aubrey began to stir, so Jeff waited patiently for her to awaken.

"Where are we?" she asked.

"Somewhere in central Turkey," he said. "Orhan and Jonathan have already gone inside that bus station over there."

Aubrey stood up and put on her coat, which she had been using for a blanket. "It's so cold," she said. "How long is the stop?" She quickly realized that Jeff probably had no idea, so she moved gingerly to the front of the bus and down the steps to where the driver was unloading some luggage for passengers getting off.

"Excuse me," she said in Turkish, "how long is this rest stop?"

"One hour," said the driver over his shoulder from inside the luggage compartment. "Go eat, and be back on the bus in one hour." He started yelling through the compartment at the porter who was on the other side of the bus packing luggage. Aubrey took this as a dismissal and turned to find Jeff gazing up at the cloud-covered night sky.

"What are you doing?" she asked.

"Just trying to see what the moon looks like, but it's too cloudy to see anything."

They walked into the busy restaurant and found Jonathan and Orhan already seated and drinking cups of Nescafe.

"Mind if we join you handsome gentlemen?" asked Aubrey pulling up a seat at their table.

Orhan and Jonathan rearranged the tabletop to make room. The other patrons of the eatery stared at them and whispered in hushed tones. Jeff felt uncomfortable at first, but then he realized that they were the only non-Turks present. He scooted his chair up to the table and accepted the cup of coffee offered by the waiter.

"How's it goin' back there, you two?" asked Jonathan through a sip of hot coffee.

"Great!" responded Jeff. "That is, if you don't mind feeling like a sardine. I can't get comfortable." He noticed Aubrey eyeing him, and quickly added, "But the company is wonderful." She smiled, satisfied, and took a sip of her hot tea.

"I've been reading through the notes again," said Orhan. "There's nothing to suggest a way to kill this jinn. They do mention ways to control it, but it does not clearly state how to get rid of it."

"So all we have to do is find the right voodoo witch doctor to tell us how, and we'll be home free," said Jonathan over his cup.

Jeff sat back on the back legs of his chair and rocked, clasping his hands over his belly. He was only half listening to the conversation when something out of the corner of his eye caught his attention. He turned to find a man dressed in black from head to toe, standing by the door that exited opposite from where their bus was parked. He focused more intently on the man, who appeared to be scanning the crowded restaurant in search of something or *someone*. Jeff suddenly became very uneasy and sat his chair back down on all four legs, resting his elbow on the table and covering the side of his face with his forearm as he pretended to be deep in conversation with his companions. When he chanced another glance over toward the man, he found that the man had moved closer to their table and was now staring menacingly at them.

"Don't look now, but I think we've got company," he said interrupting Orhan's dissertation. The other three, as was usually the case, ignored his warning of discretion and turned abruptly to face the man, who had now moved within a few tables from them. When he met their stare, he swiftly approached their table, pulled an empty chair from an adjacent table, and sat down. The four travelers nervously searched each other's faces.

The man studied each one at the table in silence, as if empirically gathering data. None of the four found their tongues to speak. Finally the man broke the mute tension and spoke to them in English.

"Good evening," he began pulling his black scarf away from his neck. "You do not know me, and I have no doubt that you are confused and maybe a little frightened by my presence, but I assure you I am a friend." This statement was met by collective looks of doubt.

# Vale of Shadows

The man continued to remove his outer winter garments—every stitch in black. After hanging his coat over the back of his chair, he clasped his hands on the table in front of him. He wore a black turtleneck sweater, black trousers with silver saddle buttons down the side of each leg, a black belt tipped in ornate silver, and black cowboy boots trimmed and tipped in ornate silver. His fingers were tobacco stained and adorned with silver rings of various design. Around his left wrist was a wide silver and turquoise studded bracelet. To top off the effect, his complexion was dark and ruddy, black hair was slicked back and tight against his head, and he was clean-shaven except for a black tuft of a beard directly below his lower lip. Jeff couldn't help but be reminded of a Mexican desperado he had seen in a movie.

The man gazed at his audience and smiled broadly, revealing a gold tooth on his right lateral incisor. Jeff wanted to smile just because of the absurdity of the man's appearance, but he kept it to himself. The man met each of their eyes in turn, and then slowly relaxed against the back of his chair. He finally settled his gaze on Orhan.

"So, you are the nephew of Ümët Aziz?" he asked, not releasing Orhan's stare from his own. "My name is Mustafa Mecit." He paused as if he wanted his words to elicit a greater effect than they had. "I have come to offer you my services," he continued, dismissing their lack of enthusiasm.

"I have never heard of you," said Orhan.

"Of course you haven't," said Mustafa. "I know of your uncle and his household. I have been away for a very long time. Wandering in search of myself, you might say. But I have come to know that you and your friend are in a very bad way. Trust no one. I, however, have every intention of proving to you that I can be trusted. Starting right now."

Jeff listened to Mustafa's accent. His English was exceptionally good, and maybe it was the Mexican desperado look, but Jeff detected a hint of Spanish influence. "Where are you from?" he asked suspiciously.

"Ahh," said Mustafa nodding his head approvingly, turning his focus to Jeff. "You do not take the obvious for granted. That is good. I am a man without a country, but I have spent twenty years in Spain and the last five years in Mexico. My early years were spent mostly here and in Albania. I have not been back in Turkey for many years." He relaxed into his chair, crossing his right foot over his left knee and further revealing the intricate silver work on his boot tips and heels. He looked back over at Orhan.

"I received a letter from your uncle several months ago asking me to come. He felt I could be of particular help in a dangerous situation that he was convinced was about to take place. I arrived in İstanbul this morning only to find the family in mourning over his death. I attended his brief funeral and was given a sealed letter with my name on it explaining what was happening with you and your friend. It wasn't hard to track you down from there." He paused, resting his gaze on Aubrey. "I was unaware that there would be such…pleasant company included." Aubrey looked away, annoyed.

Jeff threw daggers at Mustafa with his eyes. "So what do you know about what is going on?" he asked, his tone less than cordial.

Mustafa smiled back at him in a way that could only be described as sleazy. Then he licked his lips lecherously and ogled Aubrey's bustline through her sweater. Jeff decided that he was going to take an intense dislike to this intruder from now on.

"I know a great deal more than you, I must say," Mustafa finally answered. "My family has had some experience with the creatures that will haunt you beginning with the full moon tomorrow. They are relentless, and they will not stop until their appointed time. Death and destruction will roil in their wake, and you, my friends, are right in the middle of it."

"You refer to whatever this is as *they*. How many are there?" asked Orhan.

"I refer to them as *they* because they are twins. Twin jinni, both equally malicious, both equally virulent. You, I am sorry to say, are in a lot of trouble." Mustafa sat back up to the table, seemingly pleased with the effect his words were having. "Your two friends here, however, are not a part of this; they should leave and go home at their earliest convenience." He nodded to Jonathan and Aubrey as he said this but barely took his eyes off of Aubrey as he spoke.

"We're staying," said Aubrey indignantly. Jonathan nodded adamantly.

"Well, I cannot make you leave," said Mustafa, "but if you choose to be a part of this, there will be no leaving later once the jinni have set their sights on you. You will be as much at risk as Orhan and Jeff."

Jeff looked at him, surprised to hear his name. Mustafa answered his questioning glance.

"Oh yes, I know about you from Ümët's letter. You are in grave danger. That means anyone who is around you is in grave danger. And while we are on the subject of grave danger, you can no longer travel on this bus full of innocent people. That is why I have come now. You will continue the rest of the way to Ephes with me."

Jeff glanced over at Orhan, who seemed to have resigned himself to the truth of what Mustafa was saying. Orhan looked absently into the bottom of his empty coffee cup, saying nothing.

"You talk about the innocent people on the bus, but what about Jeff and Orhan? *They* are innocent. What about them?" asked Jonathan.

107

"Innocent," chuckled Mustafa in mock disdain. "They are not innocent. They will have to pay for the transgressions of their fathers. Their blood carries the weight of a great deal of guilt. Are you familiar with the Bible?"

They all nodded halfheartedly except for Orhan, who shook his head negatively. Mustafa continued. "The book of Job in the sixth chapter and the fourth verse sums it up quite nicely." He paused to build the suspense. "It says, and I quote, 'The arrows of the Almighty are in me, my spirit drinks in their poison; God's terrors are marshaled against me.'"

# 11. Cave of the Seven Sleepers

Ehes, Turkey
11:30 a.m.

Mustafa pulled his Fiat Albea rental car into the parking lot at the ruins of Ephesus. Orhan had insisted that he sit in the front seat with Mustafa while Jeff, Aubrey, and Jonathan sat scrunched into the back seat. They had all slept during the long drive. Aubrey had laid her head on Jeff's shoulder early on, and he had no desire for her to move. When she finally did wake up, Jeff massaged his painful neck muscle, and rotated his head. Despite the stiffness, he wouldn't have traded the last few hours for the world.

Jonathan slouched over with his head against the side window sound asleep, drool trickling from the corner of his mouth. He managed to stay in the same position despite the bumpy parking lot. Jeff caught Aubrey's eye as they tried to work the stiffness out of their necks, and they smiled at each other shyly.

"Thanks for being my pillow," she said with a gleam in her eye as she cocked her head seductively, looking back toward Jeff.

"It was my pleasure." He kept her gaze for a few seconds more, and then looked off awkwardly out the window, wishing he could come up with something clever to say.

Mustafa found a parking place close to the entrance and made a motion with his hands that they should all get out. It was only then that Jonathan woke up and looked around, bleary-eyed.

109

"We here already?" he asked through a stretch, and a yawn. His rhetorical question was answered by complete indifference as the others got out of the car. They walked passed a bazaar that catered to tourists and proceeded toward the gate that led to the ruins. Jeff stopped to pick up a multi-breasted statue of Artemis Ephesia, goddess of fertility. He held it up discreetly for Aubrey to see, but she only countered by picking up a statue of Priapos, the male version, giggling maniacally at Jeff's obvious embarrassment. They hurriedly ran to catch up with Mustafa, Orhan, and Jonathan who had already purchased their tickets and were walking through the gate.

A tour group was forming to get in line, so they pushed passed them to buy tickets. Then they began making their way along the surprisingly crowded walkway through the ruins. It was quite a bit warmer than Istanbul, but still nippy, and the snow of Istanbul had turned into the rain at Ephesus. Jeff would have rather had snow. Orhan had picked up a map and was studying it as they walked, but Mustafa took the lead and wound his way quickly through the meandering tourists. As they got to the Marble Road that ran parallel to the ancient Agora, the dampness made the way slippery, particularly for Mustafa in his cowboy boots.

Jeff felt like he was being dragged along by Mustafa's pace. There was so much that he wanted to see in the ruins: the Celsus Library, the latrina and baths that once had hot and cold running water, the brothel, the theater; there just wasn't any time. Jeff looked out toward what had been the magnificent harbor of antiquity but now was a valley full of orchards. Earthquakes and sedimentation over the centuries had filled in the harbor to the Aegean. The Harbor Street that once ended at the docks now lay five kilometers from the Aegean Sea. Jeff was amazed to learn that archeologists estimated that it would take another five hundred years to excavate the entire ancient city.

They soon passed the theater and continued on toward the Cave of the Seven Sleepers. "Most tourists do not venture beyond this point, especially during cold weather," said Mustafa slowing his pace so that the others could catch up with him. "We should have the place to ourselves. We are early. Hopefully we have beaten Ermal here. I want to be hidden when he arrives."

The rest of the group looked at each other and shrugged.

"Do you expect some kind of trouble from Ermal?" asked Orhan.

"I expect trouble from every direction now," Mustafa replied. "I do not trust your uncle's Gypsy." He had become noticeably sullen. Jeff noticed that he seemed nervous and out of sorts—nothing like the arrogant jerk he had been at the restaurant. Jeff hoped secretly that he was just tired from the long drive, but he sensed that Mustafa dreaded what was about to happen. He was like a man who had just jumped off a fifty-foot cliff and was about to have to do it again.

They hurried beyond the last group of tourists to a more remote area of the ruins, where Mustafa began to proceed more cautiously as he neared the cave. Aubrey took Jeff's hand and squeezed it, not letting go as they approached.

The cave was bricked into seven niches. The ruins of an ancient church sat over it. It was obvious that no one was here, nor had there been anyone here for some time, as evidenced by a lack of footprints in the mud. The company decided to wait in one of the niches to get out of the rain. Only Orhan carried an umbrella, and he stood as sentinel in the mouth of the niche using it as a shield against the now driving rain.

Time passed slowly as the dankness began to invade their bones. Even though they were dressed against the cold, the moisture-laden wind seemed to cut right through them. Jeff could hear Aubrey's teeth chattering uncontrollably as she snuggled under his arm into his chest.

111

The rain beat against the stone and the brick, dancing a percussive rhythm on the taut skin of Orhan's umbrella. Jeff became mesmerized by the cadence of the beat. He strained to keep awake, trying to concentrate on any sound other than the wind and the rain that would herald the approach of Ermal. He thought to himself that this would be a great afternoon to have chicken noodle soup and to take a nap.

He was jolted to alertness by the sudden movement of Mustafa as he jumped from the shadow of the niche at a lone figure that had just entered the cave. Ermal stood before them pulling back the hood of a large water-repellent cape. The Gypsy turned to face them calmly, clearly not surprised by Mustafa's abrupt advance from the shadows. He stared at the group with cold, dark eyes. Jeff saw little resemblance to the docile servant he had encountered at the *yalı* of Ümët. The man before him now was powerful and wary. He fixed each one with a stare in turn. Aubrey and Jonathan lowered their eyes, shying away from his penetrating gaze. They sensed they were unwelcome.

He made no pretense at a formal greeting. Coming deeper into the cave to get out of the blowing rain, he approached Orhan first.

"You have no time," he warned. "The jinn has been released. Your only hope of survival rests in your ability to do exactly as I say." Seeing a hint of the master/servant relationship they had once had in Orhan's expression, Ermal stood squarely in front of the young Turk almost nose to nose.

"I am not your servant," he stated. "I never was. What you took to be servile submission was simply the best way for me to protect you and your uncle." Orhan was momentarily speechless, so Ermal continued. "My family for generations have been the guardians of people who abused, mistreated, took for granted, and summarily dismissed us as inferior. We stood in the way of great evil to protect and preserve. It is now time for you to listen to me as if your very life depended on it, because it does."

Ermal confronted Mustafa next. "You, my brother, have been gone too long." With that the two men embraced and kissed each other on both cheeks. Orhan and Jeff stood dumbfounded. Jeff was the first to break the silence as the two men talked in hushed tones beneath the hearing of the others.

"You are his brother?" asked Jeff. "I thought you said you didn't trust Ümët's Gypsy."

Mustafa turned to him, looking amused. "I don't. I never have. At least not since he stole the heart of my childhood love."

"Moza?" asked Orhan, surprised.

"Moza," confirmed Mustafa smiling affectionately at his brother still in his partial embrace. "She is the only women I have ever truly loved. I have spent my life experimenting with innumerable substitutes, but no one has come close to filling the void in my heart." He then feigned a poetic posture. "Alas I am destined to spend my life lonely in a crowded room."

Ermal pulled away from Mustafa and stood in front of Jeff. "You should have stayed in America, but I respect why you came. The danger for you *all* is imminent." He said this scanning Aubrey and Jonathan, including them in the threat.

"My brother and I along with several members of our clan will do what we can to protect you." He stepped deeper into the cave facing out so that the others could see his face more clearly in the dim daylight entering the mouth of the cave. "We are protected here. The power of the jinn cannot touch you in this place. They will have to seek you out as you would them, but do not be deceived as to their intent and their ability to achieve it. They mean you mortal harm. Others will die just as a matter of course, but you are the true target of their malice." He paused for a moment to make sure he had their undivided attention before proceeding.

"Your families had a great deal to do with the betrayal of the jinni centuries ago. It has been a carefully designed act of destiny that your families have been in close contact with each other through out the generations. It was no accident that Altin and Ümët were school friends. It has been no accident that you and Orhan were university roommates. It is no accident that you felt compelled to come to Turkey. You have been brought together for a purpose.

"The ancestors of my brother and I were pledged centuries ago to protect against the fury of the jinni and the curse passed down. You will only survive by cunning and ruthlessness. We are in a battle that we cannot win unless we follow very specific protocols."

Jeff couldn't help but catch the distinctly military swagger that Ermal had adopted. He began to eye the two brothers with a new acceptance. Looking over at Aubrey, who had been listening as best she could through the drum of the wind and rain, he noticed she was no longer shivering. For the first time he could see fear in her face. He realized that it was simply a mirror of his own.

"What must we do?" asked Orhan.

"It is our deepest feeling," began Mustafa, "that this has gone on long enough. We therefore believe our best course of action is to be on the attack, not on the defensive. Defensive postures were the mistakes made in the past."

"As I said before," interrupted Ermal, "the jinni means to destroy your line. They not only want to, they need to. The only thing that has saved your families from total annihilation is the intervention of our ancestors."

"Their course of action was to run and hide," continued Mustafa. "They tried to outlast the jinni. Some survived; most did not."

"How do we attack them?" asked Jeff. He could sense a chill penetrating his garments that he realized was not from the wind and rain but from his own nervous perspiration.

"We have charms, incantations, and spells that can bind the jinni long enough to destroy them," said Ermal. "Each of you must be thoroughly acquainted with our armamentarium so that you all become soldiers capable of fighting and protecting each other."

"That was the tragedy of the generations past," said Mustafa. "They became fearful, panicked, and isolated, and one by one were destroyed by the jinni. The jinni enjoy making sport of the killing, which we can use to our advantage. They often tease and taunt their victims before killing them."

"Your uncle's research was right about one thing," said Ermal. "The jinni thrive on fear. Killing is a means to an end. The more killing that goes on, the more fearful the survivors become. Cruelty prolongs the terror. We will make that work for us. They will come after you just as they have done every generation for the last five hundred years. They will assume that you are no different than the thousands they have slain in the past. They will provoke you to terror before they get around to killing you. At that moment we will strike at the very heart of their evil and destroy them once and for all."

* * *

Jonathan tried to keep focused on the conversation, but he had not used the restroom since they had stopped hours ago along the Aegean. The cold wind and rain only made matters worse. He decided to go behind a fallen column outside of the cave.

Uneasiness came over him as he realized he was being watched. He felt the hairs on the back of his neck begin to prickle. He didn't dare look around him, but he quickly zipped his fly and tried to walk nonchalantly back to the entrance of the cave. As he approached, his attention was drawn to movement

115

amongst the ruined foundation of the church on the hill above the cave. A thick black form balanced itself on a fallen column just above Jonathan's head. He didn't want to look, but he knew it wouldn't go away by ignoring it.

He slowly turned his gaze and met the flaming eyes of a massive beast. The rain blurred his vision as he swallowed a scream and bolted the last few steps to the mouth of the cave where the others were continuing their discussion unaware that he had even left. As he stumbled in out of the rain, his companions turned a glaring eye on his interruption.

"Uh...uh...I hate to say this, but something's out there just above the cave on the side of the hill," he stammered.

"What is it?" asked Ermal.

"I don't know, but it's big and black and ugly," Jonathan said, still shaking.

The two brothers pulled out odd-looking crossbows from under their coats and crept stealthily toward the entrance of the cave. Their weapons looked ancient but had modern modifications. The elastic cord was carefully woven in a tight braid. As Mustafa passed in front of him, Jeff noticed that his crossbow had a trigger on the handle, and the tips of the bow were sharp and knife edged. Mustafa positioned himself slowly just under the lip of the cave's entrance and peered cautiously up the hill without exposing himself too far from the cover of the cave. As he did so, he cracked open the handle of the crossbow and placed a .22 caliber bullet into the chamber, snapping it shut again. He reached into his pocket, never taking his eyes from the opening above him, and placed a well-polished peach seed in the sling, then pulled it back into the cocked position.

He grape-vined side-stepped into the rain raising his sling-rifle into shooting position as he squared toward the hill backing step by step until he could clearly see the ruins of the church above. Ermal mimicked his brother but stayed under the overhang of the cave to cover him. Jonathan and Aubrey cowered together in a niche deepest in the back of the cave. Jeff picked up a fist-sized stone, as did Orhan, and stood their ground just behind Ermal.

Jeff was startled to see the rain-distorted dark forms of several creatures making their way up the low slope from the valley behind Mustafa. They circled predatorily in a semicircle fanning out facing up the hill. As they got closer, he could see that they were men similarly dressed and armed as Mustafa and Ermal.

Suddenly a cascade of small rocks and muddy water plummeted over the mouth of the cave. Mustafa reacted quickly, taking aim and releasing the sling as he pulled the trigger to send the projectile with fierce velocity. The report gave off a compressed echo, dampened by the precipitation. A ferocious snarl was replaced by a quick yelp. Mustafa dove headlong into the cave a split second before a massive, black, dog-like beast leaped onto the spot he had just occupied. The beast turned swiftly toward the cave, snarling lips pulled back to reveal long, saber-like fangs. It glared hatefully with flaming eyes threatening attack, but was stayed by an unseen force. It reared and thrust forward as if straining against a leash.

Ermal squeezed the trigger of his weapon, releasing the peach stone with deadly accuracy between the flaming eyes of the beast. The other men closed in from behind and shot the monster in similar fashion, aiming for the head and behind the foreleg. The beast writhed furiously, lashing out in all directions, but was unable to breach the threshold of the cave. It made a final lunge at the occupants but rebounded and fell crushed as if it had banged into a thick glass wall. It snarled vehemently in its death throes, never taking its hateful glare off of Jeff and Orhan, who were frozen in horror.

Mustafa reloaded his sling-rifle and stepped forward out of the cave to stand over the fallen beast. He rolled the massive carcass onto its side with his boot and aimed point-blank at the heart. The smooth peach stone embedded itself deep into the monster's thoracic cavity causing a combustion of light to spear the dim afternoon haze. The beast let out one last hair-raising cry, not of agony but of pure, unadulterated anger. It raised its head to stare at Jeff and Orhan one last time, and then flopped back down into the mud as it was quickly consumed by a lapping fire and dissolved into ash before their eyes. The rain carried the ash in rivulets of mud and water over the embankment to the valley below.

The company stared in awe, speechless, as the other men came into closer view from the periphery and congregated around Mustafa and Ermal. Jeff counted four newcomers. They all had similar facial features to Mustafa and Ermal, and long, dark hair matted to their faces, which held the look of determined warriors. There was no doubt that these men were all Roma.

They began to talk amongst themselves in the tongue that only the Gypsy knows. They made occasional animated gestures toward Jeff and Orhan, with sidelong glances that made Jeff uneasy. Finally, after several moments, Ermal approached them.

"Is it over?" asked Jeff.

"No," stated Ermal flatly. "This was just a minion of the jinn. It had the spirit of the jinn, so it was bound by the same laws that the jinni are bound by. That is why it was unable to enter the cave." Ermal replaced his weapon in a hidden holster inside his cape. "The fact that it saw you means that the jinn now knows were you are. He saw you through the beast's eyes. The jinn will come with all haste to slay you."

"Well, thanks for those cheery words," said Jeff looking around toward Aubrey and Jonathan, who were still in the back of the niche.

"The jinn will not be so easy to kill," said Mustafa. "He will be quicker and more powerful."

"What are these weapons you were using?" asked Jeff. "And what were those projectiles? They look like fruit pits."

"We call them sling-rifles. And these are the stones of a fruit," said Mustafa. "In this case I believe the English word is *peach*. It is only by the stone, or pit as you call it, of a fruit that a jinn can be killed."

"Who in the heck figured that one out?" said Jeff incredulously. "That seems like a pretty arbitrary way to kill something that is supposed to be so powerful."

"It has to do with the nature of the jinni," said Ermal. "They are created beings, spirits of fire. They are not of our natural world; therefore the intrusion of our living nature into their being, such as the fruit stone, is intolerable, and thus death ensues. It is much like the effect chemical poisons have on our systems."

"I still don't understand why they are after us," said Jeff. "What exactly did our ancestors do to tick them off?"

Jeff had just finished his question when two more men arrived from the direction of the ruined city, their black winter garments soiled and wet. They approached Mustafa and pulled him aside speaking in hushed voices. One of the men held his left wrist tight with his right hand. A trickle of blood ran from under his coat sleeve and down to his fingertips, dripping to the floor at his feet. The man's hand quivered slightly as he fought back the pain.

Mustafa noticed the pooling of blood on the floor. He took the man's injured arm in his hands and pushed up the cuff of the coat and sweater revealing a four-inch gash in his forearm just above the wrist. The man winced as Mustafa moved the arm into the light. Ermal was quickly at his side with a first-aid kit he had pulled from his black leather shoulder bag. Ermal washed the wound with mineral water from his water bottle, and the injured man clenched his teeth as the water effervesced from the carbonation.

"Petro, this is going to need stitches," Ermal said, addressing the injured man as he opened a package of 3/0 silk suture.

Petro looked away as Ermal began to stitch his arm. Jeff and Aubrey looked on with interest, but Orhan and Jonathan averted their attention to outside the cave, trying not to seem soft. Ermal deftly sutured the wound closed. When he was finished, the gash was a fine red line. Mustafa placed an antibiotic salve over the wound and then expertly bandaged the arm.

Jeff raised an eyebrow at Aubrey as he inspected the field dressing and let out a low whistle of approval. "It looks likes you've done this a few times before," he stated.

"More times than we would like to count," said Ermal. "We were lucky this time. It was only a small scratch."

Jeff mumbled under his breath to Aubrey, "If that was a small scratch, I'd hate to think what they consider more serious." Aubrey nodded in agreement.

Mustafa and Ermal turned their attention back to Jeff and Orhan.

"Our men killed two more beasts up the hill in the residential ruins. There can be no doubt now that the jinn knows you are here," said Ermal. "Our company will form a perimeter, but we must be ready to leave. First of all, however, you must be told the answer to your question.

"Your ancestors were at war against each other nearly six hundred years ago. Orhan, your family fought for and led armies for the Sultan Mehmet the Second. He was known as Mehmet the Conqueror. In those days an unsuccessful general would more than likely lose his head over a loss in battle. Your ancestor was a successful general until he tried to conquer Albania. He ran into a huge obstacle in Gjergji Kastrioti, also known as Skënderbej. This man was of Albanian noble birth. He was taken as a hostage of the Ottomans during the reign of the previous sultan, Murat the Second, and educated as a soldier. He had many successful campaigns for Mehmet, but after the Turkish defeat at Nish he abandoned the Ottoman army, returned to Albania, and became Christian. He took over the fortress at Kruja and over the years repelled thirteen different Ottoman invasions.

"This is where Jeff's ancestor gets involved. Although your family has been Turkish for many generations, the truth is your roots are Albanian. Your ancestor, like Gjergji Kastrioti, was of noble birth. His name was Përparim Lleshi. His family, however, converted to Islam, and therefore he was not sent as a hostage to the sultan. When Skënderbej returned to take power in Kruja he gathered around him the nobles of Albania. Jeff's ancestors swore allegiance to him, and thus became enemies of the Ottoman Empire.

"It was a terrible war that lasted nearly twenty years. Both sides were desperate to defeat their enemies. The Ottoman generals were pushed from behind to succeed in battle or die with dishonor at the edict of the sultan. The forces of the Albanians were fierce, and they were on their own ground. The Ottoman general, Selim Bey—your ancestor, Orhan—resorted to magic to try and defeat his enemies. With the help of sorcerers from the eastern lands of the empire, he called into service the power of the jinn. He was able to enlist a marid, a particularly evil, malicious jinn that had a bloodlust for human flesh. It had a devastating effect on the resistance armies of the Christian Albanians.

"As is the case with all new weapons that are meant to bring swift and final victory, the Albanians were able to match the jinn of the Ottomans with one of their own. In a daring raid, they attacked and killed an entire garrison near what is today Lake Orhrid. They put to the sword all but a single sorcerer named Baba Moush, who promised equal power to the Albanians if they would spare his life. Thus, the conjuring of the power of a second jinn as powerful and malicious as the first. Both sides suffered great losses for a period of about six months. The jinni, however, went beyond the bounds of their masters and began to work together to fulfill their own desires for carnage. Soon they killed indiscriminately. No side was safe. It became obvious to the leaders of both camps that if something were not done, soon they would all perish.

"With the aid of the eastern sorcerer, a mighty spell was prepared to bind the jinni forever; but in order for it to work, the jinni had to be in close proximity to each other. So the generals of both armies secretly met and made a pact to meet in a river valley that is now in Gramsh province of Albania for one last great battle. It was, however, a ruse to trap the jinni and bind them. At the signal from their commanders, the two armies collided in a mock mêlée. The jinni rampaged through the valley killing many from both sides. When they met in the middle, it was clear for all to see that they were actually twins. Terrified at this revelation, the soldiers began to fight in earnest—first against their enemy, then against their brothers. The power of the jinni increased at a startling rate as the frenzy of terror and war increased. Total mayhem ensued. The armies of Albania and Turkey were on the verge of complete annihilation.

"Meanwhile Baba Moush made his trap on the summit of Mount Tomori. He began his incantations to drive the twins each to two golden cubes prepared by the sorcerer's black art. The cubes were inscribed with binding spells inside and out. They were embedded with diamonds, rubies, emeralds, and sapphires to bribe their gods to honor the incantations and give the spells power. From the mountaintop the chanting of the sorcerer echoed north through the valley. The jinni were quickly caught in its snare. They writhed and spat venomous threats as they were literally sucked in by an implosion from the golden cubes on the top of Mount Tomori.

# Vale of Shadows

"All fighting ceased as the warriors stood in awe at the terrible sight. The turbulence from the implosion caused all manner of atmospheric and seismic activity. Christian and Muslim fled in panic into the hills surrounding the valley. By the time it was over, the jinni had been captured and sealed in their respective golden cubes.

"But more treachery was yet to come, as each general had schemed to steal the two golden cubes for themselves. They laid an ambush for Baba Moush, waiting for him to accomplish his task. Përparim Lleshi lay to the west side of the summit while Selim Bey lay to the east. When the storms and earthquakes ceased, the two generals sprang from their hiding places to seize the cubes. They had no regard for the sorcerer as he tried to warn them of the danger the cubes contained. Selim Bey was the first to reach the sorcerer. He was enraged that he had been betrayed by the magician's aid to the Albanians. With a single stroke of his scimitar, he cleaved Baba Moush in two. But the magi had not trusted his "allies" and had prepared an incantation implemented at the event of his death. An incantation of revenge on his betrayers. As a result the jinni were not eternally bound as was promised, but were to be loosed once in each generation to bring death and destruction on the linage of the two commanders.

"There has been twelve such unleashing. This year marks the thirteenth and final time. The sorcerer was powerful in prophecy, and mathematics and astronomy were second nature to him. His curse was always meant to conclude after thirteen cycles. The number thirteen is significant for it was the number of his fellow magi that were slain by the Albanians, but he held the Ottomans equally culpable for their conquest of Persia.

"On the top of the mount hand-to-hand combat ensued between the warrior chiefs. Both were powerful and skilled in war, but alas, a sortie of Turks crested the summit and came to the aid of their general. Lleshi fled down the mountain with the cube he had stolen tucked safely in his tunic. He came upon a sortie of his own men making their way up the mountain and turned to see the Ottoman general gazing down at him. The battle was over. Each side went own its way.

"The cubes remained in the possession of the two leaders, one in Albania, the other in Turkey. There was still conflict between the two nations, but these generals never faced each other again. It wasn't until some years later that the impact of the sorcerers curse was first realized. The jinni have never reunited but have carried out their own vengeance on the descendents of their betrayers, each bound to the proximity of their golden prisons."

"The whereabouts of the golden coffers are the key to our success," interjected Mustafa.

Ermal nodded. "Yes. We believe that if we can find the golden cubes, then we can destroy them physically or by altering the curse with incantations of our own. Our family is not without certain skills in magical arts. We have been preparing for this very time for many years. We are ready, but the weight of the burden lies with you two descendents of Përparim Lleshi and Selim Bey."

Ermal paused and studied Jeff and Orhan in the afternoon light that now cascaded into the cave through a break in the clouds, as if trying to ascertain their strength and resolve. Could they endure to the end? Would they show cowardice like so many generations before? The next few hours would reveal much.

# Vale of Shadows

# II

On the Day of Judgment
It will be asked of the angels,
"Did you cause men to worship you?"
They will proclaim their innocense.
"In no way did we put ourselves before men.
It was in the jinni that some worshipped."
The Creator will proclaim
With sadness in His heart,
"The condemnation of the one
will be the same as for the other.
I will tolerate no other gods before me."

Abi bin Mustifi
Salim Bey's Imam warning him of his folly

# 12. Ölüm Unleashed

## Mountains of West-Central Turkey
### 12:30 p.m.

Light stabbed impudently into the darkness of the coffer, and the lid popped open like it had been released from a magnetic seal. The marid stirred from his slumber. His flaming spirit issued from its confines. Before him stood a troop of mercenaries gathered to do his bidding. As he straightened to full height, they bowed to the ground in reverence as they had been taught. He gazed out at his entourage, satisfied that they had protected him once again from his enemies while he languished in abysmal oblivion.

His fiery form rose and towered over his servants, who still groveled with foreheads to the ground. Men who were the descendents of men who over the centuries had sworn to protect the jinn, and in return they were given power and wealth. He took on a distinctly humanoid appearance. A conflagration lapped along the floor from his pedestal-like lower body, and his minions shielded their eyes from the brilliance of his presence. The small cave that had been his resting and hiding place for the last four decades absorbed his glory into every crack and crevice. He allowed his stature to diminish to better fit the size of his habitat, and at the same time transformed into a creature of solid human shape. Only his eyes gave him away, blazing with inner fire.

127

# Rob Dakin

He summoned the commander to rise and face him by the power of his will. The man stood bravely, but fear clearly etched his expression. He had never stood before the jinn before. He was following in the footsteps of his father, who had trained him from childhood for this very moment. The man was determined not to fail his legacy. He summoned his strength to stand before his master unflinchingly.

The marid studied him intensely, reading the man's past through his thoughts. The commander grimaced under the intense scrutiny of the jinn's mental probing. He fought the pain, determined not to flinch and show weakness. The jinn found mild pleasure in his agony, but after a few moments the test was over. The jinn released his servant, satisfied that he possessed adequate strength to be of useful service to him.

He walked through the ranks of the men standing now at attention. As he passed by the torch sconces on the cave wall, the flame of each exploded toward him in showers of sparks. The men flinched but quickly regained their composure to stand firm before their demigod's inspection. He mused at their display of weakness. Finally he made his way back to the rock table on which his golden coffer sat, and faced his troop commander.

"You will call me Ölüm," he said with a voice of deafening resonance. "In the tongue of these mortals it means *death*, and it is death that I will most surely wreak on those who betrayed my twin and me." He met each man's eyes in turn with his fiery gaze. "You have all sworn allegiance to me. Failure to meet my expectations will result in a fate worse than your meager deaths. Obey, and be rewarded. Fail, and be eternally eviscerated by the insidious demons of hell, a torment that will know no end."

"We are at your command, my lord," said the commander.

"What shall I call you?" asked Ölüm. "Besides worthless maggot.'"

"I am called Jason," he said mustering boldness.

"Ah...a worthy name for a *great* warrior. You will prove yourself true to your name, or you will die trying. I will not tolerate weakness in my commander. If you ever show timidity in my presence again, I will strike you dead where you stand."

"I understand," said Jason forcefully. "I...we will be ruthlessly fearless in your service."

Ölüm nodded his approval. "How many men are you?"

"We are fifty men," answered Jason. "We stand ready to receive your orders."

Ölüm summoned three of the men standing in the back ranks by telepathy. They made their way forward through the lines of men and stood before Ölüm. The jinn spread his arms wide. Flames shot from his fingertips and ricocheted about the ceiling of the cave, and fire came to rest on each of the three men. The flame consumed their bodies, enveloping them in blinding light. Soon they stood before Ölüm as spirits of fire transformed into the likeness of the jinn.

The others stood their ground unwavering, remembering the warning given to Jason. But they stared in silent awe at their comrades. Each steadied the excitement growing in him. The promises made by Ölüm of great power and reward would be kept. They stood eager to do their master's bidding.

Ölüm placed his massive hands on the head of the first flaming spirit. The spirit's form changed in a ripple of light refraction to slowly become a great, black, dog-like beast. His eyes burned with fire. Ölüm went to the other two, transforming them as he had done the first. The three beasts stood at their master's side. Ölüm looked at each one with pride.

"You are now worthy to serve me," he said to them. "Go track down my enemies. You have all the skills you need to accomplish the task. Strike fear in them. Show no mercy to anyone who opposes you. You go in my name."

With that the three beasts bolted out of the mouth of the cave. Heavy snow was falling. Soon their dark silhouettes vanished into the white flurry. They raced with supernatural speed through the ravines of the mountains, angling their way to the southwest. As men, they had successfully intercepted communication that pointed to Ephes. As beasts they burned to overtake their prey. Nothing would stop them.

* * *

Ölüm knew that his will would be done. He turned his attention back to Jason.

"What have you accomplished during the pre-time?" he asked.

"We have successfully accounted for all of the descendents of the Ottoman and the Albanian," answered Jason proudly.

"Where?"

"Within reach, my lord. The Albanian is even now with the last of the Ottoman's line in Ephesus at the Cave of the Seven Sleepers. Your servants are on their way and will arrive there shortly," said Jason. He stepped forward, puffing out his chest and added, "My only wish and my only request are to avenge the death of my father at the hands of that treacherous Gypsy. Let me be the one to kill him and his family." He flashed an arrogant smirk toward Ölüm, surprising himself at how demanding his tone was. He did not mean to presume to demand anything from his master. He knew it was a mistake as soon as the words left his mouth.

Ölüm glared at him with contempt. "For this curse to be released, I must kill them all," he said. His voice was pungent with hate. "Every cycle for five hundred years I have gotten close to my goal, but always someone escapes. They propagate, increasing in number, and become more spread out with each

130

period of time. I will not fail this time to annihilate the issue of Selim Bey and Përparim Lleshi." He paused for a moment fixing hateful eyes on Jason. He boiled with anger as he towered over his minion. "Nor will I tolerate any other agenda but my own." Ölüm flexed his massive humanoid physique. Fire danced from his skin and splattered off the walls and ceiling of the cave. The men standing at attention recoiled from the heat. The smell of singed eyebrows, moustaches, and hair wafted throughout the grotto.

Jason, who stood closest to Ölüm, took the brunt of the conflagration. His flesh blistered and bubbled, oozing yellowish serum, and his facial hair and scalp were blasted away. He tried to keep his feet, but the agony was too great. He crumpled in a heap before the feet of Ölüm, writhing in pain. Smoke roiled in wisps from his garments. The other men watched in expressionless horror as Ölüm towered over them, indifferent to the pain he had caused his lieutenant.

Three men in the back ranks took their eyes off of Ölüm and glanced at each other in uncertainty and fear. Immediately tongues of fire lapped out at them from Ölüm's fingertips, brutally consuming them to ash.

"I will have no weaklings in my army!" Ölüm bellowed. "If you wish to live, show no fear." He gazed down at the charred features of Jason. His black, necrotic flesh hung in tatters from the cooked muscle revealing scorched bones below.

Jason's wretched spasms and convulsions slowly ceased. He gasped his last breath, staring with fire-seared eyes up at his master. His last thought before darkness took him was the terrifying realization that he had been wrong in his allegiance to Ölüm. A scream of terror caught in his scorched throat as his spirit floated into utter blackness. The excruciating agony of his death did not diminish. His soul would languish in torment for all eternity.

* * *

Ölüm stepped over the smoldering corpse, glaring disdainfully at the men left standing. He walked over and stood in front of each one of the men, staring deep into their eyes, probing their minds for strengths and weakness. After careful inspection he settled in front of one in the middle rank, circling him warily, bumping up against him in an attempt to provoke him. The man stood firm. Unwavering. Expressionless. Ölüm stopped in front of the man once again. He perused his stature from head to toe. Finally a faint smile curled his lips. He reached out and brushed the man's hair back, revealing hard but distinctly feminine features.

Ölüm glowered at the woman standing before him. "Who are you?" he demanded.

"I am called Ursella, my lord," she said unflinchingly. "I have come to serve you."

"You feel you are worthy to serve me?"

"I am more worthy than any man here," she retorted, looking straight into Ölüm's eyes. Her eyes reflected his fire.

"Yes, I believe you are," Ölüm said reflectively. "You will be my new lieutenant. Do you understand what must be done?"

"I am at your bidding, my lord. I have only just arrived a short time ago from Albania. I understand what you must do to end the curse, but what would you have me do for you as your lieutenant?" She said this without hesitation. Ölüm was impressed by her boldness.

"I want you to go before me," he said. "I want you to go in my strength and power. You will be given a portion of my power to transform yourself into my likeness. You will use this power to throw our enemies into confusion. You will in essence become me." Ölüm watched her expression, but he could not read her. Her inner strength kept her features expressionless. Ölüm's confidence in Ursella increased.

As if on cue, Ursella stepped forward, separating herself from the rest of the men. She kept her eyes forward, allowing herself just the faintest glance at the charred remains of her brother. Ölüm stood before her, grasping her head between his massive hands, and pulled her face up toward his. He hesitated, and then placed his lips firmly over hers. A firestorm passed between them. Ursella's body convulsed, but Ölüm held her head firm. She levitated, sustained by the stream of flame that issued from Ölüm.

Lightening arced across the cave ceiling sending static blue fingers into the bowels of the earth. The men standing at attention bowed their heads against the glare, but none dared to close their eyes. Sonic pulse waves thundered in rapid succession, deeply resonating through the caverns and out through the mountain valleys. Tremors shook the ground they stood on. Dirt and gravel cascaded from the dome of the cave to fill the space with billowy clouds of dust. The rumble of a distant avalanche echoed down the ravine.

The fire infusion abruptly stopped, and Ölüm lowered Ursella gently to the floor. She slumped, weakened, against his chest, but then mustered an inner strength to stand on her own. She looked down at her torso, arms, and legs. Nothing seemed to have changed. She stared up at Ölüm confused. He met her gaze with a smile.

"You appear as you have always appeared," he stated, "but now you carry the fire of my ancestors within you."

Ursella held up her hands and admired her fingertips as she began to sense the empowering spirit of Ölüm coursing through her veins. The chill from the winter mountain air that she had felt moments ago was replaced by a warmth that seemed endless. She was no longer the same woman but was in fact a new creature—one capable of great deeds. She turned her attention to her master. A bond now existed between them. She felt drawn to him, willingly enslaved. Ölüm studied her flaming eyes. She would do all that he required.

133

His attention was suddenly drawn forward, toward the mouth of the cave, and he stared absently observing a scene far away. Pondering a moment, he then looked back to Ursella. "The three that have gone before us have been destroyed," he said. Ölüm strode out into the blowing snow gazing westward and summoned Ursella with his mind. She came and stood next to him, following his gaze.

"I see clearly now," she said. "They are in the cave at the ruins of Ephesus."

Ölüm smiled at his protégée. She was becoming powerful. He mused to himself that she might very well be the most worthy human he had ever met. Although she was alien to him, he began to appreciate her strength. Could she finally be the link that would free him from this bondage? He perused her from the corner of his eye. She sensed his thought and returned his with her own.

"Soon you will be free of this curse, my lord. We will not fail."

The two were joined by the troop of minions that had exhumed themselves from the cave. Ölüm faced them, raising his hands into the flurry. Fire passed from him to them. After the initial jolt, they stood ready. Without further delay they raced off toward Ephes, carried by the wind.

# 13. Whoops! There Goes a Perfectly Good Ruin

Cave of the Seven Sleepers
2:00 p.m.

Rain continued to blur the landscape, and as a stiff wind blew in from the Aegean Sea the smell of salt water mixed with the smells of winter rain. A distant, mournful cry floated on the wind from the inland hills. The company was standing in a vortex of clashing weather fronts. Ermal and his men studied the sky trying to discern the direction of the cry. The wind made it difficult to pinpoint, but it seemed to be coming from the northeast.

Another cry, closer this time. The men sprang to the top of the hill, positioning themselves in the ruins of the church. Mustafa motioned for Jeff, Orhan, Aubrey, and Jonathan to go back into the cave. Aubrey clung to Jeff's arm, her gloved fingers pressing through his winter parka into his upper arm. He looked down at her and then at her grasp, indicating she was squeezing too tightly.

"Sorry," she apologized, loosening her grip but maintaining her grasp.

A forlorn wail carried into the cave, and then another. They could hear the sound of men shouting right above them. Suddenly a bloodcurdling scream was abruptly cut short just outside the cave in the direction of the city. The mangled body of one of Ermal's men was tossed into the gape of the cave. Aubrey shuddered and buried her head into Jeff's chest, letting out a quick sob.

Jeff pried open her grip and quickly guided her into one of the back niches. The three men picked up loose bricks from the muddy stone floor and prepared to throw them at whatever came around the corner. Jeff felt a presence next to him and turned to find Aubrey squeezed in between Orhan and himself with her own brick raised. She met his questioning gaze.

"We're all in this together," she said trying to sound brave.

The foursome was startled by a thud in the back of the cave. Through a hole in the roof of the cave the body of Petro was flung, dismembered and mangled. Jeff glanced at Aubrey, who was steeled with determination. He realized at that moment that he loved her. He loved her fierce strength and her vulnerability. He loved her loyalty and determination and intelligence. And he thought that he would rather die with no one else by his side.

"What a time to fall in love," he mumbled under his breath. The comment was lost in the wind.

The pinging reports of .22 caliber bullets firing in the sling-rifles staccatoed through the ruins, and another body fell at the mouth of the cave, near their feet. This one, however, they did not recognize.

"Chalk one up for the good guys," said Jonathan, trying to lighten the moment. But he was suddenly toppled onto his back with a cry of surprise as the fallen man grabbed his ankle and yanked violently. The man crawled towards him, a bloody gash showing crimson across his face. Orhan quickly straddled the man's prone torso and bashed the brick into the back of the man's skull. His eyes rolled into the back of his head and his grip went limp as he slumped dead over Jonathan, who kicked himself free of the dead man's clutch and clambered to his feet.

Two men wrestling in the mud rolled into view. The one on the bottom was Mustafa. His assailant straddled his back with a stranglehold around Mustafa's throat pinning him in a headlock. Mustafa flailed frantically to reach his enemy, but he was brutally pummeled face-first into the ooze.

Jeff erupted with a primal cry, raising his brick as he charged. The intruder saw his attacker too late. He released his grip on Mustafa and tried to ward off the assault, but Jeff smashed the brick into the side of the man's face. He careened over onto his side, dead before he hit the mud, as Jeff helped the dazed Mustafa to his feet.

Mustafa pushed him away roughly. "You must stay within the protection of the cave!" he said angrily as he staggered back towards the fray on the top of the hill. Jeff reluctantly obeyed, backing into the grotto. His eyes fixed on the man he had just murdered.

"Evil times are on us, Jeff," said Orhan. "You did what you had to do." His words were little consolation; Jeff felt sick to his stomach. Killing was completely contrary to his whole way of life. He bent over, placing his hands on his knees for support.

"I'm going to throw up," he groaned. Aubrey came to his side and carefully supported his midsection as he heaved the contents of his stomach into a pool of rainwater. Aubrey looked over at Orhan with tears running down her face. After a second retch, Jeff stood straight and wiped his mouth with the back of his gloved hand.

"I'm ready to go home now," he said halfheartedly. He carefully peeked out into the open, and then darted over to retrieve his brick lying next to the corpse. Meanwhile, Jonathan searched the body of the first dead man, retrieving a .22 caliber Lugar, and then dragged him out into the rain, leaving the body piled next to the other.

"I don't know why I did that," he said wiping the mud off his hands onto his pants legs.

"We will only survive by being as ruthless as our enemies," said Orhan.

A shadow blocked the light coming into the cave as Ursella strode belligerently into view. She stood with her fists clenched against her hips and studied her prey with flaming eyes that exuded hatred for them. Gingerly she stretched out her hand toward the cave, testing the power of the unseen barrier that restrained her. Her fingers bumped abruptly against the invisible shield. Smiling warily at the entrapped friends, she smoothed her hands over the mouth of the cave like she was touching glass.

"Do you really believe this pathetic force can keep us out?" she asked disdainfully. "Do you really think that you are safe here?" She laughed manically, and then her flaming eyes flashed with determination at the foursome. "You will surely die in spite of your magic."

\* \* \*

Rifle and handgun fire erupted from the church ruins. Ermal and his men had realized that the majority of their foes were untransformed mortals, so only common weaponry was required. They kept their sling-rifles close at hand in the event that the jinn and its morphed minions came onto the scene. Ermal was amazed at the reckless abandon of the minions. They threw themselves into the fight driven from behind by the will of Ölüm.

From behind the minions came an oozing blackness. Mustafa thought at first it was the heavy rain playing tricks on him, but soon he realized it was the force of darkness that he had been anticipating. A great jolt of air blasted toward the ruins, pummeling the defenders to the ground in agony. Unsupported bricks in the walls of the ruins fell on top of two Gypsies, killing them instantly.

The two brothers and the rest of their surviving clan lay as dead men in the muck of the rain-drenched stones. The shock of the air concussion had knocked them out. The minions moved from their hiding places to pick their way through the ruins.

138

They kicked each body, checking for life. There appeared to be none, but the heavy downpour made it difficult to tell. They let the bodies lie. No one doubted that Ölüm's barometric pulse had been completely lethal.

\* \* \*

The shock wave was heard as a thunderous boom but had little effect on the occupants of the cave. Ursella glanced up the hill with an ear cocked, listening, a faint smile etched her lips. She stared back at Jeff and Orhan, her eyes burning with brilliant flame.

"That should just about do it," she exclaimed. "Your protectors are all dead. You are all alone. Who will help you now?" She stood back, awaiting the arrival of her master.

Jeff and Orhan stared back at her, speechless. After all, what was there to say? They had nothing the jinn wanted but their lives. They had no other bargaining chip. Jeff slowly reached under his coat around to his back hoping that Orhan was blocking Ursella's view just enough to pull out the sling-rifle he had picked up from Petro. The sling-rifle was already loaded with a peach stone and a .22 caliber bullet. He stealthily untangled it from his garment and slid it low around to his side directly behind Orhan. Jonathan saw what he was doing and slowly moved forward to position himself slightly in front of Jeff, at the same time turning and easing out the Lugar, holding it against his hidden side.

A tumble of rock announced the arrival of three of the minions. Ursella took them in with less than a glance. They were inferior to her. Reaching out, she grabbed one of the men by the scruff of the neck.

"These men are willing servants of our lord Ölüm, and are not bound by your pitiful spells." With that she hurled the man toward Jeff with the power of her will. Caught off guard, the man hesitated just long enough for Jonathan to raise the Lugar into the man's face and pull the trigger at point-blank

139

range. The man's head popped back from the recoil of the bullet striking him in the forehead, and the minion fell straight back out of the cave like a falling tree landing with a splash at the feet of Ursella. She stepped back, startled, but then quickly regained her composure.

The other two minions dove up the hill away from the entrance just as Jonathan capped off two more shots. The bullets ricocheted off of the rocks just missing the closer of the two men. Ursella laughed at their cowardice. She picked up the body of the dead man at her feet and raised it over her head without effort, then tossed it onto Jonathan's outstretched shooting arm sending him crashing to the floor.

Jeff used the distraction to aim the sling-rifle at Ursella. With a sharp crack, the stone embedded itself into her shoulder. She gave a cry of surprise followed by a grimace of pain. Her mind raced for answers to the onslaught of questions now raised by her obvious vunerability. Ursella glared at Jeff with lethal intent.

He quickly reloaded ready to fire again, but Ursella sprang around the corner out of sight. Rock and mud fell from the brow of the cave and down the side slopes as the rest of the minions converged for the kill. A rattle of bullets skipped across the floor stones as a human minion fired his weapon through the hole in the ceiling. A fragment glanced off the angle of rock and burrowed into Aubrey's left calf. She screamed in pain clutching her leg with both hands. Jeff was immediately at her side.

"I'm OK," she said through clenched teeth pushing him away. "Watch out!"

Jeff ducked into the closest niche just as a barrage of bullets spattered from the ceiling. Orhan wrestled the dead minion off of Jonathan, grabbing the dead man's nine-millimeter Walther P99. He aimed up at the hole, firing the semi-automatic with accuracy: there was a muffled gurgling sound, followed by a thud. The hole in the ceiling darkened as a minion fell across the opening.

Jeff used the opportunity to pull Aubrey to a niche farthest from the entrance. He carefully pulled her hands away from her wound to inspect it. Aubrey protested with tears, biting her lower lip to keep from screaming. The bullet had embedded into the soft flesh of her calf, but since it was not a direct hit the butt of the bullet was just under the skin. Jeff took his scarf from around his neck and tied a quick field dressing over the wound to help stop the bleeding.

"We'll have to remove that fragment later," he said.

"Promise?" responded Aubrey. "Promise me there will be a later." She fought back panic as she looked squarely into his eyes. Jeff felt the depth of her question.

"I promise," he said giving her hand a gentle squeeze as he kissed her forehead. She leaned back against the bricks of the niche. From where she sat, the entrance was almost completely out of view.

Jeff hurried to help Jonathan up, who was still dazed from the force of the weight that had knocked him to the ground. Jonathan flexed his fingers, hand, and arm to see if anything was broken. Although painfully stiff everything appeared to be intact. He joined Orhan in covering the edges of the cave entrance with his Lugar.

A great commotion arose outside the cave, out of view of the three men. A minion landed on his hands and knees in the mud within clear range, clearly being sacrificed by Ölüm to test the firepower of those within the cave. He stood in stark horror at his precarious predicament. He scrambled first toward the cave, and then back to cover, not knowing which way to turn, but he was pounded back out into the openby an unseen force, landing flat on his back. Orhan and Jonathan held their fire, knowing that the ruse was meant to test them.

# Rob Dakin

The man knew he was dead either way. The promise of the master for wealth and power was nothing more than a lie, and the recognition of his expendability shook him violently to his core. Looking into the cave, he saw that this great enemy was just three men not very much different than himself. The brutality of the master was beyond his desire to serve any longer. He raised his nine-millimeter Beretta, aiming it at Jeff. Before anyone could react, he turned his aim toward the minions who were crouched out of sight and got off three quick trigger pulls. Three thuds and splashes followed, and a string of curses in Turkish filled the air.

The rogue minion was flipped into the air by an unseen force like a rag by a pit bull. He hit the ground sprawling face-first into the mud. With his last bit of effort, he raised himself to his knees tossing his nine-millimeter at the feet of Jeff. From the brow of the cave, Ölüm drove a powerful, flaming bolt through the man's chest. He slumped backward over his legs, immediately bursting into a conflagration that lapped up the puddles of water around him, transforming them into sizzling steam. It took only seconds for the intensity of the heat to melt him to ashes.

Flashes of lightening arced across the sky originating from a point within the ruined church, and peals of thunder echoed throughout the valley. The cave acted like an amphitheater as the sound resonated off the brick and stone producing a continuous, rolling growl. Jeff, Orhan, and Jonathan tried to prepare themselves for what would come next. The intensity of the electrical storm increased, and the three had to cover their eyes from the brightness of the flashes. Soon the earth began to shake under their feet. Though they couldn't see it, a crack in the earth generated somewhere out in the Aegean was crackling its way inland and swallowing everything in its path. It continued through the valley of orchards heading straight toward Ephesus. Trees and hillsides slid into the abyss.

# Vale of Shadows

Wave after wave of seagulls screamed inland, and small animals raced to higher ground as the crack widened and zigzagged its way toward the hill of the Cave of the Seven

Sleepers. Water from the sea filled the fissure with deadly force. The earthquake was relentless; rock and debris fell like rain.

As he saw the crack approaching, Jeff ran back into the niche to retrieve Aubrey. He helped her up and supported her with her arm around his shoulder. She was groggy from the pain in her leg, the blood loss, and the cold rain. They hobbled over to Jonathan, who then supported her other arm.

"What's happening?" asked Aubrey trying to gain more bearing.

"I don't know," said Jeff, "but it looks like we're in for more trouble." His words were punctuated by the grinding rumble of the earthen crack that was now just feet from the mouth of the cave.

"Be ready to jump when the fissure reaches us!" shouted Orhan. The others could barely hear him above the roar.

The crack heaved up a stone slab as it reached the cave, and two minions hiding to the north side of the cave groped helplessly as the earth tilted out from under them. They fell with trailing screams into the depths. The floor of the cave jolted up and back, falling away from under the feet of Jeff and Aubrey and separating them from Orhan and Jonathan. They made a frantic dive for higher ground, but the rain-soaked stones gave them no traction. Jeff clung with all his strength to Aubrey's waist as they began to slide together down the slab. With a loud pop, the stone broke in two, exposing a root vine. Jeff lunged toward it, catching it tenaciously. The slab fell out from under them into the chasm. He dangled by the root with Aubrey in his grasp.

Orhan and Jonathan were thrown back onto the other side of the widening gap, and the roof of the cave collapsed into the gorge, leaving them exposed. Rain peppered Orhan's eyes as he looked frantically through the downpour for any sign of Jeff and Aubrey. Through the torrent he spotted them hanging from the vine just below the lip of the newly developed cliff. He sensed Jonathan crawling up beside him on his hands and knees. The two men looked timidly over the precipice. Seawater lapped and foamed fifty feet below them.

The earthquake continued until the crack reached halfway up the mountain, and then it angled off to the south toward the center of Ephesus. Soon the trembling stopped. Orhan and Jonathan pressed themselves flat against the slab and looked warily for any sign of the jinn and his minions. There was no cover for them to hide in. Fallen debris of rock and brick lay strewn across the damaged landscape.

Suddenly there was a clatter of activity across the chasm above where Jeff and Aubrey hung. Through the dense rain, Orhan could make out the fiery form of the jinn hovering over the toppled ruins of the cave. Bellows of steam rose from the unquenchable fire of his countenance. Five minions had secured ropes to the fallen columns of the church and rappelled down the steep slope to search the remnants of the cave.

Orhan strained to see into the shadows of the cliff face. The root that Jeff had grabbed was barely visible, but there was no sign of his friends. Jonathan nudged his arm and pointed to a spot twenty feet below the cliff edge. There in a small pocket of earth huddled Jeff and Aubrey, out of direct view of their pursuers at the top, but the men on the ropes would soon discover their position.

Orhan and Jonathan slithered to a large boulder. They could still see the scene across the ravine but now had a better hiding place.

"What are we going to do?" whispered Jonathan. "There's no way to get to them."

144

# Vale of Shadows

"Those men are almost on them," stated Orhan. "The jinn is up there behind those pillars. Can you see him?"

"Yeah. It looks like he's looking for someone else. You think it could be Ermal and Mustafa?"

"I don't know," said Orhan, "but I can't believe as prepared as the two brothers were they would be killed so easily."

The rain began to fall harder as a thunderstorm moved in. Orhan aimed his pistol at the minion who had rappelled the deepest, and fired. The shot was muffled by a timely crack of thunder. At first Orhan thought he had missed his target, but the man slowly slipped from his perch and fell noiselessly into the foaming waves below.

"Great shot," exclaimed Jonathan trying to keep from raising his voice. "Do it again."

The men on the ropes froze in place when they saw their companion fall. Fortunately for Orhan and Jonathan, they assumed that he had simply slipped in the rain and lost his hold. They continued their descent. Suddenly another one arched his back as if stung and slipped from the rope into the abyss. The others looked frantically around but saw no danger.

The storm had settled nearly overhead. Jonathan counted the seconds between the lightning and the thunderclaps. Flash. One-thousand-one, one-thousand-two, one-thousand-three, clap. He was now able to cue Orhan to fire his Walther P99 at the same time as the thunder, masking the sound. Another minion slipped off his rope. Soon there were only the men peering over the edge, but none of them had a clear view due to the ruggedness of the upheaval in the terrain. They remained oblivious to the loss of Ölüm's henchmen on the ropes.

\* \* \*

Jeff and Aubrey sank as deep into the nook as they could. There was no firm support; the rain washed away the floor of their pocket in torrents. The little cave began to collapse around them, and soon there would be no haven. Across the mouth of the cave, a large object fell from above. Then another. Jeff couldn't tell what they were. A third one fell, but this time the object was screaming in terror. Jeff cautiously peered out and down just as one of the jinn's men fell into the foaming seawater below. He looked back at Aubrey with hope in his eyes.

"Something is happening up there," he said.

Aubrey weakly blinked the rain out of her eyes. The cold and loss of blood were beginning to take their toll. Jeff reached for her hand and gave it a tender squeeze.

"We'll get out of this," he said. "I promise."

Aubrey smiled faintly at him as another portion of their cave floor sank down the precipice and into the sea. As they scrambled to dig in for a better foothold, Aubrey gasped, "I have faith in you, Jeff."

Jeff gazed over the edge. The water was less tumultuous, and was climbing slowly up the gorge. He estimated that the surface was now only about fifteen feet below their perch. He strained to see up the canyon and could just make out a bend that angled back toward the city ruins. Formulating a plan in his mind, he looked back and forth from Aubrey to the water.

"Aubrey, do you think you could swim a little ways?" he asked. "I think we could maybe swim through the canyon and find a way out near Ephesus.

"I don't know," she moaned feebly. "I don't feel so hot."

"I know, hon, but we're trapped here, and this cave is disappearing by the second. That genie is out there somewhere. Here, I'll help you."

He crawled up under Aubrey's arm and lifted her just enough to sidle up to the edge. He searched her dazed eyes nervously. "I love you, Aubrey," he said as he leaped, carrying the both of them into the flow.

# 14. There Goes the Neighborhood

Jeff and Aubrey broke the surface gasping for air. The cold water took their breath away, leaving them numb. Jeff struggled against the undertow of the outward-bound current as the initial surge of the sea began to abate back to its origins. With the weight of Aubrey and their heavy clothing, fatigue set in quickly. He kicked with his legs and stroked with his free arm, but the force of the flood was too great. Instead of fighting it, he tried to conserve his energy and concentrated on keeping Aubrey's head above water. Aubrey tried weakly to help, but she was fading fast.

Suddenly Jeff was grabbed from behind just as his head began to bob under. He fought frantically, but the grip was more than he could overpower. To his great surprise and relief, he realized that the grip was helping him stay buoyant. He craned his neck enough to see Orhan grasping him from behind just as he was doing to Aubrey. Jonathan swam up and took Aubrey from Jeff, keeping her head above water. Jeff offered a tired nod of thanks and stopped fighting against his friend. The current took them quickly toward the sea, but they were able to angle toward the edge of the gorge, which was now dropping and forming climbable banks in the old harbor valley.

A tree from the orchard floated close enough for Jonathan to clasp and pull over to within reach of Aubrey, Jeff, and Orhan. They clung exhausted to the trunk. After a short rest, Jeff and Orhan pulled Aubrey up on top so she could straddle one of the branches. They then hauled themselves up into the branches, getting clear of the frigid water. No one spoke; they were unable to stop their teeth from shattering. It wasn't long before they sensed that their "ark" was taking them safely away from the jinn and his minions.

Jeff peered through the light drizzle back toward the collapsed ruins of the Cave of the Seven Sleepers. The water level had dropped enough so that he was unable to see the top of the cliff, but even from a distance he could see the blazing fire of the jinn combing back and forth through the debris in search of his prey.

The tree floated easily over shallow cataracts as the water withdrew to the Aegean. Before long the tree began to snag on underwater obstacles. The water carried the foursome safely through the peaks that guarded the inlet of the ancient harbor. With a jolt the tree stuck hard into the mud. Jeff and Orhan looked at each other with a smile. They had survived. They had won this round.

Aubrey moaned quietly, slipping from the tree into the soft muck. She lay slumped on her side where she fell. Jeff and Orhan struggled to free themselves from their perches to go to her. Their muscles and joints ached with the endeavor. Orhan was the first to reach her and roll her over on her back. Her breathing was shallow, and her skin was clammy with a pale greenish hue. Jeff gently brushed her wet hair from her once beautiful face, now corpse-like.

Jonathan crawled over on his hands and knees and gazed at her. "She's in shock," he exclaimed. "We need to do something."

Orhan stood looking around. The rain had stopped, but the afternoon light was beginning to fade to dusk. Down farther into the valley, Orhan spotted a small village not far from where the tree had dumped them. "There is a village," he said stooping down to kneel at Aubrey's side. "Help me get her up. We will take turns carrying her. We need to find shelter quickly."

Jeff and Jonathan helped Orhan put Aubrey on his back piggyback style. There was no time to do anything else. They knew they had to reach shelter before the jinn gave up searching the rubble of the ruins, and came looking for them in the valley.

149

Their soaked clothing weighed them down and clung to their skin with a frigid grip. Orhan was slightly warmed by exertion as he carried Aubrey a hundred meters through the rough, muddy terrain. He stumbled as he climbed up a steep incline, but Jeff and Jonathan were right there to keep him from falling. The cold wind began to bite deeper as the light of day disappeared beyond the horizon.

Orhan waved off any attempts from the others to take Aubrey, and they stumbled and fought their way through the rolling landscape until they finally reached the first building of the village. It was a small tea barn. They unlatched the half-door and rushed into the shadows without hesitation. The powerful aroma of the herbal tea revived them a little from their fatigue, but the cold made it impossible for them to feel anything but despair.

Jonathan pulled out a bundle of the dried tea and made a makeshift mattress for Aubrey. Everything they possessed was soaking wet. Jeff pulled his cell phone from his pack, which he managed to still have draped over his shoulder.

"I never did get that stupid ring tone changed," he said with resignation. "Oh well, it's trashed now." He flung it back into his pack and pulled out his flashlight, checking to see if it worked. When it did, he turned his attention back to Aubrey.

Meanwhile Jonathan stared out into the village from the half-door. The village appeared to be abandoned except for a faint wisp of woodsmoke on the air. He could see no sign of life from his vantage point. He turned to find Jeff and Orhan tending Aubrey's wounded leg.

"We've got to get that bullet fragment out of her leg ASAP," Jeff said studying the hole in her flesh. "All I have is my Gerber."

"It will have to do," said Orhan. "She's unconscious now. It would be best if she were not awake."

150

# Vale of Shadows

Jeff strained to see in the dimly lit barn. "I can't do it without light," he complained. "I need to be able to see, or I'm not even trying." He pounded on his flashlight to try and stir up more power.

"I can smell woodsmoke on the breeze," said Jonathan. "I'll go see if I can find anyone to help."

"Be very careful," said Orhan. "Stay low against the buildings and bushes. Don't let anyone see you until you know for sure it is safe."

"Yes, Mother," Jonathan mocked. With that he quietly slipped out the door and disappeared around the corner in the direction of the rest of the village.

\* \* \*

Jonathan decided to track into the wind and follow the smell of the smoke. He crept stealthily, careful not to spend too much time out of the cover of the shadows. He passed by the first house, which had been abandoned for some time. The stick-lashed gate lay broken off to the side, and an overgrowth of untended vines cast a deep eerie gloom over the unkempt courtyard. Jonathan proceeded along the fence-lined path until he came to another house in a similar state of disrepair. As he scurried past its front walk, his jacket was grabbed from behind. He let out a cry of surprise as his heart went into his throat, freezing in mid-step, and turned first with his eyes and then with his head, reluctant to see what was behind him. To his great relief his jacket had been snagged by a rosebush thorn. He let out a trembling sigh as he freed himself, and then continued to creep down the side of the path.

The path climbed up and to the right as he wound around a bend. In the distance he caught a faint flicker of orange light through the window of a small house off the main path. He stayed in the shadow of a dormant mulberry tree, studying the cottage from his hiding place. A wisp of smoke rose from the chimney and fingered its way eerily with the current of the breeze. The slope that led up to the house was overgrown with the skeletons of untended grapevines and fruit trees.

Jonathan darted from the shadow and pressed against the wall of a small livestock barn. The wood was weatherworn and dilapidated. The roof had collapsed from a rotten beam leaving a silhouette shaped like a double-humped camel. He peeked around the corner toward the house. The smell of woodsmoke wafted all around him as a down draft from the nearby mountains forced the smoke closer to the ground.

He could see the front of the house more clearly. He moved along a hedge of thorns that bordered a small sheepfold, coming up quietly onto the front porch. The clouds suddenly cleared, and the brightness of the full moon cast a ghostly shade under the trees and buildings. Jonathan slunk toward the worn, green-painted door. His heart raced with adrenalin, and he stopped and checked his heart rate with his hand over his chest. "I can't believe I'm doing this," he muttered. He paused, hesitant to knock on the door, and crouched against the white stucco wall then slid around to the front window. He raised his head slowly to peer into the room.

Through lace curtains he could see an old man sitting hunched over in a short chair in front of the fireplace. The man appeared to be napping; Jonathan could see the gentle rise and fall of his shoulders as he breathed. He waited for a few moments to be certain that the man was alone. The old man looked harmless enough, so Jonathan gently tapped on the windowpane with his fingernails. The man remained motionless and continued to sleep. Jonathan rapped a little harder and still got no response. Finally he knocked on the glass with his fist.

The man stirred, and then looked up blinking his eyes in confusion. He remained seated but looked around the room not sure of where the noise had come from. Jonathan tapped on the glass again. The old man squinted and stared at the window, but he clearly could not see Jonathan through the white lace curtain and beyond the glass into the darkness of night. Jonathan knocked again and called out in as nonthreatening a voice as he could. The old man rose and walked cautiously to the window, pulling back the curtain. When he saw Jonathan, he took a step backward but kept the curtain pulled aside. Stunned at Jonathan's appearance, he stared at him with his mouth open.

Jonathan pantomimed that he was going to go to the front door. The old man's gaze held Jonathan's as he backed away and let the curtain fall back into place. Jonathan went around to the front door, which remained closed. He listened intently for any sound from inside. Hearing none, he knocked on the wooden door causing it to jar against its hinges loudly. Startled by the loudness of the rattling of the old door, he backed off the intensity of his pounding. After what seemed an eternity, he heard the old man shuffle behind the door and then fumble with the latches. Slowly the door was opened a crack just enough for the old man to stick a side-by-side double barreled shotgun out and aim it defiantly at Jonathan's head.

"*Kush është jeni ju?*" the old man shouted through the crack. "*Çfar doni?*"

"Now what?" Jonathan moaned exasperated. He didn't recognize the old man's language as Turkish. "I don't understand you!" he shouted back through the crack keeping his eyes on the muzzle of the shotgun. "Do you speak English...or Turkish by any chance?" He lowered his head trying to think of another way to communicate. "I'm sorry, but I need your help."

The old man kept the shotgun aimed at Jonathan as he slowly opened the door wider. The two men glared at each other in the gloom of the night. The old man studied him for a moment, and then lowered the shotgun. Jonathan gave a silent sigh of relief.

"*Çfar doni?*" the old man repeated suspiciously.

"I'm sorry, I don't understand, but my name is Jonathan Michaels. I'm an American. I have a friend who is hurt in the barn down on the edge of town" He pointed frantically in the direction of his friends. The old man seemed to consider his words, and then stepped out onto the front porch to face him. He eyed Jonathan up and down in the dimly moonlit porch.

Then he shouldered his shotgun and walked past Jonathan in the direction that he had pointed. Coming to the tatters of his own front gate, he stopped and turned, looking back expectantly. It took Jonathan a moment to realize that the old man was leading him back to the barn. He hopped off the porch and joined the old man on the muddy path.

Jonathan matched the old man's pace, which was too slow for his liking as he picked his way deftly through the mud puddles. Still soaked from his earlier ordeal, Jonathan sloshed through without regard for his shoes and socks. They continued in silence until they turned the bend and began walking down the main trail of the village. When the tea barn lay just ahead, the old man froze in his tracks and moved quickly to the shadows of the trees lining the path. He lowered his shotgun to his hip, pointing it in the direction of the barn. Jonathan jumped in behind him."

"What is it?" he asked. "What do you see?"

The old man pointed with his chin. "*Shtrigë*," he hissed. He walked cautiously, raising his gun up to his shoulder and keeping to the moon shade of the trees.

Jonathan strained his eyes to see ahead. The full moon illuminated the village in a surreal, otherworldly landscape. Peering intently into the shadows of the trees and buildings, he suddenly perceived movement just ahead. He blinked his eyes to focus and could just make out a hunched form skulking from window to window in the abandoned cottage that Jonathan had first come to after leaving his friends. The figure went around to the front door. Jonathan heard the rattle of a locked chain, and then a clank.

# Vale of Shadows

The figure entered the path. An old woman, shrouded in a black, hooded cape came toward them. Her face was partially concealed by the cowl, but he could see her burning red eyes scanning the terrain. She hobbled like an old crone, gasping and cackling as she went. She had not yet seen Jonathan when he was suddenly and forcefully yanked through a small gap in the stick fence. The old man pulled him down to the ground with amazing strength. The two men lay in the mud as the witch passed by on the other side of the hedge.

The old man signaled with his finger over his lips for Jonathan to stay quiet as they rose and sneaked down the fence on the field side until they reached a collapsed portion allowing them to cross over to the tea barn. Jonathan held up his hand for the old man to wait as he peered cautiously through a broken panel in the half-door. He whistled softly like a lark into the darkness beyond. The door was slightly ajar, so he squeezed through the small opening and remained in a squatting position resting his back against the doorjamb. The moonlight stabbed like ghostly white fingers through the rickety, rough board roof. He allowed his eyes to grow accustomed to the gloom. Panic swelled inside him as the horrible truth began to overwhelm him: his friends were gone.

# 15. Blood Feud

Dusk, atop the ruined ruins of the
Cave of the Seven Sleepers

Ursella cursed as Ölüm pried the burning peach pit from her shoulder with a pair of tongs. She was angry that she had been so easily damaged by her enemy. She had underestimated them. "That will never happen again," she swore under her breath.

Ölüm held the fruit stone up in the fading light of day to examine it. A seething hiss escaped his pursed lips. He threw the pit into the chasm and turned to survey the remains of his surroundings. He had lost more than half of his men, but what angered him the most was that his enemies had escaped. He searched throughout the ruins then turned his attention to the newly formed river that exploded from the Aegean. No sign of his prey.

He strode toward Ursella, glaring at her with disdain. He blamed her for this failure. Considering his options he realized that she was still his best ally. That fact alone kept her alive.

Ursella sensed his animosity and glared back at him defiantly. She was not going to take the blame meekly. She rose to face him. Stern and with resolve, she stepped to him. Fire leapt between them. She stood unflinching, daring him to accuse her. He met her resolve with his own. Lightening blasted in sabers of brilliance all around them. Finally Ölüm stepped away from her and smiled.

"You are no weakling," he said admiringly. "I will not hold you at fault." With that he turned to a minion standing near and evaporated him with a burst of fire from his eyes.

Ursella looked on with scolding in her eyes. "If you continue to kill your own soldiers you will soon have no one left," she said. "Take your hatred out on your enemies. We will follow you, but we will only be able to serve you if we are alive."

"You know nothing of what it takes to serve me," Ölüm hissed.

"Do you forget that I have been united with you through fire? I do know what it takes. I also know that your enemies are more cunning than their predecessors. You need human help, or you will fail once again." She knew that this outburst might cost her life, but Ölüm's temper was more detrimental to their mission than anything the humans could accomplish. "We need to proceed with our plan. Hunt them down and kill them. You have destroyed their sanctuary. They have nowhere else to run."

Ölüm considered her words and his temper subsided. He looked around at the men still standing at attention around him in the rain, waiting for his command.

"Spread out and find the Gypsies," he ordered. "Ursella, you search the valley."

One of the minions approached. "My lord, we have tracked the Gypsies back to their automobile. They joined other Gypsies and left in three vehicles traveling back through the mountains."

"Are they headed toward the sea?" asked Ölüm.

"No, my lord. They are heading into the mountains toward the northeast." The minion paused. "In the same direction from which we came."

Ölüm considered this. The imminent danger to his own survival did not escape him. "I will follow the Gypsies," he thundered. "You aid Ursella." He set his sights to the northeast and began to morph into a pillar of flame, but was quickly quenched by the rain. He tried again, but to no avail. He was powerless to transform himself. He looked around for someone he could blame for his impotence but realized the fault lay with the Gypsies.

"They have placed a spell on me," his wrath spewing in each syllable. He looked closely at the ground around him and saw what he was looking for. In the muddy gravel of the hill top was a ring of pulverized brick powder from the Cave of the Seven Sleepers making a wide arc around Ölüm and his men. "I will destroy them and all their kind." His hatred boiled over into contorted writhing. "Clear this abomination away immediately," he spat.

Ursella observed the handful of men that stood ready to leave with her. "My lord, I will seek our enemy better alone. Let these men make their way to the coast to block any escape from that way. I will go into the valley."

"Do as you wish, but do not fail," warned Ölüm.

The rest of the men set out toward the road that wound through the mountains. Ursella watched them leave with satisfaction. Then she carefully traversed a muddy path that led down into the valley. Much of the chasm had already begun to cave in on itself, narrowing the gap. The once raging river was now a trickling stream that formed intermittent pools of seawater all along its retreat.

She came to the base of the cliff, her clothes and boots a filthy mess. The going was too slow for her impatience. She tried to call on the wind to take her as before, but the spell of the Gypsies had also stolen her power. She cursed their interference as she slogged through the bog that sucked at her boots with every step. Her resolve was weakening with despair. The power she had felt in Ölüm's presence was a mere shadow of its former strength. The magic of the Gypsies had been carelessly underestimated.

# Vale of Shadows

The gloom of winter dusk blurred the landscape. Finally she crawled over an embankment that jutted out from the foot of the northern mountain that stood guard over the ancient harbor. Below, she spied a small village in the distance its terracotta shingled roofs reflecting the rising full moon. She scraped and clawed her way through the thickets and hedges that outlined the fields. As she strenuously pushed through one particularly dense hedge, she snagged her cloak on a thorn. The extra effort it took to free herself catapulted her face-first into the dormant stubble of wheat that protruded like frozen spikes impaling her hands and cheeks. She let out a cry of surprise followed by a long string of Albanian curses.

She scrambled to her feet and found herself staring at a small tea barn, its silhouette accented by the moonlight against the dark shadows of the trees beyond. No one seemed to be about. She pulled the hood of her cloak over her head, concealing her face in the depths of its folds, and searched the ground for a stick that could be used for a cudgel. She stooped, hunched at the waist and swaying slightly from side to side as she walked like an old hag.

Her disguise complete, she peered through the half-door of the barn straining her eyes and ears for any sign of life. The aroma of the mountain tea overwhelmed her senses, and she cursed her weakening power. Perceiving the barn to be empty, she slowly made her way toward the rest of the village. The faint smell of woodsmoke reached her nostrils as she entered the main path. The first house she came to was abandoned and had been for some time as evidenced by the disrepair of the gate and window shutters hanging precariously from rusted hinges. The fruit trees had not been tended for many years and stood choked by the skeletons of ancient vines. As she continued up the path following the scent of smoke, slight movement behind a hedge caught her eye. She paused, but did not look around. She made her way up to a bend in the path, and then paused in the shade of a fruit tree peeking back down the way she had come, studying the dimly illuminated landscape with anticipation.

Ursella lurked menacingly in the shadows. Her prey was here; she could feel it. A sound up the hill startled her. She swung around to run towards the noise when she was suddenly and violently stopped in her tracks. She fell flat on her back into the muddy rutted pathway. Her vision blurred, and she felt herself fading into unconsciousness. The shadow of a man stood over her. She raised a feeble hand to defend herself, but her strength was quickly fading; darkness infringed the periphery of her sight. The weathered face of an old man appeared through the blur as he leaned closer. She stared up at him, her brow furrowed in confusion. Even in her state of stupor she recognized him. She struggled to rise, but then fell back as darkness overtook her.

* * *

Road leading away from Ephesus

Mustafa and Ermal raced down the road in their Fiat Albea. The headlights rose and fell on the back of the transport truck in front of them as the road undulated into the mountains. Mustafa rotated his sprained wrist gingerly as he gripped the steering wheel. He concentrated on the distance between his car and the truck, trying to keep his mind off of the pain that radiated the length of his arm.

Ermal studied a map by the illumination of the overhead dome light. He gazed intently at their route, ignoring without success the throbbing behind his eyes. He grimaced as Mustafa took a curve too quickly, causing him to strain to keep his position in the front seat. The cracked rib under his left arm made breathing laborious, and any movement was excruciating. He gently palpated the area over the rib, sucking through his teeth as he touched the tenderest spot. He knew he was lucky to be alive. They all were.

160

# Vale of Shadows

He hoped that the incantation he had placed over the ruins would slow up the jinn long enough for them to reach their destination. He also hoped that it would weaken the jinn enough for them to gain an advantage. His clansmen in the trucks ahead of him and behind were all in various stages of injury and incapacitation. No one had escaped unscathed in their battle with the jinn and his minions.

The moon that had broadcast the scenery was now shrouded by silver-lined, dark clouds. The brothers could feel the temperature dropping as they climbed higher into the mountains. They had left the main highway some time ago and were now winding northeast through the narrow, two-lane, pothole-ridden switchback ribbon of cracking concrete and asphalt the Turks called a "main road."

Mustafa was driving faster than was safe, but time was not something they could carelessly waste. The truck ahead of them swerved and swayed from side to side, the driver clearly disregarding lane restrictions. At this time of day, the road was abandoned except for the occasional horse-drawn cart filled with firewood. One such cart driven by a villager down the middle of the dark road nearly caused the lead truck to plummet into the canyon as the trucker braked and skidded to a stop inches from the ledge of the thin shoulder. The villager continued undaunted, never looking back.

Ermal's map indicated a side road that would take them faster to Alia. He wanted them to stay as inconspicuous as possible as they approached the lair of the jinn. He and his clan had spent years searching for the location of Selim Bey's golden cube. The information that they had gathered narrowed their search to two possible regions. They had staked out the areas with members of their Roma clan. When the jinn and his entourage swept through the valley on their way to Ephesus, the Gypsy trackers had been ready and waiting. It took them only about an hour to find the cave deep in the mountain ravine. The location was confirmed by the presence of a number of charred corpses, and the golden cube itself.

Ermal looked over at his brother, the glow of the dashboard lights illuminating his face from below in an eerie, ghostly green. He turned his attention back to the mesmerizing swaying of the red lights on the back of the truck ahead. His head pounded as he massaged his temples. He thought back to their narrow escape from the top of the ruin after the sonic blast had knocked them all unconscious.

They had been left for dead. Ermal pondered their good fortune, but the lack of efficiency by his enemy confused and troubled him. Why hadn't the minions of the jinn made certain of their death? He and his men slowly came to their senses at about the same time as a horrendous earthquake smashed the ruins apart. They used the diversion to escape back to their vehicles and join the rest of their force waiting in reserve.

The brick powder from the Cave of the Seven Sleepers they had worked into the mud near the ruins had the power to disable the jinn for a short time. It had been conjured with incantations by a Gypsy soothsayer who had been considered old during the life of Ermal's great grandfather. Her magic was the strongest of all conjurors. Ermal had not been told the exact effect the powder would have on the jinn, but he trusted the old crone's expertise. Her craft had helped him in the past with the affections of a certain young lady he had hoped to steal from his brother. He tried to smile at the years-old memory, but every muscle in his face hurt.

The men who had tracked the whereabouts of the cave had contacted the reserve forces in Ephes. Soon all parties were on their way to the small village of Alia in west central Turkey. The golden cube had been carefully removed and taken to the outskirts of the village awaiting the arrival of Mustafa and Ermal.

# Vale of Shadows

For the first time in over five hundred years, the golden prison of the jinn was in the possession of honorable men. They would soon accomplish what their fathers could not: the total destruction of the marid. It was within their grasp. Ermal tried to get comfortable in the cramped front seat of the Fiat, but no position gave him any relief. Dozing off was out of the question. The only thing left for him was the hypnotic effect of the red taillights on the truck in front of him.

* * *

Mustafa drove deep in thought until he began to notice a throbbing ache in his left arm. He looked over at Ermal, who had slunk down in his seat and was staring out into the darkness. His reflection on the glass from the dashboard lights revealed to Mustafa a brooding disposition. Mustafa knew that many things had gone wrong this day, and that Ermal would take the blame on himself to the point of depression.

Mustafa gingerly palpated his sore upper arm with his sprained right hand. The area was painful to the touch. His fingers felt damp. He pulled them away and examined a smear of blood covering them. He glanced over to Ermal to see if he had noticed, but his brother kept his attention outside of the vehicle. Now that Mustafa had noticed his injury, the throbbing seemed to increase, making it difficult to navigate the winding road.

"I just noticed that I am still bleeding," he stated without emotion.

"Where?" asked Ermal.

"My upper left arm. I must have been shot. With everything else that hurts, I must not have noticed it."

Ermal leaned over to examine Mustafa's arm but was not able to adequately see it. He noticed a blood smear on the door panel adjacent to his brother. "We need to pull over so that I can take a look. I don't want you bleeding to death," said Ermal. He lifted the walkie-talkie to his mouth, "Pull over as soon as you can."

The truck in front of them immediately pulled over to a wider spot in the road at the top of a hill. Mustafa and Ermal stood in the light of the headlamps of their Fiat. Mustafa removed his coat while Ermal studied the wound. A bullet had grazed across his deltoid muscle. The wound was not deep, but the edges had already become puffy and red.

"It is good that we stopped," said Ermal. "With all of the filth we have been wallowing in, this wound is becoming septic." He washed the area with a sterile saline and wrapped it tightly with a dressing and bandage.

The pressure made Mustafa's arm feel better. He rotated it slowly at the shoulder and gave his brother a smile.

"That ought to do it," he said

The night was crisp. At this higher altitude, the rain had turned to soft falling snow. The moon peeked through the clouds and cast the mountain valley in a serene bluish hue. The other men stretched their legs as the cold air revitalized them. Two of their clansmen lay in the back of the last truck. Their wounds would soon prove to be mortal.

Suddenly Ermal froze in his tracks. Mustafa and the other men caught his abrupt stop and turned their attention back toward the valley from which they had just come. Off on the horizon, a blazing comet appeared low over the trees following the silver ribbon of road. At the speed it was advancing, the Gypsies knew they could never outrun it. The men climbed frantically up the hill that jutted up from the ditch on the inner shoulder of the road, hiding behind shrubs and boulders.

The comet swooped along the road until it rounded a bend, and then slowed near the position of the trucks but did not stop. It proceeded cautiously, swinging wide out over the valley and hovering in place. The men could clearly see the form of the jinn within the flame. After what seemed an eternity, the jinn circled high overhead and then with lightening speed vanished down the road ahead of them.

Mustafa and Ermal looked at each other with horror in their eyes recognizing the gravity of the situation. The jinn would reach Alia before them. They bolted for their vehicles, clamoring to get started. Mustafa sped ahead of the trucks to take the lead. Speed was of the essence regardless of the treacherous roads. In the rearview mirror, he could see the intermittent headlights of the trucks behind him struggling to keep up as they wound their way through the valley. The distance between them grew greater, and soon he could no longer see them.

As he came up over a rise, he hit a patch of ice that caused him to slide up onto the raised shoulder of the inner curve. Immediately they came upon a series of switchbacks that descended back into the valley, but the agility of the Fiat allowed him to gain control. Ermal cautioned him to slow on the perilous curves. Downshifting, Mustafa reluctantly reduced his speed.

The second truck entered the patch of ice and swerved into the inner shoulder, but its speed and weight caused it to bounce up on the two outer wheels and career harshly to the left. It banged back down on all four tires just as it plummeted over the edge of the cliff crashing through trees and shrubs. It hurtled passed the first section of the switchback sending sparks flying from the metal rim of the exploded front left tire. Smashing through the next lower grouping of trees and shrubs, it popped out onto the second section of the switchback cutting directly across the path of the Fiat.

Mustafa slammed on his brakes, but the massive bumper of the truck caught the front driver's side cowling and spun the car violently into the rear tire of the truck. The Fiat jolted to a stop sidewise in the road, steam spewing from under the hood. The brothers watched horrified as the truck flew through the air and struck a tall pine, bursting into a ball of flames. It catapulted past the last switchback and was obliterated into a cascade of cauliflower-shaped fire. The second gas tank exploded as it finally smashed into the rocks below.

Mustafa and Ermal sat dazed, unable to move as the second truck squeezed past them on its way to the lower switchback. Screeching to a halt, the men jumped out and slid down the snowy face of the ravine. Smaller explosions popped as ammunition ignited, and the would-be rescuers were sent diving for cover behind boulders and trees as the truck continued to erupt wreckage in chunks.

The Fiat rattled and ground its way to the second truck. Mustafa kicked open his door and stumbled out into the brisk night. Ermal had already limped to the edge of the cliff and was peering down at the other men when Mustafa joined him. They stared in shock and disbelief at the horrendous sight below. The charred and smoking remains of his comrades and family lay tossed across the ravine floor. Most were completely beyond recognition. The ghastly sight was sickening. The men recoiled from the stench of burned flesh with a cry of anguish and anger as they ascended the slope. There was nothing any of them could do.

Mustafa offered his hand to Besnik as he crested the edge, but his hand was slapped away by the bitter man. Besnik stood nose to nose with Mustafa, stepping on his silver-tipped cowboy boots. He glared at him with hate in his eyes, flexed his fingers into a fist, and knocked Mustafa onto his back with a right cross. Besnik stepped over Mustafa straddling him not allowing him to rise from the wet pavement.

"You have now caused the death of two of my brothers," he spat with malice. "For the sake of the clan, I was told I had to forgive you for the first, but for this loss you will die. When our business with the jinn is complete, I will kill you." He glared at Ermal as he pushed past him and went to grieve with other men near the second truck.

# Vale of Shadows

Ermal offered his brother a hand up. Mustafa brushed the mud and snow off of himself as he stared, confused, toward Besnik. He knew that Besnik was just venting his anger, but a public threat had been made. The vendetta could now only be satisfied with blood.

He rejoined Ermal, who was prying the hood of the Fiat open. The radiator hose had been split from the impact. Ermal motioned to Mustafa to hold the hose while he wrapped duct tape around it.

"I don't understand what Besnik means by the death of *two* brothers," said Mustafa as he stared back over his shoulder at Besnik. "I know of only of Simion in the truck."

Ermal finished the last wrap of tape, and then said, "He blames you also for the death of his younger brother, Orin."

"What do you mean? I know nothing of the death of Orin," Mustafa defended himself.

"No, I don't suppose you would since you have been gone for so long," said Ermal glancing over his shoulder at the other men. "Besnik is a professional. He will keep his word and see the plan through, but you are well aware that a blood feud must be satisfied eye for eye, tooth for tooth, and skin for skin. One of you will die. Be careful it is not you, my brother." Ermal caressed his younger brother and gave him a kiss on the cheek. "There is nothing more we can do here," he called over to the others. "We must meet the jinn in Alia."

\* \* \*

The two vehicles proceeded with more caution, as the higher they ascended in altitude, the icier the roads got. Mustafa continued to drive, as Ermal's cracked rib made it difficult for him to stay in one position for very long. After a short time of silence, Mustafa asked Ermal about Orin.

"When you decided to leave our village to go on your 'adventures,' you will remember that you did so against the express wishes of the queen. She was so angry with you that she banished you in your absence and placed a tribal taboo that no one was to speak your name."

Mustafa looked shocked. He had no idea what had transpired after he left all those years ago.

Ermal continued, "Besnik's younger brother, Orın, idolized you, however, and when he turned seventeen, he left to find you. Again this was against the wishes of the queen and his parents, but one night he stole away despite their threats of confinement and even a whipping. Orın never found you because he was murdered by Serbs six years ago. He was killed along with some refugee Kosovar who where trying to cross the border into Albania.

"The clan took his death very hard. The blame rested finally on you for leaving in the first place and putting such a careless notion in his head."

"I knew nothing about this," Mustafa pleaded.

"I know you didn't, but the family, especially Besnik, has held a grudge against you ever since. The blood feud will now be embraced by all of Besnik's family. If he should fall at the hands of the jinn, then another will take his place to restore honor to the family."

"This is crazy," Mustafa protested. "We are all part of the same family. I didn't have anything to do with Orın running off. I was long gone for many years. He was just a small child when I left. How could he have idolized me? He would not have even known me."

"I am afraid stories of you trickled back to us," said Ermal. "The king spent many evenings telling the children, including Orın, stories around the fire of his adventurous son's exploits. Most of them were probably embellished by his vivid imagination. It was only the queen, our mother, who objected. Father secretly admired you for going into the world of the *gadjo*, but he could not oppose the will of the queen. As you remember she really wore the pants." The two brothers allowed themselves a faint smile at the memory of their parents' tumultuous relationship.

"It *is* probable, however, that none of us will survive this ordeal, in which case blood feuds will be the least of our worries," said Mustafa. He wiggled his jaw from side to side trying to get his temporal mandibular joint back into place. Besnik's punch had evidently dislocated both sides, as his jaw joints popped and ached with each movement. "Where do you suppose Jeff and Orhan are?"

"I am hoping they escaped toward the sea. If they are still alive, they will have the jinn's minions after them. If they are dead, then we have already lost, and it is just a matter of time before we are confronted by the unified front of our enemy. He knows us and knows of our plans; he won't rest until we are dead as well. We must destroy that box. If he is successful in killing off the last of the line of Selim Bey and Përparim Lleshi, then the spell will be broken, the curse will be lifted, and the jinn will be free to roam unrestrained. He may be able to rejoin with his twin. I fear the devastation that will follow will be unprecedented. We must succeed even at the cost of all of our lives and the lives of our families."

Mustafa nodded in agreement. "I pray that the others are alive. I have this unexplainable feeling that they are. Have you considered why the jinn did not try to interfere with us back there?"

"Yes. The fact that he left us alongside the road has bothered me greatly," said Ermal. "Is his power so great that he views us as insignificant? Or has he indeed accomplished the final destruction of the ancestral line?"

"Or there is another possibility," interrupted Mustafa. "He is not as powerful as we thought, and he fears us."

"Yes...I suppose that is also a possibility, but I will not count on it. If we actually do have an edge, I do not want to waste it by becoming overly confident."

"Well, we shall soon see. We are almost at the cut-off to Alia."

"The road that leads to the village looks more like a trail on the map. The truck may not be able to pass through the mud and snow," said Ermal. "You may have to hike the rest of the way in those fancy cowboy boots of yours."

Mustafa smiled at his brother's jab against his flamboyant apparel, but grimaced from the pain in his jaws. As they drove on in silence, Mustafa pondered Besnik's hatred, and the unfairness of it. He was not responsible for Orın's death. He would not take responsibility for it. Anger began to swell in him. Besnik would not succeed.

# 16. Spies, Lies, and Cults

Aydin Village
Evening

Jeff took his small Maglite from his pack and studied Aubrey's wound while Orhan tried to make her comfortable by rearranging the *çai* fronds under her head. She was cold and wet, and feverish, and she went through bouts of violent, uncontrollable shivering. Jeff gently massaged her cheeks fearing her teeth chattering would chip a tooth.

The full moon broke through the clouds and pierced through a crack in the roof of the barn. The extra light allowed Jeff to see the wound more clearly. He gently squeezed the calf muscle, rolling the wound into the light coming through the ceiling. Aubrey let out a soft groan.

"I'm taking this fragment out right now while I have a little light. Here, hold my flashlight." He thrust the light into Orhan's hand. "Hold the beam right over the center of the hole." Jeff took out his Gerber tool kit and opened up the needle nosed pliers. He took the lighter he had in his pack and heated the tip of the pliers. Looking down at Aubrey, he took a deep breath. "Sorry, honey, this is going to hurt." He wiggled the tip of the pliers into the wound and immediately struck the bullet fragment just under the tissue surface. Aubrey moaned quietly but remained semiconscious. Orhan looked away, causing the light to lose its focus. "Keep the light steady," Jeff demanded.

"Sorry," apologized Orhan. "I'm feeling a little queasy."

Jeff glanced up to see his friend a pale hue of green. "Even after everything we've already been through? I just need you another minute. I almost have the fragment." Just as he said

171

this he squirmed the bullet out of the flesh of Aubrey's calf and held it up with satisfaction to the light.

Jeff made a bandage out of a bandana he had in his pack and tied the wound as best he could. He began to look for a place to start a fire when he caught movement through a missing plank in the wall. Across the field in the hedge beyond, a shadowy figure lurked. Jeff made a hissing, low whistle to get Orhan's attention. Orhan sidled over to him in a low crab crawl.

"We've got company," Jeff said nudging his chin forward in the direction of the missing plank. Orhan crawled on his stomach to get a better look through the gap. In the trees across the field he could see a silhouette cast against the moonlit backdrop. He scooted back to Jeff and Aubrey.

"It looks like an old woman, and she is coming this way. Let's not take any chances," Orhan said glancing around for a way to escape. Suddenly over in the corner he spied a gap from a broken section in the wall that was partially covered by a stack of çai.

The two men carefully but quickly dragged Aubrey through the opening into a small, brush-covered sheepfold made of roughly stacked stones. They pressed themselves against the wall using the shadow from the height of the low wall as cover. Soon they could hear the rustling of the old woman at the half-door of the barn. Straining their ears to hear any sound that would give her position away; they could sense her presence on the other side of the wall as she hobbled up the muddy path toward the village. Jeff peered through a small gap in the stacked stones and saw her hunched over like an old hag walking with a knobby cudgel. The gnarled knuckles of her hand gave the illusion that she was decrepit, but the hand gripped the end of the walking stick like an iron clamp.

She seemed to slither through the concealing shadows. Jeff felt the hair on the back of his neck stand up as she passed.

His eyes met those of Orhan, whose expression told him that he felt the same.

Aubrey moaned softly, and Jeff quickly cupped his hand over her mouth, praying that the hag had not heard her. She suddenly struggled under his grip, eyes wild with fear. Abruptly she recognized Jeff looming over her and stopped fighting against his hand. He went eyeball to eyeball with her, warning in his gaze. She calmed and nodded her head as he relaxed his grip over her mouth. Straining her neck to take in her surroundings, she caught Orhan motioning with his finger over his lips to remain silent. She looked back up at Jeff and saw the deep concern in his eyes. "I'm OK," she mouthed silently.

From within the barn came a snapping sound of a *çai* twig. Jeff's heart raced as he crept back toward the opening in the barn wall. The hag was not alone. Fear seized him, but he knew he couldn't let the others be taken. He rose up in a squatting stance and squeezed back into the darkness of the barn, letting his eyes grow accustomed to the new level of moonlight. He was still crouched behind the mound of tea when a dark figure eased into the barn and stood hunched over directly in front of him. His fight or flight mechanism kicked in full throttle as he dove headlong into the midsection of the intruder, driving him into the dirt floor. Jeff scuffled to gain control, but the strength of his opponent surprised him. Suddenly he was flipped over onto his back and pinned to the ground as his assailant straddled him. Icy, hands clasped his throat. He fought frantically to free himself, but his foe was too heavy to overpower.

Jeff suppressed an urge to cry out to Orhan for help. He kicked with his knees into the other man's back, jolting him just enough to wiggle out from under him. He landed a boot into the side of the man's head and toppled him over onto his side. Jeff wasted no time in grabbing the man from behind in a chokehold. The man flayed uselessly to reach Jeff's head, but the strength of

Jeff's headlock and the bulkiness of the man's wet overcoat made it impossible for him to free himself. Jeff tightened his grip. The man gasped in desperation.

"Jeff! It's me, Jonathan!"

Jeff continued squeezing the man's throat.

"Jeff! Stop! It's me."

He suddenly recognized his friend and released his hold. Jonathan fell forward on his hands and knees, rubbing his bruised throat. "You just about killed me," he gasped.

Jeff bent over and helped Jonathan up. "I'm sorry, but there's a—"

"I know," interrupted Jonathan, "a witch is out there; we saw her from the hedge across the way.

"She may be with the jinn and has tracked us here." Jeff suddenly reconsidered Jonathan's statement. "What do you mean by *we*?" he asked.

"I found this crazy old man in the village. I think he's the only one left here. I can't understand a word he says. It's not Turkish. I don't know what it is. Where are Aubrey and Orhan?" Jonathan asked with nervous excitement.

"On the other side of that wall in a sheepfold," said Jeff. "Where's the old man now?"

"I don't know. I came back over here after the witch or whatever she is passed by. He was still crouched behind the hedge across the path."

"We've got to find him. Maybe he can help us," said Jeff hopefully.

The two men crawled back through the hole in the wall to reach Orhan and Aubrey. Aubrey was sitting up with her back against the stone wall.

"You look better," said Jonathan softly as he sat next to her.

"I feel a little better," she said. "My leg doesn't hurt as badly."

Orhan moved from his lookout spot to sit closer to the group. "The woman went up around that bend, past that empty row of houses." He pointed over his shoulder in the direction the woman had gone.

They were suddenly startled by a presence hovering over them from the other side of the wall. Jeff jumped up, grabbing a sickle handle that was lying half buried in the straw. He swung it blindly at the figure in the dark of the barn shadow, and his stick struck hard wood with a crack that reverberated painfully through his cold hands and fingers. His stick was grabbed by a strong grip, keeping him from being able to bring the handle back to swing a second time.

"*Mos*," said the old man letting go of Jeff's club.

Jonathan jumped to Jeff's side. "This is the guy I was telling you about," he whispered as he looked nervously up the path. "I found him in one of the houses up on the hill."

The old man motioned for them to follow him. Jeff looked suspiciously at Jonathan, who just shrugged and clambered over the stone wall. Jeff and Orhan helped Aubrey swing her legs over the wall, and then the two stiffly crawled over onto the path beyond. The old man strode hunched over as he fought his way up the muddy path. "*Hajda*," he said over his shoulder, beckoning them to come.

"See, what did I tell ya?" whispered Jonathan out of the side of his mouth to Jeff. "Some kind of gibberish. I don't know what it is."

"It's Albanian," said Aubrey, out of breath from hopping on one leg. The others stared at her in the moonlight, not understanding her words through the huffing and puffing. "He is speaking Albanian," she said more slowly. "*Prit* (wait)!" she called up to the man. He stopped and turned around meeting her eyes. "*Shqiptarë jeni ju* (you are Albanian)?"

"*Po* (yes)," he said nodding his head. "*Do të shkomjë në shtepia ime* (we will go to my house)."

175

Aubrey hobbled up to where he was standing and shook his hand. The old man tipped his head forward in a slight bow. Aubrey waited for the others to come up and shake the man's hand. "He is Albanian. He wants us to follow him to his house. I believe we will be safe with him." She turned to walk with the elderly man, who supported her with a firm but gentle hand, helping her around and over the water-filled potholes that pocked the path. Jonathan and Orhan walked ahead, wary of the jinn's woman.

As they rounded the bend, they stopped suddenly, shocked by the scene in front of them. There, bound and gagged with a cord, was the witch lying on the ground. She was a much younger woman than her previous disguise and posture had suggested to them. Her limp form and the trickle of blood that oozed from a small gash in her forehead suggested she was unconscious. Jonathan approached her with caution and nudged her with his boot.

"She's either out cold or dead," he surmised looking with new respect at the old man standing there.

"She will not harm you," the old man said in surprisingly good English. He stared down at her with what looked like pain and sorrow etched into his weatherworn face.

"Your English is very good," stated Aubrey. "Do you live here in this village?"

"No," he nodded. "I live in Gramsh province in Albania. I arrived here not many days ago. Finding this village abandoned, I made myself at home in one of the houses."

"Why are you here?" asked Orhan.

"I came to find my children. They fell in with some bad company, I am afraid. I followed them to Turkey."

"Do you have any idea where to find them?" asked Jeff.

"Yes. My daughter, Ursella, is the woman you see bound before you. She has not become wholly evil, or I would not have been able to overpower her in the manner that I did." He indicated the butt of his shotgun. "I pray that I can claim her back from the power that invaded her." The old man bent over and easily slung Ursella over his shoulder like a sack of grain. He waved off any help and trudged toward his newly acquired dwelling.

Entering the house he carried her to a rickety futon and gently placed her down, covering her with an old blanket but keeping her bound hand and foot. He went to the fireplace that had nearly burned out and stacked a bundle of tea fronds on the glowing embers. Soon the room was filled with the herbal smoke. A down draft from the chimney pushed the rising smoke out of the flue back into the room, causing it to become even denser. The four friends began to cough and gasp for air. Jeff tried to restrain the old man from placing more çai on the fire, but Aubrey stopped him, pointing through the smoke to the futon where Ursella lay.

The smoke lay over her in a dense cloud that enveloped her. Her form seemed to fade before their eyes, becoming a translucent apparition. She writhed and retched under the heaviness. She was still bound and gagged, but her eyes suddenly flew open, bright with incendiary malice. She strained against her bonds, but her strength was being slowly and insidiously drained by the herbal essence.

The company watched in terrified awe at the violent convulsions of the woman. The old man took a burning bundle from the fireplace and waved its smoking end under Ursella's nostrils. She choked behind her gag. He cut the cloth from her mouth with a sharp blade he had concealed in his coat. She gasped for air but only aspirated the fuming herb. Soon a fluxing fireball washed from her gaping mouth and hovered over her. She let out a bloodcurdling scream and slumped unconscious on the futon as the fireball darted up the flue of the chimney.

The old man took the bundle away from her face and carried it out onto the front porch. He pounded the remaining bundles into sparking embers with his shoe. Jeff and Orhan managed to pry open a shuttered window, and soon the smoke cleared the room and the air became breathably crisp.

The old man knelt beside his daughter and cut her binding cords. She lay sleeping before him as he tenderly brushed her matted hair away from her face. He smiled up at Aubrey, singling her out from the rest. Tears began to flow down his cheeks leaving a streak through the soot and grim. He sighed deeply as he turned his attention back to Ursella.

"My name is Anton Rustemi," he said not taking his eyes off of Ursella. "I have waited many painful years for this moment. I have given up everything and lost everyone that I held dear, but now I finally have my daughter back." He paused for a moment and sighed deeply. "There is still much to be done in reclaiming her spirit, but the first step has been taken."

With that, the old man tucked the dusty blanket tighter under her chin and rose to face the foursome. He seemed taller now, as if a great burden had been lifted from his shoulders. He stood before Jeff and Orhan and studied their faces.

"I know of your ancestor," he said turning to Jeff. "I know what line you are from in spite of the deceit and intrigue over the centuries to hide your true identity."

"What do you mean by that?" asked Jeff, irritated that people knew more about him than he knew himself.

"You are the descendent of Përparim Lleshi. Your family has traveled much to conceal this fact. Relocations from Albania to Macedonia to Bulgaria to Turkey, and finally to America. Now you are back in Turkey. You cannot run from your destiny, no matter how hard you try."

"What destiny has in store for me has little to do with what is going on in this madhouse," said Jeff. "I choose my own way...make my own destiny. I live and die by my own action or inaction. I'm not bound by the deeds of my ancestors, and I am getting tired of everyone thinking I am."

"Ah...I *see*," said Anton mockingly with a slight smile. "So all this is just chance? You just *happened* to come back to your ancestral roots just in time to be murdered by the jinni to fulfill a curse that was made over five hundred years ago?"

Jeff stared at him blankly, anger welling up inside of him. He didn't know what to believe any more.

"The truth is you are more of a man of honor than your predecessors. You came here to help people in their time of great need. You—"

"Wait just a minute," Jeff interrupted. "How do you know all of this? I've never been to this part of the world before. You say you just got here from Albania. I've never been there either. How is it you know anything about me?"

"How indeed," said Anton. "You don't believe that destiny has brought you here? Well, I do. In fact, I know it has. You. Orhan. Myself. Even my daughter Ursella. Here for a purpose. A task, if you will. Regardless of what you believe or disbelieve, you are here to travel the road destiny has placed before you."

"I believe in God," said Jeff stubbornly.

"You believe in God? That is good. Then let us change the argument. God has placed you on this road. You are here because God wants you here. Now do you feel better?"

Jeff didn't feel like arguing. He was tired, wet, and hungry. "OK, I'm supposed to be here," he conceded. "Now what?"

Anton smiled and took Jeff's hand in a firm shake. "Now you go to Albania."

"What? I can't go to Albania," Jeff protested. He glanced over at his friends for support.

"First of all, however, you will all get out of these wet clothes and have something to eat," said Anton. "There are garments in that room to your left. As soon as you have changed, we will eat.

* * *

The companions found shirts, trousers, and sweaters stuffed in a canvas bag that had been left by the previous occupants of the house. It felt good to be dry again. Anton was hunched over a pot dangling from a hook in the fireplace stirring it with an old wooden spoon.

"It smells great," said Jonathan, the first to reenter the room.

"Do we even want to know what you're cooking and where you got it?" asked Jeff following closely behind with Aubrey, and Orhan.

"Possibly not," said Anton not turning around, "but it *is* chicken. Albeit rather scrawny. I stole it from a village up the coast as I was coming here."

"Your English is good," said Aubrey as she sat next to him. "How have you come to speak and understand it so well?"

"It is a long story. It starts when I was a young man. A teenager, actually. My village and I, including my father and two brothers, went to fight against the Nazis that invaded our country during the Second World War. We lived in the north. In the mountains of Tropojë. We were partisans, and we fought alongside British commandos and American Rangers. I was very proud of my involvement against the Nazis. I lost one of my brothers and many friends from our village, but in the end we were victorious. We were heroes, and after the war we wanted democracy. Soon it became clear that we had driven out one tyrant only to replace him with another. Stalin turned Yugoslavia over to Tito, and Tito turned Albania over to one of his lieutenants, Envir Hoxha. We were put under the thumb of Communism. We resented it very much and fought against it, but in the end we were fighting against fellow Albanians. My father and brother continued to fight against the Communists. They and others were such a pain in the government's side that no roads were built in that area. No power plants. No electricity.

No running water. The north was kept in the dark ages as punishment for the resistance.

"I eventually left, and moved south to Gramsh. You might say that after a time I lost my way. I finally joined the Communist party and became a valuable asset because of having worked so closely with the Americans and British during the war. Our old allies had become enemies almost overnight. I spent most of my younger years living in the West, spying if you will.

"I first became aware of the legend of the jinn after I was sent to investigate a Catholic priest who was skulking around in northern Albania in the early nineteen sixties. He had been making an unauthorized investigation into some bizarre murders in the mountain villages. I had the power to arrest him for subversion to the state, but he fled back across the Adriatic to northern Italy before I could capture him. I followed him there and 'convinced' him to let me read his journal. At the time we had little interest in murders in the northern mountains. Those people had a way of vindicating justice in their own way. My superiors and I deemed an un-influential priest and troublesome villagers not worth our time. I left the priest his journal with a promise that he would be arrested and executed if he were ever caught on Albanian soil again.

"I remained a stalwart party member, forsaking my roots in the north, until I witnessed a great treachery against the people of my adopted province. It shocked me back to the treachery of the Nazi. Envir Hoxha built a factory in Gramsh that manufactured the Kalashnikov AK-47. I was on assignment in Great Britain at the time.

"Hoxha was a very paranoid man even for a Communist. He wanted his factory to be secret to the outside world. Gramsh was very remote. Almost overnight those who were religious or politically opposed to the party disappeared. Then whole villages of people disappeared or were killed

181

outright. Hoxha was thinning out the population in the valley to keep tighter control on the security of the factory. My wife was one of those killed, but my two children, Ursella and Jason, had been taken away and hidden by my wife's brother.

"When I came home to find this horrific treachery done by my own government, I stopped being a loyal party member. It has actually taken me years to track down my children, who were raised by my brother-in-law as his own. They were very young and the fact that I was away in Western Europe most of the time caused them to not even recognize me as their father. My brother-in-law was involved in clandestine activities involving the occult and sorcery. My children learned much from him and looked to *him* as their father.

"When I finally found my children, they would have nothing to do with me. My wife's brother had told them lies about me, and they did not even believe that I was their father. My brother-in-law had done a most unspeakable thing in Albania—to steal another man's children. My years working with the Sigurimi, the Albanian secret police, did away with any moral compass I may have had, so it was only natural for me to kill him. Unfortunately he had made provisions for members of his 'cult' to hide my children from me once again.

"After the collapse of Communism in Albania in nineteen ninety-one, it became easier to travel, and I never gave up on my quest to find my children. Of course, by this time they were grown and capable of remaining hidden from me if they wished. I was able to track down a member of the cult not long ago still living in Gramsh. I forced him to tell me where my daughter and son were. I am now an old man, but I have not forgotten how to make a man beg for mercy. He told me everything, including plans to aid a genie and fulfill an ancient curse.

"My prisoner told me that the only safe haven in Turkey was the Cave of the Seven Sleepers at the ruins in Ephesus. The genie had a target for his malice, the progeny of the ancient betrayers who were known to be in Turkey and bound to show up in Ephesus.

"I decided to take a chance that Ursella and Jason would be allied with this genie and would eventually come here. I was here this afternoon when the earthquake cracked open the earth straight from the sea to the ruins. I knew it had to be the work of the genie," Anton finished.

"How do you know about Jeff?" asked Orhan.

"The members of my brother-in-law's cult had prepared a very extensive portfolio of the history, genealogy, locations of the members of this generation, and an elaborate collection of magic spells and incantations. It was a long journey by bus to arrive here, which gave me plenty of time to read everything this group had compiled. They even had current photographs of the two of you, places you frequented, and names and addresses of your friends. An itinerary of Jeff's airline flights was included. They knew exactly how to find you. I will add that according to their information, you two are the last of the line. If the genie destroys you, his curse will be lifted and he will be free to roam as he pleases. The men who stole my children from me have aligned themselves with this genie. They are my enemy, which means that the genie is also my enemy. We share the same enemy. That makes us allies." He smiled at the three men and then gazed over at his sleeping daughter. "So much time lost," he sighed. "I am old, but you will find me a worthy ally. I didn't survive the Nazi, CIA, MI6, and the Communists to be daunted by this adversary." He went over to Ursella and took her hand as he knelt beside her.

Jeff felt better having Anton on their side. He also felt better after eating some of the broth. Aubrey and Jonathan had been sitting in the corner of the room eating while listening to Anton's story. Finally Jonathan spoke up.

"Are you aware that we have had a group of Gypsies helping us?"

"No, but I am not surprised," said Anton. "The notes I have stated that a clan of the Romany had been sworn to protect the lineage nearly as far back as the origins of the curse. They were to have been exterminated. I have spent a great deal of time in my younger days tormenting the Gypsies, but I now realize that most of my prejudice came from political and bigoted propaganda. They will be valuable in dealing with the genie's power. The knowledge that I used to extract the genie's power from Ursella was from a handbook I found with the portfolio. It contained, among other things, magic from the Gypsies."

"We have been separated from the men who were helping us," said Jeff. We haven't seen them since the earthquake. We don't know if they are alive or dead."

"Do you know anything about them?" asked Orhan.

Anton shook his head. "No. I came here on my own. I only know what I was able to extract from the man in Albania concerning my children."

"Well, speaking of Albania, there is supposed to be another jinn or genie bound and loosed in Albania during a full moon cycle like this one in Turkey. Do you know anything about that?" asked Jeff.

Anton looked troubled. "Only that the time for its release is not the same as the one here in Turkey. Apparently there has been a schism in the time frame of the curse. Apart from that I know nothing," he said. "It seems that our best course of action would be to find these lost Gypsies of yours to determine their fate. Hopefully they are alive and can help us with what we need."

It had begun to rain again. The depression that had settled in on the four companions seemed to be taking its toll. The rain came down harder now, and the wind blew more fiercely. The prospect of leaving the warmth of the fire only drew them deeper into the melancholy. They finished eating their broth; the only sounds were the wind howling through the valley and the occasional slurp of spoon to mouth. No one wanted to meet anyone else's gaze. They stared off into their own little corners pondering their plight. Secretly they recognized the need to find Mustafa and Ermal as soon as possible, but that meant going out into the cold, abysmal night without sleep.

Finally Anton spoke up. "We will rest for two hours then make our way back up to the ruins."

No one argued with his plan, but each quickly settled as close to the fire as possible. Jonathan had found a stash of old, dusty blankets in an armoire and distributed them among the others. Aubrey snuggled close to Jeff.

"How are you feeling?" he asked.

"Better," she said. "It hurts, but it isn't making me sick to my stomach like it was before." She laid her head on his chest as he wrapped his arm around her. It was not until that moment that he realized how sore his shoulder and arm were from clinging to the roots at the cliff. It seemed so long ago. Had it really been just a few short hours?

He watched the flickering dance of the fire shadows on the wall through eyelids that grew heavier and heavier. Aubrey breathed softly in shallow sleep. The others lay sprawled in various contortions on the floor. Jeff fought the urge to nod off. He strained his ears for any hint of danger from the abandoned village. Were they really safe? Could Anton be trusted? Could Ursella *ever* be trusted? He stared over at the sleeping woman on the futon. She tossed fitfully as if tormented by her dreams. He turned his attention to the woman resting comfortably against his chest. He smelled her hair and smoothed it tenderly. Soon he fell into a deep sleep unaware of the shadow that passed soundlessly through the wooden door.

# 17. Mercurial Fortunes

Ölüm sped through the ravine like a flaming meteorite, a long tail of fume in his wake. He slowed his streak only slightly as he passed the bodies of his dead minions that had been left to guard the cave and the golden cube. He crashed into the cavern in a panic. The cave was empty. The cube…gone.

He stormed out of the cave in a thunderous blast, streaking to a great height in the sky looking for any sign of the thieves. They had obviously been gone for quite some time. He bellowed out a dead-waking wail that tumbled rock and snow from the high peaks and ridges of the mountains. Then he spun in a violent cyclone of destruction, ripping up trees by their roots and casting boulders like they were pebbles. His temper tantrum pounded and reverberated in a concentric shock wave that rippled for miles in every direction.

He knew his doom. His golden cube, although a prison, was also his lifeline, now in the hands of his enemies. His mind raced over his options. He had very few. He had to retrieve the box, forsaking all else, or he was dead. He stormed in ever-widening circles, hunting for movement on the ground like a hawk. His mind went back to the three vehicles on the road. He had ignored them, thinking they were no threat to him.

Over the ridge to the south he caught the beam of a headlight just before it disappeared around a curve in the road. Then another beam. He raced toward them but kept his distance to the rear and followed, keeping low to the tops of the trees, allowing them to lead him to his goal. He transformed himself into a wisp of cloud to be less conspicuous in the bitter night.

The vehicles, a car and a truck, slowed as they entered a small village. Other vehicles were carefully hidden behind buildings and under trees. Ölüm touched down to the ground a short distance from the village in an open field. He moved as mist toward a barn where a villager was feeding hay to several cattle. Entering the barn, he transformed into a cow and stood among the other bovine waiting to be fed.

His presence startled the hungry creatures, but they reacted so subtly that the herdsman was unaware of the additional member to his herd. Ölüm pushed his way past the other cows, his eyes blood red. He continued in his disguise taking up a position at a vine-lashed stick fence near the two vehicles that had just arrived. He watched in seething hatred the two Gypsy men exiting the car, giving orders to the others. He recognized them from the ruins. They would die first. Ölüm peered into the shadows reconnoitering his enemy's numbers and positions. He counted fifteen who were already hidden and another ten who had just arrived.

Ölüm wanted revenge. He craved terror. He summoned the other cows to the fence; they obeyed stupidly. With little coaxing he stampeded them, smashing through the fence. They ran maddened by the power of the jinn straight for the men that had just jumped from the back of the truck and were beginning to make their way into hiding.

The first man squawked in surprised terror as he was plowed over and crushed underfoot. The others turned toward the stampede only in time to be tossed and trampled. Suddenly there was a burst of gunfire as the Gypsies regrouped after their initial surprise. The cattle fell dead in their tracks from the barrage.

Ölüm took several hits but was impervious to the bullets. Mustafa, who had jumped to the top of the cab of the heavy truck, noticed the ineffectiveness of their weapons on the larger-than-normal cow at the rear of the stampede. He rolled onto his back and pulled out the sling-rifle he had buried within the folds of his coat. Loading a peach seed, he rolled back over onto his stomach to find that the jinn had again transformed, this time into a pillar of fire.

The gunfire stopped as the last of the cattle fell dead into the snow. The Gypsy men ran out from their hiding places surrounding the jinn. Peach seeds pelted the flaming creature, causing it to writhe and contort in pain. Ölüm shot off into the direction of the other houses trying to gain cover away from the barrage. As he did so, he shot past three men behind a barn, burning them to ashes. Their disintegrated forms dissolved where they stood.

Ermal and Mustafa organized the rest of the company into packs like wolves hunting their prey. Suddenly the village became alive with activity as the villagers hearing the ruckus came out of their homes carrying rifles, shotguns, and axes. They swarmed toward Ermal and his men, thinking they were the threat to their village. One Gypsy took an ax blade through the chest from an overzealous Turk. He died instantly sliding down the wall of a barn into a heap.

Mustafa screamed at the villagers to look over their shoulders, pointing behind them at the fiery form of Ölüm. The men of the village turned in shock, some dropping their weapons. Ölüm dove straight for them, slaying three villagers in an instant. He was pelted by shotgun pellets and bullets from the terrified villagers, who reacted bravely despite their fear—fear that grew to titanic proportions as they realized their weapons were completely ineffective. Mustafa and his men kept the jinn at bay with their deadly sling-rifles. Ölüm kept dodging the projectiles though some of the stones hit him in non-vital areas causing him tremendous pain and making him unable to mount a full-fledged attack. This only increased his fury as he swept along the treetops looking for a weakness in the men's defenses.

While Mustafa and his men kept Ölüm distracted, Ari rushed to Ermal's side carrying a small backpack. He pulled Ermal into an outdoor toilet and shut the poorly fitting, weatherworn wooden door. The fighting raged outside. A heavy thud landed on the roof of the outhouse causing the two men to wince; the body of one of the villager's rolled off into the dung heap behind the shack. Ölüm was targeting the less protected villagers and growing in power with each kill.

Ari pulled his backpack off and fished inside it in the dark. He removed a jewel-inlaid golden cube. Ermal could see the exquisite craftsmanship by the glow of the jinn's fiery wrath seeping through a crack in the wooden planked wall.

"This is what you seek," said Ari handing it to Ermal.

"Yes, this is what we seek," said Ermal taking the box quickly from his clansman. "We have no time to waste." He peered out the crack and saw Ölüm hovering over one of the houses just off the square of the village. Mustafa and his Gypsies were doing all that they could to keep the jinn busy, even at the cost of their own lives. Ermal could see two of his men lying in charred heaps from Ölüm's fiery blasts.

Ermal placed the cube on the concrete floor. Ari stood guard at the crack. Ermal removed from an inner vest pocket of his cape a lambskin parchment. He squatted with his back to the wall and placed the parchment on his knees. He pulled out a small Maglite and placed it between his teeth, focusing the beam on the inscriptions written on the lambskin. Ari reached down and took the flashlight keeping the beam centered.

Ermal began to chant in a low resonating voice, "*Ek tha do mosh. Usk ple neter. Ke se mosh. Usk ple neter.*" He repeated the incantation more forcefully, "*Ek tha do mosh. Usk ple neter. Ke se mosh. Usk ple neter.*" The cube began to clatter against the concrete floor. Suddenly the lid exploded open with a blindingly brilliant charge of light that obliterated every aspect of darkness within the shack. Rays beamed out through the cracks, grabbing the attention of Ölüm. He whirled around toward the tiny structure when the tail of his fire was suddenly seized by the power of the magic. He began to slowly spin in a vortex of wind and fire as he was drawn helplessly toward the golden cube.

He fought with all his might to free himself from the grip of the spell. He thrashed and flailed in a ferocious fit, hurling torpedoes of fire in all directions trying to dislodge the grip of his enemies. Many village men fell incinerated in their tracks. Mustafa and his Gypsies leapt for cover while still firing their sling-rifles at the desperate jinn.

Ölüm screamed in hateful anger as he was drawn closer to the imprisoning golden cube. The peach stones found more vital areas to wound, and his screams turned to panic and fear.

The cube began to whirl and levitate within the shack. Ari reached to steady it with an outstretched hand, but the power melted the flesh from his bones like wax. It overtook him so quickly that only a soggy gurgle escaped before he was completely consumed. Ermal was rammed into the planks of the wall. The brilliance had blinded him. Unaware of Ari's fate, he tried desperately to continue his chant. His voice rose to a feverish pitch as he screamed over the thunderous cacophony.

Lightening streaked across the sky, and a continuous roll of thunder echoed through the mountains. The gas tank of one of the trucks blevied in a catastrophic explosion sending searing debris raining down on the few men left standing. Mustafa was thrown into a stack of hay that ignited instantly despite being covered with a layer of wet snow. He thrashed his way out of the conflagration, his hands and face blistering from the heat, and lay dazed in a mucky pool of melted snow and animal feces. Looking up, he saw Ermal pinned against the plank of the outhouse, the brilliance of the cube casting a strobe effect across his silhouette.

190

# Vale of Shadows

Ölüm's malicious screams gave way to a forlorn wail as he was drawn into the bondage of the Gypsy's incantation. A pitiful whimper was the last sound he made as his final resistance failed. The lid of the golden cube clamped shut tight, sealed by a power greater than that of the jinn or Gypsy. The jinn had been vanquished once again by the treachery of men.

Ermal fell through the shattered doorway of the shack and lay as if dead in a fresh stack of hay that had not been incinerated in the battle. His face and hands screamed in agony from the heat of the power; his clothes smoldered and steamed as he lay in the wet straw. He could hear no sound save for the drumming within his skull. He tried to blink his eyes open, but the lids were crusted and swollen. There was no part of him that was not racked with excruciating pain. He was too weak to move; alone in the darkness of his mind.

Mustafa stumbled over to him and rolled him over onto his back. Ermal's face was blackened, cracked, and bleeding. A faint groan was all that indicated he was still alive. Several other men made their way over to the leaders, the few villagers that were left trailing behind.

Besnik entered the outhouse. The inside of the planks were charred black, and glowing embers smoked sporadically along the edges of the boards. He reached down and picked up the golden cube carefully, expecting it to be hot to the touch. He was surprised to find it cold and undamaged by the heat. He noticed the lambskin parchment crumpled in a corner, also undamaged. He picked it up and handed the cube to Juli, one of his clansmen, while he carefully rolled up the parchment.

Mustafa cradled his brother in his arms. There was no medicine that could ease his suffering. Besnik knelt beside them and placed his open palm reverently against Ermal's chest. Ermal coughed weakly, but his body still convulsed and jolted with the effort. The Roma stared down at their fallen captain. No one spoke.

Desultory clouds drifted across the face of the full moon, and light snow began to fall around the men standing at Ermal's side. Women from the village came out of their homes; some searched the dead for their loved ones while others brought blankets to their men. Women began to wail at their gruesome discoveries. Women whose husbands were still alive went to those who mourned to comfort them. The Gypsy band stood in the midst of but separate from the villagers. Their grief was not the same.

Ermal's labored breathing ceased with one last gasp as he arched his back and then fell silent. Mustafa had been staring absently at the golden cube still held by Juli, barely able to behold the atrocity that had been done to his brother, but as Ermal gasped Mustafa lowered his gaze briefly. Then he looked back up at his men. Only eight left. Tears began to sting his own swollen and blistered face as they streaked down his cheeks. He knew what they had to do, but with so few men and the cost in lives to get this far, the task seemed impossible.

He gently lowered Ermal's head to the ground and stood to face his men. They gathered around him ready to acknowledge his succession. After studying each man in turn, he finalized his gaze on Besnik.

"I am sorry for the loss of Orin," he said. "I was not aware of what happened to him until a short time ago. Our job, however, is not finished here." He addressed the other men. "We have two options. One is better than the other. The first option, which is the most obvious, is that we destroy the coffer of the jinn and be rid of him once and for all. We have the magic to do so. That will fulfill the vows of our ancestors, and the promises we made to see the end of the jinn in our lifetime." He paused as the men nodded and grunted in agreement.

"The second option is not so obvious but is one of equal honor and importance. It was Ermal's wish that if we succeeded in rebinding the jinn we would continue our quest to include the rebinding and ultimate destruction of the twin. This is what I intend to do. The great cost that we have all endured to reach this goal has been grievous. I will not view anyone badly who chooses not to enter into this new endeavor. It will more than likely result in all of our deaths, but the legacy of the curse continues so long as one of the jinn is left to wreak havoc."

Besnik was the first to step forward, followed by Juli. The two men stared down at Mustafa's dead brother. Besnik met Mustafa's questioning eyes. "We will follow you," he said after a time. "We will fulfill the wishes of Ermal."

One by one the rest of the men came forward to pledge their allegiance to Mustafa. He looked around the circle with gratitude.

The Roma were invited into the home of the mayor of the village to tend to their wounds. Salves and bandages were placed with expert care by the mayor's wife, who had been a nurse when she was younger. After a quick meal, the Gypsies helped bury the village dead but refrained from burying their own. "We will give our brothers a proper Gypsy burial." Mustafa had said.

So the villagers helped them carry their dead to a truck that was undamaged and gently placed them in the cargo hold. An old canvas tarp was all they had to cover the bodies. Mustafa grabbed Ermal's backpack from the Fiat and placed it in the cab of the truck.

The moon began to peek out from the clouds as they headed back down the road to retrieve those killed in the accident at the switchback earlier. Besnik sat in the front seat with Mustafa, Juli between them; the other Gypsies followed in a second truck. The three men traveled in silence, deep in their own torment over the loss of life. The bejeweled golden cube rested firmly on Juli's lap, and an eerie anxiousness settled over the men as they pondered the cube's content. Besnik perused the parchment by the light of the overhead dome. Finally he broke the silence.

"Do you know what to make of this gibberish?" he asked.

"I know," said Mustafa simply. "I learned much from the queen and the queen mother before I left. In order to determine the location of the other box, we must have this one intact. We can destroy this one only by an incantation that is on that parchment, but if we want to destroy both of the twins it must be done simultaneously." Mustafa noticed the questioning look on Juli's face. "The twins were bound together in the same spell. The resourcefulness of the sorcerer Baba Moush allowed the twins to be captured by one incantation and separated and locked into the two different gold cubes. How that was done we do not know. His black art was raised from regions we do not want to imagine. They were greater than any we have seen before or since. We can only hope that our ancestral traditions will give us the wherewithal to accomplish the task ahead. It will all come down to whether or not our magic is powerful enough."

Mustafa glanced at his rearview mirror to see the position of the other truck, but the mirror had been shattered during the battle. He looked in the passenger side mirror and caught Besnik staring at him. He didn't sense any particular malice, but even in the poorly illuminated cab the coldness in Besnik's eyes let him know that the matter of Orın and Simion was not over.

The trucks pulled over to the side of the narrow road where they had lost the other truck earlier. It was easy to find the spot from the rock-strewn path across the pavement and the hewn-out foliage piercing into the ravine. The men solemnly and silently disembarked, slipping and sliding down the wet embankment and causing little landslides of shale and gravel ahead of them. Finally coming to the wreckage, they began to wrap the remains of their friends and family in tarps and hoisted them one at a time to the top with a wench mounted on the truck Mustafa was driving. Besnik found the body of his brother Simion and carried him over his shoulder. Out of respect the men were careful not to drag the corpses recklessly to the road but tried to guide the bodies carefully around any snags that occurred from the broken trees and bushes.

After the last of the bodies were loaded into the second truck, the men stood awaiting Mustafa's orders. After a time of reflection Mustafa spoke.

"Brothers…this is a hard time. We will find a suitable meadow to bury our fallen, but we have no time to grieve. Our customary wait of three days to mourn and feast cannot take place at this time. We must honor them by ending this curse. We must look diligently for the young men, Jeff and Orhan. Their fates are still tied to the outcome of our odyssey. I purpose we search for them along the coast west of the ruins. Hopefully they have found shelter and are unharmed, but the fact that the jinn was alone indicates that his minions are still at large. We will deal with them when the time comes. It was Ermal's plan to continue on to Albania and meet members of our clan there. They have been searching for the location of the twin. I pray that they have not had the level of tragedy and loss that we have."

Without further discussion the Gypsies loaded up in the trucks and began the drive back to the region around Ephes. Each man remained deep in his own thoughts. Most were trying to mentally overcome the pain from wounds inflicted on them during the battle with Ölüm. There was no thought of quitting, however, as each considered it his duty to see the task completed for the sake of their fallen clansmen.

Juli carried on the task of holding the golden cube on his lap for safe keeping. The weight of it seemed to fluctuate from time to time; sometimes it felt very heavy and at other times it felt very light. He did not want to contemplate the reason behind it; he was too tired. He decided to keep the matter to himself. *After all,* he thought, *Mustafa has enough to worry about.*

After driving for two hours without conversation, Mustafa finally addressed Besnik and Juli.

"I do not wish to bury my brother in the snow. I want to find a meadow lower, out of these mountains."

"I agree," said Besnik. "It would be better if they did not have to endure the cold forever."

The matter settled they drove until they reached lower elevations closer to the Aegean Sea. The full moon was once again released from the bondage of the clouds. Off in the distance, an opening broke in the rugged terrain becoming a gentle, undulating roll in the landscape. A field not bordered by a fence appeared off to their right as they rounded a bend in the road. A grove of poplar and cypress trees marked the northernmost edge of the field. There had not been any sign of an inhabited village for several miles. Mustafa pulled his truck out into the field. Finding a suitable area of ground that overlooked the field, they pulled to a stop and unloaded the bodies of the dead.

They went to work quickly to dig graves. As was their custom, they buried their men standing, symbolizing the ever-wandering lifestyle of their people. Their various superstitions kept them from talking about death in the presence of the dead. Knowing that Death was surely close-by, they did not want to call attention to themselves. They quickly finished their task and loaded back into the trucks to leave. No time to utter words over the graves. No time for a priest or an imam. No time to feast and talk about the lives of those they'd lost. No time to bury them with useful trinkets that would aid them on their journey in the beyond life. Each hoped secretly that fate would allow them time to mourn later.

They took what they needed from the second truck, and then pushed it off to the side of the field concealing it in the stand of trees. The thought of returning to retrieve the bodies gave them hope for a future.

\* \* \*

Mustafa fought against the gremlins of drowsiness. He'd had no sleep since arriving in Turkey. He tracked his vision back and forth beyond the beams of his headlights and cracked his window open enough to let a stream of cold air whistle into the cab. It had little effect reviving him; exhaustion was beginning to take rule over his body. He glanced over at Besnik and Juli. Both men's heads bobbed against their chests with each bump in the road. Mustafa hadn't seen a sign along the road for...well, he couldn't remember the last time. Because of the smell of the salt sea lightly on the wind, he knew that they couldn't be far from the coast, but exactly where they were he had no idea.

Finally realizing that should they encounter the captive jinn's minions before he had a time to rest he would lose the confrontation, he pulled the truck over onto a wide shoulder that sloped steeply into a meadow. The sudden cessation in movement caused Mustafa to fall into a deep sleep.

The truck sat silent along side of the road. The glimmer of the Adriatic shone in the midnight moonlight just over the rolling ridge on which the meadow sat. The Roma slept deeply, floating and tumbling in the darkness of narcotic stupor.

\* \* \*

Ölüm fumed in the vapors of his golden prison. Nestled in the nescient grasp of Juli, he conjured his own sorcery. Although hampered by the spell of the cube, he was not without a small portion of power over hapless victims in close proximity. His phantom had twisted and seethed its way from Gypsy to Gypsy, a wisp of blackness hovering ravenously over its prey until the men slumped into a state of drowsiness then suddenly plunged into a deep level of dreamless sleep as if anaesthetized for surgery.

Ölüm remained trapped, but he desperately hoped he had bought enough time for his followers to find and release him. He concentrated in ruptured agony, casting the strength of his will beyond his confines into the ether summoning any and all who could be influenced by the power of his mind. His phantom finally dissipated, not having the substance to presevere on its own.

* * *

Clouds canvassed the moonscape, and spearlets of light fanned out in rays reflecting off of the cold, dark water of the sea. One such ray stabbed through the windshield of a dormant truck, reflecting the jewels on a golden cube in a frenzied dance. Powers stirred within, escalating in strength, and the cube became lighter in weight and levitated shallowly off the knees of the sleeping Gypsy. As suddenly as they had appeared, the clouds roiled, covering the moon. With the brilliant rays extinguished, the golden cube dropped quietly back into the folds of the Gypsy's lap.

# 18. Dawn of Recreance

He cried out, but he got no answer. He screamed, but he was consoled only by the reverberating echo of his own voice fading into the deepest, darkest blackness enveloping him. *Am I alive?* He thought, *or dead?* He strained to contain the panic spreading over him like a dense fog. *Where am I?* He struggled to move his arms and legs only to find that they were bound, immobile by an unseen restraint. No. Not bound. Not *there*. As in, he had no sensation of having arms or legs at all.

Terror seized his mind, obliterating all reason. He cried out to no avail. His heart throbbed in an arrhythmic pulse that heaved against the inside of his chest, pounding to be released from its skeletal prison. Helpless. Hopeless. He screamed out to God, but his words were thrown back into his face as if he were screaming into a pillow pushed tightly over his mouth. He coughed and choked and gagged, the air sucked from his lungs by the heavy blackness that invaded his very essence. He felt wrapped in a cocoon, the stench of which burned his eyes, nose, lips, and tongue. He was dead, he concluded. Dead and in hell, beyond the presence of God. The horror of his torment swelled insidiously inside him.

Then the blackness began to give way to soft hues of gray. He was moving. More specifically, he was floating. He couldn't tell for sure, but he seemed to be floating at a great height. The darkness boiled around him with florettes of light piercing the umbra. Finally he popped through the shadow into the light like he was emerging from a dense smoke. He searched all around him only to discover he was free, freer than he could have ever imagined possible. He was unencumbered by physical parameters, his terror of a few moments ago replaced by unfathomable awe.

His disembodied spirit reveled in its newfound freedom and he began to pick up glimpses of terrain and movement below. Wisps of cloud breaking up to reveal...what? Not cloud, but smoke. He became an unwilling spectator to a horrific calamity that was unfolding beneath his ethereal perch. The clamor of war rang out. The clash of steel. The cries of agony, fear, and anger climaxing in a hideous song. He no longer wanted to be a part of this scene, but he had no power to remove himself from it. He stared in disbelief at the cruelty that was being manifested by one human being against another.

He tried to call out a warning, to dissuade them from their wonton slaughter, but the limitations of existing only as spirit frustrated his attempts. Once again he felt helpless. Hopeless. A prisoner without understanding. Why was he here? Where was here? Why was he in such a miserable state? His mind reeled with torturous presumptions. He was doomed. He was damned. He was, after all, in hell.

The sound of war grew greater, and he realized that he had descended to a lower altitude; he could now make out the players in this desperate tragedy. A war between two armies. Armies of ancient means. Circular banners flew furtively in the breeze. To the north, flags with deep red backgrounds and black, double-headed eagles emblazed across them whipped in the wind. Various other stanchions supported emblems of rank and knighthood, but the double-headed eagle on red stood out above all others. To the south long, triangular-shaped streamers with crescent moons played on the breeze like darting finches. Foot soldiers from both sides stood in rank on the east and west slopes that outlined the river basin.

# Vale of Shadows

It was late summer, and the river was little more than a stream that snaked its way through a wide river basin of sandbars and small islands. Lined up in row after row on the sand bars were the ornately costumed cavaliers of Selim Bey. Their magnificent Arabians stamped their hooves and chomped at the bit; they flared their nostrils in anticipation of battle. The cavaliers robed in green, red, and yellow wore elaborate headdresses adorned with jewels and gold. Their shields bore *cartouches* of the sultan, lances long with streamers denoting their own personal allegiance to God and the sultan, written in the calligraphy of the Ottomans.

In the opposing ranks were the cavalry of Scanderbeg, commanded by Përparim Lleshi. They stood in defiance of Selim Bey, ferocious in their resolve to keep the sultan's empire from spreading through their land. Noblemen on horse led their ranks. The foot soldiery made up of peasants had been pressed into service by their lords, but each had a stake in the outcome. They would fight bravely with honor despite being outnumbered and out-skilled by the Ottoman empire-building machine.

Lleshi galloped into the foothills on the west side of the river valley. He prodded his charger through the steep terrain, making his way toward the foot of Mount Tomori and being careful not to be spotted by the Ottomans he was flanking. The great mountain of myth and legend loomed ahead to the south. A Turkish scout spotted him, but too late. Lleshi hacked through him like a scythe through wheat. Behind him, down in the valley below, the calamity of war rose to a fever pitch. Lleshi stopped to look back over his shoulder. The massacre of the jinni had begun.

Lleshi spurred his steed forward, a superb courser, a gift from Scanderbeg. He had to reach the summit before it was too late. Baba Moush was as treacherous as Selim Bey. He goaded his mount with his spurs up the steep slope, finally coming to a fall of boulders that forced him to proceed on foot. The climb was hazardous without a trail. The main ascent was around on the other side, to the southeast, but five thousand Turks stood in his way. The August sun beat down relentlessly; his armor became an oven, but he pushed himself beyond the bounds of human endurance for the prize at hand.

Suddenly an earthquake rattled through the valley causing a cascade of rock and gravel to avalanche down the mountain. Lleshi pressed himself into a small alcove of rock, narrowly missing being crushed by a gigantic boulder that had dislodged from near the summit. The temperature plummeted as dark, ominous clouds masked the sun, and lightening struck violently like hail sending horsemen and foot soldiers from both sides scurrying for cover. Thunder clapped directly overhead, smacking the armies with barometric shock waves, and a mighty wind blew in from all four cardinal directions causing a vortex to settle on the summit of Mount Tomori. Lleshi could feel the pull of the wind sucking him towards the top like a marionette on a string.

Through the gale a vicious cry echoed from mountaintop to mountaintop. Lleshi looked down the valley to the north to see the jinni caught in the grip of an unseen force drawing them insidiously toward the crest of Tomori. He could now see the silhouette of Baba Moush standing with his arms raised to the heavens, calling out his incantation above the howl of the wind.

Lleshi crawled to within twenty yards of Baba Moush and spied the two jewel-encrusted golden cubes. They were open, and into their mouths a tremendous flow of wind, dust, and debris was sucked. The jinni were now within a hundred yards of the summit. They writhed and spat vile curses at Baba Moush as they were drawn inexorably toward their prisons. For the first time, Lleshi could see their countenance. Twins? Terror gripped him unexpectedly. The power of the sorcerer was ominous. Lleshi cowered behind an outcropping of rock, afraid to behold the sight. He took a timid look over the edge to see a last vision of the jinni as they were pulled into the cubes.

Movement from the east side of the summit drew his attention. Selim Bey ran from his hiding place with scimitar raised. He let out a war cry, which startled Baba Moush causing him to turn toward his assailant. Lleshi used the diversion to run and grab up one of the cubes. He had no time to take the second box as Selim cleaved Baba Moush in two and was now running toward *him*. Lleshi fended off a blow with his own drawn sword, and parried with a thrust at his enemy's head, being careful not to drop the cube. Out of the corner of his eye he caught the rush of several Turks cresting the ledge and running to defend their commander. Lleshi threw one more blow toward the head of Selim Bey and then turned to run. He jumped back over the western ledge and slid and rolled down the steep face of the mountain clutching his stolen treasure. He could hear shouts of command from Selim as the Turks continued their pursuit.

He careened out of control through loose shale until his descent was abruptly halted by a firm snatch on his halyard — the powerful clutch of one of his own lieutenants. The Ottoman sortie stopped some ways up the slope when they saw the Albanian troops at the side of Përparim Lleshi. Lleshi stared up the hill one last time to see Selim Bey staring back at him from the summit. They each had a prize. It would have to be left at that.

\* \* \*

Jeff's spirit continued to be drawn to the activity of his ancestor. He watched in abject silence as the armies slowly withdrew from the river basin. Lleshi was surrounded by his commanders. Final orders were given, and the peasants began their journey home. The professional soldiers continued through the Gramsh valley making their way down the long road back to Scanderbeg's fortress in Kruja.

Time seemed to speed up like he was fast-forwarding a videotape. Jeff saw part of the army turn towards the east to their garrisons around Lake Orhid, but he was compelled to follow the movement of Lleshi and the golden cube. The scene quickly averted to Kruja and a welcome by Gjergj Kastrioti himself. Jeff could see from his lofty perch that the golden cube was nowhere to be seen, as Lleshi had hidden it from his lord before making the long winding ascent up to the cliff side fortress at Kruja.

Jeff eavesdropped on the conversation between his ancestor and the great Albanian hero. Lleshi was being commended for his gallantry against the Ottoman invasion. Although he had lost many men in the process, his campaign was proclaimed a success. The Turks had left. The reason did not matter. They were gone, and Lleshi had been instrumental in that departure.

Chronological sequence was ambiguous at best, as next Jeff was watching Lleshi conspiring with one of his lieutenants on the parapet of Scanderbeg's castle overlooking the central valley of Albania far below. The glimmer of the setting sun on the Adriatic Sea to the west caught Jeff's attention as he strained to hear what the two men were whispering. Suddenly Lleshi was riding at the head of a long column of his regiment to the north. His coconspirator was not present. Jeff searched the faces of the men. The lieutenant was not among them. He rose to a loftier height to get a wider view of the terrain, and there to the south, heading into the foothills that surrounded the lakes in the valley, he spotted the man he was looking for riding alone cloaked in black.

Jeff recognized him by the silver Moorish spurs he had seen the man wearing on the parapet. Jeff glanced back and forth between the column to the north and this lone rider in the south. He felt an urgency about this man. The hiding place of the golden cube was his destination. Jeff was certain of it.

# Vale of Shadows

The apparition of the past was fast-forwarded to the lieutenant riding hard out of a ravine galloping at full speed to the north, but angling away from Kruja as if he were trying to avoid the fortress. Although he was detached from the events below, Jeff was startled by the sudden collapse of horse and rider as they fell to the ground in a violent crash. Bandits were quickly on him as he rose to his feet dazed from the fall, sword already in his hand. He held something concealed under his cloak with one hand and brandished a Janissary saber, a prize from victory in battle, in the other. Three bandits leapt from the bushes but were quickly cut down in mid stride by the warcraft of the Albanian.

Arrows flew true to their mark from the trees, striking the Albanian in the chest, abdomen, neck, and thigh. He cried out in fierce determination to keep his feet. A fourth and fifth bandit fell headless at his feet. He turned just in time to counter the thrust of a sixth bandit, hacking off his head and sword arm with one slice. A seventh bandit swinging down from a tree branch was impaled on the Janissary saber driven through his heart to the hilt. The weight of the bandit toppled the lieutenant over his dead horse. He withdrew the lance that had felled the brave beast and threw it with fading strength into the foliage of the tree above him. An eighth assailant crashed to the ground with the lance piercing his stomach and emerging between his shoulder blades.

The Albanian staggered over to retrieve his saber, placing his boot on the chest of his fallen enemy and pulling the scimitar free. He staggered and collapsed backward, but kept himself upright by using the saber for support. He swooned in and out of consciousness trying desperately to maintain his readiness for another attack. A barrage of arrows pierced him like porcupine quills. He remained in a kneeing position as he finally succumbed to the assault and slumped over his saber...dead. The golden jeweled cube fell from his grasp and rolled out into view from under his cloak.

Jeff continued to watch as three bandits made their way timidly out from the cover of the bushes and trees. A fat bandit clothed in ragamuffin garb was the first to see the prize.He bent down to fetch it, but his size slowed him as a leaner, more nimble thief grabbed it first. The two men began to squabble over the cube. The third bandit, taller and more warrior-like in his appearance, pried it from the clutches of the other two, slapping them both to the ground with his open hand like dogs. They snarled and hissed curses at the leader, springing to their feet each wielding a dagger. He stepped aside to avoid their clumsy attack, bringing out his own sword and severing their heads from their bodies in two quick strokes.

He clutched the cube to his chest and looked warily around for any other would-be attackers, but he was alone. All were slain save for him. He rewrapped the cube in its linen cloth and placed it in a leather satchel that he had slung over his shoulder. Traveling by foot, he made his way along sheep trails that wound and zigzagged in a northeastern direction. Careful to avoid roads and villages, he made his way into the Balkan Alps.

Jeff continued to watch, puzzled and amazed at this revelation of the past unfolding below him. He had nearly forgotten his disembodied state as he was again drawn to the journey of the cube, following the bandit chief as he marched stealthily into the mountains along paths less traveled. Through the entire journey the cube remained hidden, wrapped in the satchel, the thief never taking it out to gaze at it even by the light of his campfire when he stopped to rest for the night.

Jeff was unsure why he was seeing so much detail in one instant and no details for others. The scene merged to the bandit coming unknowingly into a parallel course with Lleshi and his regiment still moving north. The two were separated only by a low ridge. Lleshi traveled a main road while the bandit chief traveled a narrow goat path.

Suddenly a cavalry of Ottoman Janissaries charged over the ridge toward Lleshi's unsuspecting troops. The event would have brought disaster on the Albanians if not for the cry of fear and surprise by the bandit, who was now caught between the two forces. His cry alerted the Albanians, and they wheeled toward the east facing their foe. The clatter of horse and armor startled the witless thief as he now realized he had enemies on both sides. He turned to run but was felled by a Turkish cavalier who mistook him for one of the Albanian soldiers. He dropped to his knees with an arrow point protruding through his chest from his back. He looked down in stunned disbelief and collapsed facedown. The satchel swung around with the weight of the cube to fall beneath him before he hit the ground.

Jeff watched the melee with an odd feeling of suspense growing inside him. He wasn't sure whom he should cheer for, or even if he should cheer at all, but he was starting to feel a certain loyalty to his Albanian ancestor. The Janissary attack proved to be only a sortie sent out to harass and confuse the Albanian column. The fracas was quickly over with only minor losses to the Turks, but a few less fortunate Albanians had been slain with arrows. Lleshi sent out a squad of horsemen to chase off the Ottomans, but they soon returned after realizing that the strategy was to divide them for a trap.

As the dead were being gathered up, the body of the bandit chief was found. A captain of Lleshi's personal guard deftly removed the satchel with his spear while still seated on horseback. He took a quick look inside but did not remove the contents. He took the satchel to Lleshi, who received it from his captain suspiciously. The captain apparently suspected what was wrapped in the linen and warned his general to open it discreetly. Lleshi took the package behind a bush and knelt down, placing it on the ground before him. He carefully unfolded the linen wrapping revealing the golden cube. Lleshi fell back on his heels startled by the sight. He inspected it with the tip of his dagger. The seal was unbroken. Puzzled, he looked around at his captain, who took him to the body of the dead bandit. Lleshi obviously did not recognize him.

Jeff could tell from his aerial vantage point that Lleshi was disturbed by this confounding event. He quickly rewrapped the cube and placed it carefully in his saddlebag. He did not understand the power that kept the lid sealed and the jinn secured, but he took caution not to inadvertently jar the cube open and release the evil within. Visibly upset, Lleshi called his troops to horse. They would travel through the night.

The next scene propelled Jeff into the future. Lleshi lay dying in a bed made of sheepskin rugs. He was surrounded by only a small number of family and soldiers. The shack he lay in was high up in the mountains, and was used by the shepherds for summer grazing of their sheep. It was winter now, and cold, with a harsh wind howling through the shutters of the shack. Lleshi was giving last-minute instructions to those around him. Jeff got the feeling that they were in hiding. No castle or fortress with all the comforts of a great general and noble lord. Only this small shack high in the cold, lonely mountains. Jeff felt a sense of remorse for his ancestor. The man looked aged and sickly. There was nothing natural about his appearance. Fear of death was blatantly etched on his face.

Suddenly, shockingly, he looked straight at Jeff, eyes wild but clearly focused on him. Jeff jumped, startled by the sudden attention. He shied away from the general's probing gaze. How could the old man see him from across the centuries? Lleshi struggled to form words, clearly trying to communicate with Jeff. Finally he uttered a single word that shook Jeff to his core. "*Come!*"

Jeff suddenly was terrified to be witness to all this. Even from the distance of the centuries, even in this disembodied spirit form he was horrified. Lleshi's locked gaze on Jeff slowly diminished. He seemed to be staring beyond Jeff now. Calmer. More peaceful. He gasped a shallow, gulping breath; then he died. Jeff looked down, stunned by what he had just witnessed. His spirit tarried there for an indeterminable moment. Then as if sensing his impatience, an old woman kneeling next to Lleshi slowly turned and stared past the confines of the roof of the shack and penetrated his soul with her gaze. She was ancient, older than old with great, deep wrinkles in her face and hair as white as snow. Her eyes, however, were sharp with a depth of discernment that could only have come over the course of multiple lifetimes. She knew Jeff's fear and smiled a toothless grin. She nodded her head and spoke softly, "Come!"

He wavered in his phantom state. Should he try to reply? He had so many questions that he wanted to ask, but he found himself dumbfounded and unable to utter a single sound. The old woman rose from Lleshi's side and turned to face Jeff. Hobbled and gnarled from the weight of extreme years, she beckoned with her twig-like finger for Jeff to come to her. Did she mean now? He stared back at her, not knowing what to do. She suddenly tilted her head back and let out a long, raspy cackle. She knew Jeff's dilemma. She simply shook her head and pointed past his vantage point toward the southwest.

He was immediately transported to another scene down in the lower hills south of the Balkan Alps. There in a village was a tomb. There was a great commotion as mourners filed by a flag draped coffin. Armed soldiers stood in regal garb, knights in full regalia. The mood was somber. Jeff couldn't explain why, but he knew he was watching the funeral of Gjergji Kastrioti, known to history as Scanderbeg, in the town of Lesh. Time was out of sequence for Jeff. He didn't know if this was before or after the death of Përparim Lleshi, or even if it was taking place at the same time. He felt the presence of the old woman inside his mind. It was she who was revealing this scene to him.

Jeff stayed in place, but the time period changed to a future date. There below him where once had been a regal tomb was a dilapidated, desecrated heap of collapsed stone. No guards were on station to protect the remains from Ottoman looters rummaging through the bones in search of a talisman that could bring them good fortune. Jeff watched in horror as a looting Turk cut a finger bone from the great king's hand and held it up with glee to show off his prize. Another was less subtle and flipped the coffin over, revealing a stone slab that had supported it. The Turks pushed the slab off of its base to reveal a second compartment. This one contained only one item: a linen-wrapped golden cube. The leader of the looters quickly seized it and placed it in his leather pack. The other Ottomans took exception to his confiscation of the sole treasure to be found, and confronted him with drawn swords. The leader hacked his way to the exit with his scimitar and quickly mounted his steed, galloping into the hills north of the village; a deserter and fugitive.

Jeff watched as the years seemed to cascade by. The cavalier had traveled deep into the Balkan Alps and settled with his prize never to participate in human interaction again. Events became very indistinct, and Jeff struggled to understand the meaning of what he was seeing. The presence of the old woman guided him gently through the sequence of time.

Suddenly an explosion of brilliant fire licked up the shades of darkness from deep within a mountain cave. Jeff was blinded by the sudden illumination, forced to consume the flare with lidless eyes. His spirit felt the radiance of the flash. There in the hidden recesses of the cavern a lavishly jeweled golden cube lay open. Jeff cringed in terror at the sight of the jinn that had been released. The light of the full moon glowed through Jeff to the earth below.

Before he could react with anything other than stupefying horror, he was violently withdrawn from the scene, sucked into a vortex of power that brought him back brutally through the pitch blackness he had originally come from. He gasped for air trying to scream, but the force of the vortex stifled all sound. He thrashed against the acceleration as he was catapulted back through time and space.

Abruptly he crashed, his senses reeling. The motion stopped. Shape and form began to solidify. He was whole again. He blinked his eyes in a flutter of confusion and bewilderment. There standing around him with looks of concern and fear were Aubrey, Jonathan, Orhan, and Anton.

He tried to focus on his surroundings, but it was as if he were peering through a dirty window. The journey had exhausted him. Once he began to get his bearings, however, he was relieved to know that he was not actually dead and in hell but was in fact alive. His confusion diminished. He suddenly looked up wide-eyed and alert.

"Man, that was some nightmare," said Jonathan.

"It wasn't a nightmare," said Jeff excitedly. "It was a vision. I know where to find the golden cube of Albania."

\* \* \*

A mercurial shadow traveled across the far wall of the room and through the outer door, its purpose accomplished.

# 19. An Imprudent Trap

Aydin Village
12:01 a.m.

The company stared at Jeff as if he had lost his mind, but he seemed so confident that they could not argue. He sat up straighter with his back against the wall next to the fireplace. Anton had kept the fire stoked, and it was giving off comfortable warmth throughout the room.

"You know where the Albanian golden cube is?" asked Orhan. "How?"

"I saw the whole thing," said Jeff. "I was there during the battle at the foot of Mount Tomori. I saw the twins and how they were betrayed by the sorcerer. I saw your ancestor and mine fighting over the golden cubes, each going his own way when the odds got bad. I watched Lleshi travel to meet Scanderbeg and then send out one of his soldiers to retrieve the cube after he had hidden it. I saw it being stolen by thieves and later fall back into the hands of Lleshi. Time went by quickly, and I saw Lleshi dying. And here's the creepy thing: he looked right at me on his deathbed and said, 'Come.' Then there was this old hag at his side and she looked right at me also and said the same thing. I saw Scanderbeg's funeral and then was fast-forwarded to a future time when some Turks violated his tomb and stole the golden cube that had been buried with him. The cube was taken into the mountains in the north. The next thing I saw was a full moon and the genie released. Then I was sucked back down this dark tunnel and woke up here, just now."

"How did you see all this?" asked Aubrey.

"I don't know for sure, but I think I had become some kind of spirit or something," confessed Jeff. The others looked at him rather incredulously. Sensing their doubt he continued, "I don't really know how, but I am sure I witnessed the events that happened over five centuries ago. I can see the cave as plain as day. It's still vivid in my mind. I don't know why, but I have a strong feeling that I can find it. It is like Përparim Lleshi spoke to me from the grave and showed me where it is."

A stirring sound from the futon drew their attention to Ursella. She was sitting up and staring at them with unseeing eyes. Finally, as if awakening from a trance, she looked straight at Jeff.

"You have been summoned," she said ominously, "but not by your ancestor. The twins have longed to reunite. The power of the jinn in its fullness is bound to the cube and to the proximity of the cube, but the shadow of their minds can travel great distances to further their will even when they are bound by the spell of Baba Moush." She paused. Her voice had been monotone as if speaking under the control of another, but clarity began to take hold and she straightened to stand. Sitting on the edge of the futon, she continued. "I felt the shadow of his mind. I am no longer of any use to him, but I touched his soul and came away with much knowledge. Knowledge that will be deadly to him. The fact that I am still alive, as well as you, leads me to believe that the Gypsy was successful in capturing him and binding him once again to the golden cube. We will *all* die now if he is released. We must find the Gypsy."

"The shadow of his mind may have been here," said Jeff, "but it wasn't the jinn who revealed the vision to me. I'm pretty sure of it. I believe it was the old woman."

She ignored him and for the first time turned her attention to Anton. "Jason is dead."

The statement came so out of the blue that it caught Anton off guard, hitting him like a blow to the stomach. The

213

others were stunned by the callousness and bluntness of her comment. After he steeled himself, Anton addressed his daughter.

"How did he die?"

"I was with him. He died at the hands of Ölüm. Why are you here?" asked Ursella indignantly.

"I came to find you," said Anton.

"When have you ever cared what happened to us?" Ursella asked accusingly. "You abandoned us. Now you are here to do what?"

"I came to find you...to help you—" started Anton.

"You came to destroy us!"

"No, that is not true. I loved you, your brother, and your mother. I had nothing to do with her murder. It was your uncle who turned you against me with lies. I did everything I could to find you."

"You lie!"

"I don't lie. Your uncle did much harm to us, as much as the government. I am still grieving, and it has been nearly thirty years." Anton paused, tears welling up in his eyes. He shook his head unable to finish.

Ursella glared at him with cold, uncaring eyes. Her disdain turned to apathy toward her father, but she remained otherwise nonthreatening.

Jeff walked slowly over to Ursella supporting himself with a hand on the wall. "So, are you for us or against us?" he asked with menace in his voice.

"I am neither for you nor against you," she said mimicking the level of his menace. "I failed Ölüm. He tolerates no weakness, and there are no second chances. Jason believed that you were dead," she said addressing Anton now. "Our uncle made him believe you had been killed by the Gypsy. But he did not believe everything our mother's brother told him about you. When he proclaimed his own desire to kill the Gypsy to avenge you, Ölüm killed him on the spot. I am of no further use to Ölüm now. He will kill me the first chance he gets."

"You should help us," suggested Jonathan. "You know a great deal about this Ölüm that could help us defeat him."

"Why should I care about what happens to you?" Ursella fumed.

"Because," reasoned Jeff, "if Ölüm is still alive, then he may know that you're with us. I think you're stuck with us whether you like the idea or not."

Ursella frowned at her dilemma, clearly not liking the options. Finally after a long pause, her face softened slightly. She resigned herself with a sigh. "I suppose you are right. We will only survive if we help each other." She rose from the futon and did a most startling thing. She went over to Anton and placed her arm around his shoulder, pushing Aubrey's arm firmly away. "I am sorry for Jason. He had become a fine man." She sighed reflectively. "I suppose we have all been victims of those who have lied to us in order to use us."

\* \* \*

The company sat in silence, each mesmerized by the dance and flicker of flames in the fireplace. The sound of rain falling on the terra-cotta roof tiles soothed them with its arrhythmic cadence. It was well after midnight. No one wanted to move, but the urgency of finding the Gypsies pecked at the peacefulness of the moment.

Gloom fell over the group, and a cold chill blew through the room as if in response. The lace curtain hanging over the inside of the outer door fluttered with the breeze eking through the poorly sealed doorjamb. There in the corner positioned under a peg coat rack was a deep shade not cast by any of their shadows. Jeff took a step toward it and paused to let his eyes grow accustomed to the dimly lit hall. Orhan became aware of it also and stepped to Jeff's side. The others, with their attention drawn to the sudden interest in the hall, stood behind them.

Jeff took another step closer. The shade deepened as if posturing a threat like a dog with it ears pinned back. Another step from Orhan and Ursella elicited a sudden flurry by the shade to the corner of the ceiling next to the door. As Anton stepped forward, the shade bounced quickly across the ceiling and headed for the flue of the fireplace, but suddenly came to an abrupt halt vacillating on the wall above the futon. Anton raised a small burlap pouch over his head and waved it in the direction of the shade. Jeff recognized it as the same kind of *hajmali* the Gypsy girl had given him—was it really just two days ago?

"It looks like it wants to escape," said Aubrey.

"It does," said Anton stepping closer to the shade now only two feet away, "but I was told this has power." He waved the *hajmali* closer to the shade.

"You have it trapped," blurted out Jonathan.

"Yes, in essence I have," said Anton, "but what to do with it now, I have no idea."

"Well, that's just great!" said Jeff sarcastically. "This reminds me of an old crazy entomology professor I once had who saw a large bald-faced hornets nest hanging from a tree. He covered it with a plastic trash bag and sealed it at the top with his fist around the stem only to find out to his great dismay that the stem was too thick to break off and he didn't have a knife. The hornets blasted out of the nest hitting the inside of the bag madder than a wet hen. He stood there all night holding that sack clinched with his fist until one of his teacher's assistants missed him in class and went looking for him. The crazy guy couldn't move his arm or shoulder for two weeks." Jeff paused taking in the glares of the others. "This just seems to be about as crazy, is all I'm saying."

"It seems to be afraid," said Orhan, motioning to the shadow.

Anton straddled the arm of the futon to get a closer look at the shade hovering in the corner. It recoiled higher on the ceiling as Anton raised his hand toward it. After studying it for a few moments, he turned back to the others. "I don't think it's afraid. It seems to be uh...well, angry."

"I don't know what we are going to do with it," said Jeff. "We better let it go before causes trouble."

Anton moved to the front door and the shade immediately moved across the walls and slipped through to the outside. The company rushed outside and stood in the pouring rain watching the shadow propel itself over the treetops toward the sea. As it passed from the house, however, it shone as a small flicker of light. Soon it trailed beyond sight.

They all stared off into the distance not knowing what to make of the phenomenon. No one spoke. Slowly Anton shuffled back onto the covered porch and started to go inside, when all of a sudden a bloodcurdling scream echoed from somewhere out in the darkness. Jeff and Orhan rushed to the front gate of the garden courtyard and peered down the lane in both directions.

"It sounded like it came from the left," said Orhan.

"No, it came from across that field straight ahead," said Jeff.

"You're both wrong," corrected Jonathan coming up alongside them. "It came from the right, down that road."

The three men proceeded with caution as they walked through the muck and mire of the rain-soaked wagon road in the direction that Jonathan had indicated. They slogged through about half a mile of mud and puddles when they came to a paved road that much to their surprise ran along the Aegean coastline. None of them had any idea they were so close to the sea. They strained to see through the rain down the road in both directions; it seemed clear to the left as it ran straight along the coast, but to the right it veered forming a bend about one hundred yards to the north. When they reached the bend, they could see that it was no more than a gentle curve that straightened past an elbow of the mountainside. There in the distance, distorted by the torrential rain, was the silhouette of a transport truck parked along side of the road. Three men sat in the front seat with their heads on their chests as if they had fallen asleep.

Orhan ran to the driver's side door and knocked on the window. No movement. He rubbed the glass with his coat sleeve to remove enough of the rivulets of water to see more clearly inside. He cupped his hands to his eyes and squinted into the dark cab, then stumbled backwards off the running board and pointed frantically at the truck.

"Mustafa!" he gasped.

The other two ran to the truck and peered in to see Mustafa, Juli, and Besnik slumped in their seats as if asleep. Orhan yanked open the driver's side door and checked Mustafa for any sign of life. He was sleeping; a soft snore escaped his mouth.

"He's alive," said Orhan, relieved.

Jonathan checked Besnik and Juli. Besnik also seemed to be asleep, but there was something odd about the way Juli sat. It was hard to determine in the dark. Jeff noticed that Mustafa sat with his foot still on the brake and the truck in gear as if he had just pulled over for a moment. The ignition was on, but the gas gauge indicated that the tank was empty.

"They must have just pulled over and fallen asleep with the engine running," said Jeff stepping back out of Orhan's way as he hopped backwards off the running board onto the road. He walked around to the back of the truck and lifted up a corner of the tarp. Inside were five other men lying in various positions of slumber. "There are more guys back here," he hollered up to the front.

Orhan gently shook Mustafa, who groaned quietly and snorted through his nose but otherwise remained asleep. Orhan shook him more firmly. Still no response. Finally Orhan shouted in Mustafa's ear and jolted him with a firm shake. Mustafa tried to open his eyes but was overcome by the effort and fell forward against the steering wheel.

"Something is wrong," said Orhan stepping back. "I think they've been drugged or something."

"Or worse," said Jonathan getting the same lack of reaction from Besnik. "Do you see what this guy in the middle is holding on his lap?"

Orhan noticed for the first time the golden cube from his vantage point. Jeff came up next to him and leaned past him into the cab.

"I saw it when I came up," said Jeff. "It is identical to the one from my dream. It's Ölüm's prison."

"Why would he be holding it on his lap?" questioned Jonathan perturbed. "I think even I would smart enough not to do that."

"I didn't see Ermal back there," said Jeff. "He was the one who seemed to have all the answers. I wonder where he is. My gosh, look at these guys. They look like they've been through a war."

Jeff had been leaning on Mustafa's shoulder in order to see the cube more clearly in the shadow of the cab. Mustafa groaned and let out a soft cry with a sudden jerk, but then settled back in the seat.

"We've gotta get these guys away from this box," said Jeff as he dragged Mustafa from his seat. Once clear from the truck, he laid the Gypsy down on the wet pavement and stretched him out. Jonathan did the same to Besnik, hauling him around the front of the truck and placing him next to Mustafa.

Orhan tried to grasp Juli in the same way but was thrown off balance by the lack of resistance he had expected from the man's weight. He struggled to reposition himself, but then in the dimness he could see Juli's severed upper torso. Orhan fell backwards from the truck cab landing on his back next to Mustafa.

"He's dead," he gasped in horror.

"My God!" exclaimed Jonathan as he peered into the cab. "He's been burned in two."

Jeff wasted no time as he began dragging the other five men from the back of the truck. Orhan and Jonathan were too shocked to help him. He finally laid the last Gypsy next to Mustafa and Besnik, panting with exhaustion.

"I'm truly sick of this," he blurted, rolling over on his back and struggling for air as the rain pelted his upturned face.

Jonathan went back up into the truck. The torso of Juli lay askew from his hips and legs, but the golden cube remained firmly on his lap. Jonathan struggled to pull out the flashlight that was buried under three layers of his clothing to keep it dry. He studied the dead man and the cube in the low beamed illumination given off by his nearly spent batteries. The cube was sealed and by all appearances intact. Although he knew there had to be a lid, there was no evident crack, as it seemed to be one piece of solid gold. He didn't dare touch it, but pushed against it gently with the rim of his flashlight. It seemed heavier than its mass would indicate from the nudge. He tried desperately not to look at the grotesque wound of the man next to him, but he couldn't help seeing Juli's face out of the corner of his eye. Juli's eyes were open and bulged in what can only be described as extreme terror, as if he had looked into the face of the devil himself when he died.

Suddenly there came a hoarse, croaking, rasping vocalization from behind him. Jeff jumped at the sound and turned to find Mustafa struggling to sit up.

"Don't touch that box!" he commanded, finally getting the words to clear his throat.

Jonathan slipped off the running board and helped Jeff and Orhan prop Mustafa up. The man was indubitably fearful. Panic emanated from his cold, dark eyes as he stared off unseeingly past the men into the truck. He fought off their help and stood shakily to his feet. Stumbling over Besnik still passed out on the pavement, he made his way over to the truck. He looked at Juli with dumbfounded horror, and then slowly lowered his gaze to the cube, muttering something in Romani that none of the others could hear let alone understand. Finally he backed away not taking his eyes off the golden cube. Jeff flicked on his flashlight and trained the beam on Ölüm's coffin. The ruby embedded in the side glistened and shone brilliantly, mesmerizing the men standing there. Suddenly Orhan slapped the flashlight from Jeff's hand, sending it bouncing to the concrete. They blinked as if coming out of a trance and looked away from the box.

"We have to be very careful," said Orhan. "The power of the jinn is not completely bound within the confines of this spell. He can still reach us."

Jeff took a zombie-like step toward the truck, but Orhan shook him hard by the arm bringing him back to the moment. They backed away, as if reading each other's minds, and then dragged the other men farther away from the truck. Soon each began to stir and sit up, the spell placed on them broken by lack of proximity to the cube.

Jeff looked around through the tops of the trees for the small sprite they had seen in the cabin.

"You see any sign of that shadow?" Jonathan asked.

"No," said Jeff. "If it was from Ölüm, then we are lucky we got rid of it when we did."

"This whole thing is just getting creepier and creepier," said Jonathan. "I expect at any minute to hear voices from the audience screaming at us to get out. 'Don't be stupid.' 'Don't go in there!' 'Do you want to die?' It's like some bad spook movie."

"Yeah, but unfortunately we can't just walk out. We're stuck here for the duration." Jeff shook his head. "I wish I had never gotten you and Aubrey into this."

"Me too, but since we're in this, what do you propose we do next?"

The two friends glanced over their shoulders at the others, particularly Mustafa who was walking around in a daze.

"I don't know, but he's not going to be much help until he snaps out of it," said Jeff. "We need to get back to Aubrey at any rate. I can't believe we just went off and left her with Anton and that weirdo daughter of his."

They went back to Orhan, who was still helping some of the men to their feet. They behaved as drunk or drugged. They did not even speak; their main focus was just keeping their feet. Jeff pulled Orhan to the side.

"We need a new plan," he said speaking covertly into Orhan's ear. "I don't think we can depend on the Gypsies for now. I want to get back to Aubrey. Stay here with Jonathan, and I'll go get her and the Albanians."

"Right. Maybe Anton will know what to do with the box," said Orhan. "I don't want to be the one to touch it without knowing how to handle it."

Mustafa staggered over to them trying hard to appear normal, but he still lacked a great deal of control over his motor skills. As he came closer, Jeff could see that his lips were cracked and parched, and his skin shone moist and clammy, taking on a greenish hue that was evident even in the dim light of the cloudy night. The rain had finally stopped, but a stiff wind off of the Aegean kept the deeper, darker clouds rolling in from the sea, obscuring the moon. Mustafa tried to form words, but no sound escaped his lips. Frustrated he spat out a curse in Romani and tried again.

"*Ve mush shecure box, no one hold,*" he stammered with slurred speech.

It suddenly dawned on Jeff what he had seen in his dream. "I think I know how to handle it," he said. "In my vision I saw Lleshi wrap the golden cube in a linen cloth. Everyone who touched it afterward kept the linen wrapped around it. Maybe that has some significance."

"You might be right," said Jonathan. "That poor bugger in the truck learned the hard way how *not* to carry it."

"The problem is we don't have any linen," said Jeff.

"I saw some linen back in the house," said Orhan. "I will go get it and the others. You stay here with Mustafa."

He trotted back up the wagon road to the village, keeping to the grassy areas along the edges to avoid the deep, water-filled muddy ruts. He had to slow his pace due to the irregularity of the ground and the heavy foliage that lined the road. Finding himself snagged on a thorn bush, he stopped to free himself when he heard sloshing through the water up ahead. He started to call out but thought better of it and decided to keep himself concealed in the shadows until he knew for sure what was coming his way.

Ursella trudged passed him, cursing under her breath in Albanian. Her head was down as she picked her way through the ruts. He thought about confronting her but he was so stunned by what he had just seen back at the trucks he didn't know what to do. *What is she doing out here?* He thought to himself. She continued in the direction he had just come from, not perceiving she was being watched. When she had progressed farther down the road, he darted out of the shadows and ran back to the house as fast as he could, not caring about the road conditions.

He slammed through the front door nearly falling into the hall. Aubrey and Anton sat wrapped in blankets next to a roaring fire in the fireplace. They jumped, startled at Orhan's intrusive entrance.

"I saw Ursella leave. Is everything all right?" he asked out of breath.

"Yes. We're OK," said Aubrey putting down her mug of hot tea on the fire stone. "We got worried when you were gone so long. Ursella went to check on you. Are you guys all right?"

"We are for the most part. We found Mustafa and what's left of his Gypsies. Most of them are dead, but they did manage to capture Ölüm. Unfortunately we found out in a most horrible fashion that the box can only be handled in a special manner." He paused for a moment and rummaged around in the old armoire where he had seen a linen tablecloth earlier as he was looking for dry clothes. Folding it under his arm, he came back out to Aubrey and Anton. "Jeff said that in his dream the cube was always covered by a linen cloth when it was being transported. We need to get back to the truck. Are you ready to go?"

Aubrey and Anton stood and moved toward the door without speaking. They all grabbed the packs that the others had left behind and headed back down the wagon trail toward the main road. The full moon shone brightly now, as the clouds had moved farther inland leaving the sky a spectacular array of brilliant constellations. As they neared the road, the breeze off of the Aegean Sea was moist and chilly with a heavy aroma of salt.

They arrived at the truck finding Jeff and Mustafa arguing over the presence of Ursella. The other men had now gained their bearings and stood in a circle around her, intent on not letting her escape.

"She is possessed by that demon!" shouted Mustafa. "I will not trust her. We have lost too many already."

"She has had the spirit of the jinn removed from her," argued Jeff.

"How? How is that possible?" argued back Mustafa looking at Ursella with contempt.

"We have met a man from Albania," argued Jeff being careful not to reveal that the man just happened to be Ursella's father. "He was able to release her from Ölüm's power. I know as well as you do that she was a minion of the jinn, but she has given us no trouble since her release."

"Who is this man? And where is he?" snorted Mustafa, still not convinced.

"I am here," said Anton walking up with Orhan and Aubrey. "I am an old man who has learned more than he should about dark and troublesome deeds. I am Anton Rustemi, and I am here at your service, such as it is."

"And what do you know of this woman and the power the jinn?" questioned Mustafa stepping closer to the old man to study him by the light of the moon.

"I admit that my knowledge of such things is only recent, but my knowledge of this woman is slightly more extensive. She is my daughter."

At these words Jeff cringed. He didn't have any idea how the Gypsy would view this revelation, but he knew it would not be good. Much to his chagrin, he was right. Mustafa started to lunge at the old man, but then caught himself and took a quick few steps backward, pulling out a nine-millimeter Beretta and aiming it first at Anton then at Ursella finally back at Anton. The other men quickly aimed their weapons at the pair.

"She killed many of my clansmen at the ruins," said Mustafa menacingly. "I will not trust what few men I have left to them."

"She will be able to give us valuable information about the jinn," said Jeff. "I don't like it any more than you, but that's the way it is."

Ursella had remained silent through this exchange. She knew the grudge of the Gypsy was justified, but the danger she faced with the jinn was greater.

"She has an evil eye," continued Mustafa suspiciously. He glared at Jeff. "If she is allowed to stay with us and causes more harm to my men, I will hold you personally responsible. Ancestral vow or no ancestral vow, I will avenge their blood with yours." He turned to Anton giving him a menacing glare. "Your's as well."

*　*　*

They decided that the best course of action would be to get some rest in what was left of the night. Orhan carefully wrapped the cube in the linen cloth making sure that he didn't touch it any more than he had to. Mustafa then took charge of it and placed it in a large inner pocket of his cloak. They gently wrapped Juli's body in a tarp and laid him in the back of the truck. Then they heaved and rolled the truck off the main road, parking it on the wagon road to the village. Besnik chose to stay in the truck with Juli to protect him from 'fell spirits' as he referred to them.

It was nearly two o'clock in the morning when they found various spots in the living room of the house to curl up and sleep. Jeff lay down next to Aubrey again and watched the dance of the fire shadows flicker along the ceiling. For the first time in his life, he was terrified at what his dreams might bring. He sighed deeply as if leaping into the unknown, then closed his eyes and fell asleep.

# 20. A Sinister Load on a Bumpy Road

Aydin Village
Early morning

Jeff woke with a start. He had slept dreamlessly, which he was very thankful for. He sat up to find himself alone except for Anton, who was putting a few more fagots on the fire. Jeff rubbed his eyes and stretched.

"Where are the others?" he asked.

"They have gone to push the truck down to a gas station. It apparently is not far, and is downhill most of the way."

"Aubrey went with them?" Jeff asked, looking around in disappointment.

"Yes. They were going to wake you, but she talked them into letting you rest." He smiled at Jeff in a fatherly manner. "She cares for you a great deal, I think."

"Yeah. The feeling's mutual. I wish I had never gotten her into this, but I'm glad she's here. Does that sound terrible?"

"No. I know exactly what you mean," said Anton.

Just then the sound of the truck's revving engine and the grinding of the gears as it bounced its way down the muddy wagon road caused Jeff to jump up and go out on the front porch. The morning was sunny and crisp. Puffy clouds rimmed the horizon, but the warmth from the sun was revitalizing. Anton came up behind Jeff and offered him a mug of hot *çai*. Jeff took the beverage and thanked him with a smile.

Soon Orhan and Aubrey came around the corner of the house followed by the others. The road was too narrow to get the truck any closer to the house.

"There you are, sleepyhead," said Aubrey as she gave Jeff a good-morning hug. "We were wondering if you were going to get up today."

Jonathan and Orhan gave Jeff dirty looks, clearly not happy they had had to push the truck to the gas station. The road was not as much of a downhill slope as Anton had thought. Ursella came next around the corner followed by Mustafa, who still had the look of mistrust on his face.

"We need to continue our journey," said Mustafa rotating his sore wrist. "I understand that Jeff has had a vision and knows where to find the cube of the other twin."

"Well actually, I'm not a hundred percent sure where the cube is, but I feel I would recognize the place if I saw it," said Jeff trying to avert his attention from his angry friends. "It's way up in the mountains in northern Albania in a cave situated in a narrow valley."

"Well, that narrows it down," said Jonathan snidely.

"Northern Albania has very steep and in some places impassable mountains," said Anton. "I know those mountains as well as anyone, but there are still areas that are so remote I am not sure if humans have ever set foot in them."

"We'll worry about that when we get there," said Mustafa. "Right now we have a very long road ahead of us if we go by land. The truck may not be able to make it all the way. To go by sea is not a good option either."

"We'll have to make do with what we have," said Orhan. "We can go as far as the truck will take us, and then rely on public transportation or hitchhike."

Anton came back out onto the front porch with a basket of biscuits he had made. They were quickly grabbed up by the hungry band. As they ate they decided the best course of action was to follow the coast road up as far as Çanakkale, sell the truck, and then cross the Dardanelles by ferry. They could then get another vehicle and travel through European Turkey into Greece and come into Albania from the southeast.

They buried Juli in a field that overlooked the small valley and the village. No one had determined why the village was abandoned, but Orhan surmised that it was due to the villagers leaving for larger cities looking for better work.

The truck was an old military transport with bench seats in the back. Aubrey sat in the front seat between Anton and Mustafa, who was driving. The others crowded into the back of the truck and tried to get as comfortable as possible on the benches. Jeff sat directly across from Ursella, who maintained an aloof demeanor. She obviously had no intention of carrying on a conversation with anyone, particularly since all of these men held a grudge against her for the loss of their clansmen. The Gypsy men sat quietly, each in his own thoughts, and in various levels of pain from wounds they bore. All without exception contemplated the death of Ursella.

The linen-wrapped golden cube rode safely in a wooden crate at the back of the truck. So far the effects experienced the night before had not recurred. Each person had his or her own "buddy" to ensure that no one fell off into anything more than a light nap.

The ride in the back was cold and bumpy. The only thing good that could be said about it was that the strain everyone used to stay seated and not be flung all over each other or out of the back onto the road actually kept them warm. Jeff looked at the faces of his fellow passengers. Jonathan and Orhan had nodded off, their heads bobbing off their chests with each jolt from the road. The Gypsy men remained alert but didn't offer an opening for Jeff to strike up a conversation with them. Ursella was the only one who occasionally made eye contact with him.

"Your English is pretty good?" He knew it was a weak way to start a conversation, but he couldn't think of a better way.

She glared at him for a moment, her facial features as hard as a backwater judge. She studied Jeff, realizing for the first time that he had saved her the night before from the angry Gypsies, and then finally said, "At the university. I learned English while I was an economics student in Korça."

Jeff looked at her, puzzled.

"You think it strange that I went to university to study economics?" she asked, finally letting her guard down a little.

"Well, no... Well, yes. I don't know," he said, exasperated. Jeff didn't know exactly how he felt about Ursella. He still harbored resentment and mistrust, but he just had a feeling she wasn't all bad. "I just can't figure out how you could have allowed yourself to become so...so evil. Were you brainwashed or something? I'd really like to try and understand before writing you off completely."

"I barely remember my real father and mother," she started. "I vaguely remember my mother dying. It was later that I learned she had been murdered in order to keep a factory secret. I lived with the man I thought was my father until he died. Later I found out he had been murdered also. I was raised to believe in no god except for the one found within myself. I now realize that I have been lied to, and surrounded by people who used me for their own ends. I was even sent to the university to study economics so that I could help my father's, I mean my uncle's, circle of 'friends' fund their various enterprises.

"No, I *would* expect someone like you to have a hard time understanding someone like me. You come from America and have had everything handed to you. You, I would guess, have loving parents who took care not to lie to you. So you were raised innocent. You and I are exact opposites. I followed my path easily because it had been made to seem as natural as breathing." She paused for a moment staring at Jeff with renewed interest. "Do you want to know something crazy? It wasn't until last night when I saw you and that girl…"

"Aubrey."

"Yes. The affection you showed to each other was the first time I had any hint of what love might be like. Never in my entire life has anyone showed me real kindness or affection. It has always been to satisfy someone else's needs or wants or to coerce me to do things they wanted me to do. No…you and I have nothing in common. So do not judge me. You can only imagine hell. I can describe it in detail, because I have lived there every day of my life."

Jeff realized that he had no argument. He looked past the men to his right and peered through a gap in the canvas at the road behind them. Pursing his lips, he began to speak, but Ursella cut him off.

"You don't have to say anything. I am not looking for pity. My life is what it is. I have no expectation of growing old, but now that I have met my real father maybe some things will be different." She closed her eyes and laid her head back against the side of the vehicle, dismissing any further comment from Jeff.

Meanwhile, Besnik listened with his eyes closed. He would *never* trust her, he thought. The death of his brother and Ermal last night had sealed her fate as far as he was concerned. He decided to bide his time for now; she might indeed be useful later.

\* \* \*

Jeff watched the others. They seemed to be doing all right. No ill effects of the cube in such close proximity. The linen must be working. He began to relax a little, or as much as he could sitting upright on a rock-hard bench that jolted with every bump in the road — and there were a lot of bumps. Catching

Orhan watching him through the barest of slits in his eyelids, he smiled at his friend, who smiled softly back.

They traveled throughout the day. Fitful attempts at uncomfortable sleep were about all any of them were able to accomplish. Mustafa continued to drive, and with no one begging to stop he pushed onward making the best time he could.

One particularly violent jolt woke Jeff up fully, and he looked around at his travel companions to find everyone else in a similar state of alertness. His head and stomach began to ache. No food, exhaustion, and the rocking, banging motion were taking its toll. He made his way to the very back and stuck his head out from under the tarp. The sky was a bright blue. The landscape to the right was winter drab but with hints of green growing from the hillsides. To the left the Aegean reflected the azure of the sky. The chill on the wind felt good at first after being cooped up in the truck, but soon it began to bite bitterly against his face. As his carsickness passed, he ducked back into his place on the bench.

"Feel better?" said Jonathan, who had his eyes closed again and his head back against the canvas.

"Yeah. It's pretty nice outside. Cold, but at least it isn't raining."

"Do you know were we are?"

"We should be somewhere between Havran and Çanakkale," said Orhan only slightly opening his eyelids. "It feels like we're heading west. We will veer north through the Gelibolu peninsula. You might know it as Gallipoli." He straightened up on his bench and stretched. "This is a famous part of the world. It's too bad we won't be able to stop to enjoy it."

"I've heard of Gallipoli," said Jonathan. "A big battle in World War One, I think."

"I saw the movie," interjected Jeff without further comment.

Orhan continued, "Yes. It was actually the only major battle won during the war by the coalition of the Central Powers. The Turkish forces were lead by Atatürk himself. He was a general at the time. Because of the fame of that victory, he was able to oppose the last of the Ottoman sultans, Mehmet the Sixth, in nineteen twenty-two. Turkey became a Republic after that time, and Atatürk led it until he died in nineteen thirty-eight. Troy is there which was made famous by Homer, and there are some very interesting museums." Orhan seemed revived now that he was talking history.

"I've read Homer, and I studied lost civilizations in college so I learned all about Herr Doktor Heinrich Schliemann and his investigations of the ruins of Troy," said Jeff. He felt that anything that could keep his mind off the journey would be a welcome relief. "Tell us a little more about Atatürk at Gallipoli? He's a pretty famous guy here in Turkey. I mean, you can't swing a dead cat without hitting a portrait of him somewhere. He's on every coin and lira. His picture is in every restaurant, hotel, and shop. So did that one battle really make him that famous?"

"Yes, in a sense it did," said Orhan. "Of course, my Uncle Ümët would have disagreed, but the rule of the sultans had been very unfavorable for many years. People were tired of the hardships of daily life that were caused by the expense of maintaining an empire. When the Ottomans aligned themselves with the Germans and the Austro- Hungarians, all the rivalry that was going on in Europe for power and lands just didn't sit well with the average Turkish peasant and city dweller. Of course, Turkey was in a key position against the Russians. We controlled the Black Sea. Nothing went in or out without passing through the Bosphorus and the Dardanelles, particularly the Dardanelles. Many battles have taken place there, but the fact

233

that Atatürk and his army repelled the British and Australians at Gelibolu made him a great hero with the sultan and the Ottomans. Unfortunately for them he felt they were selling Turkey to foreigners one piece at a time.

"When the Central Powers were defeated by the allies, Turkey was divided up amongst the conquering nations. We were overrun by French, Italians, British, Greeks, you name it. Atatürk blamed the weakness of the sultan for getting Turkey into the war on the wrong side, for one thing, and then allowing Turkey to become the tramping ground of the Allied powers. It didn't take long for him to win the military and the people to his way of thinking. So in nineteen twenty-two, the sultanate was abolished. The sultan went into exile, and the old Ottoman Empire that had ruled for six hundred years came to an end. In its placed is the Turkish Republic that you have become so fond of today.

"There were a number of battles fought to oust the foreigners. It got particularly bloody when it came to the Greeks and the Armenians, but those stories change depending on which side you talk to."

The truck suddenly came to a stop. The Gypsy men sat up in their seats and began arranging their gear to exit the truck; and Ursella, who had been sleeping, woke up with a start. Apparently she had fallen into a deeper sleep than she intended and the sudden lack of motion startled her. She slid to the edge of her seat holding an ornate dagger she had slipped from under her coat. Besnik watched her warily, but she made no sign of aggression toward anyone in the truck. Finally after seeing that there was nothing to be alarmed about, she replaced the dagger in its scabbard and repositioned the flap of her coat.

Mustafa lifted the corner of the tarp and peered into the back. Jeff could see Aubrey walking off the stiffness in her legs along the road behind him. Anton came to Mustafa's side.

"We will take a short break," said Mustafa. "Get out and stretch your legs."

With a great deal of effort they all spilled out of the back of the truck. They had traveled for almost six hours without rest. Jeff looked around for Aubrey and saw her making her way up a shallow ravine. Ursella pushed past him and followed her.

"OK," he said. "Boys over here. Girls up there."

The sea was no longer visible, but the brisk air was still scented with brine. The road was winding in a more northerly direction. Jeff strode over to where Mustafa was standing with the other men. They looked up at him indifferently, ignoring his presence, but Jeff felt their sullen mood. He decided it best to attribute it to the loss of Ermal and his men and tried not to take it personally, but the bitterness that was emanating was unmistakable. He steeled his courage and interrupted their discussion.

"Where are we exactly?" he asked trying to seem friendly, low-key, and unobtrusive.

Mustafa glared at him for a moment, and Jeff hoped that his expression did not give his feeling of total intimidation away. Then Mustafa half folded the map he and Besnik were looking at and handed it to a Gypsy Jeff had heard referred to by the name of Nicoli.

"We are fifty kilometers from Çanakkale. I would not have stopped, but Aubrey needed to," he said. "We will cross by ferry as soon as we arrive there."

"I'm sorry about Ermal, and the others," said Jeff hesitantly, still not certain if Mustafa was angry with him.

"He knew the risk. His was a good death. He saved all of us." Mustafa reflected for a moment. "I am afraid that you will find I am not the man Ermal was. I do not have his knowledge or skill in this matter."

Jeff gave a silent sigh of relief. At least Mustafa's mood was not against him or the other three. Jeff tried to cheer him up.

"I think Anton may be of some help, maybe even Ursella."

"We will never trust her," said Mustafa matter-of-factly staring back up toward the ravine in which Aubrey and Ursella had disappeared. "Even by her death she will not atone for our loss, but you may be right. They do seem to possess some knowledge that may be of use to us."

Aubrey stumbled back onto the road from the muddy ditch the ravine ran into. She limped tiredly to Jeff but kept him between herself and Mustafa. The gesture was not lost on Mustafa, as he scowled at her and walked back to the other Gypsies. Jeff noticed and pulled her gently to him in a protective manner

"Are you all right?" he whispered.

"No, I'm not," she said irritably not being as discreet as Jeff in the volume of her response. She realized that she had blurted out her frustration, drawing attention to herself, and leaned into Jeff more closely. "I am not all right," she repeated in a whisper that only Jeff could hear. "And neither are you. I'm not riding up in the front with those two any more. I will ride in the back with you." She dismissed any argument from him by walking off and standing with her back to him beside the road, looking out toward the field to the west. The sun was moving into early evening. Jeff went to her side, glancing over his shoulder toward the Gypsies. He couldn't tell if they had been made suspicious by her outburst, but regardless they had resumed their discussion over the map.

"So what's wrong?" he asked.

"I sat between those two idiots for six hours with my leg throbbing and them arguing over I don't know what all. One was yelling in Albanian and the other yelling in Romani. I thought I was going to lose my mind. When they did speak English it wasn't good news. Apparently the other genie in Albania has not even been released yet. The cycles aren't always the same. The pedigree moon is the key. Some years there is only one and other years there are two. If there is only one in a year, then they are released at the same time. But if there are two in a year they are released at different times. It's a real mess to try and understand, and I don't think they really know what is going on." She turned to face him tilting her face up to his. "They want to use you and the box as bait." She embraced Jeff, putting her arms around him and holding tightly. "Jeff, I'm scared."

He knew there were no words to comfort her. Lies of good fortune would only make things worse. He held her firmly and tried to ease her fears by being strong, but in his own heart and mind he knew that things were going to get a whole lot worse before they got better. Just then they were interrupted by Jonathan, who greeted them from up the road. He was eating an apple.

"Hey, you guys want some fruit? There's a roadside vender with a table set up just around the bend."

"Yeah, we'll be there in a minute," Jeff yelled back. He kept his arm around Aubrey's shoulder and turned to walk up the road. "Whatever happens I won't leave you. I promise."

Orhan came around the bend in the road carrying a sackful of apples, which he immediately began dispensing to the others. After greedily consuming them, the company reloaded into the truck. This time Besnik and Nicoli sat in the front with Mustafa. Anton came to sit next to Ursella. She started to shift away from him, but then relaxed giving him the faintest of smiles.

* * *

The short break had rejuvenated them all and before long they were slowing again with the sound of traffic suddenly all around them. The smell of the sea was strong. They had finally arrived in Çanakkale. Mustafa made his way to the marina and stopped the truck.

Jeff helped Aubrey out of the back. Her wounded leg was stiffening up making it painful to move. She stamped her foot lightly to get the circulation flowing again. "It actually feels much better," she said trying to sound brave.

Jeff looked at the other men, six Gypsies counting Mustafa, plus Ursella and Anton, and the four of them. He shook his head in dismay. How were they going to confront another genie, let alone capture it with just twelve people? The cost to take Ölüm had been excessively high. He looked across the marina at the flotilla that made up this small fishing village. The outline of the shore on the other side of the waterway was marked by the lights of buildings barely visible in the haze of coming night.

Mustafa called Orhan over to him as they approached a fisherman who had just docked his small *caiques* at the pier. After a brief exchange, the man pointed toward the ferry landing. Orhan came back to where Jeff was standing with Jonathan and Aubrey while Mustafa went back to his clansmen who were guarding the truck.

"We're going to walk over to the ferry pier and wait for the others while they try to find someone who will buy the truck," said Orhan. "We need to get across to the other side as soon as we can. The minions of Ölüm are still out there somewhere. He wants to be on the European side before they have a chance to set up an ambush."

"That makes sense to me," said Jonathan. "About how far is it across to the other side?"

"It narrows to about a kilometer," said Orhan. "Not far. The ferry will take us over, and then we can look for other transportation to go the rest of the way to Albania."

As they walked, the truck chugged past them, gears grinding until they fit. The tarp was pulled and lashed to the side revealing Mustafa's men sitting expressionless on the benches. They began to give Jeff an eerie feeling. They were too mechanical. Too aloof. If they were all really on the same side, it was an uneasy alliance at best. Jeff didn't like things he couldn't understand, and he definitely did not understand these Gypsies. He came to the conclusion that he was probably never going to understand them, and the main reason was that they didn't want him to understand them. "You learn by watching, not asking," Orhan had said. "You will never learn anything from the Gypsy if you ask a direct question. It is engrained in them from birth to be allusive and deceitful to outsiders. It is how they have survived so much persecution over the centuries. If you want to learn anything about the Gypsy, you simply watch him, but be careful that you don't let him see you watching him." That advice, given while they were sitting in the grand living room of Ümët in his shoreside *yalıs*, seemed so long ago. Life was so simple then. How long ago was it? Just five days ago? Maybe six? Jeff couldn't honestly remember for sure.

Aubrey took his hand in hers as they walked. The moon shone brightly on the masts and yardarms of the small sailboats and fishing vessels. As they neared the ferry pier, a large oil tanker made its way slowly through the straights on its way to the Marmara Sea, and then to Istanbul and the Black Sea beyond. Ursella walked alongside Jonathan and Orhan, while Anton trudged more slowly to the rear. Intent on reaching their rendezvous with the Roma, no one noticed the scurried movement of dark assailants in the shadows amongst the shacks and crates along the dock.

Time was running out.

# 21. Swift Current to Danger

Çanakkale, Turkey
7:00 p.m.

Ursella was the first to notice the shift in shadows. Her eyes went wide searching through the darkness. A single lamp lit a small area fifteen meters away, but they were at its fringes. She pulled her dagger out from under her coat and brandished it in the direction of the nearest shack. Her action alerted Jeff and Orhan, who quickly pulled out the weapons they had been carrying since the ruins. Jonathan and Aubrey were the only ones oblivious to the danger, as they were watching the oil tanker thread its way through the narrow straights of the Dardanelles.

A man ran out from behind a crate, charging Aubrey and Jonathan with a long fisherman's pike. He raised it, preparing to spear Jonathan between the shoulders, when Jeff, drawn to the commotion, shouted a warning. Jonathan turned quickly in time to side step the thrust and grab the wooden handle, using the man's momentum against him to fling him head over heels into the prow of a small *caique*. The minion struck his head against the gunwale and went limp.

Aubrey crouched to the ground and covered her ears against the loud reports of the gunfire. Through a hail of bullets coming from three different directions, she ran hunched over to a small rowboat that had been pulled up onto the dock and turned upside down.

Orhan and Jeff fell in behind a crate and began firing in all directions, not really sure of where their enemies lay. Ursella grabbed her father roughly by the wrist and dragged him behind the safety of a weathered, brine worn shack.

Jonathan kept the pike as he slid in next to Aubrey. "Are you OK?' he asked poking his head out from behind the rowboat to get a better look.

"I'm all right," said Aubrey through clenched teeth. She grabbed the knap of Jonathan's coat and tugged him down behind the boat. "What are you trying to do? Get your head blown off?"

Jeff shot off all fifteen of his rounds. When the action locked open after the last round was ejected, he realized that he not only had no more ammunition, but he had absolutely no idea how to reload even if he did.

"I'm out of bullets!" he shouted in Orhan's ear over the pops and staccato of ricochets peppering all around them.

"Don't yell so loud. Do you want *them* to know you're out of bullets?" hissed Orhan with a frown. He handed Jeff a full clip from his pack. "Mustafa gave me these earlier."

"OK, but how do you load it?"

Orhan rolled his eyes and slinked down on his rump snatching the Beretta from Jeff.

"Here, you push this button. The old one snaps out. You push the new one in like this, and then pull back on this lever like that, and you're ready to go," he said demonstrating as he explained. He didn't give Jeff a chance to ask questions as he thrust the weapon back into his friend's hands and repositioned himself behind the crate.

Suddenly the two men were slammed backwards toward the water by an explosion just a few meters away. Jeff found himself completely exposed as he had been flung halfway between his crate, which now lay in shambles, and the rowboat that Aubrey and Jonathan had ducked behind. His ears rang, and his head throbbed. The explosion had thrown Orhan onto his back, and he lay unconscious on the concrete marina pier. Jeff tried to focus, but everything seemed to be moving out of real time. He looked around and could see Aubrey coaxing him toward her position. Slowly the chaos of his surroundings became clearer as the percussion of the impact decrescendoed. He staggered to his knees and crawled frantically to the rowboat.

Jonathan passed him in a low shuttle and grabbed Orhan under his arms, dragging him back to the cover of the *caiques*. He laid him out next to the dock edge. Blood trickled from his ears and nose, but otherwise he seemed intact.

Another explosion to the south obliterated a marina hut. In the flash two silhouetted bodies were flung violently into the water. Jonathan looked over his shoulder to see a motorized launch skipping across the wake made by the oil tanker. Gunfire emanated from the bow: Mustafa's men firing at the flash points of the minion. Jeff could see Besnik at the port side of the launch lobbing another hand grenade into a stand of crates. Several men fled from behind them as the explosion knocked them to the ground. A quick AK-47 burst from Nicoli shattered one man's shoulder and raked across another's chest.

The launch banged into the pier right behind the rowboat. Mustafa was at the helm and shouted for them to jump in. Orhan was gaining consciousness as Jeff and Jonathan dragged him into the boat; Aubrey fell in over top of them. She rolled over just in time to make way for Ursella, who had Anton firmly tucked over her shoulder for support. She was half dragging him as he struggled to keep up. When they collapsed into the bottom of the launch, Mustafa peeled to starboard and into the swift currents of the channel. The smoke from the explosions and the gunfire wafted over the water into the darkness helping to conceal their getaway, as the launch was running without lights. The patter of bullets pinging off the water chased them into the strait, but their assailants were temporarily blinded by the glare of the fires that still burned from the grenades, and none of the bullets found its mark.

The launch slammed into the wave troughs created by the massive tanker, catapulting the escapees in contorted acrobatics. A wash of oil mixed with water sloshed over Orhan's face and he gasped for air and finally regained consciousness, but remained prone, too weak to sit up. Jeff and Aubrey tried to keep his head out of the water that was pooling in the bottom of the boat.

Ursella sat next to her father. Her right hand still held the blood-covered dagger. Blood oozed into the corner of her eye from a wound grazed across her right temple.

Anton was out of breath more than he should be, even for his age, and he was cradling his left arm with his right hand. The light was very dim, but as Jonathan moved to his side he could see the abnormal angle of Anton's wrist. He gently pushed Anton's coat sleeve up his forearm to reveal a fracture. It had not broken the skin, but the malposition of the two ends protruded to a near puncture of the flesh.

"We were nearly killed by one of those grenades," said Ursella. "I barely got him out of the way."

Jonathan glanced at Mustafa and caught the faintest sneer cross his lips. "We need to try and keep his arm immobile," said Jonathan. "I don't know if any of us can set a break that bad or not. I sure don't want to try. I think we need a doctor."

"No doctors," said Mustafa above the drone of the engines. "We have no time. When we meet up with other members of our clan, we will have someone look at it. Until then, keep it steady."

The launch headed back through the Dardanelles toward the Aegean. They skimmed through the rough waters in the middle of the channel. Mustafa felt it best they still cruise without their running lights. The strait was fairly abandoned except for an occasional ferry that darted from one shore to the other.

Jeff clamored up next to Mustafa at the helm. "I thought we were going to cross to the European peninsula," he said.

"We're going around it. We have enough fuel to make it to Greece," he answered. "We found out from a child at the pier that Ölüm's henchmen had crossed to the European side a good hour before we arrived. They have had plenty of time to set up an ambush on both sides of the water. We will simply bypass them."

Jeff settled on the railing of the launch and gazed over to the Gallipoli peninsula on the European side of the strait. The wind was cold on his face, but it had a salty humidity about it that made it bearable.

Orhan, although dazed from the concussion, appeared to be feeling better. He sat up with his back against the side wall. Aubrey and Jonathan studied him with concern.

"I'm all right," he said trying to alleviate their fears. He tenderly wiped the streak of blood from under his nose, giving the smear a nonchalant dismissal.

Jeff waddled over to him trying to keep his balance from the surging of the launch.

"Hey...how are you doing?" he asked sinking down next to his friend.

"Better, I think. I don't really remember what happened. How did I get here? And where are we?"

"Well, long story short, the Gypsies came to the rescue, but they started chucking grenades and you were too close. We are heading out to the Aegean right now. Mustafa said there's an ambush set up for us on the far side, so we are going around it. We're supposed to be heading for Greece." Jeff patted his buddy on the knee. "I'm glad you're OK. It looked pretty serious there for a while."

The boat bounced arrythmically from bow to stern and port to starboard. It suddenly crashed into heavy surf as it came around the point at the tip of the peninsula marked by a lighthouse that herald the entrance to the Dardanelles from the Aegean. They set their course north between the island of Gökçeada and the peninsula.

"We seemed to have made pretty good time," said Jeff coming up next to Mustafa, who was sitting on the wooden crate from the truck.

"Yes. We did," said Mustafa his mood obviously lighter. "We had the surface current with us through the strait." He noticed Jeff's thoughtful expression. "The current in the Dardanelles runs in both directions. The surface current flows from the Marmara Sea to the Aegean. A deeper undercurrent flows from the Aegean to the Marmara."

"Hmm...I didn't know that," said Jeff studiously. After a thoughtful pause he said, "Is anyone else as hungry as I am?"

"We will land at Kaleköy, on that island to our left. We can get food there before we continue on to the coast of Greece," said Mustafa. "How is Orhan?"

"I think he'll be OK," said Jeff. "His color looks better anyway. Jonathan and Aubrey are trying to keep him awake since he may have a concussion."

Orhan was sitting up, and he looked stronger. He was talking to Aubrey when Jeff made his way back to the group.

"Well...how you doing?" Jeff asked.

"I'm so hungry I could eat pork," Orhan said.

"Whoa, that *is* hungry! We're going to stop at a coastal village called Kaleköy on the island over there. We can eat something there," Jeff explained.

The north wind blew in their faces, taking their breath away as Mustafa veered the launch toward the island's coastline. The spirits of the companions became lighter with the hope of landfall and food. Mustafa strained to see into the darkness ahead. His spirit remained agitated with the growing feeling that their troubles had only just begun.

Rob Dakin

# III

Chant the lyric of the enchanter.
Cry out the litany of the necromancer.
Withstand the turbulence of a conjured foe.
Hold fast to the wisdom of the enlightened soul.

# 22. A Portal through Space and Time

The blackness of the horizon was complete and gave Jeff an eerie sensation of emptiness. Above the drone of the twin Chrysler engines the sound of the surf washing up on the beach was the first indication that they were nearing the coast of the largest island in Turkey, Gökçeada. No lights were visible from the small village of Kaleköy as Mustafa had angled the craft to a remote area of rocky beach south of the mouth of the small harbor.

Besnik jumped into the surf up to his knees and tugged the boat up onto the pebbly beach. The rest jumped out on dry ground. Jonathan and Jeff helped Orhan keep his feet as he rolled over the side of the launch while Anton showed a surprising agility for his age and jumped past Aubrey's offered hand.

Mustafa and his group conferred for a moment out of earshot of the others. A short time later, Besnik and another Gypsy named Ilir ran off down the beach toward the harbor. Mustafa came over to Jeff and Orhan but kept his attention inland on what appeared to be a hill.

"We will make for the ruins of a fortress up on that hill," he said. "There we will build a fire and rest for the night. Besnik and Ilir will bring food. We thought it best to keep a low profile. The village is not large, only about ninety people, so we do not want to draw any more attention to ourselves than we have to."

The group began the trudge up the slope. The landscape was barren and rocky. Finally they arrived at the crest of the hill, and stood in the roofless stone wall ruins of an ancient fortress overlooking the bay. Most of the castle had collapsed, leaving sections of the wall jutting up into the sky like snaggly teeth in a bad dentition. Inland to the ruins were red terra-cotta shingled cottages. Some were made of stone, others of concrete blocks. The moon illuminated the village as it flowed down the hill and spread along the banks of the small inlet. The beam of a lighthouse across the bay made its cyclic journey to sea and back to land again.

Aubrey was the first to find a windbreak behind one of the walls. The others quickly joined her, as there was nothing to do but wait for Besnik and Ilir to return with food. The houses closest to the crest of the hill and the old fortress appeared to be vacant, so Mustafa gathered what brush and sticks he could and made a small fire. Soon the dark shadows of the group danced along the ochre and amber hues cast by the flame against the stone wall.

Mustafa and Nicoli stood away from the others in the open, the wind whipping their hair and outer cloaks in a frinzy. They studied the horizon all around, and then Mustafa pulled out his map. The wind forced them to splay the map over a flat stone and hold it down with their four hands and a number of midsized rocks. Finally they stood up and rotated their stance in a circle peering off in every direction. They soon made their way back into the shelter of the ruin wall and confronted Jeff and Orhan.

"We are not on Gökçeada," said Mustafa. "This is a much smaller island and doesn't even appear on the map. Our heading was dead on for Gökçeada."

"What do you think happened?" asked Orhan.

"I'm not sure," said Mustafa. "But I had a suspicion that we were traveling faster than what our instruments indicated. It felt at times like we were being pulled through the water."

"So you're thinking we were diverted here?" asked Jeff.

"I don't know. I hope not. But it is possible," said Mustafa.

The sound of loose shale trickling down the slope alerted them to the arrival of Besnik, Ilir, and most importantly, food. The men ran to the glow of the fire and crouched down quickly to warm themselves. Two canvas sacks were filled with strips of dried spiced lamb, bread, simit, cheese, and flasks of hot tea, which were distributed and eagerly consumed.

"We were planning on stealing what we needed," started Besnik with a greedy mouthful of cheese and bread, "but an old man and woman were sitting out on a bench in front of their home and invited us in. They gave us everything we needed. They have invited us to come in for the night."

"That sounds good to me," said Aubrey. "I don't really want—"

She was interrupted by the presence of an old man, who suddenly appeared at the edge of the firelight. When he saw that they had seen him, he took a step closer. His appearance was that of an old fisherman. In a deeply creased face from years of sea and wind, his eyes were deep and dark, shadowed by a prominent forehead covered to within an inch of his bushy eyebrows by a woolen stocking cap. He stood before them with his oilskin overcoat unbuttoned but pushed shut by his hands, which were in his pockets. He wore black rubber boots to mid-calf that buckled with a toggle clasp but were unlatched. His eyes roamed across the firelit faces that stared at him, ultimately fixing their gaze on Orhan and Jeff. His eyebrows furrowed into a frown.

"Come," he said, and then turned, disappearing into the night.

The group looked uncertainly at each other. Finally Besnik rose to his feet and walked in the direction the old man had gone. One by one they all followed. The air was abruptly frigid away from the warmth of the fire and the protection of the wall. They descended a narrow path until they came to another stand of houses that were lifeless and vacant. Farther down near the water, they could pick up the scent of woodsmoke as they entered the inhabited part of the village. A small cottage stood before them. The old man stamped his boots against a stone slab then entered, opening the door and standing to the side allowing the others to enter.

Mustafa pulled Besnik to the side as the others ducked through the low door.

"Beware," he whispered. "This is not Gökçeada."

"Where are we then?" asked Besnik deeply concerned and eying the old man suspiciously.

"I really have no idea, but we think we were drawn here somehow. Be extra alert."

The interior was gloomy in the outer central hall, but as they began to pull off their shoes an inner door opened and the heat from a wood burning stove spilled out and surrounded them with warmth. An old woman, hunched over, shawl-draped, and wearing a black dress with worn pink house slippers, greeted them with a nod and bade them enter with the sweep of her gnarled hand. Strands of gray hair dangled from under a black scarf that sat loosely upon her elderly head as if she had hurriedly replaced it before they arrived.

Without words they were welcomed and offered a place to sit on three threadbare futons with sagging cushions that sat up against three of the walls. The old man indicated that they should continue to finish eating the food they had brought from the hilltop. The pair then left shutting the inner door behind them.

The atmosphere in the tiny room was relaxing, and the stove gave off enough heat that soon the company began peeling their outer garments off in layers. Orhan quickly fell asleep with his head back against the high cushion of the futon. He had eaten his share and felt much better. His friends reluctantly allowed him to sleep, but watched him closely for danger signs from a possible concussion due to his injury earlier.

Jeff looked around the sparsely decorated room. An old calendar dating back to 1996 displayed a picture of a Greek Orthodox Church. On the wall above the stove hung an iconic portrait of Mary the mother of Jesus decoupaged on a polished piece of dark pine. A tapered basket of plastic flowers hung on the wall above Jeff's head. From the ceiling a single light bulb hung by its cord, giving the room a faint, yellowish glow. The floor was made of rough, uneven wooden slats that were covered by a well-worn Bergama wool carpet.

Soon the old man pushed his way through the green wooden hall door that rubbed heavily across the floor and creaked with the strain of the effort, rousing Orhan. The old woman followed carrying a stack of sheets and blankets. Without speaking she indicated to the two women that they were to go to another room where beds had already been prepared. The men stood as the old man lowered the backs of the futons to the bed position and the old woman began spreading the sheets. Orhan helped the old man, who spoke to him in Turkish.

"You will have to share two to a bed, and the rest of you will sleep on the floor," he said. "We will make a cushion for you. It will be comfortable. You will see."

It did not take long for the men to pair up, and soon they had all stretched out and turned out the light. Almost immediately the raspy snores of the Gypsy men filled the room with an unmelodious din that ground into the nerves of Jeff and Orhan. Jonathan, on the other hand, joined the Gypsy chorus with his own version.

"It's really great of this couple to put us up for the night," whispered Jeff. "I wasn't looking forward to sleeping out on top of that hill."

"Yes, it is," Orhan agreed. "They are actually brother and sister. They are Greek, I think. There was a strange accent in his Turkish. Most of the islanders are Turkish, but there are a few

Greeks here. The old man said that he was near the water this evening as some of the fishermen came in. There were two strangers asking around if they had seen other strangers come from the sea, and telling them that they would be paid if they reported anyone else coming to the village. The old man said he didn't trust their look, so he and his sister sat out on the bench and watched for us. I thanked him for his hospitality, but he just waved me off and said, 'We are not barbarians. We would not let someone sleep out in the cold.'"

\* \* \*

The old man peered through a crack in the door to see that his guests had turned in for the night. The old woman stood at his side.

"Do they suspect anything?" she whispered in his ear.

"No. They believe the story I told them," said the old man. "We will wait for the others to come. Once we have the two alone we will take them."

The old woman smiled. "This is good this plan of yours. Soon it will all be over."

The old man changed his attention from the crack to the room down the dark hall where the two women slept. He pursed his lips in determination. *"That* woman I will deal with myself. She will not be given a swift death like the others."

They crept to the door of the room in which Aubrey and Ursella slept. A small crack existed between the edge of the door and the doorjam. The old man looked through it to see the two women curled up back to back sound a sleep. He stared at the older one with hatered in his eyes. *Your time will come soon* he thought.

\* \* \*

Suddenly an explosion rattled the windowpanes, and the wooden floor bucked under them from the concussion. Immediately Mustafa and his men were up with weapons drawn. Besnik shined his flashlight at the wooden crate in the corner. It remained where they had placed it.

Nicoli ran into the house from the outside. He had slipped out unnoticed while the old man was preparing the room. "They have destroyed the fortress ruins!" he said to Mustafa. "There are men combing the abandoned houses, coming this way."

"How many?" asked Mustafa peering out from behind the curtain that covered the window.

"I estimate eight to ten," said Nicoli. "They used grenades to blow up the campfire. They are careless fools. They did not even check to see if we were there."

Ursella came in from the other room and overheard Nicoli's comment.

"They are careless because they think they have the power of the jinn behind them," she offered. "If they are the same from the Ephesus ruins and Çanakkale, they may be unaware of what we have in our possession."

"We will make that work to our advantage," said Mustafa. He ordered the rest of his men outside to intercept Ölüm's minions. "You two must stay here," he said to Jeff and Orhan. "*You* will come with us," he said nudging his chin toward Jonathan.

After several minutes an eruption of gunfire could be heard up the hill. Aubrey, who had remained behind with Jeff, sank into the corner of the room away from the window. She felt an odd tingling sensation running through the muscles of her legs and up her spine, turning into burning pain. She jumped away from the corner to find she had inadvertently sat on Ölüm's crate. The pain, although temporary, caused her to fall over the arm of one of the futons.

Jeff and Orhan had not been paying attention, but Anton was quick to catch her before she hit the floor. Jeff was rushing to her side when the front door burst open and an armed gunman jumped into the hall. He took a shooting stance aiming his weapon at the prone form of Aubrey, who was just recovering from her fall. A shotgun blast from the outside reverberated through the plaster-covered stone walls as the gunman was thrown into the room from the impact of the pellets. A Gypsy appeared at the door and checked his fallen victim, and then ran back out into the night.

A rattle of machine gun fire peppered through the front door spraying the hall with bullets. Jeff saw a shadowy movement through the frosted glass of the window and fired his Beretta at it. The bullet missed but was close enough that the second assailant dove behind a fish-gutting table in the yard.

"He's behind that table!" shouted Jeff to Orhan.

Orhan picked up the AK-47 of the fallen minion and positioned himself at the front door. The gunman turned the table over for protection, but it was top heavy with elongated legs and rolled all the way over landing with its legs sticking straight up into the air, offering no cover at all. Orhan used the advantage and aimed his weapon, killing his advisory instantly. The blast of the AK-47 rang painfully through Orhan head as he was still weakened from his earlier encounter on the dock. He stumbled backward into the hall pressing his hands over his ears.

Jeff scurried over and forced the front door closed. One of the hinges had been bent from a bullet, wedging the door against the frame. A hail of bullets sent a splinter of wood from the jamb, impaling the meat of his left hand before he could pull it out of the way. He fell back against the inner wall of the hall and looked down at his throbbing hand to find a splinter the size of a pencil protruding from his flesh. The pain paralyzed him for a moment as he pulled it out.

A third minion came from the direction of the marina and managed to position himself on the other side of the door out of sight of the windows. He peered cautiously through a bullet hole in the door. Jeff saw a change in the light. He fired his Beretta at the newly formed peephole, and a howl of agony could be heard as the man ran bleeding from a deep bullet crease running across his cheek through his ear. He rounded the corner of the house running into Ursella and knocking them both to the ground. He lay stunned by the impact. She ended his pain with her dagger.

The rest of the fighting was taking place up the hill. Jeff wrapped his hand in a cloth he found near what remained of the food the old man had brought them, and then went outside into the moonlight. Ursella stared up at him as she wiped the blood from her blade on the dead man's coat.

"We have just about finished Ölüm's men," she said coldly. "The few that are left have been driven with their backs to the sea. They have been very stupid in the way they have been attacking us."

"I'm thankful for that," said Jeff. Ursella glared at him with annoyance.

"The Gypsy soldiers have proven very valiant. They deserve more credit than they have been given. Without them you would have all been killed days ago."

"I know," said Jeff. He cautiously walked in the direction of the most recent gunfire and made his way up to the ruins of the castle. The wall that had protected them had been obliterated by the first assault's explosives. He gazed down at the rock beach where they had landed a few hours ago to see their launch still burning. Two other launches lay beached nearby.

Mustafa and Besnik had a minion on his knees on the rocky beach with his hands bound behind his back. They were obviously interrogating him, but he was not cooperating. Besnik smacked him to the ground and then pulled him back upright, ready to hit him again. He looked defiantly at the Gypsy, blood slithering down his face from cuts in his forehead and lip.

Mustafa grabbed the man by the hair and yanked his head back so they were eye to eye.

"If you continue to refuse to tell us what we want to know, you will suffer horrible pain," he said menacingly.

"There is nothing you can do to make me tell you anything, you Gypsy pig," said the man, spitting in Mustafa's face.

"The pain I speak of will not come from us," said Mustafa straightening up and calmly wiping his face. "We possess Ölüm." He paused to note the surprise in the man's expression.

"You lie!"

"No. We have your master bound in his jewel encrusted golden cube."

The man glared up at him. The description of the cube was enough to convince him that Mustafa was not lying. Mustafa continued, "The power that we have over him at this time is limited, and I believe temporary. I am sure that the jinn will be interested in learning who it was that betrayed his hiding place. I am sure he will be very displeased with *you*." Mustafa glared back at the man, whose eyes betrayed his fear. "It won't really matter to Ölüm if you were the betrayer or not. He hates all humans anyway, but he seems to be particularly fond of causing great suffering to those he is most displeased with."

A long silence followed as the man contemplated his predicament. He finally spoke with reservation: "What is it you want?"

"I want to know how many more there are of Ölüm's soldiers. I want to know what you know of the jinn. Basically I want to know everything that will help us survive."

The man seemed defeated. "To your first question, that is simple. I am the only one left. The others, as you have seen, are dead." He paused to consider how much he was going to reveal. Finally he decided to come clean with all the information he had. Mustafa's threat had evidently worked. "Others will be waiting for you along the Greek and Turkish coasts. They will be alerted by a signal, or lack of a signal, sent from our group if we failed to stop you."

"Has the signal been sent?"

"No. My commander was overconfident. He's dead now." Clearly the man was in pain and defeated. "So just kill me already," he demanded.

"All in good time," said Mustafa. "What was your plan here tonight? Or did you even have a plan? You just came in here blowing everything up and shooting up the place."

"We were commanded to kill all who were with the American and the Turk."

"And what of the American and the Turk?"

"They were to be taken away by someone here on this island."

"Who?" shouted Besnik in the man's face as he gave him another slap.

"I don't know," coughed the man. "They have power. They made you come to this island."

Mustafa turned to Besnik with alarm in his eyes. "Where are Jeff and Orhan?"

"They were at the house last I saw them."

"Go and make sure they are safe," commanded Mustafa as he turned his attention back to the man.

"So you were unaware that we had Ölüm?"

The man shook his head. "We did not know that. The last we saw him was at the ruins in Ephesus."

Mustafa contemplated the possibility that the power of the jinn over his followers may not be as great as he had thought. He turned back to the man still on his knees on the jagged rocks. "Do you wish to live? Or would you rather die for your master?"

"I would rather live. I feel no allegiance to the jinn. We have been betrayed by his weakness," said the minion.

Mustafa hoisted him up to his feet but kept his wrists bound. He saw Nicoli inspecting the bodies that lay strewn along the beach and the hilltop. They had lost three of their clansman. Now all that remained of their company were the three of them. There would be time for grieving...later.

* * *

The old man looked at his sister as they studied the body of the minion lying on the front porch. He gave the man a shove with his foot to make sure he was dead.

"Reckless fool," he snorted. "He could have killed the progeny."

"Is that not what we want, Avni?" said the old woman. "To end the line of the betrayers?"

"Yes, but not yet. In order for the curse to be broken in its entirety, they must die on the altar together," said Avni as he pulled from his pocket a strand of precious gems. "These fools of Ölüm nearly destroyed the plan."

The old man placed the strand of gems in the stove causing a ripple in the air at the center of the room. Brother and sister jointly took up the wooden crate and stepped into the center of the disturbance like they were walking through a waterfall. As their shapes faded to nothingness, the room decayed into ruin.

* * *

Besnik ran up the hill to find Jeff and Orhan investigating the area around the ruins.

"You are good?" Besnik said in heavily accented English.

"Yeah. We're OK," said Jeff.

Mustafa pushed the minion up the hill until they reached Besnik, Jeff and Orhan. The minion glared at Jeff through dark, deep-set eyes. His hair was shoulder length and matted with blood from the gash at his scalp line. He stood defiantly, his open oilskin cloak revealing a heavy wool sweater underneath. His black wool trousers fit snuggly in his knee-high black rubber boots. Jeff couldn't help but notice that the man appeared to be educated; he emitted an air of sophistication even through his disheveledness.

Aubrey, Anton, and Ursella appeared at the ruins arriving from three different directions from the village. Mustafa made a mental note of their number. He realized that they had all arrived at the hilltop, but that meant that no one was back at the house guarding the crate of Ölüm. The same thought dawned on Besnik and Nicoli.

The three Gypsies ran off toward the house leaving the minion standing next to Jeff. Seeing Jeff's relaxed stance the prisoner knocked Jeff to the ground with a shoulder butt. Before Jeff could react, the man was running down the hill to the beach. Anton, still cradling his broken arm, helped Jeff to his feet as the man ran off into the darkness of the shore.

"Well, he can't get to far bound like that," Jeff said under his breath as he brushed himself off.

Jonathan came out into the open from an abandoned house and washed the blood from his hands in a mud puddle that pocked the path. He glanced over his shoulder at the pair of legs that lay across the threshold of the doorless building. A cold shiver ran down his back as he tried to forget what he had just done. He jogged to the top of the hill where he saw his friends staring in the direction of the escaping minion.

The entourage marched back down the hill into town and wound its way through the narrow alleys to the house. When they arrived they saw that Mustafa, Besnik, and Nicoli had stopped when he rounded the corner of the house. The house was in complete disrepair and abandoned like the other buildings in the area. Mustafa looked to Jeff for confirmation that they had come to the right house.

"This *is* it," confirmed Jeff, "but it isn't like it was just a few minutes ago." He stuck his head through the front door, which was off its hinges and leaning against the jam. "Hello? Is anybody here?"

His voice echoed through the empty structure. He yelled again louder, but the sound merely bounced off bare concrete and stone walls. He stepped inside to find the house in a dilapidated state. The room where they had lain down just an hour or two ago was empty except for the skeletons of three futons against the walls, their springs rusted and contorted from years of weather and disuse. In the ceiling a gaping hole with jagged and broken rafters dangled above their heads, opening to the cold starry sky above. The stove that had given them warmth was cracked and leaned precariously to the side from a broken pedestal. There was no hint that there had ever been a fire burning there. Leaves and other debris were piled in the corner blown in by the wind through broken and glassless windows. The floor was bare and dirty with no sign of the Bergama carpet.

Jeff and Orhan looked at each other bewildered. Jonathan pushed his way through the bedroom door that rubbed heavily on the wooden planked floor. There, where Ursella and Aubrey had slept, was the shattered frame of a bed.

"This place is completely empty!" he yelled over his shoulder from the doorway. "Are you sure we're in the right house?"

"I'm positive," said Jeff. The company stared at each other, their blank looks of confusion quickly replaced by looks of terror as they all realized at the same time what was missing. There in the corner, a pile of leaves lay in place of the crate that had carried Ölüm.

"Where is the crate?" blurted out Ursella angrily.

"There's no way we just all dreamed that we slept here," said Jeff. "That old man and woman were as real as us."

"So where are they?" asked Aubrey. "Did *they* take the crate?" She went over and stooped behind the carcass of one of the futons, struggling to remove something wedged between one of the slats. When she straightened she had the pine icon of Mary that had been hanging on the wall. "Recognize this?" she said holding it up for display. "This *is* where we were."

Besnik stepped in from the hall and rummaged under the futon he had slept on. Pulling out his leather pouch, he turned to the others. "I left this here when the explosions started."

"There is deep magic here," said Mustafa. He backed slowly out of the door, his eyes roving warily along the floor and ceiling looking for signs of danger.

Jeff and Aubrey met each other's worried expressions. He reached over and took her hand and backed out of the house with his Beretta ready. The others followed until they were all standing out in the small courtyard. Only Besnik remained inside; investigating.

The house stood before them, a silent sentinel of a terrible secret. The gloom that flooded outward from its miserable condition thickened the air with a putrid sweetness. Everyone gasped and turned to suck in fresh air from the sea as a cold, harsh wind blew in from the bay.

Jeff looked at his triathlon watch. It was a quarter past two in the morning. He took a deep breath and turned back to the house, which seemed to loom larger than before. More ominous. More sinister. Something was wrong. Very wrong. He suddenly had an inexplicable sinking feeling that he and all the others were in grave and immediate danger. His head began to swirl. He tried to focus on Aubrey to see if she was all right, but the forms of the others were blurred and shadowy. He tried to cry out, but the sound was smothered in his throat. Nothing seemed real or tangible. He couldn't be sure of anything. A low, resonating hum throbbed inside his head, and he staggered clumsily toward the side of the house as his outstretched hand groped for support. The house was drawing him in. Beckoning. Commanding him to move toward it. He fought against the pull, but his will was too weak. Suddenly through a bright and radiant light his hand found the post that supported the awning of the front porch. A blinding explosion deafened him, knocking him to the ground.

* * *

Jeff looked up to see the house in refurbished splendor. It was whitewashed and clean. Flowers edged the stone walk, and grapes hung from vines supported by wires that crisscrossed above his head supported by the awning of the front porch and a trelliswork of intricately laid stone. The putrid stench from before had been replaced by a pleasant aroma of flowers and fruit. He gazed around him; he was still sprawled on the ground, but there was no sign of the others. He slowly got to his feet and walked in an uneasy circle around the periphery of the courtyard. Over the stick-thatched fence, he saw a valley spread out before him with tall, rock-capped mountains on either side. A small village rested at the foot of smaller, tree-covered mountains pocked with grassy meadows. He could see sheep grazing in the distance, and a continuous tinkling sound of sheep bells carried gently on the wind.

It suddenly dawned on him that he no longer was in the village along the cold island coast. He turned back to the house, eying it suspiciously, and took a couple of unsure steps toward the front porch. As he approached, the green-painted front door swung open and an old man hobbled out followed by an old woman. They smiled at him with mostly toothless grins. The old man offered his hand as Jeff took a step up. He stared at the hand, not sure if he should take it but also not sure that he shouldn't. Finally he reached up and grabbed the man's hand firmly to return his shake. He looked over the old man's shoulder at the woman, who beamed a cordial look of assurance.

The old man pulled Jeff to his chest and kissed him on both cheeks. Jeff didn't see the old man's look of confussion as he gazed over his shoulder expecting to see another.

"You are most welcome, son of Përparim Lleshi. We have been expecting you."

* * *

Besnik come out of the house just in time to see Jeff and Orhan stagger drunkenly toward the porch. They moved as if they were in a zombie-like trance. Jeff had already touched the post of the porch and seemed to fade before Besnik's eyes, but Orhan was trailing slightly. Besnik dove at Jeff but went right through him, into Orhan's midsection, tackling him to the ground. Orhan struggled to get out from under Besnik as his hypnotic stupor was snapped. The others came to help them to their feet. When they turned back to the house, Jeff was gone.

# 23. Family Secrets

Curraj i Epërm, Albania
12 August 2000

Jeff pulled himself away from the grasp of the old man and looked around him for the others. He took a step backward off the porch and looked around the corner of the house. No sign of his friends anywhere. He came back around to the front to find the old man and woman still smiling at him. They were the same as they had been on the Turkish island, but were dressed in summer clothing. He suddenly felt hot and overdressed.

"Where am I?" he asked taking off his coat and scarf. Feeling the Beretta in his pocket, he decided to keep it concealed.

"You are in a village in northern Albania," said the old man. "It is called Curraj i Epërm."

Jeff looked over his head through the netting of grapevines to the mountain surrounded valley below. He turned slowly to see that high peaks surrounded the valley on three sides. By the position of the sun he could tell he was facing south down the long valley. The front porch faced the west.

The house sat on the slope at the foot of the mountain to the east. The rest of the village dropped down below into the valley. He could see the terra-cotta shingled roofs of other houses popping up sporadically through the trees like tiny islands in a green sea. He pulled his sweater off and draped it absentmindedly over a post next to the porch step. A million questions flooded his mind, but he was speechless and could barely form the words for even one.

"Who are you?" he finally managed to ask.

"You may call me Avni, and this is my sister, Lida."

"Where are my friends?"

"They did not make the journey."

"What do you mean they did not make the journey? Where are they?" Jeff demanded.

"They are in another place and time," Avni said matter-of-factly. "They are still where you once were and at the same time you once were. They will have great difficulty joining you now."

"So am I a prisoner?"

"No," chuckled Avni. "You are free to come and go as you like, but after hearing the story I have to tell you I am sure you will be convinced to stay."

"OK, but are my friends safe?"

Avni stared off into the corner of the porch ceiling like he was seeing a vision. He nodded his head slowly at first, and then more confidently. "Yes, they are all safe. In fact, they are safer now than they were when you were with them. Yes," he said reflectively, "they are safe."

Jeff fired off a staccato of questions. "So where am I exactly? How did I get here? Why am I here? What time of year is it? Where are my friends exactly in 'place and time'? And who are you really?"

Avni smiled at Lida and looked back at Jeff with an amused expression. He went into the house and brought out a wooden chair, motioning for Jeff to have a seat. Lida hobbled into the house and fetched out another chair for Avni, and then went back into the house. The two men sat staring at each other, Jeff with a suspicious air and Avni with the demeanor of a loving grandfather. Avni seemed content to sit in silence, but Jeff had far too many questions to sit patiently. He, however, calmed himself to respect Avni's hospitality.

# Vale of Shadows

Soon Lida shuffled out of the house carrying a hand-beaten copper tray with two small glasses full to the brim with a clear liquid.

"Ah," sighed Avni with satisfaction. "We will first drink *raki*, and then we will talk." He handed Jeff a glass then took one for himself. "This is from my own grapes," he beamed. "*Gezuar.*"

Jeff watched him put the glass to his lips. He caught the faintest sign that Avni only pretended to take a sip. He grimaced and smacked his lips, and then looked up at Jeff expectantly. Jeff brought the glass under his nose; the vapor alone burned his nostrils. He flinched. Avni laughed giving him a nod of encouragement. Jeff wrinkled his nose and brought the glass to his mouth. He paused, unsure of whether he should willingly poison himself, and then took a gulp of the *raki*, which was a great deal more than he had intended. The liquid seared its way down his throat and burned clear up to behind his eyeballs. He coughed violently, causing the *raki* to spurt out his nose, which burned even more. Avni laughed and patted him proudly on the back.

"Bravo, my friend," he said smiling back at his sister.

"Holy cow!" Jeff gasped. "What is this stuff?"

"It is called *raki*," Avni repeated. "I distill it from white wine. It is very strong, yes?"

"That's an understatement," coughed Jeff. He returned the glass to his lips again and gave it a sniff. "This is just awf—" He stopped in mid sentence noticing Avni's proud look. "Um...awfully good," he lied nodding his head but secretly hoping he didn't have to drink any more.

Avni sat back in his chair and combed his fingers through his thinning hair. He pretended to take another sip of his *raki*, and then much to Jeff's relief placed it onto the tray that Lida had sat down on a small table in the corner. Jeff pretended to take one last sip just to be polite, and then placed his glass next to Avni's. He returned Avni's smile and patted his knees nervously with his palms taking in the view of the village and the valley. Lida returned and offered him a bowl of Turkish Delight. Jeff took one, but she remained in front of him with the bowl still extended, so he took another. He nodded his thanks.

"Let me tell you the story of why you are here," began Avni holding Jeff's gaze. "You are, as I said earlier, in the village known as Curraj i Epërm. We are located in the northern province of Tropoja in Albania. It is in the Balkan Alps. It is, as you suspect, mid August. You have been brought here by an ancient magic. The house where you first met us on the island was indeed not as it seemed. It would have been good to allow you and your friends to enjoy the comforts of its warmth, but the manner of the attack by the soldiers of the jinn caused us to change our plans. My sister and I felt the urgency of transporting the golden cube of Ölüm to a safer haven."

Jeff suddenly felt alarmed by the way Avni phrased his statement *the manner of the attack* as if he had expected the attack all along. And to mention the jinn so casually made Jeff realize that he was in great danger despite the cordial appearance of his host. He knew he had to be careful not to give away his suspicion.

Avni continued. "The space in which the house on the Turkish island existed is a portal of sorts capable of transporting one through time and space. The attraction you felt to the house was an ancient call. So now you are here. In a blink of an eye you are hundreds of miles and eight months from where you started."

"So what has happened to my friends?"

"They are where you left them," said Avni. "At this moment in their time and place they are searching for you. I am afraid your friend, the young lady, is most distraught over your disappearance. I wish there was something that could be done to ease her anxiety, but I fear there is not."

Jeff wanted to ask *why just me? Why not Orhan also?* But he doubted that he would be told the truth. He began to be afraid of where he was and who he was with. Jeff was unable to mask his fear which Avni easily detected

"This is too weird," protested Jeff. "What am I supposed to do now? How am I supposed to live in this new dimension?"

"Much of what you need to know will be explained to you in good time. We have three days before the full moon cycle that will release Ölüm's *twin*." Avni paused at this statement, and Jeff couldn't help but catch the subtle smirk as he said the word *twin*. "In the meantime there is much we need to discuss to prepare you for the release of the jinn. When you are not in 'school,' you are free to wander the village, but do not stray from the borders of the valley."

Jeff leaned back in his chair and balanced on the back legs rocking gently. Avni nudged with his chin for Jeff to drink more *raki*. Jeff took a deep breath and a shallow swig. Avni reached over and patted him playfully on the back.

"It is good, yes?"

"Well, it'll take some getting used to, but…"

"It's OK, you don't have to drink if you don't want to," Avni said through his nearly toothless grin.

"No, I'll drink it," Jeff said with resolve. He steeled himself for another snort.

"*Me fund,*" said Avni, making a chugging gesture with his head and hand.

"All of it?"

Avni smiled with affirmation. Jeff threw the rest of the *raki* down his throat in one quick swallow. The pain that racked his mouth, nose, throat, and eyes nearly caused him to fall from his chair. Avni was quick to congratulate him with fond pats on the back and by rubbing his head with his palm.

"You are indeed a true Albanian," he gloated. He settled back to continue his story.

"I know you have had many explanations of what is going on here, but I assure you the entire story has not been properly revealed. You see the release of the jinni have gone virtually unrecorded. There was no detailed history of the curse from one generation to the next. What they had were stories of terror told by ignorant peasants, embellished by wild imaginations, and so dismissed by the more educated. In the end both ignorant and educated alike died horrible deaths that went virtually unnoticed.

"I am sure you are wondering how this all involves you. Your ancestor and the ancestor of Orhan, unfortunately, were not good men. They were bloodthirsty murderers. They may have started their individual careers as honest, brave soldiers in the service of their lords, but they each developed a lust for death that was sated only by the brutal killings of thousands — yes, I said thousands — of men, both the innocent and the not so innocent.

"They separately acquired knowledge of the formidable power of the jinni and tried to sway the outcome of battle by trickery and treachery. With the help of black sorcerers, they connived an alliance with the jinni promising them what they truly desired most. Përparim Lleshi and Selim Bey had no intention of honoring any bargain with either the jinni or the sorcerers. As we now know all too well, their bloodlust came back on their own heads. Both men died after living lives of paranoia and fear. Their treachery has been handed down from generation to generation.

"You have been told that the curse can only be broken in one of two ways. The first, which benefits you and your progeny, is to destroy the two jinni together. The second, which benefits the twins, is to finally destroy all of the progeny of their betrayers down to the last man, woman, and child. The jinni have been actively trying to destroy your families one time in every generation for the last five hundred some years. Their problem has always been the lack of fidelity among your grandsires, who would sometimes have anywhere from fifty to a hundred children with multiple wives. They in turn would procreate, and within just a few short generations the number was well...staggering.

"There is, however, a third alternative, and no one knows it but my sister and me."

"You said that the jinni were promised something that they really wanted," said Jeff. "What is that exactly?"

"Ahh, that is the crux of the third alternative," beamed Avni. "You see, what they were promised and what they desired most was to be given their freedom. Free to never be bound by the whims of man again. Free to live their lives in peace among their own kind. Free to revert back to the way of life that they enjoyed before the black arts of man enslaved them in their corruptible intrigues. They were promised this freedom on the condition that they bind themselves to the warcraft of opposing sides.

"Their freedom had been taken from them nearly a thousand years ago, four hundred years before the war between the Albanians and the Ottomans. They were passed from master to master, each promising freedom after just one more task, one more favor, one more wish. The sorcery of Baba Moush and his cohorts was stronger than the jinni had encountered in the past. They erroneously perceived this as a sign that the sorcerer had power to keep his promise, but as we know he used that power to drive the jinni deeper into slavery."

"So how can this third alternative be accomplished?" asked Jeff. "And if it is accomplished, what is to prevent the jinni from wreaking havoc unhindered and at will?"

"Good questions," stated Avni proudly. His blatant show of affection was making Jeff more uneasy. He could feel something sinister seething just under the surface of Avni's demeanor. "The only way to accomplish the third alternative is to have both of the jinni together, freed from their golden cubes and confronted with the proposition that they will be released unconditionally."

Avni sat back against the wall with his chair balanced on two legs. *Very "un-old-man–like,"* thought Jeff. Avni folded his hands across his stomach and smiled at Jeff again with that grandfatherly grin.

Jeff's attention was drawn to a commotion in the yard between the house and a small shed. Lida was trying to corner a chicken against a woven stick fence. Just as she was about to nab it, it darted past her and ducked under a hedge. She picked up a stone from the dust and flung it, stunning the chicken. Before it could rise and dash off again she grabbed it by the neck and gave it a quick twist with her surprisingly powerful hands. The chicken flopped aimlessly around the yard and finally came to rest near the front porch next to Jeff.

"Good, we will have meat for supper," said Avni. He continued, "I am sure you have many questions, which I will try to answer for you. I must tell you first of all that we are hoping for the survival of the jinni."

Jeff looked at him stunned. "Why would you want that?"

"Because the jinni are not as they seem. We are hoping there is some redemption available for them. After all, they were captured and enslaved by evil men a thousand years ago. They became what they are today because of *them*."

"I don't understand any of this," said Jeff perplexed. "Who are you really?"

"I have told you who I am, and who my sister is. I suppose now would be a good time to tell you a little more about us."

Jeff watched Lida out of the corner of his eye start a fire out in the yard and begin burning off the remainder of the feather stubble after plucking the chicken. He tried to pay attention to Avni, but in all his years he had never actually seen a chicken go from running around in the yard to cooked and presented on the table. He forced himself to focus.

"My sister and I are not...well, we are not what we appear."

"Who *is* around here?" said Jeff sarcastically. He could tell that Avni was skirting around something that he was hesitant to say. "Just tell me what you have to say. I mean, it can't be any more bizarre than what I've already seen and heard." He sat expectantly with his fingers clasped around his crossed knee, but the urge to run was growing.

Avni smiled. "I should tell you now that my sister and I are in the neighborhood of one thousand five hundred years old." He paused to let that sink in. "We are in fact not...human. Lida and I have taken the form of humans simply to make you feel more comfortable."

"I don't think anything you can say will make me feel comfortable from now on," interrupted Jeff. "So what are you?"

"We are...in fact...hmm . Let me just say that we are on your side, and that we will aid you in any way that we can." Avni lied. "Before I go further, I must know that you understand this. Do you understand, Jeff?"

"I don't know. I don't know what I understand any more." Jeff knew that Avni was not on his side, and he began to feel with certainty that Avni was simply stalling for time. The trap was set and Jeff knew he was walking right into it, but he saw no other options.

"I understand your dilemma. There is no easy way to say it, so I will just say it. Lida and I are jinni."

Jeff stared at Avni blankly as if he had just spit in his coffee. He remained motionless for what seemed an eternity, and then blinked his eyes coming to himself. He had no words as terror unraveled itself within his bowels.

Avni's countenance suddenly shone brightly, lighting up the porch and the courtyard. Jeff covered his eyes with his sleeve against the glare. When the brilliance faded, he lowered his arm and gazed with wonder at the two beautiful creatures that now stood before him. Avni and Lida were still in human form, but the years had shed away and they now faced Jeff handsome and gorgeous. They looked to be no more than thirty years old. Avni was strong and muscular, and Lida stood tall and curvaceous.

Jeff tumbled backward off the porch, shock and surprise mixed with terror. Avni quickly came to his aid and helped him up.

"Whoa. Be careful, my friend," he said with a deep resonating voice. "Do not harm yourself."

Avni guided him gently to his chair. His strength flowed through Jeff fortifying his legs as he walked.

"Enough with the mysteries," said Lida. "It is time to tell him the whole truth."

"You are right, my sister." Avni stood behind his chair and cleared his throat. "Unless we are able to sway Greslokmu, whom you know as Ölüm, and Freslokmut, whom you have not yet met, to listen to this third alternative you and hundreds of others may die during this cycle along with Orhan and everyone with him."

"We trust that we can convince them of your sincerity to grant them freedom," said Lida. "It will be what we have longed for these one thousand years. This is the thirteenth cycle since the inception of the curse. The wickedness of Baba Moush will rage against everyone involved in a relentless insidious storm of events. We must become allies."

The words tumbled out of Jeff's mouth. "OK, I see why you would want to help a fellow jinni, but—"

"They are not just 'fellow jinni,'" interrupted Avni. "They are, in fact, our brother and sister. We are what you would call quadruplets."

# 24. Pestilent Wind

Unknown Island off of the Turkish Coast
Aegean Sea
23 January 2000, 2:30 a.m.

"Jeff!" shouted Jonathan. "Where are you, man?"

Jonathan and Besnik ventured cautiously back into the house. There was no sign of Jeff. The last anyone had seen of him was when he staggered back up the front porch, and then just seemed to dissolve away into the house. Aubrey looked frantically around the back but only found a crumpled outhouse with the twigs of dead weeds growing up through the hole. Tears began to roll freely down her cheeks.

"Jeff! Please answer me," she pleaded. She finished her circuit and ended up back with the rest of the group, who were still standing in the courtyard. "Where could he be?" she asked no one in particular.

The wind began to pick up from the sea and howled through the buildings and alleyways. The temperature dropped quickly as a thick, cold mist began to fall. Anton stepped to Aubrey's side and tried to comfort her by placing his good arm around her shoulder. She shrugged away from him and started to go back into the house. Anton gently restrained her.

"He is not there," he said in a sad consolatory whisper.

"How do you know?" she sobbed. "Where is he?"

"He has been taken away. I don't know where, but you will not find him on this island."

She looked from Anton to the house and back to Anton. She knew he was right. She felt as if she had no strength left.

275

At that moment Jonathan stuck his head out of the front door and called to Mustafa. "Besnik has found something."

They entered the front room to find Besnik stooped down in front of the stove. He motioned for Jonathan to give him his flashlight. As he searched inside, the beam fell across an object buried in a layer of fine ash. He pulled it out, brushing off the soot on his pants leg, and held it up for the others to see.

Aubrey leveled her flashlight on the shiny object. It was a long, stranded bracelet made of gold; the light refracted off delicately cut rubies inset in a serpentine pattern. She gasped as Jonathan whistled.

"What do you make of that?" he said.

Aubrey leaned in for a closer look. She turned it over in her hands slowly as they studied it in the light. It was made up of twenty-two rubies weighing about three carats each. The jewels were set with gold filigree. As they looked more closely, they could see that the borders were edged with sapphires arranged in the colors of the rainbow. At the completion of each sequence of rainbow-colored sapphires, a diamond was set, each weighing about one carat. The clasp was made with an emerald encircled by small emerald baguettes held in place with gold filigree.

Aubrey held it up at eye level so the light shone through the gems. As she did so, a flash of brilliant light stabbed through the darkness of the room and beamed like a laser against the wall above the door. The flash dissipated as soon as she moved the light away.

"This thing is heavy," she said dropping her arm down to her side to adjust her shoulder. "It's gorgeous, but you would have to be Brünhelda to wear it."

"Let me see," said Jonathan taking it from her. "Wow! You're right. It weighs a ton. How could anyone even wear this thing?"

"I bet it wraps up around the wrist and forearm like this." Aubrey carefully draped it over her arm and displayed it to the others. "I wonder if this bracelet has anything to do with Jeff's disappearance."

"Maybe. I don't know," said Jonathan.

"I have no doubt this has had something to do with the magic here," said Mustafa. He eased the bracelet from Aubrey's hand and held it up. "This is much heavier than it looks."

Mustafa rotated the bracelet into the cross beams of Aubrey and Besnik's flashlights. A powerful beam of white light rocketed into the sky through the front room window.

"What was that?" he exclaimed

"Shining the light just right on these gems causes it to shoot off a bright shaft of light," said Jonathan. "Look, when we shine through the rubies and the emerald it comes out white. You would think it would be red or green, but it isn't." He studied it intently by the light of the flashlights. "Here, let me see that," he said taking the light back from Besnik. He tried to concentrate the beam into the center of one of the rubies. Squinting through the glare off its surface, he could make out an irregularity in the center of the stone. "There is something in the middle of it." He steadied the beam on the next ruby. "There is something here also, and in this one, and this one." He fingered the stones one by one through the light. Each ruby contained an irregularity, but the light was too dim to make it out.

"Can you tell what they are?" asked Orhan straining to see into the rubies over Jonathan's shoulder.

"No, but they seem to be all about the same size and shape. Wait a minute...they actually look like little figures," said Jonathan, looking closer.

"Figures? What do you mean figures?" asked Mustafa, pushing closer.

"As in people. Shapes of people," said Jonathan. "They look like...yeah, they definitely look like people dressed in old clothes like you see in pictures of the old Ottomans. This light is so crappy I can't really see a thing."

Mustafa took the bracelet from him and shone his own flashlight into one of the red gems. Instantly a stab of light impaled the ceiling as his beam caught it just right. In that instant he thought he could see the figure move, but he knew it had to be his eyes playing tricks on him from the glare and shadows.

"Great mother! Did you see that?" he exclaimed. He tried to recreate the angle of the light. It bounced off aimlessly at first, and then the ray caught the angle of the cut, and the spear of light shot out again. This time, however, Mustafa kept the bracelet and flashlight steady to hold the angle. The light flared brightly in a pinpoint against the far wall. All eyes were on the center of the ruby. As the light washed over the figure, a slight movement could indeed be seen. It was imperceptible at first, but it became more and more animated the longer the light shined on it.

Suddenly a loud crack like a peal of thunder split the silence. Mustafa was thrown backwards into the bare springs of one of the futons. As the others covered their ears against the blast, the bracelet fell to the wooden floor, shuddering with porcupine quills of light slicing through the room like a mirror ball in a disco.

Stunned, the group shielded their eyes and ears as best they could against the blinding light and an increasingly deafening thrum reverberating from the priceless artifact. After several seconds the brilliance collapsed back into the bracelet, and all was dark and quiet again.

Orhan bent over and picked up the bracelet, sticking it in a large coat pocket. "I think we better be careful with this until we know more about it."

Besnik helped Mustafa up from the frame of the futon and looked at him closely eye to eye. "This is the amulet of the jinn," he whispered. "It is a source of great power to those who know how to use it."

"And I suppose you know how to use it," said Mustafa sarcastically.

"No, but Ermal did...and so does your mother," hissed Besnik. "We must go to her."

"My mother will not help me. She has regarded me as dead," said Mustafa bitterly.

"She won't for your sake. For the sake of Ermal, however, she will help us," said Besnik. "We must leave this island now," he said to the others.

With that the group quickly marched back up to the fortress hill. They descended the other side and made their way to the beach and the launch craft of the minion. As they began to board one of the boats, Anton staggered along the rocky beach to catch up with them.

As he gasped for air he whispered to Orhan, "We need to leave this place immediately. There is great danger coming. I struggled to keep up with you, but I heard a sound behind me. When I turned I saw a ripple in the air around the house. Something is coming." He hurriedly climbed into the launch without help and looked around. "Where is Ursella?"

It dawned on the Orhan that Ursella was not with them.

"Has anyone seen Ursella?" he asked.

Mustafa looked down the beach in both directions. When he looked back up the hill a cold shiver shot down his back.

"Get the others into the boat," he whispered to Besnik out of the corner of his mouth.

"But what of—" started Besnik.

"She's gone," interrupted Mustafa. "We will be, too, if we don't leave now."

The two men kept their gaze on the hilltop ruins as they backed slowly to the boat. Each man had his hand on his weapon under his coat, ready if needed. They quickly turned and pushed the launch off into the surf. Nicoli was already at the helm and started the engine, peeling out into the sea as soon as they were clear of land. They ran straight for the Turkish coast for about a mile and then cut the engine, allowing the boat to drift.

Mustafa studied the shore with a Bushnell night vision monocular he found stowed in an emergency equipment cabinet. The fires still burned from the fight they had had earlier, but they were beginning to die down. From the direction of the village, Mustafa saw two figures move slowly to the crest of the hill. They stood staring out to sea, their silhouettes backlit by the flicker of flames.

Suddenly Mustafa jumped and tripped backward, nearly knocking over Anton who had come up behind him. There in the eerie green glow of the night vision monocular, Mustafa saw the figures staring right at him. Their eyes shone like bright beacons cutting through the darkness. They seemed to penetrate straight through the monocular into Mustafa's mind. He jerked it away from his eye in a panic. When he got the courage to raise it to his eyes again, the two figures were gone.

Mustafa studied the shoreline and concentrated on the inlet to the bay, his brow furrowed. He lowered the monocular and then raised it again. He turned to Nicoli who was standing ready at the helm.

"Take us out of here," he said looking again through the apparatus. A cold shiver again descended down his back. He knew they were being watched even though they were a mile out in a black sea.

Nicoli reved the engine turning the bow against the drift and back out to sea. Even in the darkness with no points of reference to mark their progress they could tell they were making no headway. Mustafa turned his head and saw that they were now actually closer to the shore.

Drawn by an unseen force the launch inched its way back toward the bay. Nicoli fought hard to gain control but to no avail. The others quickly lined up along the gunwales to peer into the darkness toward the village. No one spoke. A ghostly dread gripped each one as the wash slapped against the prow.

The boat finally eased past the lighthouse that guarded the bay which lay in ruins. They knew there was nothing they could do against whatever power that pulled them back to the island. In desperation they pulled into the marina and tied off at a dilapidated wharf.

A rush of wind bellowed from the sea. The group struggled to keep their balance in the bottom of the boat. The ferocity of the wind and waves escalated by the second. Soon the launch was thrown clear of the water and landed at a tilt on the dock.

"We have to find shelter," screamed Orhan over the horrific noise.

All but Anton and Nicoli were able to scamble out of the boat toward a building that sat at the edge of a small plaza. Orhan tried to help Aubrey keep her feet, but the gusts from the sea knocked them both to the ground. Mustafa and Besnik grabbed them and half drag them to the shelter of the building.

Jonathan crawled on his hands and knees to make it to the others, but the wind was now blowing in from the land as well and clashed violently with the wind blowing in from the sea. He turned to see a definite line of debris tumbling and roiling toward him. He braced himself against the blow. The air pummeled him, knocking him back against the wall of a shack. He tried to release himself from the grip of the gale, but he was pinned as if by a powerful wrestler. He gasped for breath, but the more he struggled the less air he was able to pull into his lungs. A shadow of torment enveloped him. He thrashed and lurched to release himself from the grip that he now realized was not the wind. The more he struggled, the more powerful the hold on him. He felt himself being raised above the rooftops of the village. His world was now full of shadows and dark shapes that lurked in the shadows.

As he fought to maintain consciousness, his vision blurred, and light beams floated around him. He strained to look for his friends in the marina far below, but all he could make out were the surreal shapes of ghostly, ghastly figures swooping all around.

He heard someone call his name and focused all his energy to turn toward the call. There in the grip of another sinister, dark shade was the limp form of Ursella dangling in midair. He tried to reach out for her, but the force that restrained him was too great. He used all his energy and then fell limp, too exhausted to struggle any longer. He gazed at Ursella levitated by the fiendish phantom and gasped one last cry. The horror of being suffocated was replaced by the resignation that comes with the relinquishment of life. His last vision was of the cold, lifeless eyes of Ursella as she was whisked into the tempest of the sea. He quickly joined her. Blackness overtook him.

* * *

Mustafa and Orhan were knocked to the ground before they could reach the building by a mighty wind that swooped at them from every direction. Besnik lost his grip on Aubrey and was hurled through the already shattered door of a house just up an alley off the square. A foul, putrescent reek assaulted him, carried on the wind, the stench of death heavy like the pungent thickness of molasses.

Orhan struggled to his feet and helped Mustafa up, and the two men forced their way to the protection of a stone wall. Besnik tried to poke his head out of the door, but the force of the wind sucked him out into the open and rolled him down the alley.

The wind buffeted the launch tied up in the marina, and Nicoli was knocked to the deck with Anton on top of him.

# Vale of Shadows

Neither man was able to disentangle himself from the gear of the launch. Anton screamed, but no sound could be heard above the shriek of the wind. The boat began to buck and heave out of the water from the tempest. Nicoli continued to fight to free himself from the spokes of the helm, but then a violent jolt catapulted him over the side and a massive wave smacked him under the surface, knocking him unconscious.

Anton could barely see Nicoli's fate through the deluge of spray churned up by the gale. Anton crawled frantically to the gunwale disregarding the pain in his arm. Nicoli was nowhere to be seen. He cried out his name, but again the sound was muted by the wind.

The thrashing of the boat cracked the mooring post, allowing it to crash onto the pier, shattering the starboard hull.

Rain fell heavily as Aubrey craned her neck to look over her shoulder. She and Besnik had been separated by a mighty gust. She had been rolled head over heels until she came to an abrupt stop against a low seawall. The dock and the launch bobbed erratically as they were pushed farther out into the bay. She saw Anton feebly clinging to the starboard gunwale, one leg in and one leg out of the launch. Aubrey called to him. Inexplicably he heard her and raised his head. Even from that distance and through the torrent, Aubrey could see the look of utter hopelessness on his face. Suddenly a tsunami-like wave pounded through the inlet of the bay from the sea. The launch and Anton were quickly consumed.

Aubrey flung herself away from the seawall and flailed her way to the closest building. She dove through the door just as the wave crashed into the row of houses washing her into the far wall. Just as quickly the wave abated, and she wallowed in the ankle-deep water that was left. Painfully she pulled herself to her feet and peered through the shattered window glass. A cyclone had formed a water spout out in the middle of the bay.

As it increased in size, debris from the shore began to be caught up in its vortex.

Her wet, matted hair began to be drawn to the cyclone. She could feel the pull on her face from the negative pressure, and forced herself to duck away from the window. The house began to shake violently. She covered her ears with her hands and squinted her eyes tightly shut. She screamed and cried, helpless and hopeless, praying for the wind to stop, but the ferocity mounted with each moment. The roof was yanked away from overhead and skidded in fragments toward the water. The torrential rain beat her relentlessly, the weight of the drops stinging her hands and neck.

Then two hands grabbed her from the darkness and dragged her out of the house and down an alley away from the bay. She tried to struggle, but terror paralyzed her. She was thrown into a stone shed that was built into the side of a hill. It was only then that she realized that her attacker was in fact her rescuer: Orhan. He slammed the heavy door shut against the storm. His drenched, exhausted body slid down the wall into a sitting position. He faced Aubrey with a grim look.

A soft amber glow filled the shed from a kerosene lamp that hung from a rafter. In the corner lay Mustafa and Besnik, exhausted. Aubrey felt sick to her stomach; she tried to rise, but the exertion was too much for her. She fell back against a roll of fishing net, groaned softly, and then fell into unconsciousness.

# 25. Holes Best Left Unexplored

Curraj i Epërm, Albania
12 August 2000

Jeff stared at his host in complete, unabashed shock. His heartbeat quickened, and his mouth became as dry as the dusty trail that led up to the house. He wanted to run. He took a quick glance looking for a way to escape but realized he was stuck on this front porch with two jinni. He studied Avni for a moment. His host's face remained congenial.

"I see that this news distresses you," Avni said kindly. "You would be more comfortable with our previous appearance, I think." At that he and Lida transformed back to the old man and old woman. "We can take any shape we chose. Is this better?"

Jeff nodded his head stupidly.

"We are family, you see," continued Avni. "Ölüm is the oldest. My sister, who is also under the curse, is the next. She is known in these parts as Vdekje, which means *death* in the Albanian tongue. Then Lida, and then me. Lida and I were set free from the service of men by a very kind and compassionate human. He had power over us through the sorcery of a Gypsy queen but decided out of the decency of his heart to use his magic to set us both free. Our other brother and sister, however, were not so lucky. They were passed from one greedy master to another until that fateful day when they were betrayed by the black craft of Baba Moush.

"We are old, even for jinni, but our memories are still strong concerning the goodness that once was a trait of all in our family. Greslokmu and Freslokmut, known in the world of men

285

as Ölüm and Vdekje or death in Turkish and Albanian, have not always been evil. Their destruction would be a terrible tragedy. That is why we have such a great desire to see this whole evil business end once and for all."

"What do you need *me* for," said Jeff. "I mean, why am I here above all others?"

"You are the descendent of Përparim Lleshi. He is one of two pillars that hold the curse together. The other pillar, of course, is Selim Bey. You saw in the vision the treachery of that day when the forces of Albania and the Ottomans clashed in the river valley of Gramsh. The force of that curse is bound to your blood and the blood of Orhan Aziz. Destroy your blood, and the curse is lifted. This has been the focus of Greslokmu and Freslokmut. They were bound in the service of evil, and so evil they have become. They will kill you and Orhan as soon as they are able.

"You are needed to put an end to this curse. You will do it through the generosity of your heart because it is the right thing to do. I will...*we* will teach you how to do this. It is very dangerous for you, however, and as is true of all God's creatures you have free will and may refuse. If you refuse then the curse will remain intact, and will end by your and Orhan's death or the death of any descendents you may have. If you look past the danger and agree to be taught how to release the jinni and give them their freedom, then you will reap great rewards. Rewards that are not obligated by the demands of magic, but rewards that are freely given in gratitude.

"So what do you say, Jeff *Smith*? Are you the strong one we have been waiting for all these centuries?"

"I don't know about that," said Jeff timidly, still suspicious of Avni's intent. "But I will do what I can." *Even if it is to buy more time*, he thought to himself.

"Good," said Avni. "I know that you are tired and hungry. So you will eat and then rest for the rest of the day. Tomorrow we will begin your training."

But Jeff caught something in the expression on Avni's face when he looked briefly at Lida that increased his suspicion. Were the jinni lying to him in order to lure him into a trap? Warning sirens continued to go off in Jeff's head.

Avni recognized the growing doubt that was sweeping across Jeff's face and quickly changed the subject to keep him from growing too suspicious. He needed to keep Jeff feeling safe for just a little while longer. "Now it is time to eat," he said graciously.

After a lunch of goat's cheese, grapes, tomatoes, thick corn bread, and the pet chicken, Jeff was allowed to take a nap for the rest of the afternoon. Avni and Lida disappeared into the house leaving Jeff to stretch out on a small cot that was unfolded on the front porch.

The breeze was pleasantly cool in the shade cast by the front porch and the grapevine trellis. He gazed out over the valley supporting his head with his forearm as he lay comfortably on his back with his legs crossed. The fatigue of the last several days ebbed from him by the moment. Within a matter of minutes, he fell into a deep, restful sleep.

\* \* \*

Lida and Avni watched Jeff sleeping through the curtain overhanging the front door. The wooden crate containing the golden cube and Ölüm sat in the corner of the living room.

"What do you suppose happened?" She asked.

"Someone interfered," said Avni. "We will go back and kill everyone who is with Orhan Aziz, and then bring him back here."

"We should have taken care of the problem ourselves in the first place," said Lida.

287

Her anger grew by the second as she thought back to how easy it would have been to take the progeny when they first entered the house on the island.

"We will not make the mistake again to depend on human help," said Avni. "We will take Ölüm to the altar chamber, and then go back to the island to finish the task."

"What of Jeff?"

"He is very suspicious. He can not escape the valley. We will use the storms to keep him in check. In the mean time we will let him think he is buying time by cooperating. It will hurt nothing to allow him to explore. It will only increase his anxiety and fear. When all is ready the outcome will be just as we have planned."

After Avni and Lida took the wooden crate to the underground altar chamber they went back to the house where Jeff was still sleeping. They stepped through the air distortion in the middle of the room; entering the portal they disappeared from Albania.

\* \* \*

Jeff woke with a start. He sat up on the edge of the cot and peered around, not sure of where he was. He put his shoes back on and stepped off the front porch into the courtyard. The house was silent behind him as he ventured out onto the narrow path that led down to the rest of the village. As he passed other houses, there was an eerie, lonely feeling.

He came to a very narrow, worn path that skirted a steep bank edging a small stream. Looming out over the trail nearly blocking his way were branches from a mulberry tree. The fruit was purple, ripe, and ready to eat. Jeff helped himself to a handful and continued into the valley. He soon came to an old bridge that spanned the stream. It was made up of wooden planks that were irregularly placed, leaving precarious gaps. He eased his way over to the other side, glad that he was not trying this at night.

# Vale of Shadows

The valley was separated into two parts divided by a promontory of land that jutted up from the valley floor about ten meters higher than its surroundings. A sheep trail wound its way to the top where two old buildings perched. Jeff climbed toward the top, shedding more of his winter garb as he went.

The plateau commanded a spectacular view of the valley and the surrounding mountains. The first building was an old schoolhouse made of red brick. All the glass in the windows had been broken out, leaving rusted bars laced with birds' nests. Jeff peered through one of the high windows by standing on a pile of discarded bricks. The starkness of the interior and the general shabbiness of the construction hinted of the condition of life during fifty years of Communism. He hopped down and walked around to the front door. Its rickety structure was chained and locked with a rusty padlock.

He stood in the shade cast by the school building and basked in the breeze that blew in from the north. The sun beat down as he stepped into the glare. On the southernmost tip of the promontory was a single-room building that had at one time been a church. The door was unlocked. As he turned the handle to enter, a cold shudder went down his spine. He stood confused for a moment. The feeling did not pass. He released the doorknob and took a step back. Only then did the sensation that cold air was blowing down his shirt stop.

He looked around. He was alone. Grabbing the knob again, he twisted it with resolve. The cold feeling returned, but this time more dauntingly. He pushed past the mounting fear, but the door did not easily open so he nudged it with his shoulder. It finally gave way with a ragged screech. Dust from the doorjamb powdered his head and shoulders as he entered an unadorned, empty room. The faded yellowish-green paint on the walls was cracked and peeling. The thud of his boots against the wood-planked floors echoed with a hollow resonance through the rafters of the high ceiling. As was the case with the school, all of the glass had been broken out of the windows.

He crossed to the other end of the room and took a step up to the small, raised platform that must have at one time supported an altar. Whisking the dust away from the floorboards with his boot, he revealed a groove concealed in the planks by years of dust and grime. He went to his hands and knees and carefully cleared the groove with the wool from one of his rolled-up mittens, following it until it finished the outline of what appeared to be a hatch. He searched for any sign of hinges but found none.

He tapped around the border and found an area halfway between the edges of one of the short sides. It sounded hollower. He stood and tapped his boot heel on the spot; a faint clinking sound came from below. Falling to his knees again, he pushed with both hands on the hollow like he was giving CPR. The clinking continued with each compression. Jeff looked around for an object to wedge into the crack, but the room was devoid of even scraps of furniture.

He went back outside and hunted around the buildings, finally finding a rusted, flat fragment of a bar that he assumed must have come from an old wagon spring. As he began to go back inside the church, he noticed that the shadows had become deeper. He glanced over his shoulder to see a blackish-green raincloud occluding the sun, and a cold shudder went through him. The wind picked up suddenly, whirling sand and dust into his face; he jumped through the doorway just as a heavy cloudburst pelted the ground. The racket of the rain against the roof was so loud that it deafened him to any other sound.

He made his way over to the hatch and quickly began to pry into the groove. After several slips and gouges, he was able to penetrate the crack enough to get some leverage. The edge of the hatch creaked slowly open, and a rush of stale air caused him to wince and turn his head away. He continued prying the wood open until he could reach in with his fingers and use his arm strength to finish the job. Finally he braced himself and flung the hatch open fully. It fell back with a crash that was muffled by the pounding of the rain.

He peered into the opening. Below was a winding stone staircase that descended into the darkness. Jeff looked around the room and glanced out the windows, unsure if he should continue his exploration. It dawned on him that he had not seen any other villagers besides Avni and Lida. This strengthened his resolve, and he began his descent.

The air was heavy and musty smelling. He pulled out his flashlight, and felt for the nine-millimeter Beretta that he had tucked in his pants under his shirt. Its presence gave him courage. He wound slowly deeper with each step. Soon the opening above was just a faint pinhole of light.

The beam of his flashlight fell into the thick featureless blackness, and light and sound seemed dull and lifeless. Even the sound of his steps on the stone stairs dropped off abruptly.

He cried out in surprise as he stepped off the last stair into knee-deep water, nearly losing his footing on the slippery rock surface. He caught himself on a stone irregularly bricked into the wall, but the impact sent a sharp pain throughout his forearm and shoulder. Fear mounted as the light of his flashlight skipped across the still surface of the dark water. Even after the disturbance of his fall, the ripple ceased quickly.

The darkness absorbed his light like a thick fog. As he stood still in the water straining to hear any sound, his heartbeat throbbed in his ears. He tried to calm himself with deep, even breaths, but the noise made by his steady inhalation and slow exhalation seemed to amplify beyond reality. Dread began to seize him.

He stepped back up on the last stone step and peered into the darkness above his head but could barely make out the opening in the church floor. Suddenly he had an inexplicable feeling that he was not alone. He began to leap two and three steps at a time as panic pushed him up the stairs. The flashlight was nearly worthless, casting almost no light on the steps ahead. He scambled and stumbled up as fast as he could.

Exhaustion began to weigh him down as he neared the top, and his struggle to keep climbing became as much mental as it was physical. He sensed something following him up the stairs, but he didn't risk looking back down. He finally clambered through the hatch and fell completely spent on the platform floor.

He lay on his back panting for breath. The air was cool and copious. He stared up through the rafters and watched a finch flit around a twig nest that had been constructed in the corner. The sound of the rain against the roof mesmerized him. His eyelids began to grow heavy. He made an attempt to stay awake, but soon a soft snore emanated from his open mouth. His legs dangled over the first step to the passage below.

\* \* \*

Jeff woke and bolted upright. He was still in the church. His legs were still dangling through the hatch. He listened. The rain had stopped, and the sun was shining through the windows. He frowned. He didn't know how long he had been sleeping, but the shadows cast by the sunlight gave him the impression that it was still afternoon.

He rolled himself onto his knees and looked down the black passage. The outline of the winding stone staircase faded only a few steps from the top. He shone his flashlight down the hole, but it illuminated almost nothing beyond what the natural light did. He shook the flashlight and held the beam against his cupped hand. It appeared to be just as strong as ever but had no effect on penetrating the darkness of the space below.

He rose and replaced the hatch, haphazardly kicking the dust around a little to conceal the groove. Then he went to the window and stared out to the east. The valley dropped down into the stream, which coursed over rocks as it flowed south. A few houses of the village could be seen through the trees, and he could see the sheep up on the hillside that he had seen before, but there was still no sign of other villagers.

He glanced back over his shoulder at the platform before he exited the church. Except for a few scuffs in the dust, no one would know he had been there. He made his way down to the stream and sat with his back against a green apple tree. He still felt groggy from his nap on the hard floor. Taking a moment to rouse himself, he watched a chicken run out from under a hedge and take a dust bath in the middle of the trail across the stream.

"Where are all the people?" he said under his breath.

He looked at his watch for the first time since he had arrived in Curraj i Epërm and blinked in disbelief. His Ironman Triathlon Timex displayed 2:16 a.m. The LCD was blinking, so he knew his watch was still working. He glared at the date: 1/24. January 24. He may have traveled eight months into the future but his watch was still as it had been in Turkey. That old familiar pang of fear and anxiety began to take hold of him again, and he looked upstream to the north and saw the roofline of Avni's house. As he studied his surroundings, he began to realize that the position of the sun had not changed in the time he had been there.

He sat and stared at his feet, contemplating what his next move should be. Nothing seemed right. Nothing made any sense. He thought back to the stories that Uncle Ümët had told him. What he and the others had read in the notes and journals of Dr. Yay and the priest. What Mustafa and Ermal had said. What he had experienced in the last few days…months?

Avni and Lida had certainly been a surprise. He knew he couldn't trust them. He suddenly felt terribly alone and ill equipped to continue this venture. He thought back to the hatch inside the church. Had he really been stalked down in the dark depths, or was it just his paranoid imagination? He wondered if he would ever see Aubrey again. He closed his eyes and tried to picture her face, but oddly his mind would only conjure a blurry silhouette. His inability to focus on the woman he loved scared him.

After a time he decided to walk back to Avni's house. He eased his way along the west side of the stream until he came to the rickety wooden bridge. A dense cornfield was to his left. Straight ahead in the distance was a high mountain pass that was well above timberline. He dragged himself up the slope and started across the bridge being careful to avoid falling through the large gaps to the stream below.

"A liability lawyer would have a heyday in a place like this," he mused out loud trying to keep his spirits up.

Thunder echoed from over the peak to the east, and Jeff stopped in the middle of the bridge and studied the terrain on the mountainside. He could see a trail wind its way up and over the summit of the mountain. It was obvious that people and animals had made those trails, but only the sheep to the south could be seen.

He continued at a leisurely pace not really knowing what he was going to do once he reached Avni's house. He entered the courtyard, stopped, and listened. Avni and Lida's shoes were on the first step of the front porch. He took a timid step up, and spying the bowl of grapes on the table helped himself to a cluster.

"Hello," he called. The door was open, and a sheer lace curtain covered the entrance. He pulled it aside just enough to stick his head in and repeated his greeting, but no one responded.

As he took a full step into the entry hall of the house, he suddenly had an overwhelming sense of *deja vu*. The interior of this house was exactly like the house on the island. He looked into the front living room furnished with three futons and a wood-burning stove. He continued into the house to the back bedroom, but no one was home.

Going out onto the front porch, he gazed out over the village, and his heart began to race at the mounting realization that he was all alone. While he had his doubts about Avni and Lida, their absence was somehow more terrifying. The rumble of the thunder over the ridge to the east resonated through the valley. In a rush of sudden panic, he called out at the top of his lungs.

"Avni! Lida! Where are you?" Only the reverberating echo of his own voice came back to him.

He ran out into the lane and headed in the opposite direction to the one he had gone before. His path ascended a steep, rocky trail that wound higher up the slope, and he soon was beyond the borders of the village and found himself on a high knoll overlooking the valley and the village below. Over his shoulder he could see a vanguard of dark clouds edging over the ridge. A sudden crack of thunder directly overhead sent him scurrying for cover under a nearby pine.

Within seconds yet another torrential downpour washed over the ridge and advanced quickly across the valley. Jeff sat huddled under the tree and watched the amazing display of lighting striking indiscriminately all along the rim and into the valley. Suddenly the hairs on the back of his neck stood on end, and he dove belly to the ground just as a blast of lightening shattered a tree directly behind him. Embers rained down all around; one singed the back of his hand covering his head. Another bolt struck a tree only yards away. The deafening explosions of energy disoriented him. He tried to stand, but another bolt hit up the slope from him, knocking him back to the ground.

He crawled on his hands and knees and tried to make for a two wheeled cart full of corn husks parked at the outskirts of a cornfield. The rain now made the path a mudslide that washed Jeff along with it. He struggled to control his descent, but the force of the slide carried him down the slope in a cascade of roiling earth. He shot straight past a steep hairpin turn in the path and was catapulted into a stand of tall corn. He came to a stop as the mud continued to flood around him. Rain beat his upturned face.

He tried to raise his head, but the effort was too much. He fell back. Rivulets buoyed his arms and legs causing him to slowly drift deeper into the cornfield. He finally came to rest on a patch of granite rubble.

The storm intensified. Jeff lay exhausted. The pounding of rain water numbed his face. He draped his elbow over his eyes and peered into the dark gray sky. Peals of thunder and flashes of lightening occurred almost simultaneously. His mind whirled with confused thoughts. Another bolt hit close by sending shards of burning wood and corn husks into the air. The two wheeled cart was obliterated.

After several moments he finally came to his senses and realized that he could not stay where he was. He rolled over onto his knees and searched above the tops of the corn. Discerning the outline of the ruins of an old house not far to his left, he scrambled through the corn stems keeping a low profile. At one point he lost his footing on a slippery rock and fell headfirst into another mud wash that carried him down the steep slope deeper into the valley. He was washed to the edge of the stream, which was now flowing rapidly and had risen to just below the edge of the bank.

He tried to grab hold of a sapling, but his grip was too slimy, and he slipped into the stream where he bobbed helplessly like a cork, snorting water from his nose and mouth. The current frustrated his efforts to level out his legs and swim as the river rushed him toward the wooden bridge. The flash flood had elevated the water level to within two feet of the bridge's bottom beam support. Jeff flung his body around in the torrent so that he was facing downstream and lurched for the bridge support, latching onto it with all his strength. The flow carried his legs under the bridge, but his grasp was firm. He rested for a moment to regain some of his strength, and then pulled himself towards the bank hand over hand until he was able to touch it with his feet.

He crawled out onto the west side of the bridge and collapsed near a corn row. Getting up, he staggered toward the promontory. It seemed to be a mile away in the downpour, but he forced himself to take one step after the other until he had reached the path that led up to the school. He scrambled through the grass avoiding the muddy waterfall it had become. Once he reached the school building, he used the wall to brace himself as he pushed through the wind and the rain to reach the church.

The door was shut tightly. He couldn't remember if he had even closed it, but the thought that he had actually left it open caused him to pause before forcing his way in. Lightening struck the lightening rod of the school, sending a surge of fire and sparks to the ground, and the heat of the explosion simmered the moisture on his face. With a mad surge of panicked strength he pushed his way into the church. The door gave way slowly as it yet again rubbed heavily against the wood planks of the floor.

Jeff fell to his knees gasping for air. He fought off the urge to vomit. Every muscle cried out for oxygen. He rolled over onto his back, and the familiarity of the raftered ceiling and the finch nest gave him a little respite from his harrowing ordeal. However, the wind seemed to suck the air out of the church as it blew through the broken windows making it hard to breathe. He shoved the door closed with his foot while still lying on his back and the fierceness of the draft lessened.

He propped his back against the door. His eyes fluttered with fatigue. Drenched and too tired to move, he sat with his legs splayed out in front of him and his arms to his side, palms up. The sick feeling he'd had a moment ago was beginning to subside, but a new feeling of hopelessness was mounting. He felt terribly alone, and afraid. Tears began to well up in his eyes as the last days events and the dispare over the darkness of his future began to become his reality. He had always had an attitude of invincibility. He was the epitome of an optimist. He knew that tomorrow could always be better than today. He had often said that he had never lived his best day eluding to the brightness of his future. But now... in this place he was confident he was going to die. He was glad Aubrey was not here, but he wished he had the support of Orhan, Jonathan, and the others.

The pounding of the rain against the roof distracted him from deeper thought, and he began to shiver. His attention was drawn to the finch, which darted through an east window and deftly made its way to the nest in the corner. As it flew through the center of the church Jeff noticed the odd configuration of the platform. He stared into the shadows with disbelief. He didn't want to face what he saw.

He steadied himself against the door as he slowly and painfully rose to his feet. He took a tentative step, and then another. He crept closer expecting at any moment for something to jump out at him. A pungent, musty, earthy smell clogged his nostrils. He snorted and placed his hand over his nose and mouth, trying to filter the stench.

To his horror the hatch to the underground chamber lay open.

# 26. No Ordinary Storm

Unknown Island off of Turkish Coast
23 January 2000, 6:00 a.m.

Aubrey stirred from nightmare-ridden sleep. She awoke to find Orhan, Mustafa, and Besnik stretched out along the floor of the shed using rolls of fishnet as pillows. The unnatural wind from the night before was over. She sat up and rubbed her sore elbow and knee. It seemed that every joint and muscle ached, but she couldn't readily recall all the details of that horrible storm.

She did not disturb the men, afraid of what the day was going to bring once they woke up. Her mind went to thoughts of Jeff and his mysterious disappearance, and she silently prayed for his safety. Her eyes stared through a crack in the brick wall where the mortar had crumbled out. Dawn was approaching.

She lay back against a grain sack and watched the three men sleep. They seemed restless, but did not wake. Her mind wandered to the fate of Anton and Nicoli. She had never really contemplated death, but she imagined death by drowning would be the worst. She was so tired. She realized for the first time that Jonathan was not with them. Anxiety grew in her chest and stomach.

The cry of gulls coming in from the sea startled Orhan awake. He sat up and rubbed his eyes, noticing Aubrey right away.

"Are you OK?" he asked.

"Yeah. I think so," she said. "I woke up a few minutes ago. I think it must be morning." She crossed her feet in front of her and said in a small voice, "What's happened to Jonathan?"

299

The somber expression on Orhan's face gave the answer before he spoke any words. "He is gone," he said sadly. "I saw him carried off by the wind out to sea. It was not natural. I do not know what it was, but I do know it was no ordinary storm. We are fortunate to be alive."

"I saw Anton and Nicoli die also," said Aubrey. "It was truly horrible. The sea just swallowed them up."

Mustafa stirred awake. The last few days had clearly taken a toll on his health. He looked gaunt and had dark circles under his already dark eyes. He coughed uncontrollably and spit up a thick, ropy mucous. His movement awakened Besnik, whose only movement was to open his eyes. Mustafa sat up with his legs sprawled in front of him. He kept his head down and stared at the floor between his legs.

Aubrey made a quick glance in his direction, but then turned back to Orhan.

"What are we going to do?" she asked.

"We need to get off this island," he said. "There may be the possibility that the second launch of the minion could still be on the beach."

"That is possible," said Mustafa through a morning cough. "If the storm was specifically directed at us, then the rest of the island may not have undergone as much damage.

"If the storm was directed at us, how did we survive?" asked Aubrey.

"Perhaps by these," Mustafa said as he pulled from his trouser pocket a small burlap pouch.

Aubrey, Orhan, and Besnik fumbled in their pockets and pulled out the *hajmali* that they had each been carrying.

"Jonathan and Anton would not have had one. I did not even think about them needing one. I am very sorry," said Mustafa. "Nicoli may have had his in his pack which I saw fall into the water as our launch bucked up onto the dock just before we climbed out."

"Be sure to keep them handy," said Aubrey. "We may need them again."

Orhan opened the door a crack and peered out into the alley. The air was cold and smelled of sea and fish. The sound of the gulls had escalated into a deafening cacophony of screeches and squawks. Orhan stuck his head out and looked down the alley toward the bay. The sky and waterfront were inundated by hundreds of white gulls that darted and dove in a wild frenzy.

"I have been around the sea all my life," he said, "but I have never seen so many gulls behaving this way."

Aubrey got up and looked over his shoulder. "Oh my gosh! What's going on?"

The air was so full of gulls that they could barely see the marina for the flutter of wings. No other sound could be heard above the din. Mustafa and Besnik pulled themselves up and stared out the door with them.

"This is very bad," muttered Mustafa.

"What's happening?" asked Orhan.

"I don't know," said Mustafa.

"I have not seen this before," said Besnik. "I have lived along the shores of the Black Sea, the Marmara Sea, the Aegean, and the Ionian, but I have never seen the gulls behave this way."

"It's as if nature is rising up against us," said Orhan. "Last night's storm, and now the gulls." He reached into his pocket and pulled out the ruby bracelet.

"Do you think the bracelet has something to do with this?" asked Aubrey.

"I wonder," said Orhan. "Maybe. I think we need to try to get back to the old man's house. There may be more answers found in the light of day than were found in the dark of night."

Besnik stepped into the alley and walked toward the square, peering cautiously around the corner. The swarm of gulls made it impossible to see the lighthouse or the ruins of the fortress at the mouth of the bay, but he could see the pier and the dock lying in shambles. All the boats were either thrown onto the shore or sunk outright with only their masts marking their watery graves. He ventured out into the square. The gulls hopped and dodged all around him.

Mustafa joined him. Each man had his weapons drawn as they made their way slowly to the edge of the pier. The gulls flew close but did not show signs of attacking them. Below the pier was a thin ribbon of rock beach strewn with seaweed and fragments of boats broken by the storm. There was no sign of Nicoli or Anton.

The cold morning air suddenly had a warm, balmy feel to it as the breeze picked up from the direction of land. The frenzy of the gulls increased. Soon they were strafing and dive-bombing the two Gypsies with wild fury. Mustafa ran and dove under a collapsed span of the dock. Besnik quickly climbed into a drain conduit, and the birds beat and pummeled themselves against the structures trying to get at them. One of the gulls managed to nip at Mustafa under the dock and gave him a cut above his right eyebrow. Mustafa swatted at the bird and struck it against the jagged end of a broken mooring post. The bird fell into the surf, dead.

A loud staccato of gunfire scattered the birds temporarily. Orhan and Aubrey were standing at the edge of the dock firing their handguns into the air. The flock of gulls was so tightly pressed that several birds fell dead at their feet.

"Are you guys crazy?" screamed Aubrey above the horrendous noise. "What do you think you're doing?"

"I wanted to find Nicoli!" screamed back Besnik. He popped off several rounds from his weapon, carelessly scattering his aim over his head. Three birds fell into the water.

Mustafa and Besnik used the distraction to climb back up onto the dock. The foursome ran back up to the village and found protection within the stand of houses. It did not take long for the gulls to get over their fright, and they swarmed again. As the group ran farther inland, they could feel the air cool, and the gulls' fury began to lessen. Soon only a handful continued the pursuit.

They forced open the door to a house and stood watching the sky. The attack of the seagulls was over. Aubrey looked at Orhan with tears welling up in her eyes.

"What is going on here?" she asked again.

He shrugged helplessly. "I don't know. I'm getting sick of this whole thing." His shoulders slumped in despair.

"We're in the middle of something far more involved than one jinn," said Mustafa. "There are too many new problems popping up."

After a thoughtful pause, Orhan asked, "Do you think Ölüm is free?"

"I don't think so," said Mustafa. "It could be something working in league with Ölüm, or it could be something completely unrelated, but obviously very deadly."

"I wish I knew what happened to Jeff," said Aubrey. "I want to go back to that house." She walked out into the alley without waiting for the men and headed in the direction of the old man's house.

The others quickly followed. The feeling of dread became heavier as they proceeded.

\* \* \*

When they arrived, the house was as it had been the night before when Jeff had disappeared. It sat dark, empty, and forlorn. The sun had risen above the crest of the hill and cast a long shadow through the courtyard. Orhan stood outside with Aubrey as Mustafa and Besnik went inside.

Orhan reached into his coat pocket and played nervously with the bracelet, rubbing the jewels between his fingers and thumb and mindlessly jiggling them up and down within the confines of the fabric. The bracelet began to warm to his touch. At first he thought it was due to friction built up between his flesh and the gems, but the warmth increased and soon became too hot to handle. With a frantic gasp he yanked the bracelet out of his pocket. The temperature increased so quickly that he feared it would burn a hole in the lining before he could remove it. He tried to hold onto it, but his fingers quickly blistered. He flung it to the ground and jumped away pulling Aubrey with him.

"What's wrong?" she yelled startled by his action.

"I was just rubbing the bracelet and it started getting very hot," he said blowing on his blistering fingertips.

Just then Mustafa and Besnik ran from the house.

"What happened?" demanded Mustafa. "The whole house just now shuddered."

"I was rubbing the bracelet inside my coat pocket when it suddenly built up a great deal of heat," said Orhan defensively. He bent down and picked it up. The temperature had dropped, but it was still warm despite having landed in a small puddle.

Mustafa took it carefully from him in his gloved hand. He rubbed it gently at first, then more forcefully. He could feel the heat through the glove, but it had enough insulation not to burn him. As the temperature increased, the rubies began to glow, casting a bright red assortment of rays in all directions. Mustafa held it up to the light and examined the small figures in the center of each of the gems. With the stimulation of the rising sunlight, the figures began to sway.

"They look like they're dancing," said Aubrey looking over Mustafa's shoulder.

With more exposure to the light, the figures became more animated. Mustafa held the bracelet aloft, allowing the rays of the rising sun to shine directly on to them. The bracelet began to throb in his grasp. He was no longer able to rub it with any coordination, so he stopped but did not relinquish his hold or the position of his hand to the sun. A deep resonating and fluctuating hum began to emanate from the rubies. It increased in volume with each second. Soon the sound was deafening.

Aubrey screamed and covered her ears against the pressure that pounded like gigantic bass woofers turned to full volume. Orhan and Besnik also flinched against the agonizing noise. Mustafa grimaced from the pain but continued holding the bracelet up, unrelenting. He meant to see this through to the end even if it killed him.

Orhan struggled against him to lower his arm out of the light, but Mustafa fought him off and pushed him back into the step of the front porch, causing him to fall. Orhan tried to regain his feet, but the pain that was mounting in his ears was crippling.

"Mustafa! Stop it!" screamed Aubrey, writhing in pain.

Besnik tried to grab Mustafa and pull him into the shade, but he was weak from the excruciating pain in his head. Mustafa fell to his knees, but with great effort he maintained the bracelet in the glow of the sunlight. He cried out in desperation as he became overwhelmed by what was now becoming an electric shock.

Aubrey fell to the ground and curled up in a ball, stuffing her fingers in her ears. The world began to spin around them as if they had been caught in the vortex of a tornado. She looked over to Mustafa, who had now collapsed and lay motionless only a few feet away. His hand holding the bracelet had fallen and lay limp at his side. Whatever power the bracelet possessed had now been unleashed and was sustained by its own energy.

Aubrey struggled to hold her head up, but the centrifugal force of the spin caused her to bob back and forth. Through the blur of motion she saw Orhan crawling toward her, and she felt compelled to crawl toward Mustafa, who now lay unconscious. Besnik made his way over to them, and the four companions huddled together in a heap in the middle of the whirlwind.

A ripple in space began to pulse from the bracelet like a pebble in a pond sending concentric waves out in all directions. Aubrey fell to her back and stared up into the funnel. After a few moments, she saw figures and shapes that at first she could not identify, but as she forced herself to concentrate she began to make out the events of life as it had once been in the village passing with incredible speed.

Orhan and Besnik struggled against the force but finally succumbed to the powerful spin and fell back as well, facing upward.

"Orhan, Help!" yelled Aubrey over the roar of the wind.

Orhan was powerless to do anything except slide his hand over and take hers in his. He realized for the first time that they were still lying on the ground even though it seemed they were floating in midair. He reached out and touched Besnik's arm. The two men rolled their heads laboriously and met each other's look of desperation. To the other side of Besnik, Orhan could see Mustafa lying on his side facing away from the rest of the group.

In the immediate wall of the cyclone, Aubrey could see the village they were in. The lighthouse at the mouth of the bay was the easiest to focus on, and spun into view in cyclic intervals like an air stem on a bicycle tire. Farther out from the whirling wall were other scenes of life. She could not tell whether they were from the past, present, or future. It startled her when she began to recognize scenes from her own life while in Turkey.

She saw herself digging with her hands through the rubble of a collapsed building. Although there was no sound other than the shrill whine of the whirlwind, she could see herself yelling frantically into the fallen fragments of concrete and brick. She relived the frenzy of when she and her team had pulled out a small child who had been buried under her building for two days after the earthquake. The shouts of joy from her fellow workers. The hope seen in everyone's eyes. Her heart ached as she saw Jeff tossing blocks of concrete and stone to the side trying to reach another survivor before it was too late. She watched herself and her friends as if they were on television. She remembered the pride she had felt after helping find survivors in the days that followed the earthquake in Adapazarı. The unspeakable sadness that came over her and the others when they pulled the lifeless bodies of men, women, and children from the rebar, concrete, and brick tombs they were encased in. The conversation she had had with her mother over the telephone when she called home to describe what she had been through with the relief efforts. Her mother in tears, begging her to come home. Wanting her not to waste her life in such a dangerous place.

The whirling of life continued. She realized that she was probably going to die here in this cyclone, but a sense of peace washed over her and a faint smile etched her lips. She realized without regret that had she not come to Turkey she would have never met Jeff. A painful stab struck her heart as she now knew she would never see him again.

Suddenly a terrifying scene came into view in the wall of the whirlwind—closer in this time, not so far out along the fringes. There to her utter delight followed quickly by horror was Jeff. She sensed that she no longer was seeing the past but was watching Jeff in the present or maybe even in the future. She could not tell. She called out his name. She didn't know if her call was audible or if she had just thought it. She called out his name again, but this time she made sure it was vocal and loud. She repeated the call several times, each time trying to muster more and more force from her lungs.

Jeff whirled in and out of view like the lighthouse. He seemed to be walking in a dark place illuminated by only a flaming torch. She called again, but this time he turned and stared right at her. She froze; the suddenness of his gaze paralyzed her. She called again. He squinted his eyes at her as if he saw her through a cloud or a sheer veil. She wanted to raise her arm and wave at him, but the force of the wind had her pinned to the ground. Then without warning his presence was gone. She began to sob bitterly and found herself being consoled by Orhan who had used all his strength to come closer to her side. She stared wild-eyed into his eyes. Had he seen Jeff? Was it all in her mind? She tried to speak, but her throat was parched.

"I saw Jeff," she finally managed to croak out audibly enough for him to hear her. "He's alive!"

"I know," shouted Orhan. "I saw him, too…and a lot of other strange things," he added.

The power of the tornado began to decrease. Soon it was little more than a strong wind that died down to a stiff breeze. Aubrey, Orhan, and Besnik lay panting on their backs. Mustafa still made no movement. Their surroundings were the same, but as they lay there in the courtyard of the old man's house something seemed very different. It was Besnik that noticed the change first.

"Look!" he said. "There are grapes on the vines."

As they regained their ability to concentrate, they noticed that not only were there grapes on the vines that hung from the grid wires overhead but the trees and bushes also had leaves on them. The sunlight shone hotter. Orhan swatted a fly away from his face. He struggled to sit upright, but when he did he could see that the village had been transformed from winter to summer.

They stood and removed their outer coats and draped them over their arms. They went to the gate of the courtyard and looked down the path toward the rest of the village. The smell of salt air and fish filled their nostrils.

# Vale of Shadows

Behind them Mustafa stirred for the first time since he had been knocked unconscious by the bracelet. He sat up but fell back from weakness; Besnik caught him just before he hit the ground and propped him up, trying to steady him. He seemed disoriented and almost completely drained of strength. After several moments he was able to regain some of his bearings and looked up at the last three of his fellow survivors. He absently took in his surroundings. Soon a frown crossed his face as he became aware of the changes. He tried to speak, but his voice was coarse and raspy as if he had not drunk water for days.

"What happened?" he asked Besnik in Romani.

"The bracelet has changed things," said Besnik. "We have not had time to investigate."

Mustafa made an attempt to stand but fell back into Besnik's arms. After being steadied he stood, but it took all his strength and concentration to stay on his feet. He feebly unbuttoned his black greatcoat.

"Why is it so hot?" he croaked. "I need water."

"It seems we have moved through time," said Besnik. "It may be late summer by the looks of the grapes."

"How is that possible?" Mustafa had a look of complete bewilderment. He noticed, as if for the first time, Orhan and Aubrey standing next to him. He tried to form his words in English. "How long have we been here?"

"Not long," said Orhan with a pause. "Or maybe we have been here for months or even years. We don't know."

Besnik brought a bucket of water from around the corner of the house that was full of rain water and gave it to Mustafa. He drank, and then passed the container to the others.

Mustafa, Besnik, Orhan, and Aubrey turned and stared at the house. It stood before them in mocking silence mysteriously transformed into a shining, whitewashed habitat. Orhan was the first to move toward the house. He stepped through the front door. The house appeared as it had been when they first saw it. Furnished, clean, lived in. He called out, but no one answered.

He looked back toward the others, who were still standing at the gate. They urged him on with encouraging nods. He walked on into the house and stood before the infamous stove. This morning a jar of freshly cut flowers sat on top of it. The scene struck him as odd because he had not noticed any of this variety of flower outside in the garden. He considered it for a moment but decided it was a small matter and let it go. When he bent down and opened the latch to the stove, it was clean of any ash or soot.

He suddenly felt the hairs on the back of his neck stand on end. He whirled around expecting someone to be standing behind him, but no one was there. He looked uneasily around the room. He couldn't shake the feeling that he was not alone in the house. He felt a presence. The feeling was so strong that he called out a greeting. He closed the door to the stove and walked around the room slowly examining the walls. The decoupaged icon, the out-of-date calendar, the plastic flowers hanging in a sconce, all were where he remembered them to be before they had lain down to sleep.

Another cold shiver went down his spine. He was certain now that he was not alone. He turned in a slow circle, his hand resting against the grip of the handgun he had tucked in his belt.

"Who's there?" he called out.

Again no answer, but this time he saw the air in the center of the room stir like he was looking though a ripple in the water. He took a wary step back toward the door and nearly jumped out of his skin when he bumped into Aubrey, who had hesitantly followed him into the house. His startled yelp embarrassed him when he realized who it was.

"I'm sorry," she apologized. "I didn't mean to scare you."

"It's OK," he panted holding his hand over his heart. "Something strange is happening. Do you see it?"

It took Aubrey a few seconds to get adjusted to the light, and then she saw the formless stirring in the center of the room.

"What is it?" she asked.

"I'm not sure, but it only started a moment ago."

"It looks like one of those trick mirrors at a carnival." She reached her hand slowly toward the apparition as if drawn to it, but Orhan grabbed her back before she could extend enough to touch it.

"Don't do that," he warned. "We do not know what it is."

"Maybe it has something to do with Jeff," she said, her eyes pleading.

"Jeff?" Orhan hadn't considered this. "Yes, maybe it does have something to do with him. I saw him in the cyclone."

"I'm sure I saw him also. It was like I was watching him from a great distance. He was walking in a dark place. It looked like he was groping to find his way. Whatever this disturbance is may have something to do with his disappearance."

"You may be right, but just the same do not go sticking your hands in things you do not know about."

"Yes, father," she mocked.

The disturbance became more apparent. It soon became a concentric wave that pulsed from its center. Orhan and Aubrey could see the stove on the other side, but it was like looking at a rock at the bottom of a clear pond while standing on the edge. Suddenly the shape of a figure could be seen emerging from its depths. It moved closer to the surface, growing in size as it approached. Orhan and Aubrey were too terrified to move, but Mustafa had moved in behind them. He recognized the danger immediately and dragged both of them out of the house.

"Run!" he shouted. "Run to the beach."

They ran with all of their might. No one dared to look back. They hurdled the rock and brick debris of the fortress ruins and with out hestitating jumped over the crest of the hill. Each managed to keep their feet as they ran with abandon.

Ten feet off the surf was the second launch of the minion turned up on its side. The three men collided into the bottom with all the force they could muster and aided by the surge of adrenaline coursing through their veins the launch toppled over onto its keel just a foot from the water.

The nauseating stinch they had smelled during the storm at the marina blew in on the increasingly turbulent wind from the land. The four companions desperately pushed and pulled the launch until they had heaved it into the water. The wind began to whip around them fiercely as they climbed into the boat.

Orhan fumbled in his pocket for the bracelet. When he didn't find it he screamed over the wind, "Where is the bracelet?"

A sickening feeling hit them all at once as they realized that it had never been picked up off the ground in front of the house.

"How could we have been so stupid?" shouted Mustafa angrily.

Besnik tried to start the engine, but it only coughed and sputtered having lain on its side for eight months. Secured to the stern gunwale was a can of fuel. Orhan poured a small amount into the carburetor and singled for Besnik to keep turning the engine over. Finally it caught and the propellers churned into the sea.

Dark clouds built with great intensity over the land and blew out towards them. The launch hurled through the waves away from the shore breaking and pitching as the wind stirred up the sea. Soon the mysterious island was just a small speck on the dark horizon.

# Vale of Shadows

The howl of the wind began to slowly subside, and a new hope began to build as the desperate fugitives began to realize they had escaped.

*   *   *

Avni stared out to sea from the fortress ruins. He had lost this round. He began to make his way back to the house when he saw the ground strewn with several small burlap pouches. This explained his inability to stop Orhan and his companions.

"Curse that meddling Gypsy," he spat.

Lida met him at the edge of the village. In her hand was the ruby bracelet.

"It is as you suspected," she said. "They used the ruby bracelet to come to this time. They are fortunate they weren't killed."

Avni grunted with disdain. "That Gypsy is becoming very tiresome."

The brother and sister turned and made their way back to the portal. This battle would be continued on Albanian soil.

# 27. The Altar Chamber

Curraj i Epërm, Albania
12 August 2000

Jeff looked around the church for something better than his flashlight to peer back down through the hatch. He went back outside and made his way through the rain to a pile of discarded lumber outside the school. To his surprise and delight he found a half-empty bucket of roofing tar lying on its side next to the lumber. He picked through to the bottom of the pile and found a dry stick under some thicker boards. He swabbed the end of the stick into the tar trying to pierce through the outer skin to the oil underneath.

Then he ran back to the church hunched over, protecting the stick from the rain with his body. As he neared the platform, he could feel his pulse beat in his ears. He knelt down and pulled his lighter out of the front pouch of his backpack, clicking it a few times with his thumb and holding it under the oiled end of the stick until it ignited.

Jeff descended down the winding stone stairs. The torchlight penetrated the darkness in a way that the electric flashlight had not. Its light flickered off the stone walled silo. He could now see that the stairs wound down the center of a handmade stone shaft. They continued to drop into the darkness below him. He studied the walls periodically in the dim orange light of the torch. The stones were cut in irregular rectangular blocks, mortar replaced by peat moss long ago.

The air became heavier and warmer the deeper he went. Something he had not noticed the first time he descended the stairs. He thought back to the times as a kid he had gone to the Cave of the Winds in Colorado and Mammoth Cave in

Kentucky. Those caves, he remembered, had gotten cooler the deeper he went. A hot breeze came up through the shaft. The flame of the torch wavered and sputtered, and he feared it would go out. Glowing embers broke away and floated like leaves on the breeze as the wood of the stick began to burn. They danced and circled, falling and then rising. Jeff hurried to get to the bottom. His makeshift torch was burning up quickly due to the wind from below.

He was not far from the watery bottom. The last ember was burning weakly and began to die out. With just a glimmer of amber light left, he reached the bottom and used what light he had to quickly scan his surroundings. To his relief there was a torch mounted in a sconce on the wall within arm's reach. He grabbed it and with the last ember ignited the new torch. It burst into a lively flame. He winced at the pungent odor of creosol.

Unlike the poor illumination of the flashlight, the torch chased the shadows into the deepest crevices of the silo. The surface of the water shimmered in the light, but Jeff could see a well-defined bottom; the water was only about two feet deep. He could feel the texture of the stone floor beneath his boots. He waded out away from the stair.

To his left a low arch opened into another chamber. He ducked through and stood upright in a natural cave that expanded well beyond the limits of the torchlight, straining to see through the surface of the water. The floor was no longer cut stone but had become a path of pebbles and small, rounded rocks like a riverbed. The added traction gave him confidence to proceed.

He fanned the torch over his head gazing up at the high, vaulted ceiling of the cavern. Stalactites hung menacingly. Jeff came to a stalagmite that jutted up from the floor in front of him and placed his hand on it for balance. It was warm to the touch. The lack of cooler temperatures at this depth in the earth

315

troubled him. As he stood he could now see the current of the water flowing in the direction he had been walking. While he was sloshing through it, he had assumed he was in standing water, but now he realized he was making his way down a subterranean stream.

He heard a voice. Faint at first, and then louder. He strained to hear where it was coming from. He knew this could not be real as the voice called his name. He turned to the direction it had come from, but nothing was there. He started to answer but was afraid to call out. The voice was gone. He continued groping through the darkness, attributing the paranoia to his growing claustrophobia.

When he rounded the stalagmite, he quickly found himself waist deep and began to panic, taking short, gasping breaths. He turned and rushed back the way he had come until he was in shallower water. He tried to control his fear, but suddenly he felt spied on from every direction. He waved his torch in an arc as if warding off an attacker, but none came. His eyes began to play tricks on him as he thought he saw black shades moving in the shadows at the edge of his light. He fumbled to find the Beretta tucked in his pants, but the more he struggled to free it from his belt the more panicked he became.

The sound of falling rocks trickled into the river ahead and to his right beyond the edge of the halo of light. Jeff froze, and then forced himself to move forward, keeping the torch well above his head. He had finally freed the pistol and clutched it with white-knuckled ferocity. As he made his way through the cavern, he began to see glimpses of a far wall looming ahead. The river made a gentle turn to the right. He continued in waist-deep water along the undulating riverbed. He sensed a presence in the darkness. Following and observing. Stalking.

The current became swifter, swirling and bubbling around him on its way into the blackness. His foot struck a larger boulder, causing him to let out a yelp as he stumbled forward. He caught himself before he went under, sparing the torch, but he lost his grip on the Beretta. He fished frantically for it, but the water was too deep for him to reach the bottom and hold the torch at the same time. He scanned the edge of the river and found a small outcropping of rock with a crack full of gravel wide enough to wedge the end of the torch. Having secured it with small stones around the base, he went back to the spot where he had lost the handgun and leaned into the water as deep as he could without getting his face wet. He groped with both hands but found that his arms were still not long enough to reach the bottom. He stood up and looked at the surface.

"I really don't want to do this," he muttered under his breath. Then he took a deep breath and plunged into the warm current. He had to expel a lot of his air in order to compensate for the buoyancy of his clothing. He was too afraid to open his eyes, so he felt along the rocky bottom until he touched the handle of his gun. He quickly grabbed it and burst out of the water sputtering the foul taste of the river in his mouth. As he did so he caught movement out of the corner of his eye near the torch.

He spun around with the weapon leveled ready to fire when he was pushed violently from behind. He fell face-first into the river and struggled madly to regain his footing on the slippery gravel. Another form appeared near the torch, but this time it did not scamper away into the shadows. Jeff fired his nine-millimeter at the figure, but a heavy arm clubbed him from behind knocking the gun out of his hand. He screamed in terror and whirled to face his assailant. As he did so the figure on the bank jumped into the water and put a strangle hold on him. Jeff fought ineptly to free himself, but the strength of the arm that held him was too great. He cried out, but the pressure on his throat began to cut off his air. Soon he found himself gasping for breath. His ears and eyes burned for lack of oxygen, his head throbbed, and he felt himself slowly losing consciousness.

The glow of his torch faded into a wash of ambient light. He soon had no more strength to fight against his attacker and feebly released his clutch on the powerful arm holding him as his own arms dropped limply to his side. Through the gloom that was overtaking him, he saw the silhouette of a figure standing before him. Jeff fell limp into the water, but his head was kept from going under by the creature that had strangled him. He thrashed out one last time, but he had no strength left.

The creature was now bent over him in the water holding Jeff's chin up. He thought that he must be dreaming as he stared into the eyes of a human being. Into a face that looked vaguely familiar. The vision of Përparim Lleshi on his deathbed played in his mind. Gazing at him with those same eyes bidding him to "come." Jeff's mind swooned into darkness.

\* \* \*

Silence. Complete, utter silence. Jeff could sense himself rising slowly back to consciousness. Little by little the pain in his throat and neck stimulated him to wake. He coughed a raspy, painful cough and raised his hand to his throat to tenderly palpate the bruise. Through his eyelids he could see the glow of light, but the thought of opening his eyes terrified him. He slowly squinted them open and peeked through the slits. Torches mounted on the walls in a ring around him illuminated the small chamber. He gazed up at the dark expanse beyond the firelight. He could discern no ceiling in the deep blackness. A soft breeze of warm air washed over him from his right, and he turned his head to see a low, arched doorway that led to another chamber. He rolled his head around to look at his surroundings, confident from the silence that he was alone.

He finally got up the courage to rise to a sitting position. He ached all over. Rubbing his neck, he looked down and noticed that the floor was dry rock. He listened intently for any sound of the river, but heard none. After a few moments, however, he heard a scraping sound in the other chamber that sent a heart-stopping shiver down his spine. He quickly lay back down and pretended he was still unconscious. Soon he felt a presence in the chamber with him. For a moment the warm breeze stopped, so he knew that whom- or whatever it was had paused and blocked the doorway. Then he heard soft breathing and felt the breeze again. The presence came and stood over him. He tried desperately not to flinch, but he could feel the panic swelling up inside of him to the point of explosion.

He realized that he was holding his breath and was about to run out of air. He dared not open his eyes, but he knew he was still being studied. He began to see floating spots in the darkness behind his eyelids. A high-pitched whine escalated in his ears and he felt the same sensation that he had felt when he was being strangled, but this time he was doing it to himself. He grabbed the outer seams of his pants legs with his clenched fists trying to hold on. His lungs burst with fire. The agony of the pressure in his chest became unbearable. He curled his toes to eke out the last bit of oxygen he could muster. He writhed and convulsed, finally exploding and satiating his deprived lungs in large gulps. He bolted up using his left elbow for support, his back to the presence. Jagged coughing ensued until his ribs hurt.

"I was wondering when you would stop that charade," said a feminine voice behind him.

Jeff slowly turned and met the gaze of Lida. She stood beside him in the form of the beautiful young woman he had seen earlier. Her eyes gleamed in the firelight. He was captivated by them. He tried to pull his gaze away, but she held his gaze with hers. He shifted his weight so that he could swing his legs over the edge of the stone platform he had been lying on. As he did so she released his gaze, and he could now see that he had been spread out on a stone altar cut out of the rock. She stepped to the side as he got to his feet.

"Where am I?" he asked still groggy from the ordeal.

"Where you should not be," she answered in a motherly reprimand.

"OK, I'll go along with that, but really, where am I?"

"In a cavern deep within the earth. You could have been killed intruding into a place where you do not belong. This isn't Kansas, you know."

"No kidding," he retorted.

Jeff felt sick. He sat back down and rubbed his forehead. Lida put a gentle hand on his shoulder. It felt like a deep, heating balm on a sore muscle. The warmth spread through his shoulder and down his arm. He felt it crossing over to the other shoulder and through the arm and hand that was massaging his forehead. The touch soothed his headache and calmed his queasy stomach. Soon he felt better and raised his head.

"You have been through a great deal in the last few days," she said soothingly. "Your stamina must endure for a great deal more if you are to survive. I wish I had better news for you, but the danger is not over."

Jeff let her words sink in. He stood back up and straightened. Lida stood nearly a full head taller than he was, something he had not noticed before. She faced him dressed in a sheer cotton blouse covered discreetly with a red embroidered vest. She wore a baggy pantaloon wrapped with a sash that wound around her waist, the end of which was tied in a decorative knot. Her feet were shod with intricately embroidered slippers made of gold thread and brightly colored silks.

"How much time has passed?" he asked finally, unable to come up with anything better.

"By the time of men, very little," she said. "The time measurement of the jinni is, of course, completely different, and in this time you have passed many months. The chronometer on your wrist probably indicates it is still winter, but as you saw earlier we are currently in late summer."

Jeff walked around the stone altar. It was hewn smooth from the rock floor and rose about a meter from the base. It was roughly three meters square. He fingered the polished surface as he circumvented the platform.

"What is this platform?" he asked, not wanting to use the word *altar*.

"Altar, actually," said Lida, overriding his attempt. "It is an altar."

"Altar for what?"

Lida smiled. She looked at him in a way that made him uncomfortable. "I am not so sure that you are ready to know that information," she said with a bemused lilt in her voice. "All will be made known at the proper time."

Jeff hated the ominous sound of that last statement. He tried to remain calm and not give away the fact that he had no faith in his new "friends." He walked over to the arched doorway and peered into the darkness. The light from his chamber cast a shallow pall beyond the threshold. His shadow loomed over the smooth rock surface of the floor.

He looked back around at Lida, who was watching him curiously.

"May I have this?" he asked as he took a torch from its wall mounting. He proceeded through the door without waiting for her answer.

The next chamber was much larger, extending beyond the torchlight. Along the floor was etched a path in the stone worn smooth by centuries of foot traffic, or so Jeff assumed. He ventured only a little way, and then turned to see Lida standing in the doorway watching him.

"Who attacked me?" he called back. "It wasn't you, was it?" He said this more as a hopeful statement than a question.

"No, it was not me. There are other beings here in the earth. It was they who secured you."

"Secured me. They almost *killed* me," exclaimed Jeff as he began to walk back toward Lida.

"They secured you for your own protection," she said calmly. "You were about to hurt yourself. They had been watching you from the time you entered the stairs."

"The face I saw, I had seen before." Jeff was now standing next to Lida looking back at the altar. He replaced the torch in its sconce. "Who was it?"

"The face you saw belonged to the enslaved remnant of your ancestor Përparim Lleshi." Jeff stared at her, aghast. "His spirit is here along with many others from your line. That is part of the curse. The jinni are bound and released, but the souls of those who bound them are here to trudge through the disparity of darkness for as long as the curse is in place. The power and bitterness of Baba Moush are far reaching, as you can see."

"In the vision I saw Baba Moush was killed by Selim Bey. I don't see how he would have had time to cast any spells. I saw him utter one quick thing, and then he died."

"Baba Moush was the leader of a brotherhood of sorcerers. All of his fellow magicians had been slain by one side or the other. He trusted no one. The magic that he concocted was put in place long before that fateful day on Mount Tomori. It was designed to be implemented at his death. Even if he had not been betrayed by the Albanians and the Turks, he had planned to destroy their leaders as revenge for the deaths of his brotherhood."

"There is so much that I don't understand," said Jeff. He studied the surface of the altar. His mind was plagued with thoughts of doom and disaster. He worried about Aubrey, Orhan and Jonathan. Finally he looked up at Lida and studied her for a moment. "So what you're telling me is that the ghost of Lleshi is here, in this cavern?"

"Yes. He is doomed to wonder the darkness. He and the others will not readily expose themselves to the light, not even the light of the torches."

"I was carrying a torch when they attacked me," said Jeff.

"They did so at great pain to themselves," replied Lida. "Lleshi knows his progeny. Many of them are here. Part of his punishment, if you will, is to know that his actions caused so much grief to his family. It is true you were strangled to the point of losing consciousness, but only to that point. Had you been any other intruder you would have been slain."

Jeff gave a deep, prolonged sigh. "OK, but what about all the other deaths between the cycles? Were they caused by the jinni?"

Lida looked amused. "My, you do change subjects quickly."

"I'm sorry. I told you I had a lot of questions. They just aren't all in order."

"The deaths were caused by the nature of man not by jinni. 'It is appointed unto man once to die...' You know this saying I think."

"I've heard of it," said Jeff. *A Bible quoting jinn*, he thought. *What next*?

Lida noticed the look on Jeff's face. "Oh, don't worry. Your time has not yet come. There still may be hope for you."

Jeff sat down on the altar and folded his hands in his lap. "So when will the jinni be released?"

"Two days from now by your time reckoning. By the reckoning of the jinni it will be just about anytime now."

"What do you mean, 'just about anytime now'?" asked Jeff alarmed.

"I mean that within the next hour or so they will both be released at the same time." She stared off into the darkness of the chamber beyond the doorway. "It will be the first time they have been united for nearly six hundred years. We have been waiting a long time for this."

Jeff took a deep gulp. He tried not to betray the intense terror he was feeling at that moment, but the pressure in his ears began to build and throb. He realized it was his heartbeat. When

he would not make eye contact with Lida, she came and stood in front of him.

"If you fail to survive, I am sure you will not be destined for this place. All who come here have led evil lives and must tarry here until the judgment of God is carried out."

Jeff perked up when he heard God mentioned. Lida noticed his shift in posture.

"Oh yes, we believe in God," she assured him. "He is the maker of all things. All creatures are ultimately accountable to him."

Jeff frowned. His Christian faith, his beliefs, all that he had been taught seemed so far from his conscious, everyday life lately. He opened his mouth to speak, but Lida interrupted him.

"You are one of the redeemed," she continued. "No one has power over your soul. You belong to God. You may lose your physical life here in these caverns, but you will not lose your eternal spirit. Does this encourage you?"

"You have no idea," said Jeff. He felt stronger, more prepared to face his dark future. "What do I have to do?"

She smiled a broad smile at him and wrapped her arm around his shoulder. He felt the exhilarating warmth from her touch he had felt earlier. "Soon Avni will return," she said, "and much that remains in darkness will be brought to the light."

Her last words echoed in his head, and his vision became tunneled. He slumped back on the altar. Lida released the pressure she had subtly applied to the base of his skull, gazing down at him with a sardonic grin.

# IV

Ek tha do mosh. Usk ple
neter.
Ke se mosh. Usk ple neter.
Binding spell
Lamb Parchment

# 28. Jinni, Passports, and Queens

They beached the boat on a rough, rocky beach and packed the supplies that were salvable from the minion in their knapsacks. After a short hike they arrived at Ecebat, on the Turkish cost where Mustafa intended to steal a car, but Orhan talked him out of it and they ended up buying a1988 Mercedes Benz 560 SEL.

"We will go by way of Korça in the south," said Mustafa. "We will see what my mother has to say about all of this. Our clan is currently outside of that city.

Orhan drove first with Aubrey in the front. Mustafa and Besnik quickly fell asleep in the back. They drove without stopping until they came to the Turkish D110 and headed west for Alexandroupolis, Greece. The desperation of their haste lay just under the surface of all their thoughts. Stops were for quick gas, food, and restroom breaks. No one needed to be prodded along. The sense of urgency hovered over them even in the shallow naps they took.

When they reached the Greek border to cross into Albania, they were delayed by a long line of traffic on the Greek side of the border. Aubrey and Mustafa took their passports to the passport control booth and waited in the growing heat of the morning of the second day. They had driven through the night making good time on the well-maintained Greek roads, but soon the delay at the border became unbearable.

Mustafa checked his watch. They had already spent forty-five minutes in line and they had not even arrived at the Albanian border. Aubrey restrained him from getting out of line and going up to the window to see what the problem was. He turned and shouted to Besnik, who was sitting in the car with Orhan, something in Romani that Aubrey was certain had something to do with a slur against the ancestry of the Greek officials.

After another fifteen minutes, Aubrey and Mustafa were finally allowed to step up to the window. Aubrey nervously handed the four passports through the window, placing her blue American passport on top. The official thumbed through her's first, searching for an entrance stamp into Greece. When he found none he quickly flipped through the other three.

"Your passports are not in order," he said to Aubrey in English. "You have no stamp to enter this country."

"I know," she apologized trying to think of something to say to get out of the problem. "I was in Turkey and I didn't have time to get a visa because of an emergency."

"You are American. You do not need a visa to get into Greece."

"Oh, well, I don't know why there...would...be a problem then," she said looking at Mustafa for help with an explanation.

"They were out of ink for the stamp," offered Mustafa. "They told us to just go, because it was the middle of the night."

The official made no pretense that he believed Mustafa's explanation. "At what border were they out of ink?" he asked, his tone deeply sarcastic.

"At the Turkish border," answered Aubrey.

"What was your business in Greece?"

"We had no business," said Mustafa. "We are just passing through to get to Albania."

"So you are coming from Turkey? What business did you have there?"

"We were visiting friends," said Aubrey. "One of our Turkish friends is traveling with us. He is in the car."

"I want your entire group to come here," said the officer.

Mustafa motioned for Besnik and Orhan to come to the booth. When they got out of the Mercedes, drivers in line behind them laid on their horns in frustration. The traffic was now backed up a half a mile. Orhan shrugged and pointed to the passport control booth, passing the blame onto them.

Another officer typed in their passport numbers. When they did not show up on the computer, he walked over to the first officer and whispered something in his ear. He looked at the four standing before him suspiciously.

"How is it you came here without going through our system?" he asked. "You will have to wait here until we get this problem cleared up."

The impatience of the other drivers escalated as they began to get out of their cars and yell at the border guards. Soon there were about thirty people standing at the booth shouting obscenities at the guards for being so slow. The sun was hot and there was no shade. Tempers began to flare as a shoving match broke out between two of the other drivers who were trying to advance their position by cutting in line.

Aubrey went up to the first officer and said, "Listen I don't know why we are not in your system, but all we want is to get to Albania. I promise you that we're not criminals, or terrorists, but we must get through."

The guard looked from her to the passports and then at the potential riot that was on the verge of starting.

"You promise you are not troublemakers?" he asked.

"I...we promise," said Aubrey, startled by his acquiescence.

The guard quickly opened the four passports and stamped them with an exit seal. He handed them back to Aubrey dismissively and waved them on through the gate. They ran to the car and hopped in. Mustafa sped the car through the raised gate before the guard changed his mind.

When they entered the neutral zone, Aubrey leaned up from the back seat and asked, "How did we get through from the Turkish border?"

"While you were sleeping we pulled over to the side of the road not far from the gate," said Besnik. "There was some trouble with two truckers. When they finally were allowed to pass through, we sneaked in between them."

Aubrey looked at his face in the rearview mirror and gave him an angry look. "We are in a hurry. We can't afford to be put in jail."

"It is the Gypsy way," said Mustafa without apology.

They drove the quarter of a mile to the Albanian border gate and parked the car in the shade of an olive tree. Mustafa and Aubrey once again took the passports up to the passport control booth. The Albanian guard took them and looked for the appropriate stamps. He then handed them two small forms for each passport, one for entry and one for exiting Albania, and told them in Albanian that they each had to fill them out before they could be allowed through.

They all grudgingly filled out the forms on the hood of the car, taking turns using the only pen they had, which belonged to Aubrey. When they were done, Aubrey handed them back through the window to the officer. He took each one in turn and wrote slowly and deliberately their information on a separate form. His lack of urgency was starting to really get on everyone's nerves. Finally after fifteen minutes the guard handed back their passports and told them that they each had to pay a ten-dollar entrance tax. When Orhan began to pay in Turkish lira, the guard waved his index finger in a negative gesture and made a clucking sound with his tongue on the back of his front teeth.

"We only take U.S. dollar," he said in English with a heavy, slurred accent.

"I have *leke*," said Mustafa in Albanian.

"No, only dollar," said the officer again.

The men looked helplessly at Aubrey. She fished through her bag looking for forty dollars for them to pay the embarkation tax. Finally she and Orhan scrounged together enough dollars to satisfy the guard. They had spent an agonizing hour and a half getting across the border.

\* \* \*

Mustafa wasted no time driving the Mercedes through the rough, winding roads on his way to the Gypsy village out side of Korça. It had been many years since he had been to Albania, and much had changed since the fall of Communism. The first noticeable change was the number of cars on the road. When he had been here last, there were very few automobiles. People were not allowed to travel very far from their villages. Most walked, used donkeys, or road in horse-drawn carts.

The poorly maintained road was strewn with potholes. Whole sections were washed into ditches as water undermined the support of the badly engineered asphalt. In some areas there was just barely enough room for one car to pass. Pedestrians walked precariously close to the edge carrying plastic bags full of produce from village venders.

Aubrey decided that it would be best if she didn't look out the window. She nervously glanced at her three companions, who were taking the ride in stride, although occasionally Orhan grabbed the back of Besnik's seat when Mustafa took a curve to fast.

They soon drove through the mountain pass that entered the sprawling valley of the Korçan plane. The road wound south, which made Orhan uneasy as he thought they were traveling in the wrong direction. Mustafa explained to him that it was very important to see his mother before they confronted the jinni.

"She taught Ermal," he explained. "She has many strong spells and potions"

The valley was broad and ran north to south surrounded by mountains on all sides. A gigantic white cross on the side of the mountain to the east overlooked the city. Out in the fields, men from the villages were cutting wheat with long scythes while the women gathered the sheaves up into bundles to be threshed. Aubrey remembered her time in the villages of Albania with fondness and wished she could be returning under better circumstances.

They entered town from the north and drove past the open market. Ahead loomed a large Orthodox cathedral. They veered to the right and followed the road that led to Erseka. The village Mustafa's mother lived in was in a neighborhood in the south part of Korça called Lagja Gjashtë. The road was lined with stark gray concrete apartments, a reminder of the crude architecture of the Communist era.

Mustafa turned off the potholed paved road onto an even bumpier dirt road and drove past an abandoned factory that looked like it had been unused for nearly a decade. The infrastructure of the entire nation top to bottom had been undermined when the government collapsed. They passed along a gray cinder block wall topped along its length with broken glass and barbed wire to keep out intruders, and then came to a gated driveway that led into a large courtyard surrounded by low concrete block and brick buildings. The compound was an unkempt disaster zone of concrete blocks, rebar, broken glass, weeds, and rough gravel strewn across the ground. A group of dark-complexioned children wearing tattered clothing were kicking a deflated soccer ball through the dangerous obstacles.

Aubrey cringed at the way they carelessly ran around the glass and rebar in their bare feet.

Mustafa parked the Mercedes next to an old, rusted-out bus, the windows long broken out and the rubber from the tires vulcanized into brittle, cracked strips that hung from the wheels. Mustafa and Besnik walked to where several old men were playing dominoes; Orhan and Aubrey timidly followed behind. The old men raised suspicious eyebrows at the intruders, and then continued with their game, ignoring them with indifference.

"I am here to see Merriam," Mustafa said in Romani.

The men looked up at him with more interest when they heard their mother tongue. A younger man stepped from the shade of an open room behind the small tables of the old men. He had shoulder-length black hair and a black, scraggly beard and moustache. His complexion was dark, and his eyes were penetrating brown. He wore a dirty tank top with khaki shorts. His worn-out sandals revealed rough, calloused feet that had had little protection from dirt, fungus, hot weather, and cold. He stepped towards Mustafa and Besnik and eyed them up and down with his thumbs hooked in the straps of his tank top.

"What do you want with Merriam?" he asked back in Romani.

"She is my mother," said Mustafa.

"She is everyone's mother," said the young man. "She is queen."

"I am her son, Mustafa."

"No, that cannot be," said the young man doubtfully. "Her son left long ago, and is now dead. Killed in Spain, I think."

"No. I am very much alive," said Mustafa, irritation growing in his tone. "Enough of this! I must see her now. Where is she?"

The young man stepped aside, thumbs still hooked in his straps, and allowed Mustafa and Besnik to enter. He watched them go by, glaring at them suspiciously. When Orhan and Aubrey stepped up to enter, he quickly squared around and blocked their way.

"You cannot enter, *gadjo*," he said to Orhan in Albanian.

Aubrey understood enough Albanian to know that they were not welcome and tugged on Orhan's arm to get him to back off.

"We can wait outside," she said, still pulling him away from the entrance. "Let's wait here in the shade around the corner." She didn't like the way the men looked at her.

The late morning sun was beginning to scorch the top of their heads, so they leaned up against the side of the building in the shade. The Gypsy children quickly pressed in on them holding out their hands in begging gestures.

"What do they want?" asked Orhan.

"Anything you have," said Aubrey. She reached into her bag and searched for something she could give them. Finding nothing she apologetically shrugged and shook her head *no*. They scampered off and disappeared around the corner into another building. Within seconds they came screaming back out into the courtyard followed by six more children who pushed and shoved their way to the front of the pack to beg. The children became more forceful. "*Jo!*" she said firmly. "Don't push."

The Gypsy men had stopped playing dominoes and began laughing at Orhan and Aubrey's predicament. Finally the press of children was becoming a near riot. With no help from the adults to calm the kids, Orhan grabbed Aubrey firmly by the hand, and shoved past the children with disgust forcing his way passed the Gypsy man blocking the door with an intimidating stare-down.

Once inside they saw Mustafa and Besnik standing over a woman sitting in a moth-eaten high-back upholstered chair.

Merriam sat with widespread legs covered by a dingy, multicolored, horizontally striped dress. Her strong, sinewy fists rested on her thighs. Her hair was raven black with strikes of gray. Her eyes were dark but gleamed with recognition as she gazed up at her long lost son, and smiled at him with a toothless smile. Mustafa began to speak, but she cut him off with a wave of her hand.

"You, I heard, were dead" she said in the language of her clan. "How is it you come here in such urgency with *gadjo* tagging behind? We have not heard any word for months."

Again Mustafa tried to speak, but again she waved him off.

"You are involved in Ermal's foolishness?"

"Ermal is dead," Mustafa said flatly. This news clearly jarred the old woman. "He died while fighting the jinn of the curse."

The old woman studied Mustafa for a moment. The news of Ermal's death had clearly caught her by surprise, but she shed no tears. She pondered the news for a moment longer and then turned to address Mustafa and Besnik together.

"I take it you two are all that is left of our clan that went along with Ermal?"

"Yes," said Besnik. "We have paid a great price to get as far as we have."

"And yet you survive to stand here before me...failed. You have failed your task, have you not?"

"No, we have not failed," said Mustafa boldly. "We have trapped the jinn. At the cost of Ermal's life it has been rebound."

"You have trapped him? Indeed," she mocked. "We have word from our clan in the north that the twins are in the northern province of Tropoja, in a village called Curraj i Epërm. It seems you have until tonight before they will be released again by the full moon."

"That is why we came to you," said Mustafa. "You know things that can help us."

"You are mad if you think you can reach that village by tonight. It is very far up in the mountains, and there are no roads. You will need a magic carpet to get there in time." She cackled a hoarse, raspy laugh and lit a new cigarette off the butt of an old one. She didn't speak again until she had drawn two deep pulls on the cigarette and expelled the smoke through her well-practiced, nicotine-stained nostrils.

"What do you advise?" asked Mustafa. "We have no time to stand here and argue."

"No, you never have had time," chuckled the Gypsy queen. "My advice to you, if you are finally wise enough to accept it, is to abandon this foolish quest and let the jinni have their revenge. Otherwise you will die senselessly for a line of *gadjo* that care nothing for you or your people." She inhaled deeply again.

"I cannot do that." Mustafa turned and motioned for Orhan to come closer. "This, we believe is the last survivor of the line of Selim Bey."

"Truly," marveled the old queen.

"Truly. The last of the line for Lleshi is already in Curraj i Epërm. If what you say is true, the the twins are together for the first time in five hundred years…"

"And for the first time in five hundred years we have the two lines together," finished the queen thoughtfully. "Four of the five chief players are in one arena once again." She nodded her head deep in thought and stared at Orhan with great interest. "It seems that things are no longer what they used to be."

"Who is the fifth player?" asked Besnik.

"Baba Moush, of course," Merriam said.

"Will his absence hinder us?" asked Mustafa.

"He will not be absent. His line has carried on through the centuries as has the others."

Mustafa stared at her waiting for an explanation. "He will not be absent?"

"The blood of the sorcerer survives," she said. "It thrives, as does his magic."

"How? Where? Who?"

"It thrives in the blood of his heir," she boasted. "Yes, it is I. The queen of this clan, and your mother. Now will you finally listen to me before it is too late?"

# 29. A Bracelet, Two Cubes, and Other Undesirable Things

Curraj i Epërm, Albania
15 August 2000

Jeff lay in the dark. Alone. No sound. No external stimuli to give him a point of reference. He had lost all track of time. Had he really been unconscious three days? He could no longer trust his triathlon watch. He pushed on the Indiglo button that illuminated the face and saw that it had changed to August 15. He tried to use the face of the watch as a flashlight. The faint light did little to reveal his surroundings.

The silence in the blackness amplified the rush of red blood cells through the capillaries in his ears. He stretched out his hand and felt along the hard rock floor he was lying on. He abandoned all fear of groping in the dark. *What could be worse than to be strangled by a ghost?* He thought. His fingers slid across the damp floor until they came to a rise. He followed it higher. A wall. He got to his knees, bumping his head hard against the low rock ceiling. Cringing in pain he kicked out with his legs and stubbed his foot against another wall. When the pain abated he felt around with his feet and hands again to find that he was in a small enclosure of rock. His heart began to race as claustrophobia began to swell within him.

He tried again to use his watch as a flashlight. The dim greenish-blue light cast just enough illumination to show him that he was entombed in a rock alcove that had three walls, the floor, and ceiling in solid rock. The forth wall at his head was a hand-built stone wall with no mortar. He pushed against the center with his right hand while supporting his weight with his

337

left. The wall flexed slightly, revealing that it had been loosely stacked.

Jeff lay down on his stomach and rested his head on his crossed arms. He puzzled over his present situation. The last thing he remembered was sitting in the chamber on the altar with Lida. He strained to recall how he had gotten here. It was all a blank. His mind raced over dark and dread possibilities. If Lida meant him harm, then why hadn't she just killed him and gotten it over with?

The air was stale and heavy, and he felt tired, almost groggy. In this dark place all he wanted to do was sleep, but a resolve suddenly came over him. He raised and pushed against the stone wall, digging his fingers into the space between two stones and prying a block loose. Placing it on the floor behind him, he removed another stone, and then another, trying to be as quiet as he could for fear of disturbing anyone or anything that might be lurking beyond the wall. The pitch blackness slowly dawned into a faint light that came from a source far above in the ceiling of the outer cavern.

Jeff squeezed through the small opening he had made and rolled down a fall of stones onto the rock floor of the cavern. He stood erect, but with caution, remembering the ache from cracking his skull earlier. He peered back over his shoulder to see that the tomb where he had been walled up was actually a niche in the rock. As his eyes grew accustomed to the light, he saw that he was standing on the outskirts of the ruins of a small underground village.

His gaze followed the shaft of sunlight that speared down to the cavern floor as it spilled through an oculus carved in the roof. The sound of flowing water could be heard beyond the lowest border of the village. He picked his way carefully through the labyrinth of piled stone walls. No section was higher than his waist, but the outlines of buildings and streets were plain to see. As he neared the river, the shaft of light became more brilliant as the sun escaped the cover of a cloud high above, and he found a well-worn path of smooth stone and followed it upriver. Peering into the surface of the water, he found that he was walking against the current. He continued to follow the path until it rounded a large outcropping of rock and entered what appeared to be another, even larger chamber.

This chamber was illuminated by a line of torches that ran along the path intermittently on both sides. The terrain of the chamber rolled in soft, even hills that looked to Jeff as though they were lush with vegetation. A passing thought to explore this odd flora was replaced by a sense of urgency to stay on the path. He continued at a quick pace, but occasionally, nervously glanced over his shoulder.

He felt a cool breeze blowing gently against his face; the draft increased in strength the farther he went. The torches flames began to snap and pop as the wind grew in intensity. He knelt down on one knee and cupped up a handful of cold water, lapping it from his palm. The water was sweet to the taste. He lapped up another handful, not realizing how thirsty he was until the water drained down his parched throat. He thought back to the warmth of the air and the foul taste of the river earlier and decided that this had to be a different underground system.

He was startled by a drumming sound that echoed throughout the cathedral-like cavern. Jeff stood up and cocked an ear in the direction of the sound. After a few strenuous moments, he could discern a definite beat that rolled and thrummed, speeding up and slowing down. He took a few steps along the path. The sound was coming from the direction he was going.

A long hill came up before him in the gloom of the torchlight. He pushed his way up, the strain taxing his leg muscles. When he reached the top, the path dropped sharply beyond the light casting a deep, dark shadow in front of him. He hesitated, studying the continuance of the path a few meters beyond the shadow, then bent over to peer into the shaded way but could discern no outline. Finally he decided to move forward as the sound of the drums grew louder.

He took a tentative step into the shadow. The ground was firm. He slid his foot along the path. It felt solid. He straightened and took a bold step forward, but as he came down the earth fell steeply away from his foot into a torturous slide. He fell head over heels flipping and contorting until he finally regained his stability enough to slide headfirst down the increasingly dark tunnel. He let out a cry of desperation and fear, but the sound was dull against the tight confines of the rock tube he was now barreling down.

The fall seemed eternal, but suddenly he plunged into cold, deep water. Flailing frantically to regain the surface, he geysered to the top gasping for air. He kicked and treaded water spinning in a circle in the darkness. Panic overwhelmed him as the cold crept into his muscles, paralyzing his movement. He gave a meager cry, more of a prayer than a cry for help. It was a struggle to keep his head above water; his clothing was weighing heavily against his fatigued muscles. In the total blackness, he began to sense that he was swirling in a spiral. He thrashed out in every direction, feeling for anything he could grasp.

Suddenly what sounded like a toilet flushing bubbled up from below his feet, and he felt himself being pulled with great force into a churning vortex of water. He caught his breath and held it, but his head never went below the surface. Instead he was dragged into another spiraling tunnel, washed along like a log in a sluice.

He soon cascaded over a cliff in a waterfall, dropping thirty feet into another pool. He sank quickly to the bottom from the force of the fall, and then popped back up out of the water like a cork. His new surroundings were illuminated by an unseen light source that glowed from the rim of a ledge near the rock ceiling sixty feet above the pool. He swam quickly to a pebble beach and pulled himself out of the frigid water where he lay on his back on the verge of exhaustion, his body cramping from hypothermal trauma.

Jeff heaved heavily, choking up the water he had swallowed. The sound of his coughing bounced off the walls of the rocky chamber. When he gained his composure, he sat up and looked around the cavern. It was smaller than the one he had fallen from. As he studied the light source, he saw that above the ridge was a line of torches following some kind of a trail through the rock formations. The trail stopped at the pool opposite the shore he was sitting on. He soon figured out that the waters of the pool reflected the torchlight, amplifying it to brighten the entire chamber. The pool was surrounded by rock pebble beaches that swooped up to the rock walls that made up the chamber. The waterfall shot out in a cascade of iridescent foam sending a gentle mist throughout the cavern.

Jeff fell back onto his back. The combination of fatigue, exhilaration, and fright had left him feeling queasy. He stared off into the dark recesses of the chamber roof, which extended well beyond the reflection of the pool. At the fringes of the light he thought he could see dark shapes hovering over him. Watching him. He remembered what Lida had said about the spirits of the wicked dead trapped in this place until judgment. The thought of them watching him didn't bother him as much as the vivid memory of the physical contact with them earlier.

He caught his breath, and then studied the chamber for a way to escape. The water entered the pool by way of the fall, but there was no apparent exit stream or river. Jeff stood up on wobbly legs and walked around the perimeter of the small pool. As he ducked behind the cataract, he noticed that the pebble beach paved a path into a narrow crack in the rock. He fished for the flashlight in his pack that was surprisingly still on his back, and tested it to see if it still worked after the drenching. He wedged his way into the crack leading with his extended flashlight. The passage ascended gently just wide enough for Jeff to squeeze through if he turned sideways. Much to his chagrin, his feet crunched loudly in the gravel.

The passage widened after about twenty meters allowing him to square his shoulders. He rounded a bend in the rock and was surprised to find an arched doorway hewn out of the rock with a frame of stone blocks set in place without mortar. A faint light glimmered through the doorway and washed over his legs below the knees. He quickly turned off his flashlight and moved back into the shadows, waiting breathlessly for a moment. Then he crept stealthily toward the door being careful to stay in the confines of the shadows.

He pressed his back against the stone frame and peered over his shoulder into the small chamber. This area seemed to have been carved out of the rock, and formed a perfect cube. A single torch flickered from a wall sconce showing the walls to be smooth and painted with a mural. Jeff ventured into the room. He was alone.

He studied a mural that had been created with a bright pallet of colors depicting a battle scene. As he studied the painting, he realized that it was an exact representation of the battle he had seen in his vision. He gasped as he recognized the detail of Ölüm's face, fierce and menacing, before he was bound by the magic of Baba Moush. The mural was divided into panels that depicted the sequence of events of that fateful day almost six hundred years ago. He saw Përparim Lleshi, whose face still haunted him from the encounter in the underground river. The finale of the pictorial was the two jewel-encrusted golden cubes still poised on the rock above the lifeless body of the sorcerer just as the two generals were on the verge of stealing them. Jeff recalled the golden cube he had seen in Mustafa's possession. It was clear the artist of this mural had intimate knowledge of the events of that day.

In the center of the room was a round opening trimmed in inlaid stone blocks. Jeff stood and peered down into a stone stair that spiraled to a lower chamber also illuminated by torchlight. He descended the stone steps until he came to the bottom. This chamber was similar to the first, but the artwork on the walls seemed odd to Jeff. Otherworldly. The figures and shapes in the pictures were not familiar. In the center of the chamber was a stone altar, ornately carved with the same strange shapes and figures that were depicted in the paintings on the walls. He realized that these must be scenes from the life of the jinni.

As he neared the altar, to his horror he saw inset into a carved depression two jewel encrusted golden cubes sitting side by side. Jeff held his breath and backed away toward the stone steps. He had no doubt that what he was looking at was the golden prisons of the jinni. Fear prompted him to back slowly up the stairs. As he reached the top he could hear the thrumming of the drums growing louder. They were moving toward him. Soon he heard the shuffling of the pebble gravel in the narrow passage outside the chamber.

He spun around looking for a place to hide. His head and shoulders protruded above the opening. Seeing no way to escape, he ducked back down the steps and found a shadowed niche under the stairs. He fell into a sitting position and cinched his knees up tight to his chest, praying that he had not made too much noise.

Soon he heard footsteps on the stone floor above. He screwed his eyes shut tight as if that was going to conceal his presence better. The footsteps began to descend to his level, followed by another set of footsteps. He pressed his head against the stone niche and opened his eyes. The shadow concealed him thoroughly. He could see the entire stone altar from his hiding place.

Two forms stepped into view. They faced the altar and reached out to hold each other's hands. Avni and Lida stood with their heads bowed in a prayerful manner. Soon they began to chant in unison words that Jeff could not discern.

The ground began to shake slightly, more like a light quiver. Small pebbles tumbled from the steps onto the floor. Avni and Lida began chanting louder. The ground shook more forcefully. A third time they shouted out their incantation.

*"Reten elp ksu hsom es ek. Reten elp ksu hsom od aht ke."*

As the final phrase was repeated, a loud clap came from the depression in the stone top of the altar and a dazzling light punctured the chamber leaving no shadow. Jeff shoved himself deeper into the niche. The light exploded with a thunderous clap, and he let out a yelp of surprise as he pressed his ears closed with his index fingers. He clamped his lips shut to keep from crying out again, but the noise was so great that he had not given himself away.

In a flash the light dissipated and the room was once again bathed in the light of the torch. Jeff opened his eyes. To his relief he was once again concealed within the shadow of the niche, his presence undetected. There before him were Avni and Lida now transformed into their natural forms as jinn. The forms of Ölüm and Vdekje, his twin sister, faced them.

Ölüm and Vdekje seemed surprised to see each other, and even more surprised to see their long-lost twins, Avni and Lida. The newly freed jinni flexed and stretched, reveling in the open space. It was Ölüm who spoke first.

"So, it seems much has been afoot since we last met. How has our union come to pass?"

"For the first time in six hundred years we are all together," said Avni. "We have been eagerly awaiting this moment when the geographical distance between you two would be no more."

"We have worked feverishly for generations of men to get to this point," said Lida. "For the first time, all is in place to not only destroy the magic of the black sorcerer but to end the bondage to men forever."

"What do you mean?" asked Vdekje. "My blood burns for revenge on the bloodline of the betrayers. You would rob me of this?"

"Your blood burns because of the spell cast on you by Baba Moush," said Avni. "You have been his puppets against *his* betrayers. We now have in place the means to free you both."

"What means is it that you speak of?" asked Ölüm.

"When the Gypsy, Ermal, conjured his magic to rebind you, he unwittingly gave us the means to transport you here to Albania, where it all began."

Lida added, "We also have the last survivors of the family lines of Përparim Lleshi, and Selim Bey together for the first time since that day."

"It is ironic that they have been working together by a design that we initiated almost fifty years ago," beamed Avni. "The blood of the betrayers has been brought together once again. The powerful magic that separated us will now work to reunite us."

Ölüm pondered the words of his siblings. "You say the sole surviving heirs of the curse are right now working together. Where are they?"

"Two are on their way. They must travel by rudimentary means to get here, but they are motivated to come with haste," said Avni.

"How have you motivated them to come when doom surely awaits them?" asked Vdekje.

Avni and Lida smiled broadly looking at each other with pleasure. "They come in haste," said Avni, "because the third and final member of their alliance is here with us now. He is of the blood of the Albanian. Lida has him kept in a safe place until he is needed. He is under the delusion that he will survive by helping us."

Jeff's blood ran cold when he heard this. He suddenly realized that he and Orhan had been playing into the hands of the jinni from the beginning. He tried to calm himself, but the adrenalin surging through his veins made him want to bolt up the stairs and out of there. However, it was obvious that the jinni had not discovered his escape, so he relaxed and listened.

"When the others arrive," continued Avni, "we will bring them to the altar that has been prepared. Their spilt blood over the ancient stones will cleanse the curse away from you, and you will be free at last, never to be subservient to mankind again."

"What power have you discovered to make all of this happen?" asked Vdekje.

"A power that we have had all along," answered Lida. "A powerful amulet that has been handed down to us from our ancestors."

"The ruby bracelet," said Ölüm with satisfaction.

"Yes, the ruby bracelet," confirmed Avni, definitely pleased with himself. "We found it quite by accident nearly five hundred years ago. The spirits of our ancestors inhabits the gems." Avni held the bracelet aloft, allowing the gems to be struck by the torchlight. The four jinni eyed it with admiration. Avni placed it reverently between the two golden cubes in the recess of the stone altar. "With this bracelet nothing can stop us from succeeding in our plan."

"That is nearly true, brother," cautioned Lida. The three others looked at her for clarification. "There is one other loose end." She paused. "The witch, Valbona."

"Valbona!" retorted Vdekje. "I have dealt with her before."

"Yes," said Lida, "but she is still very much a threat. The spirits of the wicked dead in these very caverns could be called on by her to rise up against us."

"Then we will deal with this witch together," said Ölüm, anger rising in his voice.

"She has never faced us all together. Her powers will crumble when met against the ruby bracelet," said Vdekje.

"We must first discover where she is," said Lida.

"That will not be a problem," said Avni confidently. "She will come to us. All the participants will be gathered together. You will see my dear ones that I have planned for every contingency."

"All your plans are good as always, my brother, but my time begins now," growled Vdekje, bloodlust burning in her flaming eyes. "I must feed my need, now."

Avni smiled at his sister. "And so you shall. Begin your terror on the village on the other side of the mountain and know that it will be your last. Soon you will act by your own will."

Jeff cringed in terror as the four jinni swooped up the stairs and out of the upper chamber. The absence of their fiery presence cooled the room, giving him a cold shiver. He timidly crawled from his hole, knowing it would not be long before his escape had been discovered. He stood by the altar and looked down at the golden cubes and the ruby bracelet. Impulsively he gathered the three artifacts and put them in his knapsack, cinching the flap tight. Then he mustered all his courage to ascend the stairs and squeezed back through the narrow passage.

\* \* \*

Jeff had to find a way to escape these caves. The lives of his friends and himself depended on it. He stood under the fall and stared out through the cascade of water. As he looked deep into the pool, he saw what looked like another tunnel just under the surface. He studied the interior of the cavern. No other way of escape seemed possible.

He took a deep breath and dove headfirst into the water heading for the tunnel. As he neared it, he could feel a strong current pulling him in. He didn't fight it and soon bobbed up into an air pocket that formed between the underground river and the roof of the tunnel. Taking another deep breath, he let the increasing strength of the current rush him to his unknown destination. Soon he found that the torrent was carrying him through spacious canopies of rock. Except for a few bruises from shallow boulders, his trip was uneventful.

Soon, however, he plunged over a large cataract into a tumultuous river below. The current became powerful and roared through the walls of the caverns as Jeff struggled to keep his head above water. Suddenly he burst out of the darkness into the blinding light of the sun. The river widened and slowed, allowing him to swim to shore. He clawed his way to dry ground and pulled himself under the thick foliage of a large plant.

He gasped to fill his lungs with air. The air was thick and earthy smelling, the atmosphere weighty and stifling; he found it hard to catch his breath. Opening his eyes and rubbing the dampness from his eyelashes, he studied the leaves of his impromptu shelter. He let out a tired laugh as he suddenly recognized the unmistakable shape of the cannabis leaf. "It figures," he mumbled to himself, "that with my luck I'd crawl under a marijuana plant." He made a halfhearted attempt to find another shelter, but the shade was intoxicating where he was, so he lay back down and rested.

After several minutes his exhaustion began to pass, although he still felt achy in his joints and muscles. He groaned to a standing position and studied the mountains that surrounded him. He could see the wide-mouthed cave that he had come through. The river gurgled and churned winding its way farther south. He had no way of knowing where he was. Walking up a low rising hill, he found that he was in a narrow ravine. The cave opened into the steep side of a mountain; the ravine walls were steep and impassable. Downriver he could see that the ravine widened into a valley, so he decided to go in that direction. At least the hike was downhill.

He hoisted the strap of the knapsack across his chest and shoulder. The weight seemed dreadful, and he hoped he was not going to have to carry it for long. As the afternoon turned into early evening, he trudged through a reed-infested bog next to the bank of the river. No other trail was available to him. He drew a little comfort from the fact that the day seemed to be progressing in normal time.

The river continued to flow through an open valley, and still Jeff did not recognize where he was. He began to play back in his mind the twists and turns he had made underground, but there were just too many gaps in his memory to know for sure in what direction from Curraj i Epërm he was.

Finally he came to a fork in the river. Ahead of him was a tall hill that jutted up between the forks. He waded over to the other side and climbed the hill to its crest. From there he could see in every direction. He found that he was actually on a small island, and that the river rejoined itself farther south. In the distance he could see a small village sitting precariously on the eastern slope of a tall mountain. A wisp of smoke from a fire suggested it was inhabited. He waded back across the river and after about a half an hour came to the base of the mountain and followed a goat trail up into the village.

He was startled by the bark of a dog that stood on a ridge above his head as he walked through a tight gorge. He heard a gruff curse in Albanian that he assumed was directed toward the barking dog. Jeff was relieved to here human voices again. He didn't care who they were; at least he wasn't alone anymore.

He climbed up the embankment to a rocky trail that led to a whitewashed stone house. The Albanian was busy milking a goat when Jeff stepped into the clearing and greeted him with a nod of his head and slightly raised hand. The man barely acknowledged him and continued milking his goat.

"Hello," Jeff said in English. The man stopped and stared at him, and then slowly rose to his feet and walked over to him and shook his hand. The man was dressed in tattered, heavy, dark wool slacks. His feet were covered with worn-out rubber goulashes, and his cotton shirt was threadbare and opened at the neck revealing a hand-knitted wool undershirt that looked suffocating to Jeff. His most astonishing feature was his scraggly hair, which Jeff realized was crawling with lice.

Jeff released the man's hand and discreetly wiped his palm on his pants leg, looking around at the house and yard. It was in much poorer condition than the houses in Curraj i Epërm. The dog growled at him as he passed by, but then lay down under a mulberry tree.

A young girl, in her mid teens, Jeff guessed, came and stood in the doorway of the house. Her face, arms, and legs were smudged with dirt and grime, and her feet were bare and dirty. She wore a threadbare pink dress with a faded blue flower pattern, and her blonde hair was tied back in a pony tail with a pink ribbon. Jeff studied her for a moment and felt that had she been born in America she would have probably been a very beautiful, vibrant, high school girl; here her options were limited. She smiled shyly at Jeff, which raised a frown from her father. Jeff smiled respectfully back at her but then quickly adverted his attention to the father.

"Curraj i Epërm?" He pantomimed with his hands in all directions hoping the Albanian would understand that he wanted to find that village. "Do you know Curraj i Epërm?" he asked again. The man just stared at him blankly, and then turned and fetched another goat and began milking it. Jeff stood helplessly and looked from the father to the daughter.

"I speak a little English," the girl offered timidly. "I learned it in school."

"Oh, good," sighed Jeff in relief. "You have a school here?"

"We used to, but now we go to school in Fierza," said the girl. "We live there during the school year." The girl's English was very good, and she clearly wanted to practice it with Jeff.

"My name is Jeff," he said tentatively offering her his hand to shake. She took it but did not meet his gaze.

"I am Besiana," she said. "Curraj i Epërm is over that mountain to the west." She waved her hand absently over her shoulder in the direction of the mountain behind her.

Jeff's heart stopped as he remembered what Avni had said to Vdekje about the village to the east just over the mountain. "Is it directly over that mountain on the other side?"

"Yes. This village is Qerg Muli. You can reach Curraj by goat trail. It only takes two hours."

Jeff felt his stomach tighten. He knew that these people were in grave danger from the jinni. The evening light was fading behind the mountain casting a long gray shadow over the village.

"How many people are here?" he asked.

"We have six families. About forty people."

"Besiana. You and your people are in great danger. You must gather everyone quickly and come with me," said Jeff, desperation rising in his voice.

Besiana recognized his urgency and called to her mother and brother, who were in the house. They came out and looked at Jeff suspiciously. The father rose from his one-legged stool and asked his daughter what was happening. She shrugged and nodded to Jeff with her chin.

"Tell him that there is a terrible evil that will come here. It comes once in every generation; every forty years or so and tonight marks the beginning of the full moon cycle. We must hide," said Jeff trying not to cause a panic but needing to express the importance of their compliance.

The father grunted his affirmation. He told Jeff through Besiana that he had heard the stories of the evil that possesses animals and men and drives them mad with fear, and then finally kills them. Jeff looked nervously at the family.

"Besiana, we need to get everyone in the village to a safe place for them to hide, or they will be killed."

"There is only one place safe," she said. "My father knows the way."

The family scrambled quickly up the trail to the next house. Besiana told the children to run through the village and warn everyone to come to the old schoolyard. Soon children could be heard running from house to house yelling for the villagers to go to the old school.

Jeff turned to see Besiana's father emerging from his house carrying a Kalashnikov AK-47 strapped over his shoulder. He trotted up past Jeff and eyed him without saying a word, joining his neighbors as they began to pool together and move toward the school. Jeff looked over at Besiana questioningly.

"My father took the Kalashnikov from the armory during the civil war three years ago," she said. "He keeps it buried under the floorboards of our house in case of another war."

Jeff noticed that several of the men had AK-47s while others carried axes and long-handled, curved scythes. They marched deliberately toward the school. Only hushed chatter from the children could be heard. The villagers seemed to be resolved in dealing with the current problem without fear. Jeff admired their courage.

As they gathered at the school yard, Jeff counted forty-eight people.

"Is this everyone?" he asked Besiana.

"Yes. My father will lead us now to the only safe place there is," she said. "We haven't much time. Darkness will be on us soon."

"Where will we go?" asked Jeff.

"To the grotto of the ancient woman. The mother known as the witch."

# 30.  Loathsome Vapors

Korça, Albania
15 August 2000

"We have no time to waste," said Merriam. She looked at the young man blocking the door. "Sami, gather the young men, and bring them here."

Sami quickly ran out the door, and after a few moments he returned with five other Gypsy men who crowded their way forward to stand before Merriam, each taking in Mustafa and Besnik with a glance.

"We are going north to Tropoja," she said. "The time has come for you to remember what you have been taught. I will go with Mustafa. You all will follow in my automobile."

They quickly turned and left the building, following close behind Merriam as she stormed out into the courtyard. Mustafa and Besnik were left standing looking at each other. Orhan and Aubrey quickly followed the Gypsies out to where Merriam was pulling a carpetbag out of a metal trunk sitting up against one of the buildings.

A dilapidated double wooden garage door was hauled open, and the six men pushed out an automobile covered by a tarp. Sami pulled the canvas off the machine to reveal a brightly painted, multicolored Mercedes Benz. The paint job and the extra features that had been welded onto it such as iconic pictures and figurines of various saints made it difficult to tell what year or model it was. One of the men jumped into the driver's seat and started the engine, which chugged and spat smoke from the exhaust. After a few revs, the diesel caught but continued to sputter. Orhan and Aubrey stared at each other nervously.

"It look good but runs bad," said Merriam in broken English, slapping Orhan on the shoulder as she passed to climb into the Mercedes SEL. "It'll make it. You will see," she said with a cackling laugh.

Without further discussion the six Gypsies hopped into the "parade" Mercedes while Mustafa, Besnik, Orhan, and Aubrey joined Merriam in the SEL. Merriam took command of the front passenger seat and then leaned her head out the window shouting one last barrage of instructions to Sami in Romani.

Mustafa pulled out of the compound, spinning his tires in the loose gravel as he fishtailed onto the road. The others followed close behind, and soon they had driven through Korça and were on their way heading north. Merriam turned to Orhan and Aubrey in the back seat. She glared at Orhan and shrugged in a dismissive manner.

"So you are the blood of Selim Bey," she retorted, more of a statement than a question. "You better sleep while you can. When we reach the north there will be no rest for any of us." She gazed at Aubrey and gave her a sinister smile. "I do not know what part you will play in this, but be assured you have not seen horror as you will see when we reach our destination." She bounced back in her seat and faced forward. After a short time she looked over at her son. "You know your father is dead. He died of a broken heart…the one you gave him. My heart is not so brittle. Do not disappoint me. I will not be so forgiving next time."

Mustafa stared ahead at the road, not meeting her penetrating glare.

It was midafternoon. The sun beat down hot on the countryside. Few Albanians were out. Most had gone inside for the midday meal and to get out of the heat. Work would resume again around five o'clock when it was cooler.

They decided to continue through Albania rather than cutting through Macedonia and Kosovo. That would have been the most direct route, but Mustafa did not want to have to cross through three more borders and passport controls. The last time at the Greek border had cost them almost two hours. Although the roads were bad and under constant repairs, they figured that with any luck they would still make better time.

They came up over a mountain ridge and wound their way down hairpin turns. Lake Ohrid lay ahead, ancient and expansive. As they entered the town of Pogradec that rose up along the shores of the lake, Mustafa deftly made his way through the traffic of beeping horns and dramatic gestures. As they cruised north with the lake on their right, Aubrey stared beyond the sleeping form of Orhan at the beauty of the lake.

"Across the lake is Macedonia," offered Besnik from her left. "This is a very old lake. There is a fish here that is found only in this lake and another one in Russia. It is called *koran*. Very tasty."

"I've heard of that fish," said Aubrey. She mused that this was the first time Besnik had spoken directly to her. "I've never had it, though. It's some kind of trout, I think."

The conversation died as the two closed their eyes again to rest. Mustafa kept their speed at an unsafe level. What traffic there was he quickly and unsafely passed, blaring his horn. Aubrey again thought it best not to watch.

The switchback turns climbing another ridge left the lake behind. Before them was another steep drop into a sprawling river valley. The road was potholed and treacherous, and again swept into the valley by way of hairpin turns. Thatched lean-tos sat dangerously close to the road with vendors selling everything from *koran* fish to benzene, corn on the cob, and cigarettes.

# Vale of Shadows

Aubrey found it hard to rest as they bumped and bounced down the road. During times that traffic came to a standstill, Mustafa pulled wide around the stopped cars and tried to nose ahead of the other vehicles. This was the common practice of every driver, which compounded the problem causing a constant barrage of horn honks. Hot, bumpy, dusty, and noisy. Aubrey looked at her watch. They had only been driving for about an hour and a half. She rolled her eyes and tried to get comfortable between the two men. Only fifteen more hours to go.

*   *   *

Mustafa finally pulled over in Librazhd and they walked into a cafe to use the restrooms and get something to drink. Soon a commotion was heard at the front door as the flamboyant Mercedes carrying the Gypsies pulled to a stop in the parking lot. The proprietor of the café rushed out and headed them off before they could enter, not allowing them to come in. Aubrey was just coming out of the WC when she saw Sami and the others being detained by the owner and one of his sons. She went over to try to calm the Gypsies, who were beginning to get out of hand.

"*Ju lutem* (please), they are with me. *A kupton* (do you understand)?" she said to the proprietor.

"Yes, I understand," said the son in English. "We have had trouble with Gypsies before. They are not welcome here."

"Please," she begged, "We have been driving a long way. We just need some food, and we will be on our way. No trouble. I promise."

"You are American?" he asked.

"Yes, we are just passing through."

The son looked at them suspiciously, and then looked at the car with a smirk. "Why does an American travel with Gypsy?"

"We have important business in the north," said Aubrey not wanting to say too much. "We will pay in dollars."

That seemed to pacify him. "OK. You pay in dollar. You can stay, but no trouble."

"Yes, thank you. No trouble. I promise."

After taking a quick break with no further incidents, they were able to get back on the road. Besnik took the wheel, but Merriam maintained her hold on the front passenger seat. The condition of the road was bad enough, but the construction made it even worse. They followed a long river valley until they got to the city of Elbasan and headed north winding up a steep pass through the mountains. The switchback road wove through olive groves that looked down on the industrial city.

A breeze coming through the open windows was becoming cooler as evening approached. Aubrey enjoyed the view as they rose higher and higher in the pass. After thirty minutes of climbing, Elbasan could still be seen in the valley below. Finally after nearly forty-five minutes, they cleared the pass and began the decent down toward the capitol city of Tirana.

A broad switchback in the road gave them a spectacular view of Mount Tomori in the distance to the south. The setting sun emblazoned the western slope of the sacred high place in an orange-pink glow. Aubrey shuddered as she recalled the story Jeff had told of his vision and the battle at the foot of the mountain over five hundred years ago. She watched until the road curved around the slope and Tomori was out of view.

Besnik and Mustafa consulted the map that Merriam provided and decided that there was no good way to get around Tirana. They would have to drive through it and hope that traffic was not at a complete standstill, as it often was. When they finally pulled into the southern edge of the city, their worst fears were realized. Traffic was backed up for nearly a mile. They nudged forward impatiently bumper to bumper, fender to fender. Aubrey languished in the back seat but gained a little hope when she saw the American compound out the window to her right. She knew that the American Embassy was not far, and from past experience she knew that most traffic bottlenecks eased slightly after they cleared through the narrow lane beyond the university and the embassies.

The towering statue of Scanderbeg mounted on an armored charger overlooked the square next to the mosque. The roundabout was congested with trucks, buses, cars, horse carts, bicycles, and pedestrians. It always irritated Aubrey the way the pedestrians walked out so close to the moving vehicles. Their fatalism dictated that if they were going to be hit by a car then they were going to be hit by a car, and there was little they could do about it.

It took them nearly another hour to finally get through to the west exit of town and head down the main road to the ancient port city of Durrës and the sea. To the north, built on the slope of a tall mountain over looking the central valley of Albania, was the fortress city of Kruja: the seat of Scanderbeg's power.

After a while, night blanketed the countryside, but the radiance of the full moon gave the world a ghostly glow. Anxiety mounted within the automobile as unspoken regret began to swell in everyone's chests; they had not arrived in time. No one doubted that the jinni had been released in the north, and that somewhere Jeff was out there all alone. Aubrey choked back a soft whimper as she contemplated his fate. She rubbed a tear discreetly from her cheek hoping no one had noticed it in the darkness of the car.

\* \* \*

Somewhere in the middle of the night, Besnik pulled over and let Mustafa drive again. They had only stopped for a short break in Fushe-Kruja, and then continued on. Despite its junk-heap appearance, the other Mercedes had kept up with Besnik's lead foot.

Merriam had made little attempt to have much input in the route that was taken, but when they came to the fork in the road at Milott she informed Mustafa that they would need nearly another day to travel by car. She told him it would be better to go by ferry down the Drin river to Fierza, and then into Tropoja. Mustafa didn't like the idea of leaving the surety of the automobiles, but he also knew how poor and in some cases, nonexistent the roads were in the north. He conceded that he would think about it but veered to the right, continuing along the road that would lead to the hydroelectric dam on the Drin from which they could take the ferry.

*  *  *

Aubrey was jolted from her sleep when she suddenly sensed the cessation of movement. She stared over at Orhan sheepishly as she noted the dab of drool on his shoulder where she had been resting her head. He smiled tiredly at her. Both of them squinted their eyes against the sudden glare of light that filled the car.

Mustafa and Besnik had already exited the car and were talking to an Albanian soldier who patrolled casually on the ferry landing with his AK-47 strapped and hanging from his shoulder. The soldier pointed to the café where they could buy tickets to go to Fierza. Merriam climbed out and went back to talk to the other Gypsy men. Their Mercedes rumbled and coughed as it idled just outside the tunnel.

Aubrey and Orhan got out and took in their surroundings. The landing was a small, flat area completely enclosed by the slope of the mountain on one side and the river on the other. A narrow, rough-walled tunnel cut through the mountain was the only access to the landing. It was only big enough for one truck to shove through in one direction. A small café was built against the rock slope. Along the dock a barge lay moored to a rusted metal and concrete stairway down to the water's edge. At this late hour, there was very little traffic, but pedestrians and vehicles began to emerge from the tunnel to catch the earliest ferry upriver.

Merriam retrieved her carpetbag and slung it over her shoulder. She marched up to Orhan and Aubrey and with a sharp nudge with her chin in the direction of the ferry herded them to the landing.

The ferry was a long, enclosed barge with windows that ran up and down both sides. The squad of eleven ducked into the low doorway to the seating area, which was furnished with tattered, spring-exposed benches arranged like church pews. The seating cabins were separated into two sections, one toward the bow and the other at the stern. Between them were the pilothouse and the latrines, called *banjos.*

Aubrey quickly made her way to the WC at amidships, portside. When she returned just as quickly and sat down next to Orhan, she answered his inquisitive look.

"That goes down on my bottom five list of worst toilets I have seen in the world," she said. "I'll just hold it."

"We have a long way to go—" started Orhan.

"No," interrupted Aubrey shaking her head. "I'll just hold it!"

The ferry began to fill with passengers. Orhan watched with amusement the number of people that went to the latrine and then quickly backed out with disgust on their faces.

"The bottom five, huh?" he said to Aubrey as he settled into the torn upholstery of his bench.

"The bottom five," she affirmed.

They watched with interest as Merriam made her way to the toilet, went in, and then didn't come out for nearly ten minutes. They crinkled their noses at each other and smiled.

The ferry, *La Gomar*, soon chugged away from the landing and began to head upstream. Dawn would come in a few hours. The pilot had told them that the trip would take nearly four hours to Fierza. The cool breeze that blew in off the river was overshadowed by the foul, loathsome, putrescent reek that emanated from the toilet and was carried through the sitting area. After several minutes Orhan realized he was not going to be able to stomach the stench. It took little argument to convince the others to move to the bow section of the cabin.

It didn't take long for the exhaustion of the long drive from Turkey to take its toll. An arrhythmic chorus of their snores soon filled the bow section. The breeze was pleasant and sedative. No one noticed the wisp of fog that crawled with long, fingerlike extensions over the starboard gunwale of the barge. It rose from the river and moved like smoke drawn through a fan until it hung menacingly over Orhan's sleeping form.

# 31. She Doesn't Look a Day over Six Hundred

Qerg Muli, Albania
15 August 2000, 9 p.m.

The cave where Jeff and the villagers hid had been hand dug centuries ago. Catholics who had fled to the north to escape the reach of the Ottoman Empire had burrowed into the mountainside in a narrow ravine that was so well hidden that only those who knew where it was could find it. No one in all those centuries had ever accidentally stumbled across it. Many believed that its secrecy had remained because of a spell placed on it by the witch. Mercenaries and partisans made it a safe haven from Turks, Italians, and Germans. Now it was used to hide from the jinni.

Two young men from the village, named Cledi and Toni, guarded the entrance. Neither one looked to be much older than twenty years of age. They were each armed with AK-47s. Darkness shrouded the ravine beyond the mouth of the cave, but a silvery pall was beginning to cover the landscape as the full moon rose over the peaks of the mountains. The villagers huddled along the walls each remaining in their family units. Gysi, Besiana's father, talked with the two guards in a low whisper. The other men stood loosely around Jeff and Besiana.

Jeff's heart was filled with dread as he watched the silver light of the moon pervade the camouflaged opening. He watched Gysi's urgency. How he handled himself and the other villagers. He was strong, and a natural leader. Jeff noticed for the

363

first time Gysi's limp. The furrowing of his brow did not go unnoticed by Besiana.

"He has had that limp since he was a young man," she said answering Jeff's question before he asked it. "He has always been a fighter. He fought with his father against the Communists when he was younger. He caused them so much trouble they slit the back of both of his legs from the heel to the back of the knee so he could not run. It took him years to learn to walk again, but he never gave up, and he never quit fighting against the Communists."

"That is something I never knew," said Jeff squatting down on a rock, motioning for Besiana to have a seat next to him. "I just figured that everyone had been a Communist all those years."

"Oh, no. My grandfather actually fought with Americans in World War Two against the Nazis. After the war he wanted democracy, but Albania became Communist instead. So he and others from this area fought against them. He was later put in prison. No one ever saw him again, but that was before I was born."

"Hmm. It seems I've heard that story before," said Jeff.

Gysi came and stood over Jeff gesturing for Besiana to interpret for him.

"The witch will be here before morning," said Besiana relaying Gysi's message. "She will know what to do. All we have to do is stay alive through the night. We will take turns as lookouts. You get some sleep, and I will wake you when it is your turn." Gysi strode away and talked with the other men who nodded their agreement and wasted no time lying down with their families.

Jeff slid off the rock and rested his head against it. To his surprise Besiana curled up next to him but was careful to maintain a respectable distance. He looked up at the ceiling of the cave, illuminated only by the ancillary light of the full moon, and placed his knapsack under his head for a pillow. The golden cubes protruded into the back of his head uncomfortably, so he discreetly rearranged the interior trying not to draw attention to himself. He didn't know what the villagers would do if they knew what he carried, but he thought it best to keep it a secret. The ruby bracelet laced around his fingers. He slowly withdrew it and held it in his hand keeping it from onlooking eyes by rolling over on his side away from the others. As he gently rubbed one of the rubies between his thumb and forefinger, it began to give off a faint glow. He quickly shoved it back into the sack under his head.

He thought back to what the siblings had said about the bracelet's power and its ability to give them success in what they planned to do. The knowledge that he was so close to something so powerful unnerved him. He knew he would be getting little sleep. As his mind went from one thought to another, he tried hard to remember a time where he had tranquility. It seemed he had been in the middle of this mess for so long.

A sudden thought occurred to him, causing him to roll over on his back with a quick jerk. More than once he had overheard or been told that he and Orhan were the last two survivors of the lines of Përparim Lleshi and Selim Bey, but what of his sister back in America? He knew that she was all right; at least, she had been last time he talked to her. When was it? Months ago? January? Surely she was OK. He hoped. He prayed. He had to find out. He rolled over to Besiana, who now lay sleeping, and gently nudged her elbow.

"Besi...Besiana." She stirred. "Besi I need to talk to you." She stirred again, but this time she opened her eyes just a slit.

"What is it?" she asked.

"Do you know where I can get to a telephone?"

"No. We have no phone in Qerg Muli. There is one I think in Curraj i Epërm. I think the mayor has one." She stared at him with confusion scowling her face. "Why do you need a telephone?"

"I need to call home. Back to America. I need to find out about my mother and sister."

"I am sorry, but we have no phone," she said apologetically. "Perhaps when the witch comes she will know what to do."

"Yeah, right," said Jeff rolling back over onto his back in frustration. He arched his back and strained his head and neck to peer over his knapsack at the men behind him. The imperative of contacting home grew into absolute determination.

He rose to his feet and went to Gysi, who was still sitting with Cledi and Toni. He felt Besiana following close behind.

"Tell your father that I need to get to a telephone," he said over his shoulder to her, keeping his gaze on Gysi. "The danger we are in may also affect my family back in America. I need to find out for sure."

Besiana repeated his request to her father. He stood and gazed out of the cave entrance to the ravine as if deep in thought.

"The jinni are out there roaming the countryside seeking whom they may destroy. It would be very foolish to venture out tonight." he said in Albanian. "There is only one phone in the region, and that is in the home of the mayor in the village over the mountain." He gestured casually over his shoulder in the direction of Curraj i Epërm. "You should wait until morning."

Jeff waited impatiently as Besiana translated the conversation. He knew Gysi was right, and he knew that his need to know right this moment about his family was irrational. *Sense the jinni were here in Albania how could they harm his mom and sister?* He thought. He was surprised to hear Gysi mention the jinni. "The jinni believe that I am the last of the line. I'm sure this is not true. If my sister is safe then that means that the jinni are not as powerful as we may think. They make mistakes. I think we should find out as soon as possible, and the only way to do that is to get to a phone."

"I understand that this information could be very useful, but you cannot go to Curraj i Epërm alone. We must go quickly and you must travel light." He eyed Jeff's knapsack. "You must travel *very* light."

Besiana took the knapsack from his shoulder as she interpreted her father's last words and laid it down next to Cledi. Jeff resisted at first but then realized that to tote that weight would be even more hazardous. At any rate he didn't like the idea of carrying the golden cubes back so close to the lair of the jinni.

Besiana rubbed down the front of her tattered dress as if pressing out the wrinkles, and then stood at Jeff's side with an expectant smile.

"What?" asked Jeff confused about her intent.

"We will go together," she said. "You will need me to talk with my father." Her resolve was beyond argument, so Jeff decided to not make an issue of it. If it was OK with Gysi, it was OK with him.

He went over and fished through his pack until his fingers came across the bracelet. Looking around he quickly pulled it out and placed it in his pocket. Gysi watched him intently.

"That will either help us or destroy us," he said quietly through Besiana. "The witch will know what to do with it. Come" With that he ducked out of the door followed quickly by Besiana. Jeff steeled his nerve and ducked after them. His heart pounded so hard that he was sure the jinni would hear it.

Jeff followed Gysi and Besiana from cover to cover. The ravine was heavily wooded, which made for good protection from any wandering eyes above. They came to the outskirts of Qerg Muli, and Gysi paused studying the village. He tensed and held up a warning hand for them to stay down and be quiet. In

367

the distance a forlorn moan echoed down the valley followed by what sounded like a human scream. Jeff found himself clutching Besiana's hand in a steel grip that caused her to writhe against his grasp. They had emptied everyone from the village. Who could be making such a terrible sound?

The moan echoed mournfully, dissipating in the air and making it hard to pinpoint where it was coming from. A shadow passed over the moon, blocking its light for an instant. It moved too quickly to be a cloud. The threesome ducked deeper into the shade of an oak tree, studying the skies above. Jeff was the first to see a dark shape gliding above the mountain peak that separated Qerg Muli from Curraj i Epërm. It swooped and banked like a large eagle hunting for prey, but even from this distance it appeared to be very large and flowed more like a tarp on the wind.

Another moan floated towards them, sounding nearer this time. This time they could tell it came from the slope above the village. Gysi wanted to get closer, but the ground to the next cover was open for several yards. The distance paralyzed them. They wallpapered themselves to the trunk of the tree and peered at the sky through the break in the leaves. The moan grew louder and more distinct.

"It is at the other end of the village," whispered Besiana. "It is coming toward us." Fear laced her voice. She reached out and grabbed Jeff's hand. He did not pull away.

The shadow passed low over the field between the oak tree and a small shed. As it did so, Jeff could hear goats inside the shed bleating, agitated by the shadow's presence. The shape darted up in a high arc and then plummeted to the ground landing in the field not far from where the trio was hiding. As it touched down, it transformed into the shape that Jeff had seen in the underground chamber. Vdekje floated smoothly toward the shed. The closer she got, the more agitated the goats became. As she reached the door, which was facing outward toward Jeff and the others, a violent gust of wind yanked the door off its hinges and sent it flying into the ravine. The goats jumped over and collided with each other to get away from her, the frenzy of their panic wild and violent.

Vdekje tore into the goats, ripping them limb from limb in a bizarre frenzy of her own. Blood and body parts spattered and flew in all directions. She retreated from the shed and stepped into the field again. Ravenous. Unsatiated. Her flaming eyes roved to and fro looking for another victim. With a shriek she launched into the air again, flying low over the village. After several circular passes, she catapulted back over the mountain to the west.

The moan sounded again. Now it was coming from the middle of the village. Gysi, Besiana, and Jeff dared not move. Terror gripped them at the onslaught they had just witnessed. The earth began to shake, softly at first, and then grew into a tumult beneath their feet. A tremendous crack like a whip sounded from the center of the village, and an exploding fireball of light rocketed into the night sky. They watched it ascend to just above the altitude of the mountain peak and then arc gracefully back down to earth, where it took the shape that Jeff recognized as Ölüm. A maniacal, cackling laugh echoed through out the valley as Ölüm turned and flew to the south quickly disappearing out of sight.

Gysi grabbed Besiana by the hand and dragged her across the field into the village and to their house. Still clutching Besiana's hand, he dove through the door. Jeff barely made it before Gysi slammed it shut with his foot. The three lay on the wooden floor gasping for air. After a brief moment, Gysi jumped up and went to a cabinet lined with plates and raki glasses. He pulled out a handful of 7.62 millimeter rounds and shoved them into his pocket, and then motioned for Jeff to grab some of the ammunition and put them into his own pockets.

369

A faraway scream could be heard crescendoing from the south. Jeff risked a quick glance out of the window. He could see his face reflecting the moonlight in the pane of glass, and pulled back slightly behind the curtain. The screams grew louder. Soon he could see Ölüm circling high above the valley. He had transformed himself into a frightening creature with the head of Ölüm but the body of a giant eagle. His wingspan was over thirty feet in length. In his talons he carried two struggling and kicking forms. Jeff watched in horror as Ölüm flew closer. He could make out two humans in the clutches of the jinn.

Ölüm dive-bombed the village, releasing a screaming man, who toppled through the air from about sixty feet and crashed through the roof of one of the neighboring houses. His screams came to an abrupt halt as the sound of breaking timbers and terra-cotta tiles rushed across the distance between the houses. The screams of the woman still in the jinn's grasp were drowned out by the frenzied cackle of Ölüm. He swooped above Gysi's house and dropped the woman from over a hundred feet. Her lifeless body bashed through the roof and into the living room, knocking Besiana and Gysi to the floor.

Plaster, wood, and tile rained down on them puffing up a cloud of dust that fogged the room. Gysi pushed himself up from under a fallen ceiling section while Jeff helped Besiana out from under the rubble. The body of the woman lay mangled in the pile of roof timbers. Through Besiana, Gysi said that he recognized her as a woman from the village of Betoshi farther south.

The shadow of Ölüm passed over the moon again like a deep, dark cloud. With a heart-stopping screech he zoomed to the south again. Gysi ran to the door and watched as Vdekje in like form flew alongside her brother. Soon the two jinni had faded into the starlight.

Jeff, Gysi, and Besiana ran from the house and scampered up the goat trail that wound up the side of the mountain. There was plenty of tree cover for them to hide under, so they were able to ascend making good time. As the cackle of the twins shot through the darkness from the south, the trio quickened their pace until they came to a steep rock face that jutted skyward from the slope. A crag just big enough for the three of them to squeeze into was within a short climb from the trail. The jinni were very close now, circling overhead. A muffled scream drew Jeff's attention toward the valley. Another villager was dropped onto the roof of a house crashing through as had the others before.

Jeff was becoming numb to the terror. He pulled Besiana from the crag and pushed her on up the trail. He climbed with determination, not allowing the altitude to weaken his Kansas flatland legs and lungs. Adrenalin drove him upward. Besiana and Gysi followed. The screams of two more villagers sailing through the air to their deaths could be heard below. A shadow passing overhead caused them to dive under a low bush. They could not tell if the jinni had spotted them or if they were just widening their flight path. Suddenly, through the boughs of a tree nearby, another villager crashed to the ground.

They stayed frozen in place unable to move. The grotesque remains of a man lay disemboweled on the rocks less than three meters from them. Besiana turned into her father's shoulder, biting her lip to keep from crying out; tears streamed down her cheeks. Ölüm careened away, joining Vdekje who was swirling high above; their gruesome cackling scratching the silent night like fingernails on a chalkboard.

When they swooped to the south again, Jeff crawled on his belly to the body of the dead man. The man's dull, lifeless eyes stared blankly back at him. He felt as if the man were pleading with him beyond the threshold of death, begging him to save the rest of his family. Jeff felt powerless. Hopeless.

The screams of the jinni returning pushed them to find better cover. They continued their climb until suddenly they crested the ridge and looked down into the wide-open valley with Curraj i Epërm below. They shuffled down the steep trail on their rumps, sending cascades of loose dirt and gravel down the slope ahead of them. They followed a gully wash in an undulating slipper slide, a well-used path marked by sheep and donkey manure. The depth of the sides of the gully and the angle of the moon cast a dark shadow protecting them from sight.

Jeff could see by the route of descent that they were going to pass dangerously close to Avni's house. He braked with his feet splayed wide into the gully walls and hissed to get Gysi's attention, pointing frantically in the direction of the house.

"That is were the other jinni live," he whispered to Besiana.

"He knows," she answered back softly, "but the jinni are not there."

"How does *he* know?" snapped Jeff in hushed anger.

Besiana frowned at him in the dark. "He knows because he saw them fly together to the south as we came over the ridge."

Jeff tried to comprehend what she was telling him, but his mind suddenly was pulled back to the urgency he felt to contact his sister. Thoughts of Aubrey and Orhan began to flood his mind. Finally with effort he shook himself back to the present.

"He is sure it was Avni and Lida?"

"He does not know them by those names, but he is sure they were not the two jinni that have been dropping villagers on us," she said indignantly. "My father says we need to hurry and stop wasting time." Without another word she turned and slid quickly to Gysi, who had already resumed his skid through the steep gully.

The slope gradually leveled to an open meadow on the outskirts of the village. The three stood and brushed their bottoms free of the dirt, twigs, and manure they had accumulated. A high-pitched shriek could be heard in the distance over the ridge above. The moon popped up over the tree line of the ridge as it moved across the sky and now illuminated their valley. They cautiously approached the mayor's house.

Suddenly a dull thud startled them coming from a small shed to the left. They pressed themselves against the side of a house gaining some invisibility in the shade cast by an overhanging eave. Another clank and rattle came from the shed, as if a metal bucket had been kicked over. Gysi leveled his AK-47 sliding along with his back to the wall toward the shed. Another bang and thud froze him in place. He nervously sighted down the barrel of his weapon. Jeff and Besiana moved quickly behind a low wall and watched breathlessly as Gysi crept closer to the shed.

Jeff felt cold sweat streaking down his back. He searched in vain for his Beretta, forgetting that he had lost it in the caverns. Beside him Besiana shivered uncontrollably. He reached out his hand and brushed across hers. She grabbed his hand forcefully and cinched up tighter to him.

Gysi gave a low whistle, and a thud pounded the door to the shed as if it had been rammed. Gysi jumped back, but refrained from pulling the trigger. Finally he heard a long, drawn-out guttural mooing sound from inside. Remembering the scene in Qerg Muli, he stepped to the side of the door with his AK-47 ready. With his support hand, he reached over and flipped up the wooden latch. The door swung open on its own about a foot and then was nudged the rest of the way open by a dairy cow. She gently nuzzled Gysi with her soft snout.

He lowered his weapon and sighed, relieved to see a healthy cow needing to be milked.

"We do not have time now, little sister," he said kindly as he pushed her firmly back into the shed and latched the door. "You will be safer in there."

\* \* \*

The mayor's house was dark and empty. A wooden chair lay on its back with one of its legs broken. A wooden table was shattered in half. Next to the chair was a broken woven basket with freshly picked vegetables strewn across the ground. Gysi knew better than to call out.

Jeff took a step up to the porch and slipped on something wet. It seemed viscous beneath his boots. He wiggled free his flashlight and cupped his hand over the lens to block the glare of the beam. On the steps and across the front porch was a trail of blood that looked like someone had been dragged out of the house and down the steps. The trail disappeared under the overhanging branches of a fig tree. Jeff began to comprehend the reason he had seen no villagers before.

"Looks like the jinni has carried the mayor off," he whispered over his shoulder.

Gysi crept into the house, stepping over the pool of blood that washed over the threshold. The scene inside was limned by moonlight sifting through the window. Broken furniture and spilled food wallowed in rivulets of blood. Besiana covered her mouth to hold back a cry as she took in the carnage.

She began cry softly. "Oh, Eli, what has happened?"

"You know this family?" asked Jeff tenderly behind her.

"Eli is my age. We went to school together," she said trying to hold back a sob. "She is my best friend."

"I'm sorry," said Jeff putting his hand gently on her shoulder.

He saw Gysi pull the receiver of the telephone off the hook and check for a dial tone. Satisfied that it was working, he handed it to Jeff. The suddenness of having the telephone in his hands flustered him for a moment, and he was unable to recall the overseas connection numbers. He tried to calm himself and strained his memory. Soon it came back to him. A series of soft clicks pulsed on and off as the central telephone company patched his call through. He waited for what seemed like hours, but finally after about a minute he heard the faint ring of the phone on the other end. It rang several times. He looked at his watched and calculated the time difference.

"Three thirty-five a.m. here," he mumbled under his breath, "makes it eight thirty-five p.m. last night there."

The phone continued to ring. He began to panic when he realized that his mother would not recognize the number on the caller I.D. and probably would not answer. Despair from the anxiety began to make him antsy with each ring. He could hear Gysi becoming restlessly impatient standing guard at the front door. Just as he was losing hope and was about to hang up he heard a faint click on the other end of the line.

"Hello?"

His heart jumped at the sound of his sister's voice. "Hello, Anna?" he practically shouted through the receiver.

"Yes. Who is this?" she asked cautiously.

"It's me, Jeff. I—"

"Jeff! Oh my God. Mom, it's Jeff," she shouted deafening him through the receiver.

Jeff said hastily, "Anna, look, I don't have much time. I just needed to call to find out if you were OK." But he heard heavy leather heels clacking across the wooden floor of his kitchen back home, and a rustling sound told him that his mother had taken the telephone from his sister.

"Jeff? Are you all right? Where have you been?" his mother sobbed. "We thought you were dead. We haven't heard from you for months. We still have the embassy searching for you in Turkey. Where are you?" She barraged Jeff with questions, not allowing him to get a word in edgewise. Finally he had to butt in.

"Mom! Mom. Listen to me. I'm all right. I'm in Albania. I needed to know if Anna was all right."

"Yes. Yes we are both fine now," she continued to sob. "Jeff, what's happening? Why are you in Albania?"

"It's a long story. I don't have time now to explain, but I promise I will contact you soon. Promise me you two are OK."

"Yes, Jeff, we're OK. Please let—"

The line went dead. Jeff stared at the phone in his hand and wiped a small tear from the corner of his eye. He had so much he wanted to say. But the knowledge that his sister was all right had given him strength and determination, and he felt relieved as if a heavy burden had been lifted from his shoulders. He sighed a long sigh of satisfaction and turned leaning with his back against the wall. The gore brought him back to reality. He was still in grave danger.

The ramifications of what he had just learned played through his mind. He now knew for sure that the knowledge of the jinni was imperfect. They had blind spots. They had weakness. This made them vulnerable. Avni had told him that he was the last of the line of his ancestors. Somehow he would work their error to his advantage.

"My sister is alive and well," he whispered to Besiana. "The jinni think that I am the only one left."

A flood of confusion expressed itself on her face. Jeff could see her bewilderment.

"I do not understand any of this," she said. "I do not even know what these horrible creatures are, or why they are killing all these people."

"I think your father knows more than he's saying," said Jeff. "Tell him that my sister is alive in America. She is OK."

She repeated Jeff's news. Gysi looked at him and smiled faintly. "*Mirë,*" he said. "Good."

Jeff could see deep concern etched across Gysi's face. The father looked nervously at his daughter when she had her back to him. Her safety weighed heavily on him. Jeff pursed his lips and nodded in affirmation to the man. The unspoken word bonded the two men. Gysi leaned out of the front door and stared up into the night sky. They had not seen or heard the scream of the jinni for several minutes. Jeff craned his neck over Gysi's shoulder, not wanting to expose himself to the moonlight any more than he had to.

The air was getting chilly. A magnificent blanket of stars shone overhead, and Jeff tried to pick out any constellations that he recognized, but the steepness of the surrounding mountains limited the patch of sky that was visible. He felt Besiana press up behind him again. The three perused the sky for danger.

Suddenly, as all their concentration was skyward, they felt a disturbance in the air in front of them. They fell back in shock as their attention was quickly drawn to a small, hunched figure silhouetted on the front porch. It straightened slightly revealing an old hag of a woman crippled by time. She took a bold step toward them and clacked her walking stick against Gysi's shin, causing him to move out of the way and let her pass to stand before Jeff. She strained her feeble neck to look up into his face, and his eyes grew wide with recognition. It was the old woman from his vision at the deathbed of Përparim Lleshi. She studied him up and down and then pushed passed him into the house.

"You have no time, Jeff," she said over her shoulder as she placed a throw pillow over a bloodstain on the futon and sat down heavily. "The quadruplets are upon you. Do you have a plan?" She analyzed his hesitance in answering her. "I see you have no other plan but to run and hide," she concluded.

Jeff stammered. Gysi became even more guarded. Besiana's fear glued her in place.

The old woman kept her attention on Jeff. "Do you know who I am?" she asked in heavily accented English.

"No," he answered, "not really. I suspect you are the witch everyone has been talking about."

She cackled a coarse laugh and went into a coughing jag. "Yes," she choked over her words, "I am known as the witch, although that is not my preferred name. You may call me Valbona. You seem to have a knack for getting into and then out of trouble. But all that will be coming to an end soon." She patted the futon indicating Jeff should come and sit next her.

He looked around and found a handmade wool rug to place next to her, and sat down hesitantly. She patted his knee with her arthritic hand and smiled through a toothless grin. Her chin nearly touched the tip of her nose when she closed her mouth. She looked the same as Jeff remembered her from his dream. Same tattered gray cloak pulled over tattered gray clothes. Same facial features. Same long gray-and-white streaked, matted hair. It looked to Jeff as if she had not changed in five and a half centuries.

"Do you truly understand what is happening to you?" she asked giving him a sidewise glance.

"No," he answered truthfully.

"Nor do I expect you ever will," she said with a sigh. "You have heard so many explanations by so many people…and *non-people*, that I can well imagine you are just about as confused as you could possibly be. Am I right?"

"Yes."

"You really have nothing going for you right now that will help you to survive. I guess you know that by now also. You have been lucky so far. You have been told that the jinni have a propensity for toying with their victims. This is what has kept you alive thus far. This is the one thing that has been in your favor, but it is soon going to wear out. The time for toying will come to an end, and they will fulfill their destiny, which of course is to kill you and Orhan. I am afraid there is really very little you can do for yourself, or that others can do for you in spite of the well-intentioned help of the Gypsies. Unless you can come up with a magic rabbit out of the hat, as they say, you will die." She paused for a moment as the cry of the jinni could be heard once again drawing closer from the south.

"You see, Jeff, you have not one or two jinni to deal with but four that are dedicated to ending this curse once and for all. They now have the two golden cubes together in one place, which puts Ölüm and Vdekje together for the first time in all these centuries. On top of that, for the first time in all those years the survivors of Lleshi and Bey are together, and the last survivors at that. The Gypsy queen is coming and that will complete the lineup with the heir of Baba Moush. At no time in the last five hundred years have all the pieces been in place to complete the articles of the curse. That is, until now.

"So, young Jeff Smith, do you have anything that we might be able to consider to be in your favor that I should know about?"

Jeff paused for a moment, not sure he should divulge his secret. He realized he had nothing else to lose, and so he decided to confide in the witch. "Well, for one thing, I am not the last in the line." He paused to get her reaction, which was as he thought it would be. Her wrinkled face gave away her complete surprise. "And..." He tapped his feet nervously. "And I have the two golden cubes."

The witch jumped up from her seat and faced him. She seemed invigorated by his news. She towered over him menacingly but then relaxed. "You truly have the golden cubes?" she asked with wander in her voice. "How?"

"It's a long story," said Jeff, "but that isn't all." He paused again. "I also have the ruby bracelet."

She gasped and fell back down into her seat, nearly missing it but catching herself before she fell to the floor. She finally gathered herself enough and stared at him with renewed admiration. "These are great assets," she managed to say. "Great assets indeed."

Jeff tumbled through the ruby bracelet with his fingers, keeping it concealed in his baggy pants pocket farthest from the witch. He pondered whether to tell her he had it there with them and decided to keep it secret for now. She was right about how many different stories he had been told and who had said they could be trusted but then ended up not being trustworthy.

"The jinni must be unaware of their loss," Valbona said. "When they find out, there will be no more toying. They will kill everything that breathes." She turned in her seat and stared deep into his eyes. Even in the dark, he felt her probing glare. "You have the ruby bracelet with you?" She waited for him to respond.

He wanted to lie, but he found himself suddenly wanting to tell her everything. He choked back a gush of confession. His mind spun in a whirl of possible answers, but in the end all he could tell her was the truth. Had she willed him to tell the truth through some power she possessed? He fought the urge to blurt out that he had the bracelet folded in his hand. Her gaze penetrated deep into his mind. He could not look away. He could feel her presence encroaching on him. The struggle between their wills clashed for several seconds.

Finally he blurted out as if he had been holding his breath, "Yes. Yes, I have it here in my pocket." His head and shoulders collapsed into a slouch of defeat.

"There, now wasn't that easier than lying?" she said tapping her walking stick once against the wooden floor triumphantly. "With the ruby bracelet in our possession, your chances for survival have just increased dramatically." She paused for a moment and gazed off into the corner of the room as if she were seeing a vision. "Orhan, however, I am afraid is in immediate danger. We must hurry if we are going to save him."

# 32. Night Flight

La Gomer Ferry
Somewhere on the Drin River, Northern Albania
16 August 2000, 3:30 a.m.

Orhan tossed and turned in a fitful, nightmarish sleep. He stopped breathing, and then suddenly bolted upright and gasped for air. He stared bewildered at his surroundings. The chug, chug of the ferry's engines cut across the surface of the dark water, echoing off of the high cliffs on either side of the river. Aubrey slept fitfully on the bench next to him. The Gypsies had curled up next to each other finding whatever space they could on the floor.

Orhan tried to squirm into the shabby seat cushion to get comfortable but only succeeded in attracting two more springs to his rear and the small of his back. Aubrey stirred at the commotion but only rubbed her nose with her sleeve and dozed back to sleep.

He slouched with his feet stretched out and his head resting against the back of the bench. His chest felt heavy as if someone were kneeing him, making it hard to breathe. He closed his eyes and prayed for sleep. After several futile minutes, he opened his eyes a slit. He sensed something hanging over him and reached out, swatting at it like a pesky fly. His arm was suddenly jerked up in the air and wrenched higher, pulling him unwillingly off the bench. He tried to cry out but found that he had no air. Something was wrapping around his torso, constricting tighter and tighter. He fought to release himself

381

from the grip but suddenly realized that he was several feet above the deck and being taken out over the river.

Orhan clutched the knobby, leathery talon that had him completely immobilized. He strained to see what had latched onto him, but all he saw was a great shadow of darkness that glided effortlessly with him into the night sky. He continued to struggle, but the more he did the tighter the grip became. After a few moments, his body went limp. He slumped back, his arms, legs, and head splayed earthward.

Far below he could see the dark ribbon of the Drin winding its way into the Balkan Alps of northern Albania. Above, the shadow became more discernible in the light of the full moon. Orhan's mind struggled to comprehend his plight. His brain was not getting enough oxygen. He strained to raise his head so he could breath, but gravity and fatigue pinned his neck in a slung down position. His last thought before passing out was that he was being carried away by a giant eagle.

He came to after a few moments and strained to see the massive shadow that carried him. He realized it was not an eagle, but something else. The night air became cooler. He felt himself going higher. Wisps of cloud floated below him, obscuring the ground, and the full moon illuminated the mountain scape from horizon to horizon. The rhythmic wop, wop, wop of the gigantic wings pounded his face and eardrums with sonic thumps.

The creature descended and glided effortlessly through mountain valleys, and the air warmed slightly. Orhan could once again smell the earth coming up and filling his nostrils with the mustiness of farms and animals. He could see tiny villages spattered along the slopes and in the deep ravines. The moonlight shimmered off another narrower river like twinkling candles. Orhan noticed the wave of the shadow cast by the creature rolling over the terrain.

# Vale of Shadows

A great and startling ululating cry burst from the creature. Orhan struggled to cover his ears but found his arms too numb to raise from their hanging posture. Another screech was answered by a similar cry resounding off the mountain faces far to the north. Orhan craned his neck to see the creature's flight path. As he did so, he saw out of the corner of his eye another creature flying in a parallel pattern off the left wing and slightly elevated.

In the grasp of the second creature was the dangling body of Merriam. She was cradled in the talons facedown, which gave her slightly more mobility than Orhan. She kicked and beat with her fists against the huge, scaly knuckles of the creature, screaming curses in Romani.

Orhan could hear the amused cackle of her captor. Suddenly the grip of the talon relaxed, and Merriam plummeted to the earth flailing and scream as she fell. The creature swooped in a high arc and dove steeply downward, skimming the tops of the trees and snatching her by the leg just before impact with the ground.

Merriam screamed in terror, and the creature cackled with delight, flying with irregular rises and falls like a roller coaster, brushing her along the treetops. At one point it rolled over on its back and kicked Merriam high into the air like a ball, and then swooped in on her snatching her at the last second.

Orhan looked on in horror. Any thought he had to beat against the talons of his own creature quickly ended as he watched Merriam's plight. He could now see the face of the creature carrying Merriam. It was human-like, but even from a distance the features were far from human. Merriam's creature turned and leered up at him as it rejoined its flight off the right wing of his creature and slightly below. Its countenance suddenly transformed into a hideous snarling beast, and then just as quickly into a beautiful young woman. Orhan stared in amazement at her stunning facial features. Noticing that he was watching, she morphed into the face of the old woman that he remembered from Turkey.

As if on cue, Orhan's creature bent its head down and stared at him. The face slowly transformed into the face of the old man. The kindness that was present in his eyes before was now gone, replaced by a ravenous cunning that sent a cold shudder through Orhan. He squirmed under the scrutiny and averted his gaze. His eyes fell on the hapless form of Merriam dangling by one leg upside down. The fight had left her as she succumbed to her captor's will.

Avni let out a blood-chilling screech that echoed through the mountains and rumbled like thunder off the granite peaks. Lida joined him in an awesome chorus that deafened Orhan. From a short distance away, two more distinct cries reverberated through the valley. The jinni glided into the openness of a mountain pasture and dropped their prey five feet from the ground.

Orhan and Merriam crashed into a soft pillow of hay that had been piled in a conical stack. Orhan slid to the ground and realized they had just missed being impaled by a pole that ran up through the stack collared by a circlet of wired stone weights. Once he gained his feet, he stumbled toward the trees that edged the field, but Avni's ominous form blocked his way. He heard a scream from Merriam and saw Lida knock her to the ground rolling her playfully like a log with her talon.

The village below the meadow caught Orhan's attention over Avni's shoulder. A valley spread out surrounded by mountains on three sides and open to the south. In its center was a raised promontory with two buildings that shone in the ghostly light of the moon. Avni side stepped to block Orhan's view. With a frightening shudder, he morphed into a handsome young man but kept his giant stature, towering over Orhan.

Lida strode up to Avni in human form as a beautiful young woman. She dragged Merriam forcefully by her long hair.

Merriam cried out struggling to keep her feet, clasping onto her hair with both hands to ease the strain on the roots. Lida stood next to her brother admiringly, her own stature matching his.

Orhan was pushed roughly aside as Avni went to the haystack and with a powerful sweep of his arm toppled the pole, sending the hay scattering. He kicked at the stubble with his foot, clearing a spot to reveal a stone slab that lay flat on the ground. Avni bent over and with both hands leveraged the lip of the slab. With his fingers he pried the stone up and heaved it upon its end, rolling it to the side. It clattered to the ground gyrating like an out-of-balance wheel until it settled with a heavy thud.

Lida grabbed Orhan and Merriam by the shoulders and heaved them toward the opening in the ground. They sprawled clumsily until she came over and grabbed them up again, carrying them the rest of the way to the entrance.

A shaft of moonlight shone down into a stairway cut in stone. Avni led the way, giving Orhan and Merriam a menacing look indicating they should follow him. The stairs were slippery with dew. The jinni needed no light for the descent, and they clearly had no regard for the safety of their captives. Orhan groped his way down the steps, timidly sliding his foot to the edge of each step and then stepping down. Merriam grasped his shoulder for support and guidance.

The going was slow, and the jinni had little patience. Lida shoved Merriam from behind causing her to topple into Orhan. He barely caught his balance, nearly falling into the darkness. A cackle of glee burst from Lida as she watched their feeble attempts to help each other.

In desperation Orhan snapped at Merriam, "Can't you do anything?"

"All my potions and spells are in my carpetbag," she muttered woefully.

"No talking," commanded Avni. "Pleading is appreciated, however," he said with a macabre laugh.

"Yes. We also like groveling," laughed Lida.

They continued their treacherous descent until they came to a smooth, paved stone path. Torches hung in sconces on the rock walls dispelling the darkness. They had arrived at a large passageway that seemed to have been partially hewn out by hand. The lit torches stretched out as far as the eye could see, spaced every five meters until they converged in the distance.

Orhan could make out the brightness of an opening as they trudged along the stone path. His mind wandered to a scene he remembered from a college literature class of Dante Alighieri's *Inferno*. The fumes of the torches sent up black wisps of smoke that danced along the ceiling of the passage.

Soon they could see they were approaching a large arch framed in cut stone blocks, and they entered into a larger, more rudimentary chamber. The stone path ended at the threshold, and the floor became a trail of foot-worn, smooth rock. The torchlight was more sparsely placed, leaving the chamber in a contortion of shades and shadows. The trail wound through a series of bends created by formations of stalagmites and branching off into various directions at a number of forks. Orhan lost the last semblance of direction and any hope of retreating the way they had come. A tremendous sense of doom washed over him, stronger than at any time before. His legs felt like lead. Each step became harder and harder to take.

Merriam also struggled to keep the pace the jinni demanded. She chanted under her breath a spell she had known since she was a child to ward off the evil eye. Much to her chagrin, it failed to help her now. Lida let loose a reverberating guffaw at her useless superstition. Merriam continued to mutter it, despite its futility, for lack of anything better.

As they rounded a large stalagmite that was as big as a three-story house, the sound of rushing water filled their ears;

soon they could feel the wet mist of a waterfall tickling their faces. The trail approached an arched stone bridge illuminated by a span of torches.

Avni stopped and studied the cavern. Orhan could tell something was not right with the way he paused. Sensing the same, Lida came up and stood by her brother. Orhan and Merriam stared at each other with looks of resigned helplessness.

Suddenly Avni bolted over the bridge in a fury. As he went his countenance began to glow a fiery red that increased in intensity as his rage fomented. Lida stayed behind, but Orhan could see through the rage of her own flaming eyes something else. Fear. He studied her in the dark. Merriam noticed it also. A faint glimmer of hope began to well up inside of them.

In the distance beyond the bridge, a terrifying, unearthly scream resounded through every crevice of the subterranean cavity. Lida took one look at Orhan and Merriam, giving them a stern warning with her eyes not to move, and flew off in the direction that Avni had gone. Within seconds another like-mannered scream bellowed through the caverns.

Orhan pressed himself into a crag in the rock pulling Merriam along with him. To his surprise he was able to continue backing into the crack, and soon found that they had followed a fissure line that secluded them from the main passage.

The screaming could still be heard bouncing off the hard rock walls. Orhan continued to back along the tight crevice pulling Merriam unwittingly along until he felt the crush of the walls give way and they stood in a broad opening. After their eyes adjusted, they could see a faint light shining through a veil that they soon discerned as a waterfall. Orhan made his way closer to find that they had actually come up behind the fall, with the main cavern on the other side of the water. The light came from the torches that lined the bridge.

From this vantage point, Orhan could see around a large stalagmite on the other side of the underground river. Another chamber lay beyond. The jinni were in a rant, sending out splashes of fire that licked along the floor and up the walls of the chamber spilling out into the cavern toward the river. The flashes were blinding even through the heavy waterfall. Orhan and Merriam shielded their eyes with their hands but still tried to squint into the glare.

"What's happening?" shouted Orhan over the roar of the fall.

"I do not know for sure, but something important is missing," replied Merriam, straining to listen to the wild ranting of Avni and Lida. "I understand only part of what they are saying, but whatever is missing is of great importance." She listened intently, and a faint smile curled the right corner of her lip. She looked at Orhan with a renewed vigor. Her head began to nod with understanding. "I hear something else in their voices," she said. "Fear."

It took Orhan a second to assimilate the information. "What do they have to be afraid of?" he asked with suspicion in his tone.

"I heard Jeff's name mentioned," she said holding up a hand to hush him. "Jeff has been here. In these caverns. He has stolen something. I can't quite make out what it is." She paused to listen.

Thunderous claps shook the foundations of the mountains as Avni bashed the rocks with his flaming fist and bolts of radiant lightening. Boulders and stalactites from the ceiling of the cave began to plummet to the floor sending voluminous clacks and tremors echoing up and down the underground river course. A massive chunk of granite crashed into the river overhead, knocking Orhan and Merriam to the ground. They skittered across the stone floor of the sub-cave like sand on a trampoline.

# Vale of Shadows

Orhan grabbed a footing of rock as he vibrated toward the edge of the cliff. Merriam frantically latched onto his legs but suddenly found herself dangling precariously over the river far below. He reached down and grabbed her by the sleeve, heaving her up beside him. Rock debris and dirt continued to cascade down throughout the cavern system as Avni vented his rage.

Orhan dragged Merriam to a more secure hold and waited out the onslaught of collapsing granite. He chanced a look over his shoulder toward the opening of their hiding place. The boulder above had partially blocked the flow of the waterfall, eliminating part of their screen. Aghast, he watched the fury of the jinni in the chamber across the river. It dawned on him that if he could see them clearly, then they could also see Merriam and him now that the fall had ceased. He squirmed to his hands and knees and crawled back into the narrow crevice. Merriam followed him as best she could, but the violence of the quake jittered her back toward the cliff. She furiously grappled for a hold on the wet slab. Orhan dove for her outstretched arm, but the distance had grown too great; she slid over the edge and disappeared into the darkness below. Her muffled cry trailed away from him as she fell.

He gazed in stunned disbelief as the last remnant of her cry was drowned in the waters below. The tantrums of the jinni began to subside. Orhan knew he was vulnerable. Caught out in the open, he knew the jinni would have no compunction about killing him on the spot. His only hope of survival was to find a niche in the blackness. He slithered backward as low as he could into the crevice.

A thunderous crash shook the ground as another boulder smashed into the river above. It jarred the blockage of the first boulder, allowing water to once again flow over the mouth of his cloister. Orhan cringed as dust and dark enveloped him.

He dared to slide his hand up the wall of the crack. He knew the eyes of the jinni were keen in the dark, but he had seen a depression in the face of the rock about waist high when the fire of the jinn lapped out from the chamber across the way. His hand fell into another crevice, and he groped as far as he could without rising too high from his belly.

He stared through the screen of water. The commotion seemed to have died down. Trusting that the veil of the cataract would shield his movement, he jumped to his feet and felt deep into the depression. It went beyond his reach. He squirmed in headfirst and prayed claustrophobia would not paralyze him. He wiggled deeper and deeper until he was confident that his feet were no longer in the passageway. He forced his mind to allow him to continue despite the mounting terror that was digging its claws into his chest.

The blackness was complete. He knew that whatever terror awaited him in front was not as great as the one that lurked after him behind. He soon was able to crawl on his hands and knees. The going was slow because bumping his head had become a common occurrence. Eventually he heard the sound of rushing water ahead, and a dim light penetrated his crawl space. He was nearing the end.

He belly flopped back down and continued his crawl to the exit of the horizontal fissure he had been following. The voices of Avni and Lida could be heard beyond the orifice, but other voices had now joined them. He slowly scooted back a little ways into the fissure. He could tell the voices were calling back and forth to each other from both sides of the river.

He knew in his gut they were searching for him. A sudden cry of surprise and a cackle of glee came from beyond Orhan's view. He inched forward to gain a better look. There in the fiery glow of the jinni stood four figures. His heart leapt in both hope and fear as he saw that Lida had Merriam pinned down by the neck with her foot. Merriam was alive, after all. But she wouldn't be for long if he didn't help her.

Orhan knew that now was not the time for panic. Panic would cost him his life and the life of Merriam. He fought the urge to shuffle back and escape, mustering all his courage to stay and face the danger and come up with a plan. His mind fell on something Merriam had said. She had sensed fear in the jinni. Orhan tried to calculate what might cause them fear. His mind was a numbing blank, and he watched in horror as the jinni began to tug ruthlessly on Merriam's arms and legs. She cried out in pain. Orhan couldn't take his eyes off the terrible scene.

Fear. The jinni were afraid. Jeff had been here. What did it mean?

Suddenly the two jinni dropped Merriam back onto the gravel beach of the river. The quadruplets turned and scanned the walls of the cavern. Searching. Searching for him. He snuggled back into the crag.

They feared.

They were afraid.

Orhan suddenly, inexplicably felt...courage.

# 33. A Good Thing It's "Borrowed"

La Gomar Ferry
Approaching dawn

The first thing Aubrey noticed when she woke up was how cool the wind was blowing across the bow of *La Gomar*. She arched her back and stretched her arms and legs in a wide-air angel oscillation. She had slept surprisingly well. She sat forward on the bench taking in her surroundings. The grayish light of dawn crept over the peaks to the east in ever broadening bands. She yawned widely and stared unblinking at the pile of Gypsy men still sleeping on the deck, glancing absently to the bench where Orhan had slept. Seeing he was not there nor on the floor, she assumed he had gone to brave the toilet.

Mustafa stirred and sat up facing her. He looked around him and immediately noticed that Merriam was not where he had last seen her. He craned his neck so he could see down the side deck toward the toilet, but no one was astir.

"Where is Merriam?" he asked Aubrey, who was fighting back a yawn.

"I haven't seen her," she replied. "Orhan isn't here either. Maybe they're in the toilet."

"There is only one toilet, and I can see from here that the door is open." He got to his feet and rousted Besnik with a gentle nudge of his foot. "Wake the others," he said while walking to the starboard side of the ferry.

The speed of the boat heading into the wind as it blew through the canyon swirled his long black hair around his face. He clasped it back with his hand as he peered over the side into the water. Besnik strode up next to him and stretched into the wind, relieving the kinks he had from lying on the floor. The two men acknowledged each other with a nod, and then Mustafa made his way passed the pilothouse to the stern cabin.

He searched the sleeping passengers but did not find Orhan or Merriam. Concern began to well up inside of him, and he rushed back to the bow cabin to find that the others had risen and were discussing the whereabouts of Merriam and Orhan.

"They are not on the boat," said Mustafa.

"Where are they then?" asked Aubrey. "They couldn't have just—" She caught herself before she said the word *disappeared*. She was all too aware of the fact that they could have easily "just disappeared."

Besnik walked back to the pilothouse and tapped on the window of the closed door. The pilot stared straight ahead without acknowledging him. Besnik rapped harder on the glass and jiggled the door handle at the same time. The noise jolted the pilot out of a trance. He stared at Besnik blankly, his eyes glazed over with a sheen of bewilderment. Finally his eyes blinked and he looked at Besnik as if for the first time. He slowly unlocked the cabin door and allowed Besnik to poke his head in.

"We are missing two of our party," Besnik said in Gegë Albanian, the northern dialect of the mountain people.

The pilot fluttered his eyelashes as if he were trying to recall a past event. He finally shook his head and said, "I don't know where they could have gone. We haven't stopped all night." The sound of his own voice seemed to snap the man out of his trance. "Last night I remember seeing something gliding over the water off my starboard bow. It was like a fog but seemed to have a will of its own, traveling independently of the wind gusts. I don't remember anything else until just now. I'm sorry." A sudden look of fear crossed over his face, and he waved Besnik to move away from the pilothouse; but when the Gypsy did not move fast enough the captain gave him a shove and then locked the door quickly. He stared out the side window toward the shore and ignored Besnik's attempts to speak to him.

Besnik decided it wasn't worth the trouble so he went back to his group. "The pilot saw something last night, but he blanked out and couldn't tell me what it was," he said. "Something has frightened him."

"What did he think he saw?" asked Aubrey.

"A strange fog is all he said."

"How much farther to Fierza?" asked Mustafa.

"We should be there soon," answered Besnik. "The sun will be up in another thirty minutes. Have you thought about how we are going to get to Curraj i Epërm?"

"Merriam said she has arranged transportation. Some cousins will meet us with a Land Rover at the dock in Fierza."

He had no sooner said this than the ferry rounded a bend in the river and came within view of the town of Fierza. A crimson band grew from the mountain peak as the sun began to crest the horizon beyond. The waterway was still dark with shadows, but the company could see the early morning activity as villagers crowded the dock to get a seat on *La Gomar* when it made its return journey.

Soon the ferry rubbed against the concrete dock ramp that protruded out into the river. The boat quickly emptied, but not before those waiting to get on began to crowd the gangway impeding the disembarkation process. Mustafa pushed through the pack of villagers none too gently. The rest of his company followed closely behind before the
swell of people collapsed on the wake he had created.

The ramp became a narrow concrete sidewalk that rose steeply to the road above the bank of the river. There, waiting on the dirt road, was a dark green Defender. One Gypsy standing at the back of the Land Rover greeted his clansmen, while another was perched on top ready to tie down any luggage. The stern looks on the two Gypsies' faces quickly faded to looks of confusion and concern when they heard of Merriam's mysterious disappearance.

They eyed Aubrey suspiciously. She now was the only *gadjo* in the group. She suddenly felt very alone and missed Jeff more than ever. Mustafa and Besnik began to argue with their cousin perched on the top of the Defender. Furtive glances at Aubrey turned into outright glares as the argument became more heated. Soon the two Gypsy cousins were shouting at Mustafa and Besnik and pointing at Aubrey vehemently. She understood that they clearly did not want her coming along on the trip.

She began to shy away from the company, not knowing exactly what to do, but then she realized she had to assert herself or be left behind. She stepped boldly to Mustafa's side.

"I'm not staying behind," she blurted out obstinately. "I'm coming with you!"

Her determination took the two Gypsies by surprise. They gaped at her with blank looks.

Mustafa gave a half smile and translated her statement in Romani. The cousin on the ground began to open his mouth in protest, but before he could say anything Aubrey climbed into the back seat of the Rover and sat stubbornly with her eyes fixed out the front windshield.

The Gypsy recognized the futility of arguing any further and motioned for the rest of the group to climb in. The bags were quickly tied off on the top rack while Merriam's six men climbed into the far back bench seats sitting three on a side facing each other. Mustafa and Besnik joined Aubrey, each taking a window seat and forcing her to straddle the transmission tunnel in the middle.

The Land Rover climbed laboriously up the steep incline of the dirt road. Soon they had wound their way above the town overlooking the Drin and *La Gomar*, which was now slowly pulling away from the landing with a full load of passengers. The sun had cleared the peaks to the east and promised another hot, dry day.

The mountains loomed high to the north as they followed a road that was little better than a trail in some sections. Other sections were black topped with cracked, bubbled asphalt for a quarter of a mile or so, and then resumed back to the rutted dirt resemblance of a road.

The Defender crawled slowly over the uneven, rough terrain. As they rounded a steep bend, a large cement truck lay parked at a tilt along the outside edge of the pass, leaving almost no room for the Land Rover to squeeze by. It was rusted and stripped of its doors and tires. The rear axle had broken possibly decades ago given the weathered state of its condition. The truck driver had tried to dump his load, but only achieved a cascade of hardened concrete that formed a surreal fall from the mouth of the tumbler to the ground.

Josef, the driver, ground the Rover into first gear and swooped precariously up the slope of the inside hill squeezing past the cement truck with a shriek of metal on metal. The maneuver creased the side of the Rover, putting a half-inch groove into the doors and side panels. The careless swerve threw the men in the back off balance, causing them to topple into each other, and the sudden shift of weight to the left side of the Rover tipped it just enough to gouge the crease deeper. The grinding noise set all of their teeth on edge. Finally they revved through the obstacle and continued up the arduous switchback.

Mustafa and Besnik smiled at each other when they noticed the distressed look on Aubrey's face.

"It is OK," said Mustafa answering her unspoken concern for the damage to Land Rover. "It's not ours." He smiled broadly at Josef, who eyed him through the rearview mirror. "We are simply borrowing it."

After an hour, the road cut back along side the Drin. They followed it until they came to the village of Lekhibaj where the road forked to the northeast and southwest at the foot of a mountain. Josef downshifted and bounced the four-wheel drive over the ditch mound, crossing through a meadow and staying to the west of the mountain line.

The meadow stretched into a long valley that was patched with trees and cut by a narrow stream. The Defender loosely followed a sheep trail. At times Josef would have to search for a way through thickets and gullies. The jarring the passengers took was brutal.

They came to a deep rut that would easily have high centered the vehicle, but there was no other route available. The men piled out, glad to stretch their legs from the confines of the cramped Rover, and went to work gathering stones and placing them in the gully to make a track for the vehicle to traverse. Aubrey decided to make her decision to come along more palatable for the Gypsies and hauled stones along with the rest of them. After half an hour, there was a pile of stones large enough for the vehicle to cross to the other side.

Once they cleared the gully, they bumped through another field that had been plowed. To the side of the field was a wooden handled plow with a steel blade. The harness and reins for a horse straddled the handle. Grazing in the grass next to the field, a small Albanian horse was hobbled with its two front legs tied together by a twelve-inch-long rope.

As they came through the trees following a cart path, a village opened up in front of them.

"This is the village of Curraj," said Josef in Albanian.

"So we're here then," stated Aubrey pleased that she understood him.

"No. We must go higher up to the village of Curraj i Epërm," corrected Mustafa. "It is still north of us."

As they skirted the village, they noticed a distinct lack of life. Josef was familiar with this area and sensed something was wrong. Pulling over, he told the others to wait while he and his brother Fredi went to check it out. The others tensed in anticipation as the suspense mounted while Josef and Fredi disappeared around the corner of a corn shed.

The sun had risen higher and was beginning to heat up the occupants of the Rover. Aubrey sat and fanned herself with a leather document wallet she had found tucked up under the front seat. One of the Gypsy men in the back opened the back door allowing a slight breeze to draft through.

Suddenly Josef and Fredi lurched back around the corner of the shed and ran toward them yelling and flapping their arms to get everyone's attention. They yanked open their doors and jumped inside, out of breath with looks of terror on their faces.

"They are dead," gasped Josef. "The jinni have ripped them limb from limb. We found only corpses." In his panic he had flooded the carburetor and the engine would not turn over. He continued pumping the gas pedal, making the problem worse.

"You're flooding the carburetor," explained Aubrey from the back seat. "You can't pump the gas like that." She paused trying to get Mustafa to translate for her. "He's only making it worse by stomping on the pedal that way," she said, frustrated.

Finally Mustafa got him to stop and Aubrey pushed Besnik through the door so she could get out. She pantomimed that Josef should pop the hood release and then propped the hood open by its stay bar. She loosened the wing nut to the air filter, pulling off the cover, and blew into the carburetor to evaporate the excess fuel. The Gypsy men had little knowledge of how an automobile worked and tried to pull her off the bumper to get her to go back inside the Rover, but she stubbornly fought them off.

After several puffs of air she jumped down and motioned for Josef to exit the vehicle. Taking his place she cranked the starter a couple of times, and the engine fired with a loud bang from the tail pipe. "My dad taught me," she said with a shrug.

Seeing the engine was running, the men looked at her with renewed respect and climbed back into the Defender. Josef started to climb into the back seat, but Aubrey made it clear that she did not want to drive and moved over for him, replacing Fredi in the front seat.

They left the village as quickly as possible, but the ground had been made soft by a hard rain the day before and they soon bogged down and found themselves buried up to their axles in mud. Attempts to push the Rover out of the muck failed despite the eleven's collective efforts.

"This is getting us nowhere," grunted Mustafa embedding himself up to his knees in the mushy earth. He stood and looked around the field. They had only traveled about four miles from Curraj before getting stuck.

"With this mud it will be quicker to walk," said Besnik. "Curraj i Epërm is only about three hours by foot according to Fredi."

With no time to waste, they decided to unload their packs from the roof of the Defender and make their way on foot. They were able to find firmer ground under a belt of trees that extended along the foot of the range. Their spirits were lifted after being freed from the confines of the Rover.

Heavy gray clouds rolled over the mountains to the east and blocked the heat of the morning sun, giving the company a little relief. They trudged forward in silence walking in single file with Josef leading the way.

Mustafa clutched Merriam's carpetbag tightly. He fought off the urge to open it and study its contents, but he knew he would have no understanding of the magic that lay inside. He decided it best to leave it for her to open when they met again. This thought spurred him on. He felt in his heart he would see her again. He had run away years ago to get out from under her domineering thumb, but now he yearned for her as a son yearns for his mother. He pondered the threat Besnik had made to avenge his brother's death after this was all over and glanced over his shoulder to see Besnik help Aubrey climb over a fallen tree trunk that lay in their path. He knew Besnik would not forsake his vow. The weight of so many enemies burdened him. Each step grew harder to take.

Aubrey tried to push the thought of the deaths back in Curraj out of her mind. She checked her watch. Only 9:30 a.m. It seemed later to her. She felt a drop of moisture on her face and looked up. Rain began to fall from the dark patch of cloud that hovered over them. To the south and west the sun still shone brightly, but the heavy cloud cover was quickly roiling over the mountain peak spreading out over the valley.

For some reason, maybe because she was so tired, she remembered a line from an old Mel Brooks movie: "...it could be worse. It could be raining." She slogged through the rain wandering if she would ever laugh again. The weight on her shoulders pulled her spirits down far more than the simple weight of her pack.

She sighed deeply and mournfully. She needed hope. She needed Jeff.

# 34. Secret Passages

Curraj i Epërm, Albania

Valbona rose abruptly and went outside the mayor's house. She boldly stood out in the middle of the courtyard and searched from horizon to horizon for the jinni. The sky was clear. She sensed something had changed; not for them, but for the jinni. She closed her eyes and concentrated deeply, holding her hand up to stop any interruption from the others.

She began to sway gently from side to side and mumbled an inaudible chant. Jeff, Gysi, and Besiana watched in silence. They did not have her confidence and stayed under the protection of the front porch eave nervously watching the sky. Finally the witch opened her eyes and walked slowly back to the porch.

"There is great trouble ahead," she said. "The jinni have captured the blood of Selim Bey and Baba Moush. They are being held in the caverns below this valley."

"I have been to those caverns," said Jeff. "I woke up in a chamber on some kind of an altar, but I doubt I could find it again."

"Did you see or talk to anyone?" asked Valbona.

"Yes. Lida was there. She was in the form of a beautiful woman."

"Their plan was to placate you until they could get their hands on the other two," said Valbona. "Now the jinni do not have you, but they have Orhan Aziz, who is the last in the line of Selim Bey. The other is the Gypsy *queen*; apparently you have not met her. She would be in the line of Baba Moush. The

401

proliferation of the Roma makes me doubt that she is the last of Baba Moush's line. So if anything happens to her there are plenty more where she came from."

Jeff cringed at her callousness. "How do you know it is a woman that is in the caverns with Orhan?"

"I *sense* the woman, is how," said the witch matter-of-factly. "I sense it is Merriam. I sense her power, but she is in trouble. We shall see."

"Well, what do we do now?" asked Jeff.

"First of all we go get those two golden cubes." She looked at Gysi and said something to him that Jeff did not understand.

Gysi took Besiana by the arm and began to walk out into the night. Valbona called after him before he reached the front door.

"We will go back to your cave by a secret way," she said.

Gysi stopped and stared at her. "What secret way is that?"

"You didn't believe that after all these centuries I was coming and going between these villages by climbing over those mountains, did you? We will go together. Please wait outside. It is OK. It is safe, for now." After she watched them leave, she turned to Jeff. "Now let me have that bracelet." Valbona held out her hand, and Jeff pulled the bracelet out of his pocket and placed it without hesitation in her outstretched palm.

"Magnificent," she said as she turned it over and over in the dim light of the moon. "Absolutely magnificent. This bracelet was not made by human hands. It was crafted by the jinni over three millennia ago." She tapped her cudgel twice on the floor, causing the piece to glow brightly. Holding the bracelet up before her eyes, she watched the dance of the figurines inside. "You see these figures entombed in the body of each one of the rubies?" she asked Jeff. "They are the spirit essence of ancient jinni. They were bound by the Master until such time as he summons them. There is great power here for someone who knows how to use it."

Jeff looked closely at the figures as they swayed within the gems by the light of the cudgel. He found himself transfixed by the movement. All peripheral vision blurred, and the features of the figures became more distinct. With time he actually began to believe they were looking at him as they danced. His head began to swim.

"Who are they?" he stammered in awe.

"They are marid. Malicious, evil jinni who have been bound as punishment for their deeds against mankind and their fellow jinn."

"Do you know how to use this?" he said, unable to pull his eyes away.

"Not yet, but I will before the day is out," said Valbona.

Jeff snapped out of his hypnosis and stared at her. "I think I know," he said. "Don't ask me how I know, but I just have a feeling I know how to use this bracelet."

Before the witch could react, he took the bracelet from her and tugged on the end ruby. When it did not separate from the strand, he clenched his fist around two adjacent rubies and pulled at first lightly and then with a gradually increasing force. The bracelet still did not break, even after he had pulled on it with all his strength.

"What is it you are trying to do?" asked Valbona curiously.

"I'm trying to get one of these rubies off," he said giving the bracelet another try.

"As I said," she countered irritably, "this bracelet was made by the Master. You will not separate these gems with mere human strength." She snapped the bracelet out of his hands before he hurt himself. "Why do you want this broken?"

"Back in the cave in my backpack is a weapon that the Gypsies gave me. It's like a charged slingshot. They told us that the jinni could be killed by something that was not of their world but that would penetrate their world. Specifically we were shooting peach seeds at them, and it seemed to work, at least in part. I'm thinking if we used these rubies instead of peach seeds, we could shoot the jinni with the sling rifles and the rubies would penetrate them, killing them." He paused to see her reaction. "What do you think?"

"I think you have a lot to learn about the jinni and magic," she said condescendingly, "but I will keep your idea in mind."

She led him out of the house. Dawn was approaching; the faintest glimmer of light was beginning to waken the valley. In the distance the painful bray of a donkey could be heard echoing off the mountain slopes, and the soft bleating of goats came from a shed down closer to the river. The air became thick with the presence of black flies.

She led Jeff, Gysi, and Besiana up the hill toward Avni's house. Jeff balked when he saw the direction they were heading, but she assured him with a kindly beckoning of her hand that it was safe. They stepped into the front courtyard of the house, which was as Jeff remembered it. The grapevines hung by the wire trellis bulging with clusters of grapes. He inadvertently started to take a handful, but Valbona cautioned him to beware of the jinni's grapes. He eyed the cluster warily, wiping his hands on his pants legs.

They went around to the back of the house where an old corn shed stood. Next to it was an open well rimmed with stone. Valbona pushed one of the wall stones inward with her hand; a soft, grinding noise came up from the ground below their feet, and then a gentle rush of cool wind hit them in the face. The witch agilely stepped over the low wall and disappeared into the mouth of the well. Gysi and Besiana quickly followed, leaving Jeff standing alone. The first light of dawn began to creep over the mountain peak above him, and he felt exposed, vulnerable. He hurriedly jumped over the wall to catch up with the others.

To his surprise he found himself on a broad stone platform that was not visible from beyond the wall. A stairway descended several steps and then leveled off into a low, narrow tunnel. Jeff quickly gained on the others, but unlike them he had to stoop slightly to clear the ceiling. He heard another soft, grinding noise behind him, and then a metallic clank telling him the entrance had closed.

Valbona lit their way by the light of her cudgel. An eerie groaning came from deep within the mountain as it settled in on itself. Jeff looked up at the ceiling nervously. He was getting tired of underground adventures. They intersected a side tunnel that shot off to the right and dropped steeply downward. Valbona waved her arm down the tunnel as they passed.

"We will take *that* tunnel another time," she said over her shoulder not slowing her pace. "That way leads to the caverns of the dead and the chamber you were talking about containing the altar."

The tunnel coursed in a straight line as near as Jeff could tell. It wasn't long before they heard a strange moaning sound coming from up ahead. It grew louder as they approached the end of the tunnel. Valbona pushed gently on a protrusion of rock, and the wall slid open revealing another short tunnel that opened into a cave. They could tell now that the moaning was in fact human voices, whispered, but amplified off the rock walls.

They had come up behind the villagers of Qerg Muli who were still in hiding. When the villagers saw the witch, they jumped in a panic, but Gysi quickly stepped in front of her to calm them. They stared at him not believing what they were seeing until Besiana stepped out into the cave. Then Gysi's wife ran to him and wept in his embrace. The other villagers came to them whispering their astonishment.

Valbona pushed her way to the center of the group. They shied away from her at first, but when they saw that Gysi and Besiana were not afraid of her they relaxed.

"We have no time to waste," said the witch in Albanian. "The jinni will be distracted for only a little time. They will renew their fury shortly."

"Why are they doing this?" pleaded Gysi's wife, Mira. "What have we done to anger them?"

"You have done nothing except be human." Valbona then gave a short explanation and history of the curse. As she spoke many of the older villagers shook their heads in agreement as they remembered the tales of terror that had been passed down to them. Jeff listened without understanding. He was confused at certain times when he was sure the villagers agreed with the witch, yet shook their heads no. Besiana noticed his expression.

"In Albanian we shake our heads for yes, and nod our heads for no. This is different in English I think, yes?"

"Yes, it's different in just about every other country in the world," whispered Jeff keeping his attention on Valbona. "I can see I could get in a lot of trouble over here with that."

"You mean more trouble than having jinni try to kill you?" she asked coyly.

"Oh, yeah. Right."

Valbona turned to Jeff. "Where is your pack?"

He took it from Cledi, who had not let it out of his sight, and handed it to the witch without opening it. She peered inside, a dark expression crossing her face. The sight of the two golden cubes took her breath away. She inhaled deeply and tried to steady herself.

"The last time I saw these was..." Her voice trailed off into an inaudible mumble as she recalled that fateful day all those centuries ago. She suddenly snapped back to the present. "Jeff, we must separate these from the jinni as far as possible. I am beginning to think that your plan may have some merit after all."

She thrust the pack back into his hands and pulled the ruby bracelet out of her tunic. The villagers gasped at the sight. As poor peasant shepherds they had never seen anything so extravagant. Valbona held it up to the early dawn light that was beginning to show through the mouth of the cave. After studying it for a short time, she smoothed the dust from a patch of rock with her foot and cast the bracelet down with a firm toss. The sharp cracking sound it made as it hit was louder than it should have been for its weight and size.

The witch waved everyone back. They watched in awe as she groomed her fingers through the air above the gems, muttering unintelligible words that floated with a peculiar resonance throughout the cavern. Valbona's voice ebbed and flowed with guttural intonations that rose and fell in a rhythmic cadence that was both mesmerizing and frightening at the same time.

With each new verse the rubies began to glow brighter. The emeralds, sapphires, and diamonds also emitted their own radiance. Soon a burst of brilliant and blinding light shot out from the core of each one of the gems. Everyone was thrown back by the bracelet's glory, forcing them to cover their eyes. Then a deafening explosion of power knocked the villagers against the wall of the cave. The concussion brought rock and dirt debris showering down on them. Jeff and Besiana were thrown to the floor in a heap next to the secret opening. A shuddering tremor could be felt and heard reverberating through the core of the mountain. Jeff cradled Besiana protecting her from the falling rocks.

A quick series of pops like firecrackers came from the center of the cave where Valbona maintained her hunched stance over the bracelet. The echo rang throughout the cave and beyond, in all directions. When the witch stopped chanting, the tumult stopped, but a low rumble continued from deep within the foundation of the mountain for several seconds.

As the dust settled, the villagers pulled themselves back up and crowded around the witch. There on the ground in front of her was the bracelet broken into individual gems. The rubies lay in a circular pattern perfectly and evenly arranged. The figures within each gem faced upward with their feet to the center. The emeralds, sapphires, and diamonds lay in neatly stacked piles in a triangular fashion just inside the circumference of the ruby circle. Each gem gave off its own glow casting the room in a rainbow of colors.

Jeff's brow furrowed as he studied the pattern. Thin spikes of light radiated in all directions from the precious stones, but upon closer examination each stone was connected to the one next to it by a strand of light. The ruby circle was completed with strands of light that arced perfectly from one to the next. The emeralds sent a green beam at a forty-five degree angle to the pile of sapphires and a forty-five degree angle to the pile of diamonds. The sapphires sent their rainbow of colored light at forty-five degree angles to the diamonds and the emeralds. The diamonds also connected to the other two piles with a beam of blindingly brilliant white light. Soon the extraneous beams faded leaving only the connecting light.

As Jeff analyzed the shape, the Greek letters omicron and delta came to mind. He strained his mind to remember where he had seen the symbol omicron circling delta before. He finally drew a complete blank, but he felt it had significance.

Valbona sensed that he recognized something about the symbol on the floor. "What do you see?" she asked in a mentoring way.

"I see omicron encircling delta," he said.

"And what significance do you believe this to have?"

Jeff thought for a long minute and finally gave up. "I have no idea," he confessed.

"How many components do you see?" she asked.

He counted the gems. "Four. I see four components."

"Really, just four? Is that all you see? Count them again more carefully," she coached.

"OK...I see four different kinds of stones arranged in the shape of a circle and a

triangle.... I see...light that also has a distinct pattern. I see the figures clearly within the rubies. Feet to the center, facing up. Uh..." he stalled.

"What do you know about how this pattern came to be?" she interrupted.

"I know that it once was a single strand, but then it exploded and came out to be in this shape."

"Does it make since to you that this pattern should be the result of an explosion?"

"No."

"So what do you surmise?"

"That the explosion was...by design."

"Is this how explosions normally behave?"

"No," said Jeff beginning to understand where she was going with this line of questioning. "Did you cause it?"

"No," said Valbona with a smile. "Now I believe you are starting to see. If I didn't cause this explosion by design, then something else or someone else did. If it was not me, then whom?"

"One who has power to create...one who has power to create order out of chaos."

"Yes! Exactly, but whom," asked the witch.

"I have no idea," said Jeff, tired of her game.

"The Master. It was he who bound these jinni in their individual stones. He obviously has created this symbol as a tool for you to use."

"How?" asked Jeff, exasperated.

"Look at the arrangement closely. This pattern specifically deals with the four jinni in question. There are indeed the four components that you mentioned. They represent the jinni as you know them: Ölüm, Vdekje, Avni, and Lida. Ölüm, the strongest of the four, is represented by the rubies. The other three are represented by the other three stones. I do not know which is which at this time. The orientation of the inner gems are significant as well. The emerald points to this ruby here," she said pointing to the ruby adjacent to the pile of emeralds. "I believe you may have been right about how to kill the jinn."

She knelt and studied the pattern again. Jeff knelt next to her as she moved her hand slowly palm-down over the circle. As she came to the intersection of the ruby and emerald, her hand began to quiver uncontrollably. She passed over the spot and continued hovering over each ruby in turn. Again when she reached the intersection of the ruby and the sapphires, and the ruby and the diamonds, her hand began to quiver; but the most violent tremor was at the emeralds.

She straightened and rubbed her hands together. "The emerald ruby holds the key," she said. She bent down and picked it up off the floor. A sudden flash emitted from the circle, and then the glowing light from each stone ceased. She placed the ruby in Jeff's outstretched hand. He looked at her puzzled. "When you see Ölüm, use your sling-rifle contraption and send this ruby into his heart."

"Are you sure this will work?" asked Jeff nervously.

"No, but it is the best plan we have," she said. "The death of Ölüm will bring about the deaths of the other three. He is the key."

"And what if it doesn't?" Jeff asked.

"Then I would suggest you run and hide and try to avoid them for the next thirty days."

He glared at her, hoping she was teasing, but she wasn't. He gulped and placed the ruby securely in his pocket.

"What about the rubies next to the sapphires and the diamonds? If the Master aligned them in this pattern, then these other two rubies should be of use also." Jeff bent down to pick one up before Valbona could warn him not to. Just has his hand neared the sapphire ruby, an electrically charged bolt arced from the ruby to his fingertips. The shock knocked him backward into Besiana. The two fell to the floor as ionized plasma arced over their bodies. They writhed in pain, convulsing in epileptic spasms.

Valbona rushed to their side, pushing Besiana's mother firmly away. She took Besiana's hand and caressed it in her own. The plasma flowed from Besiana into her own body, but by the power of her will it dissipated harmlessly. Soon Jeff and Besiana lay gasping and exhausted. The force enveloping the pair sparked spasmodically for a few more seconds, and then ceased.

Jeff looked up into the eyes of the witch and gave her a nod of thanks. He struggled to his knees but was too weak to stand. Gysi gave him a firm hand up while also helping Besiana to her feet.

"I suppose now you will know better than to assume things that you do not understand," said Valbona. "This pattern must remain intact exactly as it lay." She looked around at the other villagers, reinforcing her warning with a stern glare at each of them before turning back to Jeff. "You must be prepared to meet the jinni now. The commotion that has been made here has been felt throughout the very root of the Balkans.

The words had no sooner left her mouth than the sound of stumbling footsteps echoed from the tunnel. The village men tensed, cocking their weapons and pointing them down the dark passage. The sound grew louder. Soon they heard the heavy breathing of someone or something running toward them. Jeff instinctively pulled Besiana behind him and fumbled in his pocket for the ruby. He placed it in the sling-rifle and aimed it at the opening.

The hurried shuffle of the runner slowed near the opening, and the villagers shifted nervously glancing back and forth between the witch, Jeff, and the tunnel. Jeff impulsively stepped closer, drawing back the sling as he did. His heart raced. He mentally fought to control the tremble in his hands as they held the weapon at point-blank range from the dark orifice.

Suddenly a battered and bruised figure stumbled out of the passage and fell sprawling face down at Jeff's feet. The sudden encounter surprised both of them, as each gave a sharp cry of exclamation. The figure groveled. He looked up out of the corner of his eye and saw the group surrounding him with weapons pointed in his direction. Exhaustion, fear, and hopelessness overtook him as he broke down and wept bitter tears.

Jeff shook himself out of his astonishment as he finally recognized his old friend. He quickly knelt down and embraced Orhan, who at first shied away from his touch but then recognized Jeff and fell into his arms. The two men wept with relief as Valbona and the villagers looked on in amazement.

After a moment the two friends separated at arm's length and stared at each other in shock and disbelief. Jeff was the first to gain his composure.

"How in the world did you get here?" he asked rhetorically.

"Long story," panted Orhan. "No time. The jinni are right behind me."

As if on cue, a rushing sound of wind could be heard coming through the tunnel from deep within the bowels of the earth. Valbona quickly shoved the stone door closed, sealing off the tunnel. She pulled from her pouch an orange powder and flung it along the edges of the door, bowing her head and mumbling an incantation that caused the orange powder to glow and then burst into a ribbon of flame running along the creases of the rock. When the flame died down, the rock door had been fused solid as if welded.

"That will only hold them for a short time," she said. She studied the cave and then shook her head. "This place is not defensible. We must find a better place."

"What place could be better than a cave?" argued Jeff.

"*Vend i shejntë*," she said, "a holy place."

"The high place," said Gysi in affirmation. "You will need time to get there. We will stay behind and hold the jinni as long as we can."

"Very brave, my friend," said Valbona, "but you will have no effect with those weapons. You will die needlessly and only fuel the craving of the jinni. No, I must stay behind while you lead everyone to the high place."

As the villagers began to exit, she turned and faced the blocked tunnel. Straightening to her full height, she stretched her cudgel vertically in front of her and opened her stance wide. She eyed the floor, careful not to disturb the placement of the gems.

Suddenly a gush of wind slammed hard into the tunnel side of the rock door. The earth shook violently as barrage after barrage of turbulent wind smashed into the obstacle. Licks of fire began to finger through the crevices in the rock. Jeff pushed Orhan and Besiana out into the ravine where the others were already making their way along the boulder-strewn gorge.

"You go!" he yelled. "I'll catch up."

"No, Jeff," pleaded Besiana. "You must come."

"Orhan, take her. You must go, Besi," he yelled above the tumult. He gently pried her grip off of his arm and pushed her toward Orhan. "You must go with your father."

He didn't give her a chance to argue as he leapt into the cave taking his stand next to Valbona. She looked at him gravely, and then smiled, her eyes steeled against the coming onslaught as the rock door began to slowly succumb to the blows. Jeff drew the ruby back in its sling.

Pieces of rock began to melt away and flow like lava down the wall of the cave. Soon a blast of hot air assaulted the two defenders as a strong draft drew through the tunnel. An opaque darkness loomed just beyond the crumbling barricade. Flaming red eyes seethed at them with malignant malice.

"Hold until you have a clear shot," ordered Valbona. "You must hit it squarely in the chest."

Jeff waited breathlessly. He aimed his sling-rifle at the center of the creature. Unbearable tension pounded against his own rib cage as he waited for the jinn to break through the last remnants of the door. His shot became clear. He held his breath to steady his aim.

Suddenly a bellow of searing hot wind pummeled Jeff and the witch back against the rock wall of the cave. They slumped to the floor dazed by the force. Jeff saw the jinn approaching. The ruby slid from the sling-rifle and clattered on the stone by his leg. He grimaced in horror as the jinn stalked slowly and ravenously toward him. Jeff recoiled against the wall as recognition of doom pervaded him. It was not Ölüm.

# 35. A Deadly Walk in the Rain

Josef found a well-worn sheep trail that cut across the slope of the mountain on a fairly level plane. It made the going easier as they continued on. After two hours they took a short break. Aubrey appreciated the rest, but she was anxious to get to where Jeff was.

The clouds had dumped rain on them intermittently throughout the morning, and thunder rumbled overhead, skipping from peak to peak. Another sudden cloudburst sent them scurrying under the cover of a rock outcropping.

Mustafa crouched next to Aubrey and smiled weakly. "We are making better time than we thought we would. Josef thinks Curraj i Epërm is just over this next ridge."

Aubrey's heart skipped a beat with excitement. The surge of joy was fleeting, however, as thoughts of what lay ahead with the jinni insidiously crept back into her mind.

A gully wash swept past their feet following the impression of the trail. Besnik stood up in the rain and studied the skyline to the north.

"What is it?" asked Mustafa.

"I hear something," said Besnik in a hushed tone. "The jinni are not far."

The news swept over each one of them like a virulent plague.

"We need to keep going," said Josef.

Without further discussion they grabbed up their packs and quickened their pace along the path. Soon they could hear the shrieks and cackles of the jinni as they circled the valley beyond the heavy dark clouds. They marched in single file

415

keeping one eye on the sky and the other on the trail. The cry of the jinni grew louder and louder. At one point Josef dropped to his knee causing everyone to dive in line behind him.

"We are very close now," he hissed over his shoulder. "I just saw a shape drop below the clouds."

The rain continued to pour. They proceeded cautiously until they came to a deep ravine cut by a stream. The trail switchbacked on itself until it dropped to the bottom. They forded the stream quickly one at a time, as the gully was open to the sky above. The fierce scream of a jinn directly overhead rang like the sharp crack of a rifle through the narrow canyon.

Fredi was the only one left to cross when the jinn suddenly swooped out from the cover of the clouds and maneuvered its glide to intercept him as he stood in midstream. He looked up and saw his attacker too late; the jinn snagged him with its massive talon and carried him kicking and screaming into the clouds.

The others looked on in horror, helpless to do anything. Josef charged out into the middle of the stream gnashing his teeth. A low, guttural groan welled up from deep inside him escalating into a heart-wrenching scream. He fell to his knees and beat the water with his fists cursing in his mother tongue, rage tearing his reason into little pieces.

Mustafa and Besnik dragged him forcibly back to the cover of the trees, but Josef was inconsolable. He thrashed from their grasp and ran back out into the stream cursing the air and shaking his fist. A gigantic sonic thump was all that was heard as the jinn careened back out of the clouds and closed in on him. Josef raised his AK-47 and spattered off half a magazine of rounds before the talon of the jinn impaled him through the heart, tossing him lifelessly among the boulders upstream from the others. The water ran blood red as it coursed among the shallow rapids.

The cackle of the jinn faded into the distance. Mustafa and Besnik had been able to duck for cover before the jinn came into view.

"Maybe it doesn't know we're here," whispered Aubrey as the two Gypsies strode back up to the others.

"Maybe," said Mustafa hopefully, "but we cannot count on it."

They hurried back up the path until they reached the level of the previous trail on the other side of the stream. The clouds were beginning to break to the north. Rain still fell on their position but had let up, although the way was now slippery, and more than once Aubrey lost her footing and skidded off the trail.

Soon the trail opened up into a sloping meadow that overlooked the valley. Curraj i Epërm stood in the distance as a silent sentinel to the massive Balkan Alps beyond. The company paused under the cover of the last trees at the edge of the meadow. There was no protection beyond that point, and Mustafa did not want another defeat like they had had at the stream. He looked to Besnik for guidance, but Besnik only shrugged noncommittally and scrunched his lower lip.

They could see that the path dropped over a rounded knoll at the far edge of the field. The ridge of another mountain intersected at what would prove to be a fork in the river below. The cak-cak-cak of an AK-47 rose up from the ravine. Two jinni glided in formation breaking the ceiling of the clouds. Another burst of gunfire pelted the jinni from below, this time from several weapons. Although the 7.62 x 39 rounds had no lethal effect, they still had the force to repel the creatures.

Mustafa and his clansmen ran from their hiding place and fired their weapons catching the jinni in the cross fire. Mustafa loaded his sling-rifle with a peach stone and fired it point-blank at Lida, who managed to veer at the last second, although the stone tore through her left wing ripping a hole through it like a paper kite. She screamed in agony and limp-winged out of range. Besnik sent another peach stone into her hindquarter, causing her to flinch and roll into a ball. She burst into flames and fell to the earth like a comet. The thunderous impact sent a column of dirt and rock debris into the air.

Enraged, Avni plummeted straight at Besnik before he could reload his weapon. Besnik dove to the ground, but Avni's talon ripped through his shoulder sending a spurt of blood geysering into the air. Besnik collapsed to the ground immediately going into shock from the sudden loss of blood.

Mustafa shot another peach stone at Avni as he came in for the kill on Besnik. The stone nicked his neck, sending Avni into a frenzy of madness. He turned on Mustafa and with a mighty swipe of his wing knocked him to the ground. His talon dug deep into the flesh of Mustafa's thigh sending him into a convulsion of pain.

Aubrey ran to Besnik's fallen body and wrestled the sling-rifle out from under him. She groped in his pocket for more peach stones and hurriedly tried to load for a shot. The other Gypsies continued to batter Avni with their automatic weapon fire. The effect disoriented the jinn enough to give Aubrey time to load. She pulled the stone back in its sling and released it, sending it squarely between Avni's eyes. He staggered backward, but regained his balance as Aubrey had not loaded the .22 caliber bullet in the chamber of the sling-rifle giving it the necessary force to penetrate the jinn's skin. Avni swatted at her, taking her legs out from under her.

Mustafa managed to get off one last shot, which hit Avni in the chest just below his throat. An ooze of lava-like blood curled down his torso.

From the far edge of the field, a rush of villagers came pouring over the knoll into the meadow firing their weapons. Avni spat and cursed at them, but their numbers were too great to overcome. He took one last slice at Mustafa with his talon, and then rose crippled into the air. The clouds quickly concealed him.

Aubrey lay on her back with her eyes closed. The wind had been knocked out of her. When Avni's deathblow didn't come, she slowly opened one eye, and then the other. To her surprise and joy Orhan stood over her with a gigantic smile plastered across his face.

"Orhan! My God. I'm so happy to see..." She broke into a sob of tears as Orhan knelt beside her and took her tenderly into his arms. The two friends held their embrace for several moments, gaining strength from the closeness. "Orhan," Aubrey stammered, "I thought you were dead."

"So did I. I am so happy to see you alive. We have no time now to explain, but Jeff is alive."

Aubrey perked up. She couldn't speak she was so happy.

"We are still not out of this, though," Orhan cautioned her. "We cannot stay here." He helped her to her feet.

Mustafa crawled over to where Besnik lay and rolled him over onto his back. Besnik stared up at the sky, his eyes beginning to glaze. His face was ashen, and a pool of blood flowed thickly through the wet grass. Mustafa carefully pulled back the tattered remains of Besnik's tunic to reveal an almost complete dismemberment of his shoulder through to his sternum.

Besnik slowly rolled his head toward Mustafa. He licked his parched lips and tried to form a word. Mustafa drew nearer and placed his ear at Besnik's lips. Besnik struggled to speak. Finally in a barely audible whisper, he managed to say, "I forgive you...for...my brother."

Mustafa buried his head in the chest of his dying cousin and wept. Besnik sighed a long, slow sigh and closed his eyes in death.

Aubrey knelt and quickly tried to control the bleeding from Mustafa's thigh, but the gash was too deep. It had severed his femoral artery. Blood pumped in a steady stream, mingling with Besnik's. Mustafa pulled the rolled up lambskin parchment from his tunic pocket and handed it to Aubrey. He anemically pointed to an incantation on the parchment. He was losing consciousness fast.

"You will...need...this," he gasped as he rolled over facedown on Besnik's chest.

There on the side of the mountain overlooking Curraj i Epërm, Mustafa breathed his last.

Aubrey and Orhan wept.

\* \* \*

Gysi and the other villagers came to the side of Orhan and Aubrey, looking on with sympathy at the two men that lay dead at their feet. It began to rain again. The clouds hung low now obscuring the view of the village. The wind came from the north, and the rain became cold. Aubrey shivered.

"We need to go to the holy place," said Gysi, with Besiana translating. "It is up on the top of this mountain." He pointed over his shoulder with his thumb. "It will not take long, but the way will be slippery from the rain."

They continued along the same path that Aubrey and the Gypsies had been following, but when they got to the knoll they took a higher fork that ascended into the clouds. Besiana stayed by Aubrey's side, and the two young women helped each other climb the treacherous slop.

Gysi led the way. Orhan followed close behind with the rest of the villagers trudging in single file. When they came to a narrow gouge in the rock face that made a natural stair to the top, the villagers kept as close together as possible.

They reached the summit, which was an island encircled by a cotton-ball sea of whitish-gray clouds. The area was flat and inlaid with stones creating a patio overlooking ranges and valleys to the east, west, north, and south. In the center of the patio was a single wooden post crowned with an iron ring. The stone around the post had a rust-colored stain that was not washed away by the rain.

"This is where the Bektashi sacrifice every year," offered Besiana to Aubrey.

"People?" asked Aubrey horrified.

"No," smiled Besiana. "Animals. Mostly sheep and goats."

"Oh," Aubrey sighed, relieved.

Gysi stood at the post and lifted the iron ring used to tether the animals. "This is where the witch said to come. We will wait for her here," he said as Besiana translated for Aubrey and Orhan.

They huddled in a tight circle facing outward in every direction. The remaining Gypsies stayed together, lead now by Sami, looking out toward the west where they had last seen the jinni. The cloud cover below, interrupted only by the occasional peaks of mountains, gave them a surreal sense that they were the only ones on the face of the earth.

Aubrey watched and waited. She had grown to hate waiting.

* * *

From a tangle of burning tree trunks and branches, Lida emerged in her true form; a fiery, amorphous shape that towered over the tops of the trees. She struggled to keep her balance. She had been badly wounded by the peach stones, which had pierced her severely in two places, and her inner fire was waning. She searched the sky for Avni, but her brother was nowhere to be seen. She had heard his cry of pain. Had he been felled also? She tried to fly from the mountainside, but she was too weak and crashed into another stand of trees. She found that the only way she could travel was to use the trees for support and pull her way down to the valley. She needed to get to their subterranean haven. In her weakened condition the rain was not helping; each drop sizzled and steamed as it plopped onto her flesh.

"The humans will pay dearly," she cursed. By the time the opening to the caves appeared ahead, the rain had just about extinguished her. She yearned for the time she could go back among her own kind. To live at peace in arid places.

She entered the dark cave, her eyes burning with fire scanning the tunnel ahead. She staggered along using the rock wall for support. Another step deeper and she tripped over an obstacle that sent her sprawling and cursing to the ground. A low moan came from the obstacle.

The prone shape of her brother, Avni blocked her way. He lay on his back gasping shallowly. A gurgling sound churned and hissed with each uneasy breath. She hovered over him, accessing his wound. A peach stone had severed a major artery in his neck. His essence of fire was flowing from the wound like lava from a volcanic cone.

He turned to Lida. Their eyes met and held each other's gaze. He gurgled one last utterance in the tongue of the jinn: "I do not regret my rebellion." Then the ember of his flame degraded to smoke. Soon his entire being was consumed by a firestorm that sparked and crackled off the rock walls, ceiling, and floor. The firestorm whirled into the afternoon rain, and then sizzled into oblivion. Avni's presence in the earth of men was ended.

# 36. The Lambskin Parchment

Jeff fumbled for the ruby. Vdekje stalked closer. Suddenly she was knocked back by a powerful blow delivered by Valbona with her cudgel. Vdekje staggered to keep her feet, and then took the form of a monstrous bear-like creature with articulated hands. She swiped at the witch, knocking her senseless against the wall. The cudgel rattled free from her grasp and clattered among the array of gems.

Vdekje watched the cudgel come to rest and noticed the pattern laid out. She recoiled at the sight and hissed a venomous curse at the witch as she stood over the pattern studying it. Slowly she realized that one of the rubies was missing from the array. Her head turned to Valbona, and then to Jeff.

"Who has the ruby?" she growled.

Straddling the witch, she grasped her by the ankle and yanked her up off the floor of the cave. She gave Valbona a violent shake, suspecting she could dislodge the ruby from her clothing. The witch groaned, unconscious. When nothing but trinkets fell to the ground, Vdekje tossed Valbona recklessly to the side and turned her attention to Jeff.

He had crawled closer to the entrance of the cave while her attention was on the rubies and the witch. By the time she got around to him, he had loaded the ruby into the sling-rifle; it was cocked and ready.

She crept toward him, confident that he could not escape. She had not seen his weapon before and was unaware of its lethal capability.

"Soon you will join the two others below," she snarled. "You will all die together and the curse will be broken."

She lunged at Jeff suddenly, swiping her massive clawed hand at his head. He ducked instinctively, causing her to rake across the rock wall and send up a shower of sparks, and then rolled to his right and came up on her left side, bringing the sling-rifle into firing position. The jinn squared around on him and swiped at him again, but this time a sharp crack and a twang exploded through the tight confines of the cave. The ruby launched true with lightening velocity, striking Vdekje deep in her heart.

She staggered backward, a look of shocked surprise etching her face, and looked frantically around the cave as her skin began to ripple with plasma of electricity. Her eyes fell on the witch, who was now conscious and standing over the golden cubes that were laid out between her feet. Her cudgel rested firmly on the golden cube that had been Vdekje's prison for over five hundred years. A smirk crossed Valbona's face.

"No retreat, Vdekje," she gibed. "The box is closed. It will never be opened again." With that the witch slammed her cudgel down hard on the top of the cube. A great metal clank rang through the cavern.

Vdekje groaned in agony as the plasma spread throughout her body. She transformed into her true form and blazed a brilliant orange-red. Black cracks began to radiate out from the penetration wound of the ruby. They spread like crawling vines hardening into black, lava-like veins. She gasped and grabbed her throat, a look of sheer terror petrifying her face.

The fire of her being ebbed to a smoldering gray smoke, and her statuesque form toppled into a heap of molten rock that flowed across the floor. The thermophilic stone drew off the heat, hardening the flow into fingerlike ridges.

The witch collapsed to the floor. The exertion of the power needed to seal the cube had left her weak and dazed. Jeff ran to her side and touched her outstretched hand that still held the cudgel. It was hot to the touch. He gently rolled her over onto her back. Valbona was feverish and delirious; the power drain had nearly killed her. She stared up at Jeff with blank,

unseeing eyes. The gaze unsettled him, and he instinctively recoiled away from the reflection that seemed to mirror eternity.

He settled on the ground next to her, and she brought her hand over her chest and pressed an object into his. He looked down at another ruby.

"This is the next one you must use," she whispered weakly. "The stone meant for Ölüm destroyed Vdekje. The jinni must now be killed individually." She coughed violently, convulsing with every hack. "You must stop him now. Here!" She coughed again, but this time a spittle of blood trickled from the corner of her mouth.

"This ruby is from the position next to the sapphires," she continued. "You must not mix them up. Take the ruby next to the diamonds and place it in your other pocket." She watched while Jeff scooted crab-like to the pattern of gems. He placed the ruby she had given him in his right pants pocket, and then picked up the ruby next to the diamonds and placed it in his left pocket. The witch nodded her approval.

"When the jinni are dead you must come back here and gather the remaining stones in a counterclockwise fashion starting with the ruby next to the one you just picked up. Keep them in the order in which you picked them up."

"What of the other gems?" asked Jeff.

Valbona tried to raise leaning on her elbow. "Your ultimate quest is not over, Jeff. Use the other stones to fund your mission."

Jeff frowned at her. "What mission?"

"I can say no more," she coughed uncontrollably and swooned back from the exhaustion. "Go," she gasped. "Go destroy the others before they destroy you." She pushed Jeff away with more force than he thought her capable of. He looked down at her, confused, but she waved him toward the tunnel. "Ölüm…" she gasped. Her head lolled to the side as her weak, centuries-old body gave out.

Jeff looked down at her with pity. He forced himself to take the first step toward the tunnel…and Ölüm.

\* \* \*

He dared not light a torch. The tunnel stretched out in front of him, a black orifice into the bowels of the earth. He carried his Maglite cupped by his palm to reduce the beam and pressed along the edge afraid to show his profile in the middle of the passageway. He remembered the tributary that jutted off to the right as they came from Curraj i Epërm. He knew it had taken them another fifteen minutes or so to reach the secret door, but that was under the guidance of Valbona and her light.

He quickly jumped to the left-hand wall and slid cautiously along trying desperately not to make a sound. After twenty minutes his hand fell into a depression in the rock. He groped in the pitch-black opening. The tributary.

Slithering his foot along the floor as it made its steep descent, he found the side of the shoot and continued on. Soon a faint glow could be seen deep in the distance. Jeff froze in his tracks staring into the blackness. His heart pounded. His right hand pinched the ruby in his right pants pocket trying to gain courage from its presence.

As he drew closer to the glow, he could see that it came from an arched chamber from which rich firelight flowed. He took another step and suddenly found himself in a larger cavern. He slowed his pace, recognizing the entrance to the altar chamber.

He took another timid step, but then a sharp, iron grip pierced his shoulder. The pain was instantaneously excruciating. He could feel the blood rushing to his face. His eyes rolled to the back of his head. Just before passing out he saw the looming, snarling face of Ölüm.

# Vale of Shadows

"I have been waiting for you, son of Lleshi."
Darkness overtook him.

*   *   *

Orhan waited nervously under the rock ledge looking out over the rain-soaked valley to the west. It had been too long. Something had to be wrong. Aubrey noticed him fidgeting.

"It has been a long time, don't you think?" she said.

"Yes. I am afraid *too* long. Maybe we should go back."

Besiana overheard them talking. She went over to her father and said something, pointing in their direction. Soon Gysi and Besiana came back to them.

"We are going back," she stated. "It has been too long. Something is wrong. Cledi and Toni will come with us."

The six of them slid back down the muddy trail with the six remaining Gypsies following behind. Patches of blue sky opened into the cloud cover to the east, but a sense of dread and urgency propelled them down the slope at a faster pace than was safe. Soon they had come to the meadow in which Mustafa and Besnik had been lost. Aubrey avoided looking over at their bodies.

The rain slowed to a drizzle. They entered the ravine and made their way among the boulders arriving at the mouth of the cave just as the witch was hobbling out. She was frail and weak from her ordeal with Vdekje, but using the power that had sustained her over the centuries she had managed to regain some of her strength.

"I was coming to get you," she said to Orhan ignoring the others. "Jeff has gone to face Ölüm."

The group entered the cave and welcomed being out of the rain.

"Where is Jeff?" asked Aubrey. "Is he here?"

"No. He has gone down that tunnel." Valbona pointed beyond the shattered stone door. She went to the mound of

427

molten rock that had once been Vdekje. The crust broke away under the probing of her cudgel dissolving into an ashen dust. Brushing through the center, she found what she was looking for and bent down to pick up the ruby, brushing off the ash. She then handed it to Orhan.

"This stone was meant to kill Ölüm. Had it done so, the other three jinni would have been destroyed as well. Since it was used to kill Vdekje, however, the jinni must now be destroyed one at a time." She stared down the tunnel and bent her ear toward it listening intently. She then turned back to Orhan. "You will go with me alone. The others must stay here." She met Aubrey's pending protest with an abrupt gesture of her hand cutting her off before she could speak. "No one is to go with him except for me."

"And what of these?" asked Gysi pointing to the array of stones on the floor.

"Under no circumstances are they to be disturbed until the jinni are vanquished," she warned. "They are meant for another time and another place. "Orhan, we must go now."

Orhan reluctantly hugged Aubrey good-bye and then followed Valbona into the darkness. She lit her cudgel with a dim bluish light just visible enough to cast a pall along the corridor. They proceeded quickly. Valbona sensed that Jeff had been taken earlier, but she kept the information to herself.

When they came to the tributary, she quickly ducked into the opening without hesitating. Orhan scrambled to keep up. When she slowed her pace, he came up behind her and whispered in her ear.

"What are we going to do when we find the jinn?"

She stopped and faced him. "The jinni have prepared an ancient sacrificial altar to kill you, Jeff, and the Gypsy Merriam. You are all of the line of the three perpetrators that started this whole miserable curse in the first place. By killing you ceremoniously together they will break the bonds of the curse and be free. If they fail this time to wipe out the linage of Selim Bey and Përparim Lleshi, they will be utterly and forever destroyed themselves. They must succeed just as you must.

"I have destroyed their golden cubes," she continued. "They have nowhere to turn."

"I believe we wounded two of them on the mountain," said Orhan. "It cost the lives of Mustafa and Besnik, but I believe they severely wounded the jinni before they were killed."

"Truly?" said Valbona, impressed. "Then this may not be as hopeless as I thought."

They came to the edge of the shadow beyond the reach of the light in the chamber. The torchlight inside cast Ölüm in an eerie orange glow. He had his back to them as he tormented Jeff and Merriam, who were tied to the altar by their arms and legs.

Valbona crept as close as she dared to the entrance. She pulled out a pouch that contained a red powder and poured it across the threshold of the chamber. She then touched the edge of the powder with her cudgel. The powder burned in a quick flash and gave off a foul stench that filled the cavern. The suddenness of it startled Orhan, and he gave out a sharp yelp as he dove behind a boulder at the edge of the light.

Ölüm spun around, also startled by the blast. He spotted the witch in the gloom and snarled, lunging at her in one quick leap, but he banged hard against an unseen wall and crashed to the floor, dazed. Valbona cackled with glee.

"You are trapped, Greslokmu," she taunted. "The ground-up brick from the Cave of the Seven Sleepers once again thwarts your passing."

Ölüm jumped back to his feet. "You have no power over me, witch. Take your tricks and be gone."

"Indeed. No power? I would say that I have more power than you can imagine."

Ölüm's face betrayed his confusion. He lunged at the unseen wall again and again. Finally realizing he was unable to pass, he relaxed and tried a different tactic.

"I may be trapped, but I am trapped with the blood of Lleshi and Baba Moush. I think I will just kill them now." He turned and grabbed Merriam by the throat with his claw-like hand and squeezed. She choked against the steady pressure he exerted.

"You may kill both of them if you like, but you are still doomed without the third one," taunted Valbona. "You cannot escape, and even if you could I have destroyed your golden box, and until all of the blood of the curse has been spilled you are still bound to it. If you kill the two you have without having the third, you will destroy not only yourself but your sister as well."

Ölüm thought on the words of Valbona and released his grip on Merriam's throat. He then pounded his fist against the invisible barrier, causing a massive tremor to shake through the cavern system.

"You are forgetting Freslokmut, Mimlokmu, and Timlokmut. They will find a way to defeat your magic," he sneered.

"Oh, didn't I mention? They are all dead," Valbona bluffed, unaware that her words were partly true. "You are all alone and destitute. Finally the earth will be rid of you and your clan."

"You lie!" he accused, beating against the barrier with his fists again.

Orhan cowered behind the boulder, not daring to show his face to the jinn. Valbona suddenly grabbed him forcefully by the wrist and yanked him out into plan sight. Orhan struggled against her grip, but it was like a vise.

"What are you doing?" he gasped.

"Be still," she commanded.

Jeff was groggy, but he recognized his friend's voice. "Orhan! Help."

Valbona and Ölüm glared at each other. The stalemate was obvious to both of them.

"I am thinking we have the makings of a deal," she said coyly.

"What do you have in mind?" said Ölüm suspiciously.

"A trade," she answered. "You give me the secret of the ancestral rubies, and I give you this human to complete your set."

"So you know of the ancestral rubies," he said disdainfully. "Even if you knew their secrets, you would not have the power to control them. They would destroy you."

"I doubt that," she boasted. "Your kind has underestimated me for centuries. Do we have a trade or not?"

Orhan squirmed against her grasp, confused as to her intent. She clamped down even harder, her fingernails digging into his flesh. Panic seized him. The realization that she was about to betray him swept over him like a tide and he swirled around hard, cocking her arm back behind her. Surprised, she loosened her hold. He kicked her from behind sending her headlong into the barrier she had created.

Ölüm paced expectantly as she crashed through the barrier. A sudden flash of energy swept through the subterranean cave system blinding everyone including Ölüm and Valbona, who grappled like sumo wrestlers. Ölüm was shocked that she had the power to withstand him. The light radiated and pulsed brighter and brighter as the two fought. The walls absorbed the energy and gave off energy of their own, increasing the luminescence.

Orhan rushed passed the combatants to Jeff's side and quickly cut the bindings from his arms and legs. He then went to

431

Merriam's side but found that Ölüm had crushed her trachea, suffocating her.

Jeff jumped to his feet and wasted no time in loading the ruby from his left pocket into his sling-rifle. Ölüm sensed the danger and spun around, keeping Valbona between them.

Suddenly a loud blast shattered the stones making up the wall behind them. Lida lunged in through the gap snarling fiercely. She grabbed up the lifeless body of Merriam, not realizing she was already dead, and pulled her free of the binding on the altar. She wagged the dead Gypsy queen like a rag doll, and then flung her at Jeff and Orhan. The brunt of the blow fell on Orhan, who toppled into the altar. Jeff swung around with the ruby still cocked back in the firing position. Lida flung herself at him just as he released the ruby.

The stone struck her with a deafening blast, throwing everyone off balance. The ruby sank slowly into her chest like a rock melting into lava. Lida screamed angrily and flung her clawed fist at Jeff's head, missing him by a mere inch. Her body jolted into an erect posture as her features began to become like stone.

Ölüm's fury raged against Valbona when he saw what had happened to his sister. He picked the witch up and crushed her to the ceiling of the chamber. The sound of old, brittle bones cracking could be heard above the rush of wind that was now imploding into Lida.

Ölüm pounded toward Jeff with vicious hatred. Jeff tried to scamper out of his path and put the altar between them, but Ölüm was too fast and furious. He latched onto Jeff's shoulder and flung him into the crown of the arched doorway. Jeff fell limp on the threshold, dazed and bleeding from a wound to his scalp.

In the confusion, Valbona beckoned Orhan to come to her from where she lay crushed on the stone floor. Orhan crawled to her, careful to keep behind the altar and away from the eyes of Ölüm. When he reached the witch, she grabbed his hand and placed in it the ruby she had excavated from the dust of Vdekje. Her eyes told him what her mouth could not. Orhan searched the floor of the chamber for Jeff's sling-rifle. To his dismay he spotted the weapon still clutched in Jeff's hand.

Orhan began to crawl on his belly toward Jeff, but Ölüm hovered over his friend ready to crush him with a mighty blow. Suddenly another explosion shook the chamber sending a shock-wave smashing through the rock cavern. Ölüm turned to see Lida flare into a thousand rays of light and then pop out of existence.

As he turned, he saw Orhan crawling behind him and made a grab at him, but Orhan sprang back over the altar out of the jinn's reach.

"Two down, one to go," sneered Ölüm. "You cannot escape."

"Sounds more like three down and one to go to me," said Orhan, surprised by his own boldness.

Orhan saw Jeff stir behind Ölüm who had now taken on a giant humanoid form. Ölüm pounced on top of the altar, cutting off any protection that Orhan had hoped to gain. He swayed back and forth following Orhan's timid movement as he crept along with his back pinned to the wall trying to gain every spare inch of distance away from the jinn.

Suddenly Ölüm stiffened and his brow furrowed. Orhan saw a deeply disturbed and confused look cross his face. Ölüm gazed around the chamber, disoriented. Orhan relaxed slightly against the wall as Jeff rose slowly to his knees, but Ölüm paid no attention to either of them. The jinn stumbled off the altar and fell against the wall next to Orhan.

"He has finally felt the loss of his siblings," croaked Valbona. "He knows that they are all dead save for him." She tried to rise, but Ölüm had fractured several of her ribs and she was having great difficulty breathing. "He will never be more vulnerable than he is now."

"I don't trust anything you say," said Orhan in a harsh whisper as he kept his eyes on Ölüm. "You were going to betray us!"

"Forgive my moment of greed. I failed…" She sucked in a gurgling raspy breath.

Jeff staggered to his feet. Blood from the gash on his head ran down his face into his eyes, nearly blinding him. Orhan chanced a dash to his side and grabbed the sling- rifle from him, quickly loading the ruby.

Ölüm snapped out of his funk and began to charge toward the pair, but Valbona managed to tangle his human legs up in her cudgel, causing him to trip. He spun around and gave her a quick, crushing kick. Her body immediately went limp and sank lifeless to the floor. Ölüm turned back toward Jeff and Orhan, who had fled out into the cavern beyond the chamber.

Orhan supported Jeff as they limped up the path to the main tunnel. The line across the threshold of red brick dust from the Cave of the Seven Sleepers had been broken by Jeff's falling across it, so Ölüm was slowed but not stopped as he proceeded through the arch way.

Jeff stumbled and fell, pulling Orhan down with him. Ölüm gained on them, spitting curses at them as he came. The two men struggled to their feet and ran. Ölüm was on them, but in his rage he had lost all sense of himself and was still in his human form which limited him in his attack. He caught up with Jeff first and pounced on his back pinning him to the ground. Orhan's adrenalin pushed him beyond reason. He turned and struck Ölüm viciously along the side of the head with a stone he had picked up from the path. The blow caught Ölüm off guard, and he fell backwards.

Suddenly an explosion of automatic gunfire ripped through the cavern. Bullets fired from the rock fall on either side of the path struck Ölüm in the chest. Although they had no fatal effect, the force of the rounds staggered him.

Orhan quickly dragged Jeff away from the jinn and helped his friend up. The continuous cak-cak-cak from the AK-47s of the Gypsies deafened them but bought them time to get away. As they ran up the slope to join the Gypsies, Orhan reloaded the sling-rifle.

The Gypsies continued their barrage, catching Ölüm in a cross fire. Enraged, he transformed into a deep dark shadow. The natural flame of his spirit burned from his eyes as he struck the ceiling of the cavern with his amorphic fist, showering down rock and dirt on the Gypsies. A large stalactite fell into the midst of Cledi, Toni, and Gysi sending them sprawling down the slope of the rock fall.

Cledi had taken the bulk of the hit and lay unconscious, bleeding from a head wound. Ölüm swatted at Toni as he tried to drag his friend back up the slope. The jinn caught him along his left side, knocking him away. Gysi picked up his AK-47 and charged at Ölüm, firing an entire clip into the jinn.

Ölüm snatched Gysi and Toni by the throats, one in each hand. They dangled helplessly in his grip. He gained power from the terror he felt coursing through their veins. Toni grimaced with pain from his cracked ribs. Gysi fought against the hold, but Ölüm only tightened his grip, cutting off the man's air.

Jeff ran to Gysi's fallen AK-47. Picking it up he aimed and fired, but the firing pin clicked into an empty chamber. Ölüm threw his shadowy head back and laughed deeply. He thrashed at Jeff with Toni's body, knocking him to the ground. Ölüm flung Toni and Gysi to the side and hovered over Jeff with a ravenous snarl.

A woman's scream caused him to pause and look up. Aubrey ran from behind a boulder wielding the lambskin parchment Mustafa had given her. She yelled through the tumult, "*Ek tha do mosh. Usk ple neter. Ke se mosh. Usk ple neter.*"

Ölüm winced. He staggered backward down the slope. His amorphic shape pulsed wildly in the air. Great schisms of fire broke through the shadow of his form and beamed out in infinite rays filling the cavern with brilliant light. Valbona had locked his golden cube, so the chant began to pull him into oblivion.

Orhan turned and fired the sling-rifle hurling the ruby into Ölüm's chest. A clap of thunder boomed off the rock walls sending a sonic resonance through the core of the Balkan Alps. The blast knocked everyone to the ground and started a landslide of boulders and dirt into the cave.

Aubrey and Orhan helped Jeff to his feet and carried him to the main tunnel while the Gypsies gathered up Gysi and Cledi and carried them quickly out of the crumbling chamber. The earthquake grew in intensity. They ran as fast as they could, but the tremor knocked them off their feet several times before they reached the secret cave.

They poured out into the open ravine just as another terrific explosion from deep within the mountain sent a blast of rock and smoke billowing from the cave entrance. The side of the mountain collapsed like a caldera. Trees and boulders careened down the slope bombarding the ravine with deadly projectiles.

Orhan and Aubrey dragged Jeff up the steep slope on the other side of the ravine. The Gypsies scrambled up along with them. Smaller subterranean explosions reverberated along the mountain ridge, and a blast of fire spewed high into the air like a geyser.

Jeff stumbled blindly through the smoke and dust. He could feel Orhan and Aubrey tugging him up out of the ravine to safety, but he could barely hear the coaxing of his friends to keep climbing. His head throbbed, his ribs ached, and his legs felt like they were made of concrete. Soon he heard another voice calling to him from above, urging him not to give up. Besiana.

He finally felt the ground level off and then drop; they had cleared the ridge. More hands grabbed him and guided him along the sheep trail. The ringing in his ears began to subside, and the air cleared from the dust and smoke. He was surrounded by the rest of the villagers, who had come to aid them.

Jeff collapsed, exhausted. He felt someone gently lift his head and scoot under it as a pillow. Opening his eyes, he blinked the dust from his eyelashes. Aubrey stared down at him with tears washing streaks down her grimy cheeks. She tried to smile through a sob when she saw him open his eyes. He met her gaze and held it. Loved it. He tried to smile, but his jaw was too sore to achieve anything more than a slight curl of his lip.

"Don't try to talk," she said. "You're safe now. We all are."

Jeff looked around at the faces staring down at him smiling. Orhan, Besiana. His mind was clouded, but he noted the absence of others: Jonathan, Mustafa. He strained to get up, but fell back into Aubrey's lap.

"Just rest for now," said Orhan.

Jeff dropped off into a deep sleep.

# 37. Farewell, but Not Good-bye

Tirana, Albania

Jeff stood with Aubrey at the entrance to Rinas Airport in Tirana. Orhan had just paid the taxi driver and made his way through the crowd of Gypsy children wanting to help with his pack. The three friends smiled at each other as the children pushed in on them. Taxi drivers waiting for fares shooed them off in the direction of other hapless travelers arriving from Italy.

Jeff gently rubbed his elbow through the sling. It had been a week since the caves in Tropoja. The soreness that he felt in every joint was a constant reminder of their ordeal. Aubrey reached over and caressed his hand lovingly.

They showed their tickets to the guard at the front door and entered the small check-in lobby. They had booked a flight to Istanbul, Orhan's final destination and Jeff and Aubrey's connecting one. They held their position in the line firmly as an old Albanian woman tried to crowd in front and then scowled at them as she wobbled to the back of the line.

As they approached the counter, the electricity went out shutting down all the lights and the computers. Jeff groaned quietly at the delay but noticed how everyone else took the brownout in stride. He stared at Aubrey as she watched a young Turkish mother helping her toddler daughter put a small pink suitcase emblazoned with a unicorn onto the scale in the next line. She turned toward Jeff catching him staring at her.

"I wouldn't mind having one of those someday," she said thoughtfully.

"What? A pink unicorn suitcase?" he said teasingly.

"No silly. A little girl," she said smiling, giving him a playful nudge as his face reddened.

After ten minutes the lights flickered back to life. The clerk behind the counter assured them in Turkish that as soon as the computers rebooted they would be able to proceed. The friends checked in together hoping to get seats next to each other.

At passport control they fanned themselves with their tickets trying to position themselves as much as possible in front of the single air-conditioning unit mounted on the wall.

"Ahh...that feels so good," said Jeff as he basked in the cool air.

"Last time I came through here a couple of years ago, they didn't even have this," said Aubrey pressing up against Jeff and absorbing the coolness with him.

They paid ten American dollars apiece for an exit tax and then placed their packs on the conveyor belt to be examined before entering the gate area. Orhan led them to gate number three of three and sat down heavily in one of the hard yellow bench chairs.

"We have thirty minutes before we board," he said as Aubrey and Jeff sat down.

The three friends waited in silence for a while, each reflecting on the past few days. Jeff took Aubrey's hand in his and held it firmly. He never wanted to let it go. His mind wandered back to Qerg Muli and Besiana, who had been a great help in his recovery. He wondered if he would ever see the people again who had sacrificed so much to save him. He hoped so.

Gysi and Cledi had been severely injured but would live. Toni had died by Ölüm's hand, and Sami sadly had not made it out of the caverns before the cave-in. Ermal, Mustafa, and so many of their clansmen had been lost trying to save Orhan and him. He reached down discreetly and pinched the ruby in the fabric of his pants pocket. He had not mentioned to his friends that he still had it. Except for his scrapes, bruises, sprains, and cracked ribs, the ruby was the only thing he had to show for his ordeal.

He mused to himself for a moment as a faint smile etched his lips. *No, check that*, he thought and tenderly caressed Aubrey's hand in both of his. He had gotten something far more important out of the ordeal. Aubrey looked at him puzzled for a second, and then covered his hands with her remaining one.

"Ahem," said Orhan clearing his throat. "Do I need to separate you two?"

"Never again," said Jeff staring deeply into Aubrey's eyes.

"It's too bad about all those other jewels," said Orhan changing the subject. "Do you think anyone will ever find them?"

"I don't know, and I don't care," said Jeff. "I never want to hear about rubies or jinni again."

"I second that," said Aubrey.

"What will you do now, Jeff?" asked Orhan awkwardly. He hated the thought of leaving his friend once they got to the airport in Istanbul. He also had time now to grieve for his Uncle Ümët and to honor his memory. It wasn't until this moment that he realized how much he missed him.

"Well, I think first I will say good-bye to my best friend in the whole world and promise him I will see him again." Jeff noted Orhan's smile. "And then I believe I will go back to Wichita with the woman I love and introduce her to my mom and sister. After that...well, I guess it's up to her." He fixed her gaze expectantly.

"Well, I guess I could grow to love you," she teased, "on one condition."

"Anything," he promised.

"No more ancient curses."

"Deal."

They shook hands on the promise. Orhan joined in, "Deal."

A voice over the intercom announced first in Albanian, then in Turkish, and finally in English the boarding of the flight to Istanbul. The threesome was nearly trampled by the rush of travelers to the gate.

"I can't wait to get back to America where they know how to stand in line," said Jeff, trying to keep his balance as the same old woman from the checkout counter pressed in front of him. He looked back at Orhan. "No offense."

"No offense taken," said Orhan, equally frustrated.

They boarded a tarmac bus that took them to the waiting Turkish Airline jet. Jeff looked out over the field at the concrete machine gun pods that lined the runway, a reminder of harder times gone by. He sighed deeply and found Aubrey's hand. The heat off the tarmac was stifling. His shirt stuck to his sweaty back.

"At least it ought to be air-conditioned on the plane," she said.

He suddenly felt a lump in his throat and an inexplicable melancholy as he paused on the gangway and took one last look at the deep blue peaks of the mountains to the north looming through the haze. He sighed and entered the air-conditioned cabin closely behind Aubrey. A strange feeling swept through him.

He would see this part of the world again.

THE END